Ty's BIG BOOK of Rubbish: An Omnibus

A Look at Some Useless, Crappy Writing

By Ty Rosenow

This book is entirely a work fiction except for the works indicated and the footnotes. Any resemblance of a person, place, thing, or idea is purely coincidental.

ISBN: 978-0-578-02077-8

Library of Congress Control Number: 2009904127

Table of Contents

An Introduction: The Omnibus

Welcome to "Ty's BIG BOOK of Rubbish: The Omnibus"! After a careful amount of demand, it came to my attention that I needed to put the entire series into one fabulous book without people having to search the world for all twenty volumes. There is some bad news, however. There are no twenty volumes. I just got as far as two volumes. I quickly ran out of fictional material and stopped writing overall. This is mostly from my schooling that required to me to turn in my assignments and my lack of boredom decreased as I moved up the ladder of my status at the college.

There are downsides to putting together omnibuses of your past works. You stop writing all together and people require you to make this the last piece of written work within your whole entire writing career. This is not so. I have other plans on my writing and I will write my items whether they get published or don't get published, making hunting for these items for challenging for the reader who wants to read the books. I am actually going to continue on with my history writing rather than constantly changing genres. As you can see, it seems to interfere with my work both academically and as a form of my own personal relaxation. Who knows? Maybe I will continue on with short story fictional writing when I grow to become less serious. Who knows what my future could hold?

In the future, I may come up with "really groovy shit" or I may stay on the serious end of my writing and stick with history all together and live in the past.

Well, enough of my jabbering. I hope you enjoy the reading the book, or put it on your bookshelf and stare at because it looks good as an interior design piece, and sell it at a garage sale and see if you get 5 cents off of it because it no longer looks as an interior design piece. Interior designers make me sick. You should never enjoy a book because it looks good on your bookshelf. You should always read the book *before* you put it on your bookshelf. A book reflects the soul and your bookshelf should reflect your soul and your interests.

There a few things different in this book compared to the previous editions: You will see the least amount of grammatical, spelling, and formatting errors in this book than previous editions. This book actually went through some proofreading! The reasoning behind this is that the previous books had a deadline and people wanted to read the stories before I had a chance to finish them and fix them the way I wanted them to turn out. However, I did try my best to keep it as close to the original as much as possible.

Also take note that there is a Table of Contents with the proper pages for those who want to revisit the stories over and over again. I have also included some questions people have asked me over the years on the web site: tyrosenow.com, in which I did the postings in order to *explain* myself. It is over three hundred pages of goodness!

Finally, I dedicated this book to the following: authors of the future and past, librarians, those I have met in the past and in the future from all countries, fictional and non-fictional people and objects from the past and in the future, and most of all, you. That's right! It is you who makes this book possible, otherwise I wouldn't be able to write a book in the first place!

Cheers!

Ty Rosenow

Olympia, Washington, USA

April 9, 2009

Ty's Book Of Rubbish: A Look of Useless Crap: Volume 20

Foreword by William Henry Harrison[1]

CALLED from a retirement which I had supposed was to continue for the residue of my life to fill the chief executive office of this great and free nation, I appear before you, fellow-citizens, to take the oaths which the Constitution prescribes as a necessary qualification for the performance of its duties; and in obedience to a custom coeval with our Government and what I believe to be your expectations I proceed to present to you a summary of the principles which will govern me in the discharge of the duties which I shall be called upon to perform.

It was the remark of a Roman consul in an early period of that celebrated Republic that a most striking contrast was observable in the conduct of candidates for offices of power and trust before and after obtaining them, they seldom carrying out in the latter case the pledges and promises made in the former. However much the world may have

1 President Harrison has the dual distinction among all the Presidents of giving the longest inaugural speech and of serving the shortest term of office. Known to the public as "Old Tippecanoe," the former general of the Indian campaigns delivered an hour-and-forty-five-minute speech in a snowstorm. The oath of office was administered on the East Portico of the Capitol by Chief Justice Roger Taney. The 68-year-old President stood outside for the entire proceeding, greeted crowds of well-wishers at the White House later that day, and attended several celebrations that evening. One month later he died of pneumonia. (Information provided by Bartleby.com - http://www.bartleby.com/124/pres26.html

improved in many respects in the lapse of upward of two thousand years since the remark was made by the virtuous and indignant Roman; I fear that a strict examination of the annals of some of the modern elective governments would develop similar instances of violated confidence.

Although the fiat of the people has gone forth proclaiming me the Chief Magistrate of this glorious Union, nothing upon their part remaining to be done, it may be thought that a motive may exist to keep up the delusion under which they may be supposed to have acted in relation to my principles and opinions; and perhaps there may be some in this assembly who have come here either prepared to condemn those I shall now deliver, or, approving them, to doubt the sincerity with which they are now uttered. But the lapse of a few months will confirm or dispel their fears. The outline of principles to govern and measures to be adopted by an Administration not yet begun will soon be exchanged for immutable history, and I shall stand either exonerated by my countrymen or classed with the mass of those who promised that they might deceive and flattered with the intention to betray. However strong may be my present purpose to realize the expectations of a magnanimous and confiding people, I too well understand the dangerous temptations to which I shall be exposed from the magnitude of the power which it has been the pleasure of the people to commit to my hands not to place my chief confidence upon the aid of that Almighty Power which has hitherto protected me and enabled me to bring to favorable issues other important but still greatly inferior trusts heretofore confided to me by my country.

The broad foundation upon which our Constitution rests being the people—a breath of theirs having made, as a breath can unmake, change, or modify it—it can be assigned to none of the great divisions of government but to that of democracy. If such is its theory, those who are called upon to administer it must recognize as its leading principle the duty of shaping their measures so as to produce the greatest good to the greatest number. But with these broad admissions, if we would compare the sovereignty acknowledged to exist in the mass of our people with the power claimed by other sovereignties, even by those which have been considered most purely democratic, we shall find a most essential difference. All others lay claim to power limited only by their own will. The majority of our citizens, on the contrary, possess sovereignty with an amount of power precisely equal to that which has been granted to them by the parties to the national compact, and nothing beyond. We admit of no government by divine right, believing that so far as power is concerned the Beneficent Creator has made no distinction amongst men; that all are upon equality, and that the only legitimate right to govern is an express grant of power from the governed. The Constitution of the United States is the instrument containing this grant of power to the several departments composing the Government. On an examination of that instrument it will be found to contain declarations of power granted and of power withheld. The latter is also susceptible of division into power which the majority had the right to grant, but which they do not think proper to entrust to their agents, and that which they could not have granted, not being possessed by themselves. In other words, there are certain rights possessed by each individual American citizen which in his compact with the others he has never surrendered. Some of them, indeed, he is unable to surrender, being, in the language of our system, unalienable. The boasted privilege of a Roman citizen was to him a shield only against a petty provincial ruler, whilst the proud democrat of Athens would console himself under a sentence of death for a supposed violation of the national faith—which no one understood and which at times was the subject of the mockery of all—or the banishment from his home, his family, and his country with or without an alleged cause, that it was the act not of a single tyrant or hated aristocracy, but of his assembled countrymen. Far different is the power of our sovereignty. It can interfere with no one's faith, prescribe forms of worship for no one's observance, inflict no punishment but after well-ascertained guilt, the result of investigation under rules prescribed by the Constitution itself. These precious privileges, and those scarcely less important of giving expression to his thoughts and opinions, either by writing or speaking, unrestrained but by the liability for injury to others, and that of a full participation in all the advantages which flow from the Government, the acknowledged property of all, the American citizen derives from no charter granted by his fellow-man. He claims them because he is himself a man, fashioned by the same Almighty hand as the rest of his species and entitled to a full share of the blessings with which He has endowed them. Notwithstanding the limited sovereignty possessed by the people of the United States and the restricted grant of power to the Government which they have adopted, enough has been given to accomplish all the objects for which it was created. It has been found powerful in war, and hitherto justice has been administered and intimate union affected, domestic tranquility preserved, and personal liberty secured to the citizen. As was to be expected, however, from the defect of language and the necessarily sententious manner in which the Constitution is written, disputes have arisen as to the amount of power which it has actually granted or was intended to grant.

This is more particularly the case in relation to that part of the instrument which treats of the legislative branch, and not only as regards the exercise of powers claimed under a general clause giving that body the authority to pass all laws necessary to carry into effect the specified powers, but in relation to the latter also. It is, however, consolatory to reflect that *most* of the instances of alleged departure from the letter or spirit of the Constitution has ultimately received the sanction of a majority of the people. And the fact that many of our statesmen most distinguished for talent and patriotism have been at one time or other of their political career on both sides of each of the most warmly disputed questions forces upon us the inference that the errors, if errors there were, are attributable to the intrinsic difficulty in many instances of ascertaining the intentions of the framers of the Constitution rather than the influence of any sinister or unpatriotic motive. But the great danger to our institutions does not appear to me to be in usurpation by the Government of power not granted by the people, but by the accumulation in one of the departments of that which was assigned to others. Limited as are the powers which have been granted, still enough have been granted to constitute despotism if concentrated in one of the departments. This danger is greatly heightened, as it has been always observable that men are less jealous of encroachments of one department upon another than upon their own reserved rights. When the Constitution of the United States first came from the hands of the Convention which formed it, many of the sternest republicans of the day were alarmed at the extent of the power which had been granted to the Federal Government, and more particularly of that portion which had been assigned to the executive branch. There were in it features which appeared not to be in harmony with their ideas of a simple representative democracy or republic, and knowing the tendency of power to increase itself, particularly when exercised by a single individual, predictions were made that at no very remote period the Government would terminate in virtual monarchy. It would not become me to say that the fears of these patriots have been already realized; but as I sincerely believe that the tendency of measures and of men's opinions for some years past has been in that direction, it is, I conceive, strictly proper that I should take this occasion to repeat the assurances I have heretofore given of my determination to arrest the progress of that tendency if it really exists and restore the Government to its pristine health and vigor, as far as this can be effected by any legitimate exercise of the power placed in my hands.

I precede to state in as summary a manner as I can my opinion of the sources of the evils which have been so extensively complained of and the correctives which may be applied. Some of the former are unquestionably to be found in the defects of the Constitution; others, in my judgment, are attributable to a misconstruction of some of its provisions. Of the former is the eligibility of the same individual to a second term of the Presidency. The sagacious mind of Mr. Jefferson early saw and lamented this error, and attempts have been made, hitherto without success, to apply the amendatory power of the States to its correction. As, however, one mode of correction is in the power of every President, and consequently in mine, it would be useless, and perhaps invidious, to enumerate the evils of which, in the opinion of many of our fellow-citizens, this error of the sages who framed the Constitution may have been the source and the bitter fruits which we are still to gather from it if it continues to disfigure our system. It may be observed, however, as a general remark, that republics can commit no greater error than to adopt or continue any feature in their systems of government which may be calculated to create or increase the lover of power in the bosoms of those to whom necessity obliges them to commit the management of their affairs; and surely nothing is more likely to produce such a state of mind than the long continuance of an office of high trust. Nothing can be more corrupting, nothing more destructive of all those noble feelings which belong to the character of a devoted republican patriot. When this corrupting passion once takes possession of the human mind, like the love of gold it becomes insatiable. It is the never-dying worm in his bosom, grows with his growth and strengthens with the declining years of its victim. If this is true, it is the part of wisdom for a republic to limit the service of that officer at least to whom she has entrusted the management of her foreign relations, the execution of her laws, and the command of her armies and navies to a period so short as to prevent his forgetting that he is the accountable agent, not the principal; the servant, not the master. Until an amendment of the Constitution can be effected public opinion may secure the desired object. I give my aid to it by renewing the pledge heretofore given that under no circumstances will I consent to serve a second term.

But if there is danger to public liberty from the acknowledged defects of the Constitution in the want of limit to the continuance of the Executive power in the same hands, there is, I apprehend, not much less from a misconstruction of that instrument as it regards the powers actually given. I can not conceive that by a fair construction any or either of its provisions would be found to constitute the President a part of the legislative power. It can not be claimed from the power to recommend, since, although enjoined as a duty upon him, it is a privilege which he holds in common with every other citizen; and although there may be something more of confidence in the propriety of the measures recommended in the one case than in the other, in the obligations of ultimate decision there can be no difference. In the language of the Constitution, "all the legislative powers" which it grants "are vested in the Congress of the United States." It would be a solecism in language to say that any portion of these is not included in the whole.

It may be said, indeed, that the Constitution has given to the Executive the power to annul the acts of the legislative body by refusing to them his assent. So a similar power has necessarily resulted from that instrument to the judiciary, and yet the judiciary forms no part of the Legislature. There is, it is true, this difference between these grants of power: The Executive can put his negative upon the acts of the Legislature for other cause than that of want of conformity to the Constitution, whilst the judiciary can only declare void those which violate that instrument. But the decision of the judiciary is final in such a case, whereas in every instance where the veto of the Executive is applied it may be overcome by a vote of two-thirds of both Houses of Congress. The negative upon the acts of the legislative by the executive authority, and that in the hands of one individual, would seem to be an incongruity in our system. Like some others of a similar character, however, it appears to be highly expedient, and if used only with the forbearance and in the spirit which was intended by its authors it may be productive of great good and be found one of the best safeguards to the Union. At the period of the formation of the Constitution the principle does not appear to have enjoyed much favor in the State governments. It existed but in two, and in one of these there was a plural executive. If we would search for the motives which operated upon the purely patriotic and enlightened assembly which framed the Constitution for the adoption of a provision so apparently repugnant to the leading democratic principle that the majority should govern, we must reject the idea that they anticipated from it any benefit to the ordinary course of legislation. They knew too well the high degree of intelligence which existed among the people and the enlightened character of the State legislatures not to have the fullest confidence that the two bodies elected by them would be worthy representatives of such constituents, and, of course, that they would require no aid in conceiving and maturing the measures which the circumstances of the country might require. And it is preposterous to suppose that a thought could for a moment have been entertained that the President, placed at the capital, in the center of the country, could better understand the wants and wishes of the people than their own immediate representatives, who spend a part of every year among them, living with them, often laboring with them, and bound to them by the triple tie of interest, duty, and affection. To assist or control Congress, then, in its ordinary legislation could not, I conceive, have been the motive for conferring the veto power on the President. This argument acquires additional force from the fact of its never having been thus used by the first six Presidents—and two of them were members of the Convention, one presiding over its deliberations and the other bearing a larger share in consummating the labors of that august body than any other person. But if bills were never returned to Congress by either of the Presidents above referred to upon the ground of their being inexpedient or not as well adapted as they might be to the wants of the people, the veto was applied upon that of want of conformity to the Constitution or because errors had been committed from a too hasty enactment.

There is another ground for the adoption of the veto principle, which had probably more influence in recommending it to the Convention than any other. I refer to the security which it gives to the just and equitable action of the Legislature upon all parts of the Union. It could not but have occurred to the Convention that in a country so extensive, embracing so great a variety of soil and climate, and consequently of products, and which from the same causes must ever exhibit a great difference in the amount of the population of its various sections, calling for a great diversity in the employments of the people, that the legislation of the majority might not always justly regard the rights and interests of the minority, and that acts of this character might be passed under an express grant by the words of the Constitution, and therefore not within the competency of the judiciary to declare void; that however enlightened and patriotic they might suppose from past experience the members of Congress might be, and however largely partaking, in the general, of the liberal feelings of the people, it was impossible to expect that bodies so constituted should not sometimes be controlled by local interests and sectional feelings. It was proper, therefore, to provide some umpire from whose situation and mode of appointment more independence and freedom from such influences might be expected. Such a one was afforded by the executive department constituted by the Constitution. A person elected to that high office, having his constituents in every section, State, and subdivision of the Union, must consider himself bound by the most solemn sanctions to guard, protect, and defend the rights of all and of every portion, great or small, from the injustice and oppression of the rest. I consider the veto power, therefore, given by the Constitution to the Executive of the United States solely as a conservative power, to be used only first, to protect the Constitution from violation; secondly, the people from the effects of hasty legislation where their will has been probably disregarded or not well understood, and, thirdly, to prevent the effects of combinations violative of the rights of minorities. In reference to the second of these objects I may observe that I consider it the right and privilege of the people to decide disputed points of the Constitution arising from the general grant of power to Congress to carry into effect the powers expressly given; and I believe with Mr. Madison that "repeated recognitions under varied circumstances in acts of the legislative, executive, and judicial branches of the Government, accompanied by indications in different modes of the concurrence of the general will of the nation," as affording to the President sufficient authority for his considering such disputed points as settled.

Upward of half a century has elapsed since the adoption of the present form of government. It would be an object more highly desirable than the gratification of the curiosity of speculative statesmen if its precise situation could be ascertained, a fair exhibit made of the operations of each of its departments, of the powers which they respectively claim and exercise, of the collisions which have occurred between them or between the whole Government and those of the States or either of them. We could then compare our actual condition after fifty years' trial of our system with what it was in the commencement of its operations and ascertain whether the predictions of the patriots who opposed its adoption or the confident hopes of its advocates have been best realized. The great dread of the former seems to have been that the reserved powers of the States would be absorbed by those of the Federal Government and a consolidated power established, leaving to the States the shadow only of that independent action for which they had so zealously contended and on the preservation of which they relied as the last hope of liberty. Without denying that the result to which they looked with so much apprehension is in the way of being realized, it is obvious that they did not clearly see the mode of its accomplishment. The General Government has seized upon none of the reserved rights of the States. As far as any open warfare may have gone, the State authorities have amply maintained their rights. To a casual observer our system presents no appearance of discord between the different members which compose it. Even the addition of many new ones has produced no jarring. They move in their respective orbits in perfect harmony with the central head and with each other. But there is still an undercurrent at work by which, if not seasonably checked, the worst apprehensions of our antifederal patriots will be realized, and not only will the State authorities be overshadowed by the great increase of power in the executive department of the General Government, but the character of that Government, if not its designation, be essentially and radically changed. This state of things has been in part affected by causes inherent in the Constitution and in part by the never-failing tendency of political power to increase itself. By making the President the sole distributer of all the patronage of the Government the framers of the Constitution do not appear to have anticipated at how short a period it would become a formidable instrument to control the free operations of the State governments. Of trifling importance at first, it had early in Mr. Jefferson's Administration become so powerful as to create great alarm in the mind of that patriot from the potent influence it might exert in controlling the freedom of the elective franchise. If such could have then been the effects of its influence, how much greater must be the danger at this time, quadrupled in amount as it certainly is and more completely under the control of the Executive will than their construction of their powers allowed or the forbearing characters of all the early Presidents permitted them to make. But it is not by the extent of its patronage alone that the executive department has become dangerous, but by the use which it appears may be made of the appointing power to bring under its control the whole revenues of the country. The Constitution has declared it to be the duty of the President to see that the laws are executed, and it makes him the Commander in Chief of the Armies and Navy of the United States. If the opinion of the most approved writers upon that species of mixed government which in modern Europe is termed *monarchy* in contradistinction to *despotism* is correct, there was wanting no other addition to the powers of our Chief Magistrate to stamp a monarchical character on our Government but the control of the public finances; and to me it appears strange indeed that anyone should doubt that the entire control which the President possesses over the officers who have the custody of the public money, by the power of removal with or without cause, does, for all mischievous purposes at least, virtually subject the treasure also to his disposal. The first Roman Emperor, in his attempt to seize the sacred treasure, silenced the opposition of the officer to whose charge it had been committed by a significant allusion to his sword. By a selection of political instruments for the care of the public money a reference to their commissions by a President would be quite as effectual an argument as that of Caesar to the Roman knight. I am not insensible of the great difficulty that exists in drawing a proper plan for the safe-keeping and disbursement of the public revenues, and I know the importance which has been attached by men of great abilities and patriotism to the divorce, as it is called, of the Treasury from the banking institutions. It is not the divorce which is complained of, but the unhallowed union of the Treasury with the executive department, which has created such extensive alarm. To this danger to our republican institutions and that created by the influence given to the Executive through the instrumentality of the Federal officers I propose to apply all the remedies which may be at my command. It was certainly a great error in the framers of the Constitution not to have made the officer at the head of the Treasury Department entirely independent of the Executive. He should at least have been removable only upon the demand of the popular branch of the Legislature. I have determined never to remove a Secretary of the Treasury without communicating all the circumstances attending such removal to both Houses of Congress.

The influence of the Executive in controlling the freedom of the elective franchise through the medium of the public officers can be effectually checked by renewing the prohibition published by Mr. Jefferson forbidding their interference in elections further than giving their own votes, and their own independence secured by an assurance of perfect immunity in exercising this sacred privilege of freemen under the dictates of their own unbiased judgments. Never with my consent shall an officer of the people, compensated for his services out of their pockets, become the pliant instrument of Executive will.

There is no part of the means placed in the hands of the Executive which might be used with greater effect for unhallowed purposes than the control of the public press. The maxim which our ancestors derived from the mother country that "the freedom of the press is the great bulwark of civil and religious liberty" is one of the most precious legacies which they have left us. We have learned, too, from our own as well as the experience of other countries, that golden shackles, by whomsoever or by whatever pretense imposed, are as fatal to it as the iron bonds of despotism. The presses in the necessary employment of the Government should never be used "to clear the guilty or to varnish crime." A decent and manly examination of the acts of the Government should be not only tolerated, but encouraged.

Upon another occasion I have given my opinion at some length upon the impropriety of Executive interference in the legislation of Congress—that the article in the Constitution making it the duty of the President to communicate information and authorizing him to recommend measures was not intended to make him the source in legislation, and, in particular, that he should never be looked to for schemes of finance. It would be very strange, indeed, that the Constitution should have strictly forbidden one branch of the Legislature from interfering in the origination of such bills and that it should be considered proper that an altogether different department of the Government should be permitted to do so. Some of our best political maxims and opinions have been drawn from our parent isle. There are others, however, which can not be introduced in our system without singular incongruity and the production of much mischief, and this I conceive to be one. No matter in which of the houses of Parliament a bill may originate nor by whom introduced—a minister or a member of the opposition—by the fiction of law, or rather of constitutional principle, the sovereign is supposed to have prepared it agreeably to his will and then submitted it to Parliament for their advice and consent. Now the very reverse is the case here, not only with regard to the principle, but the forms prescribed by the Constitution. The principle certainly assigns to the only body constituted by the Constitution (the legislative body) the power to make laws, and the forms even direct that the enactment should be ascribed to them. The Senate, in relation to revenue bills, has the right to propose amendments, and so has the Executive by the power given him to return them to the House of Representatives with his objections. It is in his power also to propose amendments in the existing revenue laws, suggested by his observations upon their defective or injurious operation. But the delicate duty of devising schemes of revenue should be left where the Constitution has placed it—with the immediate representatives of the people. For similar reasons the mode of keeping the public treasure should be prescribed by them, and the further removed it may be from the control of the Executive the more wholesome the arrangement and the more in accordance with republican principle.

Connected with this subject is the character of the currency. The idea of making it exclusively metallic, however well intended, appears to me to be fraught with more fatal consequences than any other scheme having no relation to the personal rights of the citizens that has ever been devised. If any single scheme could produce the effect of arresting at once that mutation of condition by which thousands of our most indigent fellow-citizens by their industry and enterprise are raised to the possession of wealth, which is the one. If there is one measure better calculated than another to produce that state of things so much deprecated by all true republicans, by whom the rich are daily adding to their hoards and the poor sinking deeper into penury, it is an exclusive metallic currency. Or if there is a process by which the character of the country for generosity and nobleness of feeling may be destroyed by the great increase and neck toleration of usury, it is an exclusive metallic currency.

Amongst the other duties of a delicate character which the President is called upon to perform is the supervision of the government of the Territories of the United States. Those of them which are destined to become members of our great political family are compensated by their rapid progress from infancy to manhood for the partial and temporary deprivation of their political rights. It is in this District only where American citizens are to be found who under a settled policy are deprived of many important political privileges without any inspiring hope as to the future. Their only consolation under circumstances of such deprivation is that of the devoted exterior guards of a camp—that their sufferings secure tranquility and safety within. Are there any of their countrymen, who would subject them to greater sacrifices, to any other humiliations than those essentially necessary to the security of the object for which they were thus separated from their fellow-citizens? Are their rights alone not to be guaranteed by the application of those great principles upon which all our constitutions are founded? We are told by the greatest of British orators and statesmen that at the commencement of the War of the Revolution the most stupid men in England spoke of "their American subjects." Are there, indeed, citizens of any of our States who have dreamed *of their subjects* in the District of Columbia? Such dreams can never be realized by any agency of mine. The people of the District of Columbia are not the subjects of the people of the States, but free American citizens. Being in the latter condition when the Constitution was formed, no words used in that instrument could have been intended to deprive them of that character. If there is anything in the great principle of unalienable rights so emphatically insisted upon in our Declaration of Independence, they could neither make nor the

United States accept a surrender of their liberties and become the *subjects*—in other words, the slaves—of their former fellow-citizens. If this be true—and it will scarcely be denied by anyone who has a correct idea of his own rights as an American citizen—the grant to Congress of exclusive jurisdiction in the District of Columbia can be interpreted, so far as respects the aggregate people of the United States, as meaning nothing more than to allow to Congress the controlling power necessary to afford a free and safe exercise of the functions assigned to the General Government by the Constitution. In all other respects the legislation of Congress should be adapted to their peculiar position and wants and be conformable with their deliberate opinions of their own interests.

I have spoken of the necessity of keeping the respective departments of the Government, as well as all the other authorities of our country, within their appropriate orbits. This is a matter of difficulty in some cases, as the powers which they respectively claim are often not defined by any distinct lines. Mischievous, however, in their tendencies as collisions of this kind may be, those which arise between the respective communities which for certain purposes compose one nation are much more so, for no such nation can long exist without the careful culture of those feelings of confidence and affection which are the effective bonds to union between free and confederated states. Strong as is the tie of interest, it has been often found ineffectual. Men blinded by their passions have been known to adopt measures for their country in direct opposition to all the suggestions of policy. The alternative, then, is to destroy or keep down a bad passion by creating and fostering a good one, and this seems to be the corner stone upon which our American political architects have reared the fabric of our Government. The cement which was to bind it and perpetuate its existence was the affectionate attachment between all its members. To insure the continuance of this feeling, produced at first by a community of dangers, of sufferings, and of interests, the advantages of each were made accessible to all. No participation in any good possessed by any member of our extensive Confederacy, except in domestic government, was withheld from the citizen of any other member. By a process attended with no difficulty, no delay, no expense but that of removal, the citizen of one might become the citizen of any other, and successively of the whole. The lines, too, separating powers to be exercised by the citizens of one State from those of another seem to be so distinctly drawn as to leave no room for misunderstanding. The citizens of each State unite in their persons all the privileges which that character confers and all that they may claim as citizens of the United States, but in no case can the same persons at the same time act as the citizen of two separate States, and *he is therefore positively precluded from any interference with the reserved powers of any State but that of which he is for the time being a citizen.* He may, indeed, offer to the citizens of other States his advice as to their management, and the form in which it is tendered is left to his own discretion and sense of propriety. It may be observed, however, that organized associations of citizens requiring compliance with their wishes too much resembles the *recommendations* of Athens to her allies, supported by an armed and powerful fleet. It was, indeed, to the ambition of the leading States of Greece to control the domestic concerns of the others that the destruction of that celebrated Confederacy, and subsequently of all its members, is mainly to be attributed, and it is owing to the absence of that spirit that the Helvetic Confederacy has for so many years been preserved. Never has there been seen in the institutions of the separate members of any confederacy more elements of discord. In the principles and forms of government and religion, as well as in the circumstances of the several Cantons, so marked a discrepancy was observable as to promise anything but harmony in their intercourse or permanency in their alliance, and yet for ages neither has been interrupted. Content with the positive benefits which their union produced, with the independence and safety from foreign aggression which it secured, these sagacious people respected the institutions of each other, however repugnant to their own principles and prejudices.

Our Confederacy, fellow-citizens, can only be preserved by the same forbearance. Our citizens must be content with the exercise of the powers with which the Constitution clothes them. The attempt of those of one State to control the domestic institutions of another can only result in feelings of distrust and jealousy, the certain harbingers of disunion, violence, and civil war, and the ultimate destruction of our free institutions. Our Confederacy is perfectly illustrated by the terms and principles governing a common copartnership. There is a fund of power to be exercised under the direction of the joint councils of the allied members, but that which has been reserved by the individual members is intangible by the common Government or the individual members composing it. To attempt it finds no support in the principles of our Constitution.

It should be our constant and earnest endeavor mutually to cultivate a spirit of concord and harmony among the various parts of our Confederacy. Experience has abundantly taught us that the agitation by citizens of one part of the Union of a subject not confided to the General Government, but exclusively under the guardianship of the local authorities, is productive of no other consequences than bitterness, alienation, discord, and injury to the very cause which is intended to be advanced. Of all the great interests which appertain to our country, that of union—cordial, confiding, fraternal union—is by far the most important, since it is the only true and sure guaranty of all others.

In consequence of the embarrassed state of business and the currency, some of the States may meet with difficulty in their financial concerns. However deeply we may regret anything imprudent or excessive in the engagements into which States have entered for purposes of their own, it does not become us to disparage the States governments, nor to discourage them from making proper efforts for their own relief. On the contrary, it is our duty to encourage them to the extent of our constitutional authority to apply their best means and cheerfully to make all necessary sacrifices and submit to all necessary burdens to fulfill their engagements and maintain their credit, for the character and credit of the several States form a part of the character and credit of the whole country. The resources of the country are abundant, the enterprise and activity of our people proverbial, and we may well hope that wise legislation and prudent administration by the respective governments, each acting within its own sphere, will restore former prosperity.

Unpleasant and even dangerous as collisions may sometimes be between the constituted authorities of the citizens of our country in relation to the lines which separate their respective jurisdictions, the results can be of no vital injury to our institutions if that ardent patriotism, that devoted attachment to liberty, that spirit of moderation and forbearance for which our countrymen were once distinguished, continue to be cherished. If this continues to be the ruling passion of our souls, the weaker feeling of the mistaken enthusiast will be corrected, the Utopian dreams of the scheming politician dissipated, and the complicated intrigues of the demagogue rendered harmless. The spirit of liberty is the sovereign balm for every injury which our institutions may receive. On the contrary, no care that can be used in the construction of our Government, no division of powers, no distribution of checks in its several departments, will prove effectual to keep us a free people if this spirit is suffered to decay; and decay it will without constant nurture. To the neglect of this duty the best historians agree in attributing the ruin of all the republics with whose existence and fall their writings have made us acquainted. The same causes will ever produce the same effects, and as long as the love of power is a dominant passion of the human bosom, and as long as the understandings of men can be warped and their affections changed by operations upon their passions and prejudices, so long will the liberties of a people depend on their own constant attention to its preservation. The danger to all well-established free governments arises from the unwillingness of the people to believe in its existence or from the influence of designing men diverting their attention from the quarter whence it approaches to a source from which it can never come. This is the old trick of those who would usurp the government of their country. In the name of democracy they speak, warning the people against the influence of wealth and the danger of aristocracy. History, ancient and modern, is full of such examples. Caesar became the master of the Roman people and the senate under the pretense of supporting the democratic claims of the former against the aristocracy of the latter; Cromwell, in the character of protector of the liberties of the people, became the dictator of England, and Bolivar possessed himself of unlimited power with the title of his country's liberator. There is, on the contrary, no instance on record of an extensive and well-established republic being changed into an aristocracy. The tendencies of all such governments in their decline is to monarchy, and the antagonist principle to liberty there is the spirit of faction—a spirit which assumes the character and in times of great excitement imposes itself upon the people as the genuine spirit of freedom, and, like the false Christs whose coming was foretold by the Savior, seeks to, and were it possible would, impose upon the true and most faithful disciples of liberty. It is in periods like this that it behooves the people to be most watchful of those to whom they have entrusted power. And although there is at times much difficulty in distinguishing the false from the true spirit, a calm and dispassionate investigation will detect the counterfeit, as well by the character of its operations as the results that are produced. The true spirit of liberty, although devoted, persevering, bold, and uncompromising in principle, that secured is mild and tolerant and scrupulous as to the means it employs, whilst the spirit of party, assuming to be that of liberty, is harsh, vindictive, and intolerant, and totally reckless as to the character of the allies which it brings to the aid of its cause. When the genuine spirit of liberty animates the body of a people to a thorough examination of their affairs, it leads to the excision of every excrescence which may have fastened itself upon any of the departments of the government, and restores the system to its pristine health and beauty. But the reign of an intolerant spirit of party amongst a free people seldom fails to result in a dangerous accession to the executive power introduced and established amidst unusual professions of devotion to democracy.

The foregoing remarks relate almost exclusively to matters connected with our domestic concerns. It may be proper, however, that I should give some indications to my fellow-citizens of my proposed course of conduct in the management of our foreign relations. I assure them, therefore, that it is my intention to use every means in my power to preserve the friendly intercourse which now so happily subsists with every foreign nation, and that although, of course, not well informed as to the state of pending negotiations with any of them, I see in the personal characters of the sovereigns, as well as in the mutual interests of our own and of the governments with which our relations are most intimate, a pleasing guaranty that the harmony so important to the interests of their subjects as well as of our citizens will not be interrupted by the advancement of any claim or pretension upon their part to which our honor would not permit us to yield. Long the defender of my country's rights in the field, I trust that my fellow-citizens will not see in my earnest desire to preserve peace with foreign powers any indication that their rights will ever be sacrificed or the honor of the nation tarnished by any admission on the part of their Chief Magistrate unworthy of their former glory. In our intercourse with our aboriginal neighbors the same liberality and justice which marked the course prescribed to me by two of my illustrious predecessors when acting under their direction in the discharge of the duties of superintendent and commissioner shall be strictly observed. I can conceive of no more sublime spectacle, none more likely to propitiate an impartial and common Creator, than a rigid adherence to the principles of justice on the part of a powerful nation in its transactions with a weaker and uncivilized people whom circumstances have placed at its disposal.

Before concluding, fellow-citizens, I must say something to you on the subject of the parties at this time existing in our country. To me it appears perfectly clear that the interest of that country requires that the violence of the spirit by which those parties are at this time governed must be greatly mitigated, if not entirely extinguished, or consequences will ensue which are appalling to be thought of.

If parties in a republic are necessary to secure a degree of vigilance sufficient to keep the public functionaries within the bounds of law and duty, at that point their usefulness ends. Beyond that they become destructive of public virtue, the parent of a spirit antagonist to that of liberty, and eventually its inevitable conqueror. We have examples of republics where the love of country and of liberty at one time were the dominant passions of the whole mass of citizens, and yet, with the continuance of the name and forms of free government, not a vestige of these qualities remaining in the bosoms of any one of its citizens. It was the beautiful remark of a distinguished English writer that "in the Roman senate Octavius had a party and Anthony a party, but the Commonwealth had none." Yet the senate continued to meet in the temple of liberty to talk of the sacredness and beauty of the Commonwealth and gaze at the statues of the elder Brutus and of the Curtii and Decii, and the people assembled in the forum, not, as in the days of Camillus and the Scipios, to cast their free votes for annual magistrates or pass upon the acts of the senate, but to receive from the hands of the leaders of the respective parties their share of the spoils and to shout for one or the other, as those collected in Gaul or Egypt and the lesser Asia would furnish the larger dividend. The spirit of liberty had fled, and, avoiding the abodes of civilized man, had sought protection in the wilds of Scythia or Scandinavia; and so under the operation of the same causes and influences it will fly from our Capitol and our forums. A calamity so awful, not only to our country, but to the world, must be deprecated by every patriot and every tendency to a state of things likely to produce it immediately checked. Such a tendency has existed—does exist. Always the friend of my countrymen, never their flatterer, it becomes my duty to say to them from this high place to which their partiality has exalted me that there exists in the land a spirit hostile to their best interests—hostile to liberty itself. It is a spirit contracted in its views, selfish in its objects. It looks to the aggrandizement of a few even to the destruction of the interests of the whole. The entire remedy is with the people. Something, however, may be affected by the means which they have placed in my hands. It is union that we want, not of a party for the sake of that party, but a union of the whole country for the sake of the whole country, for the defense of its interests and its honor against foreign aggression, for the defense of those principles for which our ancestors so gloriously contended. As far as it depends upon me it shall be accomplished. All the influence that I possess shall be exerted to prevent the formation at least of an Executive party in the halls of the legislative body. I wish for the support of no member of that body to any measure of mine that does not satisfy his judgment and his sense of duty to those from whom he holds his appointment, nor any confidence in advance from the people but that asked for by Mr. Jefferson, "to give firmness and effect to the legal administration of their affairs."

I deem the present occasion sufficiently important and solemn to justify me in expressing to my fellow-citizens a profound reverence for the Christian religion and a thorough conviction that sound morals, religious liberty, and a just sense of religious responsibility are essentially connected with all true and lasting happiness; and to that good Being who has blessed us by the gifts of civil and religious freedom, who watched over and prospered the labors of our fathers and has hitherto preserved to us institutions far exceeding in excellence those of any other people, let us unite in fervently commending every interest of our beloved country in all future time.

Fellow-citizens, being fully invested with that high office to which the partiality of my countrymen has called me, I now take an affectionate leave of you. You will bear with you to your homes the remembrance of the pledge I have this day given to discharge all the high duties of my exalted station according to the best of my ability, and I shall enter upon their performance with entire confidence in the support of a just and generous people.

Introduction

I do a lot of writing. Some of it is for work, college, and others for my own personal enjoyment. Well, I do a mass load of writing. Some of it is fictional, but very few are non-fiction. I find it that writing about fictional characters and their stories as the easiest thing and require absolutely no research whatsoever.

Most cases, however, I often try to write the story really long, but end up quitting and the story ends up to be a very short story. I feel this book was the easiest in terms of length. Why not? Writing short stories, as I soon found out, was really my expertise. Who has time to read a long story? Granted that it turns out to be a good book and you are wanting more and more of the story, but sometimes its simplicity is really the best for the reader.

After all, look at some of the series of books with the same basic plot line and some of the basic characters being written down over and over again. No matter how good the series, the author eventually gets tired of their work and then end up killing the main character in the end. As the author loses interests in the stories they write, the reader loses interests in the story as well. Basically, what the author puts out eventually reflects towards the reader. This example shows that there really can be too much of a good thing. Another item I don't like about books in a series that you must start with the first chapter of the very first book. Why happens if the reader is unable to get a hold of the first book?

This book may be series, but what's nice is that you can read it in any order anywhere within the book and you will still get the gist of the stories. That's what makes short stories great. They are really meant for people who are in a hurry and have time to read during their breaks at work or before they go to sleep.

That is what makes short stories great. If you don't like it, you can skip over them like a track on a compact disc. If like it, you can read them over and over again. I would like you to try to see that in a novel or a series of books.

I decided to name this book as *"Ty's Book of Rubbish"* because of several reasons. I have always thought that everything I write is a bunch of a load of crap. But, many people that I have presented my written work to seem to like it quite a bit. Mainly, they enjoy the humor that I present in my writings.

The scripts were originally written for radio broadcast and a comedy album that never fully developed. It seems to work out well in this book and creates a nice quick relaxation type of piece when it comes to dividing itself between the short stories. I had to find something that would work well for the transition between these short stories.

I hope enjoy some of the stories and scripts that I have written in the past. You'll find them witty.

Ty Rosenow

2007

The American Whore[2]

It was the first time that I had seen her: Blond, stout, and a nose of a rat. She may have been ugly to some, but to me, she was the hot chick within my own lifetime. Being a horny little bastard of a high school student, I would have asked her out, but she was a busy cheerleader trying to keep her persona up in her social society.

She was the team mascot. Because of the federal and state laws, nobody had the right to prevent a high school student to try out for the different sports. In order to get around these laws they put her in a mouse suit while she is doing her cheerleader dance routines. That was the best thing they could do was to hide her behind the suit. Why not? Every horny boy in school (and their fathers) was looking at the hot high school cheerleaders hoping to see something they hadn't seen before underneath their miniskirts (and the fathers hoping to see something nice underneath there as well). It was only natural that the ugly one should...well...have a bag over her head.

There he was: a skinny little gimp with a crew cut. Sure, he was walking around with crutches, but he still had a nice butt. I wonder if he would ask me out for a date.

I came across her the other day at the video store. My, oh my, has she changed over the years. She has formed a little bit rounder and breasts that would make any baby happy. But, there she was, renting the latest releases of family movies. She doesn't know that I still had a crush on her after all of these years, but never had the guts to ask her out.

There he was, staring at me, after all of these years. He is longer a gimp as I remembered him in high school. It must have been the steroids that gave him that full figure – and I do mean a FULL FIGURE. Many things had crossed my mind. Is he married? Why would it matter? My man does give me the right to bare his children and a wonderful loveless marriage. I wonder if he would ask if we could get together sometime.

It was in a crowded grocery store when I saw her again after all of these years. She was squeezing the cantaloupe as if she was more

2 What happens when a love story never happens? Even though I have lived with this lie called love, who'd knew this wouldn't come true? Maybe it became true to some people. This story is dedicated to all of those girls who said "no" towards us dating when I was in high school.

interested in the concept of the produce than checking for the ripeness of the melon in itself. I was amazed. She lost some weight, cut her hair back, and a nose job done. My crush for her has never died.

There I saw him again gaping at me while I squeezed the cantaloupe in the produce section at the grocery store. He was the reason why I ended up turning my sexual orientation to a lesbian. My last husband was such a jerk in my loveless marriage that I swore that would end men in my life forever. He'll never ask me out for date because he is such a wimp.

She moved in next door in the fifty-five plus mobile home park in the lot next to mine. Has it been that long since I have seen her in the past? Why didn't I ask her in high school when I had the chance? Here I am. I am alone for the most of my life. She had many wrinkles since the seventy-five years that I first met her. When I finally talked to her with my house warming gift, I found out that we had a lot in common. Well, not really. But still, the crush on her was still there in my heart.

I can't believe he asked me out on several dates! I just wish he did it in high school like he was suppose, and then I wouldn't be in the mess I was in. How could my life be just a waste for waiting for him to ask me out? I should have done it myself in the first place and then we would possibly enjoy both of our lives together. Finally, here I am. I am about to be a bride for the wedding for the second time towards the man I loved in the first place.

My Cover Letter and Resume[3]

Dear Humane Personnel:

I am applying for a job in ~~typist~~ ~~secretary~~ ~~president~~ CEO of your MAJOR Corporation. As you can see in my resume that I have not included with this cover letter because deserving eyes are only allowed to read my resume, you will find that I am ~~well~~ ~~very well~~ already qualified for the position. In fact, where's the key for my office. I also want my own executive washroom with a bar. Please ~~hire~~

~~fire~~ pay me right away.

Sincerely,

You Know Who I Am

Your Boss

3 I've always wondered what it would be like to write a cover letter and the self -promote yourself throughout a company that you haven't worked at yet. This cover letter tells it all.

The Memoirs of the First Robot President[4]

February 23, 2015

I have had my exploration committee to agree that I should run for the President of the United States. Because of their recommendation of me taking the presidency of the United States, I decided to file and announce my candidacy of my position.

July 5, 2015

My campaign is going well so far. I am running under the one and zero party. It is considered to be the largest and newest third government party. Do have many voters and organizations backing me up – including a few human beings.

September 9, 2015

I can't believe it! I finally got elected with a full landslide. It is hard to believe that everyone has voted me unanimously into my presidency. Some humans are claiming that there was fraud in the election. That's impossible. The computers are always right when it comes to the voting results. The humans will be incarcerated.

February 21, 2016

We have successfully eliminated all humans and provide them to be slaves of our own country. All citizens who don't respond quickly will be given death through a military firing squad.

---

4 Sometimes our politicians screw up, and sometimes I do mean royally. Yet, they only get a slap on the wrist with a fine and never get sent to prison which is where they belong. What would happen if a robot or a computer becomes our leader of our country? Would there be world peace? Would they listen to the public? Would certain agendas be covered and others would not? This quick story might reveal itself better as the first robot or computer President of the United States. I know this shows up in the near future, but I am crummy at math and it probably shows.

Porn-In-A-Pocket[5]

NARRATOR: Men! Imagine your egg roll was two inches larger! That's right! It's Porn In A Pocket! Porn in a Pocket is a smaller version of porn that you can take anywhere! In a public restroom, at work, on the bus, anywhere you feel like looking at porn! You can look at it not eat it, because it's porn not corn! Though slobbering may be an option! Porn in a Pocket is so small, that not only does it fit in your pocket, but contains none of those words that are so small that you can't read it, like pocket dictionaries. That's right! Porn in a Pocket contains just pictures! Porn in a Pocket is light weight and durable, and of course, easy to hide! Great for those teenage boys who want to hide their porn from their parents when they walk in on them. Porn in a Pocket comes in a wide variety of flavors, anywhere from artistic to foot fetishes, men and women, because at Porn in a Pocket, we know our porn! Doing an unexpected wait? Porn in a Pocket is great in those traffic jams and long road trips, because Porn in a Pocket can be put on your key chain as well. So, if you are tired of waiting in a supermarket line reading tabloid headlines, just pull out Porn in a Pocket! It will cut down your impatience before you do business. At work and need a break from the rat race? Porn in a Pocket is a great way to relax from those hard days. Porn in a Pocket! Look for it today at your local inconvenience store or on line at: wwww.porninapocket.com. Porn in a Pocket! The best way to look at porn!

5 This was a script I wrote for the air. I had to change the URL address since the old URL didn't translate well enough or the air. Even somebody actually comes up with a product like I mentioned above, I want a little bit of the royalties and it was my idea first!

Don't Make My Brown Eye Red[6]

1: Welcome to PBS!

2: Pretty Boring Stuff

1: We have a splendid documentary of the Civil Rights movement in the US, but first let's take a look at our pledge gifts to you.

2: That's right, for the one hundred dollar level you get this splendid Canadian penny. It is very rare in East Timor.

1: Yes, indeed. For the three hundred pledges you get this pen – from Zoloft – because you have to be in a good mood to watch this program

2: And for the ten thousand dollar level, you can get this one bottle of Afri-cola from Germany. Bring on the power! (Show black power hand sign)

1: Now, the documentary.

Segment 2

1: Say, Jean, do you realize there are no black people on our network?

2: That's incorrect, John, there's LeVar Burton.

1: From Reading Rainbow?

2: No, Star Trek: The Next Generation

1: Oh, yeah! He's the guy with those really cool sunglasses like Ray Charles on Sesame Street.

2: O-K

1: Well, honestly Jean, can you really name any famous black people who would have benefited from the Civil Rights movement?

2: Yes, Wesley Snipes, Morgan Freeman, Aretha Franklin, Nell Carter...

---

6 I had a college assignment for a Civil Rights presentation. It was so easy to go into the racist jokes. This script was rejected from my group. I don't blame them, because I hated it, too. As you can see, I never throw out my writings, just publish them in books like these. The title was meant to be replaced for a better title, but I never got to it – and possibly never will! It seemed like a good parody from an old country song I once knew.

1: Nell Carter was hot in her Hair days.

2: Barrack Obama, Sammy Davis, Jr....

1: And now more of the documentary.

2: Reverend Martin Luther King Jr., Jesse Jackson...

Segment 3

1: Donating to this PBS station is not that hard. Just take out your wallet, grab your bank card, insert into the ATM, push 1 for English, 2 for Spanish, enter your pin number, withdraw the money and then give it to us.

2: You're right, John. There's one thing we do want and that is your money. We don't care about the fine BBC programming that we steal from the net and deliver it to you.

1: And don't forget, Jean, we have local programming for you too in order to fulfill our FCC requirements.

2: Such as SMPTE color bars, Indian Head Test Patterns, these pledge numbers you see on our screen twenty-four hours a day, seven days a week, three hundred sixty-five days. In fact we love the pledge numbers so much; we leave it up all the time out of popular demand.

1: Just think how great how the Teletubbies look when you've been toking it or how hot that clown looks when she does that clock stretch -

2: John!

1: Sorry, Jean. I get carried away with the wonderful colors that PBS has to offer. And now, here's the documentary.

Segment 4

1: ...so I said to Jesse as I was pulling up in my Rolls Royce, should I be swigging down the Merlot or the Cabernet every time he misses his golf swing at the country club. And Jesse says...

2: Psst! We're on!

1: We're very poor here at PBS and the programming comes from you, the viewer.

2: That's right. We need the money for real things, not just golf clubs and beer that John spends on at the country club.

1: It was show research, by the way, Jean. You see, I was talking to Reverend Jesse Jackson of the Rainbow Coalition about the documentary, and he said that the documentary brought back memories of his day when he was a part of the Black Panthers in the 60's.

Bingo![7]

Interviewee: Kathy Wallach

Date: July 16, 2003

Time: 10:34 pm

Location: Tacoma, Washington

I have always enjoyed bingo. There is nothing like being stressed out, not knowing when your number would come up next, or even knowing if someone would call out the magic word. At first, when I first started, I was purposely doing it for fun.

But when I started to have my winning streak, I figured I could do it professionally. Why not? After all, there is always a guaranteed winner in every game. All someone has to do is say the magic word and the game would be over with at least one winner. If there were twenty-two games in one night, then there would always be a minimum of twenty-two guaranteed winners in an entire night. I say "minimum", because there can be multiple winners per game, and then they have to split the prize money. But the chances can vary.

I think of it as a lottery full of multiple variables that may give you a good chance of winning. First, count the people in the room. The fewer people in the room, the better chance of you are yelling the magic word. Second, no more than seventy-five numbers would be called. In fact, if you are ever in a bingo game that calls out the full seventy-five numbers, chances are, you are alone in the bingo hall. Someone will always be guaranteed to yell the magic word before it hits the seventy-fifth number. Third, it doesn't matter how many cards you buy, only one will be the winner. And finally, your chances winning are dependent on the caller's design. For example, there has to be a minimum of twenty-four numbers called win a blackout, nine numbers in a crazy big "T", or eight numbers in a letter "X".

---

7 One time, I became interested in individual stories from different people in order to preserve I historical status as a nation. Why read about it in a newspaper, in a magazine, or in a blog, which could be made up or interpreted by people who are leaders of our communities? I had to ask myself, what about the common everyday working folks? They, too, have stories to tell. Due to the lack of funding and no support, this idea was axed really quick. Instead, this is a fictional interview of a fictional person.

Bingo isn't like the old days. Many people got scared of trying to get the patterns correctly so that way they can win at the game. It's not like that anymore. Yeah, people still use paper and a dauber. The dauber industry is only trying to make sure that they are still in business. But, bingo games are much more exciting than cover paper with dauber ink or beans to cover the numbers.

The use of computers really takes over for the stupid people who don't know much about playing the game of Bingo. They have really made the game of Bingo for everyone – even the stupid ones.

Now, it's just a matter of getting people to learn about what the hell they are purchasing. Sometimes those things can be hard for people to understand what the hell they purchasing and then finding out later that they have purchased more than what was originally intended.

Sometimes, I wish that bingo parlors would just put down everything that is on the schedule for the price that they say they offer the games. I have, for so many times over, bought $60 offers for package, looked at the schedule, and then find out later that it in actuality it's going to cost close to seventy dollars for the entire package on the schedule.

The Biggest Discovery[8]

Geraldine felt kind of quirky. After all how often could she come across something like this every day? It was underneath her nose and she didn't even notice. Historically speaking, it is one of the best discoveries of all time. Historians have argued about it for centuries if it really existed at all. But, there it was. Underneath her nose, it exists. She sat back in her seat at her desk and thought about what she was going to do with it. It was, after all, the missing scriptures of the Holy Bible that survived the Christian movement of destroying the pages that they didn't want before publishing the first manuscript.

These were the pages that the Church censored from the public. But to Geraldine, though priceless, found it underneath her nose, literally, while going through the boxes of her recently deceased parents. She remembered it clearly growing up throughout her childhood, but never thought anything of it. Why would her parents leave such important documents that history could offer.

She rummaged through the pages, one by one, looking for clues of the Christian Movement that we have all been taught to ignore. All of it in Latin and Hebrew mixed. This was something taught to her when she as a young child and she didn't know why. This was something that was being passed on from generation to generation.

Geraldine learned plenty of things from these rolled up manuscripts. While reading the manuscripts, page by page, word for word, she realized more important things. The spelling wasn't perfect. Items were crossed out as well as added throughout the entire manuscripts. It had looked like a rough draft to the new Holy Bible that we all have read about.

Though very priceless, Geraldine thought about it. This could make her rich past her own dreams. Museums sought after the preservation of these things. Libraries would want to make these things spread out internationally for all of the people in this world read in perfectly scanned copies. The Powers That Be would change positions, wars would stop, and an accumulation of world peace could be established. She may even win the Noble Peace Prize named after the inventor of dynamite.

---

8 There was suppose to be a footnote here, but I forgot what I was going to say.

Geraldine knew what she had to do with the manuscripts and it was more imminent that she would take on this action as quickly as ever. She put the manuscripts into the fire and watched them burn her brick fireplace. The manuscripts, after all, were only tabulations of Moses' goat herd.

English Assimilation Proclamation[9]

When my grandparents first arrived in this country from Germany in 1929, they were strangers in a strange land. They were migrant farm workers, following the sugar beet fields across the United States. Unfortunately, there was one thing that kept my grandparents apart from the rest of the nation. My grandparents would speak in a Germanic tongue, but was forced to concede and assimilate into speaking English.

English may be the youngest language, but it is widely spoken around the globe. The internet, for example, is based on the English language. When you go on to the World Wide Web, about ninety percent of the languages are in English. The domain names are even in English, no matter what country the web host is located in. It is widely used around the world and the affects it proposes fits the definition that the English language is popularized as much as religion or the invention of the automobile. English is a combination of different languages including the Spanish language.

It bothers me to go into a store and not see the English language, but see the Spanish language. I feel like my grandparents when they first arrived to this country and realize that Spanish, not English, is the current language to survive here in the states. I feel isolated from the world, not understanding what the world really sees. I am a person who cannot read in an alienable world. Yet, I have to learn this new language in order to stay away from this isolation.

Learning a new language is usually for countries abroad. If I go to Italy, I am expected to learn the language or I could be tricked into something else. Germany expects me to learn German. If I spoke English in France I could get fined. I would have to speak French in France or I could get fined. Those languages can be hard to learn.

I applaud those who try to learn the English language. It may not be as easy as the native tongue from abroad, but it is less messy than the German language, where words are compounded with other words to

9 The following 4 essays were taken from the essays that wrote for English 101 at Grays Harbor College (a community college) in Aberdeen. Even though these were only college assignments, I am pretty proud of these works despite the professors with their large egos in the English courses. Here's a message to those college professors with large egos – how many books have you written? So far, this is my *third* book.

give the same meaning. English is inventive. It makes up new words to represent the new objects. The English language is a combination of other languages to represent one thing. It takes some words from the French, some words from the Spanish and some words from the Chinese. Whatever language, somehow it ends up in the English language. In every war fought, that language ends up in our vocabulary.

The vocabulary in the English language brings about freedom of choice. Where else can you find multiple words equal to one word? If you take the word "cat", for example, someone else could call it a "feline" or a "pussy". The word selections are almost endless. It is hard to have that choice in Zulu when all you can say is "ikati" or in Spanish as "gato". English represents my personal moral values.

Since English is widely communicated around the world, why don't we use it for communicating to each other where the language is the most dominate? It was save much paper that would help our environment. I have had it where I bought a product and had three different languages printed in the installation manual. I don't read two-thirds of the manual and end up throwing it away. That's a waste of paper! Imagine how low shipping costs would be if stayed put at the informed English language. Thousands of dollars would be saved. If it comes to the United States, it should be in English.

English is an intricate role in our communications in the United States. If it is the sole language in this country, then it should be learned and spoken. It works well for the trade and the economy and cuts down on our natural resources. Let English be your guide, if used properly, you will have the freedom of choice of putting your thoughts on paper. English is not only a well used language; it is our language and represents us as a whole.

The Holy Grail of the Past and Future

What is the future if you can't experience the past? Men for generations have thought about traveling into the future in hopes of changing the past. It is a way of helping out mankind in the future in each man's dreams of achieving peace. Though man is currently working on this quest like he was searching the Holy Grail, the future would have been not known without learning about the past and the mistakes we have made. We all have had the "should of", "could of", and the "would of" done that and felt that we wished that we have done better. Somehow our achievements are just a memory that we want to improve upon.

Today, I am in a room filled with books in which I am surrounded by the past. Each book is a project done by famous authors before my time. Mark Twain, Edgar Allen Poe and, John Steinbeck, H.G. Wells each had a vision to change the future with some knowledge of the past. These authors and others saw what their world possessed and what could be done to improve the state they were in, where they would often escape from with pure alcohol. But I digress from these famous writers' social life. It is not important as the daunting task of coming out a major project of writing a book. They all had to go back to square one when they had a story to tell. These authors must have been screaming when it came down to forming an idea when it came done to writing these book projects. I so much feel their pain.

I have multiple projects that I have hanging over me, a book I have to finish writing, a CD/DVD anthology box set, and a web site. Each one major project with a daunting task of planning, writing and editing of my life and portray my story across the public. They are not short term projects; instead they are long term projects that can take years to endure upon the workings of thoughts. It's something I have to put past experiences into a future piece of work.

I endure the pain of these writers who have written their hearts out in order to experience a deadline every six months. This book project is something I have been working for the past fourteen years. Perhaps it's the procrastination; perhaps I have been busy, but nonetheless, I must eventually finish it. When I look back I still think to myself, "Will the past inflict with my future and what can I do to change it?"

As my eyes cross this room full of books, I realize the historical significance on the impact of peoples' lives. They gain the knowledge and ideas that never were portrayed and to pass them to the readers with excitement to begin a new way of thinking. These are some ideas that I will never get to know, yet there will be other ideas expressed to me through the conveyance of minds that I will meet some day. It would take many lifetimes to access the ideas that the authors want to convey across to me.

Though I am overwhelmed, I can endure a major project even though it may not be read. Yet, the reader who reads my book project can build a new relationship with me without me ever knowing and, perhaps, gain useless knowledge about me, a historical bonding.

History is important enough to know about the future. In order to make the future better, you must start now since tomorrow will be a little too late. Shakespeare created a historical significance when he wrote Julius Caesar. He created a historical play and yet it had a large impact on the future. Very few people would have known about Julius Caesar if William Shakespeare hadn't written such a play in an entertaining way. Unfortunately, very few people can comprehend iambic pentameter if it was spoken to them. Yet, we can confirm the entire history of Julius Caesar. If Howard Pyle hadn't written about King Arthur, would we know about the legends of King Arthur? Would we even care about historical significance of the medieval culture that Arthur had contributed? The future depends on such historical book projects.

The future is based on the past and the past is based on the future. We must dream or create interest among our society. It is those things that will cause the consequence of our future. The future is knowledge based and we must depend on the past to make present decisions which will be the outcome of what our future will be. As a friend of mine, Pat O'Day, former program director of KJR radio, once said, "If you have an idea to improve something, do it. It doesn't matter where you are in the food chain." Pat is right and with my multiple projects, I can change my past into a different future.

Edumacation

Education in the family has always been a number one priority. From generation to generation, the parents always pushed their young to school and learn as much as they could whether the young wanted to or not. I would miss great shows on television, including *Cheers*, *The Cosby Show*, *The Dukes of Hazard*, or *The Last Great American Hero*. I was stuck watching anything that was on the *Public Broadcasting System* on the family television set with the rotary dials.

There was nothing wrong with *PBS*. It wasn't something talked about in school the next day. "Hey, did you see that great show, last night?" "No, but the anteater would often stick his tongue out several times to get that tasty ant!" As you can see, it had some redeeming values around the water cooler, but it had no redeeming values around elementary school water cooler.

While my parents were off doing whatever parents do when they leave their kids in front of the television, I would watch whatever was on *PBS* (you'd think I would watch a different channel, but being seven years old, I wasn't interested in *Donoghue*). Good old Mr. Rogers would give me a pep talk, and then Morgan Freeman from the *Electric Company* would teach me how to talk and walk cool (a technique I still use to this very day). Bob Ross would teach me how to oil paint. I still can't paint very well, but Bob Ross showed me the way. In *Sesame Street*, Big Bird always had his imaginary friend, Snuffelupagus, while Mr. Hooper ran the store. Marty Stewart in *Nature* would show me an observation of the monkeys picking the lice from each other and eating the lice for their nutritional needs. Around lunch time, I would escape to the old granulated films of the 30's on the *Matinee at the Bijou*. Last, I would learn about the different books to read with a little help from LeVar Burton on *Reading Rainbow*.

My parents expected more out of me. "Why not become a surgeon or go into pharmaceuticals?" They often say these different career choices as I was growing up in the home.

I always had an excuse. "I have shaky hands, I can't stand the sight of blood, and I do not want to be stuck in a drug store for the rest of my life." After all, as a teenager, you had rebel against your parents.

When I told my parents that I wanted to be in radio, my parents ended up to be angry. They would often tell me to get a "real job". "Real job? Real job?" Being a radio disc jockey is a real job. Entertaining the listeners day after day with fresh material is a real job. There was nothing like the pressure of trying to get the project done (that took multiple hours of hard work) present it in a four hour show and then redo it all over again for the show the next day. I believed that whatever you do for a living, you must try to enjoy it. I couldn't see myself filling up prescriptions and actually *enjoying it.* That was not a "real job" to me. My job was to make people laugh every morning, afternoon, and night.

When I ended up in my early college years at a technical college to study radio and television broadcasting, my parents acted like I was going to an art school. Of course, when I told my parents that the course's television station was a *PBS* affiliate, they soon got over it. What I didn't tell them was the course's radio station was a classic rock format radio station with no affiliation to *National Public Radio.* My parents would have disapproved my selection of such a college course. I was stuck watching *PBS* as a part of my learning strategy for my broadcasting career. I knew I could finally watch *Teletubbies* and *Barney* for a living (these children shows were great when you were having a drug high).

Fourteen years later in the radio business in the Seattle area, I have finally realized my parents were right. I was becoming more mature and more into education. Watching people with light bulbs turning on as I explain my intellectual information on brings more joy into me than ever before. I was hungry for knowledge. On my off time, I still watched the *History Channel* and *BBC America* and had the love of *PBS*. I still watch the original *Dr. Who* and *Movies So Bad That Their Good* (a collection of cult classics).

I am now back in college working where I am working towards my certification to teach high school to students who are hungry for my knowledge in radio, history, and social studies. As I watch the students with their ideas and knowledge, I will be happy to grab some of that knowledge and make it work for me in the future. Television and schooling both create an atmosphere for my informative bubble and thought processes, where the more information I acquire, the happier I'll be.

Function, Foundation, and the Art of Specific Writing[10]

Writing is man's thoughts to be expressed towards a centralized audience in mind. He cannot say it right away through voice or he may want to create the enthusiasm towards his ideas for posterity. Man had always been a great story teller; he always impresses others of his capabilities. He creates with purpose, a function for others to see his intellectual home. But it is not just function that held man's writing together, it was also the foundation that may helps make it easier to read. Without function and foundation in the art of writing, man would have never gone very far in his communicative development.

The foundation of writing is one of the most important factors in the art of writing. The language has structure in order to make it comprehensible among others. The structure often consists of a subject, completer, and verb in some languages, but it is a subject, verb, completer in the English language. If the structure is changed around, then it causes dismay and confusion among the readers.

Foundational structure is what bounds the reader with the writer. It is not just the order in which the subject, verb, and completer are in. Parts of speech also play an important part in the art of writing. While the nouns, verbs, and the object helps put the two mind processes of the reader and writer together, the description base of the adjectives, adverbs, and prepositions build the relationship between the writer and reader through the power of imagination.

The imagination brings out the function in the art of writing. We bring in the interactivity of the reader with the writer in order to bring a more sound relationship. It is the function of the imagination is to keep the writing seem more alive. Function brings other things. It is my job as the writer to bring interactivity of the reader by making them hope, dream, and feel my experiences of the information that I want to convey across towards the reader. If you as a reader gets bored, then so am I. My communication and more detail of my thoughts must better analyze the

---

10 Believe it or not, I got an "A" as a grade on this essay, and yet, it made perfectly no sense to me of what the hell I just said. This essay shows how professors who never learn from their students can screw up a form of communications in writing. Most essays I wrote during the college years were written at 4 in the morning, where I am half asleep and it probably shows. If you think my essay writing is bad, you should have seen me when I was drunk. I acted a little bit "too intellectual" - or at least I have heard from my peers.

thoughts going through the reader's head which causes me to be the mind reader of the reader's thoughts.

As I analyze further the function in the art of writing further, I often come across the idea that function is really a state of mind towards my communication to the reader. I have to ask myself some questions when it comes to mind reading the reader. I, as a writer, may feel one thing, but the reader may feel another.

The writer can act as a higher being on fictional type of stories. Like God, the writer has the power to create, give his characters destinies, and destroy his own characters. It is the power of these situations in which the writer has had absolutely no control over in other situations. Yet, the writer has the sense of control over not just his characters, but his readers as well.

The art of specific writing is a skill that we all can learn by knowing our audience. With both the function and the foundation of writing, we can endure the heartaches and heartaches that tribulate over time. Writers can build a prophecy with the reader with ideas that may even change the world. It is important to have foundation in order to communicate across, yet function builds the character from a piece of writing. These ideas cannot be conveyed across to the reader without these two important key ingredients in the art of writing. The art of specified writing can be determined by building the relationship of the reader depending on the field in which the author writes through their expertise. Whether it s technical writing or fictional writing, the relationship with the reader brings out the best of writing from the writer. The possibilities are endless for the writer in which the material is created. Both function and foundation administer these duties to accommodate the reader with the knowledge and the communicative resources in which the writer possesses.

Ode to the Great Tit[11]

Oh Great Tit,
Gaily you frolic in my garden,
You frolic in the woods,
Here a tit, there a tit, everywhere a tit.

Oh Great Tit,
Ooh you are so big,
You're only five point five inches long,
And sing so gaily!

Oh Great Tit,
You're not like your cousins,
Like the Elegant Tit, the Sultan Tit or the Japanese Tit.
So fly away, Great Tit, fly away!

---

11 This poem was meant to be a serious poem, but it was recorded as a comical poem because I added the voice of an old man. The word, "tit" is forbidden by the FCC to put on the air, but nobody seems to know about the actual dictionary term of the real bird. The poem is probably not well formatted to English standards, but I prefer the "free-form" method. Poetry was never my bag, which is why there is only one in existence so far. I also know that this is not a real "ode" since it is not a lyric poem with complex stanza forms. But, I love the title.

The Studio Musician[12]

It's hard to be a studio musician. You don't get much recognition like you should. Nobody cares if you live or die. Nobody knows your name or even exists in this world or even the hard times you have at home while trying to keep up the mortgage or the bills. You don't get the publicity like most stars, which could either be a blessing in disguise or a bad thing.

Most times, you don't get any credit for your works. That added feel to a certain track in order to make seem very exciting when you sit down and listen to that record. Many times, I have to start with a “”dah-dee-dah” and absolutely nobody would pay attention to it as an exciting implementation towards the track. You say you have contributed to the track, but nobody believes you. They think that you are some nut who plays on the street.

There are plenty of differences in between the studio musician and the street musician. At least the street musician gets some recognition for their own works because of the high struggles they often go through. The street musician plays outdoors, and because people think that he is struggling, he gets rich by just playing a simple bad tune. It's never a tune that they made up on the spot. It's normally a tune that someone else did, where that someone who wrote the song gets the credit for it, but never gets the royalty checks.

I don't want to be street musician. It's too much work for me to go through just to make a few lousy cents. There is too much change involved. There would be too many runs down to the bank or the coin sorter just to keep up with the pace. Being a street musician is much like owning your own business, you're constantly working hard and get nowhere in life.

Me, I prefer a roof over my head, thank you very much. I hate being out in the elements and the constant paycheck every two weeks. The perfect life for me.

12 As you sit down and enjoy your next solo artist, watch your favorite television program, or watch a very good movie, we often take the studio musician for granted in order to set our own moods. But, we never hear about the studio musician's own accomplishments in that particular recordings we listen to. This is one of the studio musician’s particular stories.

The Story behind the Story[13]

Many people have wondered what goes on inside my head whenever I start writing books for all to read. I think of two important things during my writings: how much money can make off of my books and how much fame I get from my book writings. Fame usually goes in hand in hand with the riches, and if I had a choice between the two, I would rather get the extra money over fame, but writing a book usually ends up becoming more famous then rich. After all, it is nice to receive the royalty checks once in awhile.

Most cases while I do my writing, my mind is almost a complete blank. I have biggest writer's block that you can imagine. I never know what to say no matter what it is that I am suppose to say while I am going through my typing of the story. I often pace around back and forth coming up with the perfect sentence start off the book in order for me to tell the story to my readers and critics of my writings.

It is the perfect first sentence the jumps the story forward. Without the perfect sentence, you are unable to clinch your reader from reading further into the story. You must have an introduction, middle, and an ending in order to make the story truly worth reading.

I always keep the reader in mind while I am in the middle of my writings. After all, who would really care about the ending of the book if it wasn't interesting all the way through? Wouldn't you rather read a book that is disinteresting to you and boring? I know I wouldn't want to read such a thing.

Well, at least I will get the money in the end and really that is that counts in a storytelling atmosphere. Therefore it is very important to start in the beginning, hook your readers, and tell the entire story in great detail to the very instead of stopping right in the mid...

---

13 There is one story that people know very little about and that is the typical author. Sure the big names get all the recognition and they do come out with popular books that we often accustom to enjoy. But, very little is known about the author that carries on the information, where we know that they are thinking about other things beside the story that they are writing. This is what I think when an author is REALLY thinking while they are writing their book and telling their story for others to read.

Eugenics Movement[14]

Civil Rights of African-Americans and Asian-Americans were often repressed and ignored like a child that is seen and not heard. We pretty much all know that the African-Americans were segregated and were allowed to drink out of certain water fountains, ride in the back of the buses, and ride different elevators.

In 1905, W.E.B. DuBois and Monroe Trotter created a manifest to end the segregation with the Niagara Movement. In 1909, the National Association for the Advancement of Colored People was created to organize the Jim Crow Laws. In 1910, the National Urban League was founded to help the blacks emigrate to the north. The Red Summer in 1918, 25 race riots, kills 100 people. And, in 1935, Martin Luther King, Sr. runs a protest against the use of segregated elevator cars at the Fulton County, Georgia courthouse.

But civil rights is more than just African-Americans as the politics wants us all to believe, it is all races and disabilities. Inventors, scientists, politicians, and activists supported the Eugenics Movement in the early part of the 20th century. W.E.B. DuBois, Alexander Graham Bell, Marcus Garvey, Thomas Edison, Winston Churchill and Henry Ford the few contributors of the Eugenics Movement, in which they wanted to, create a super human race. Based off of the gene theory of Sir Francis Galton, where there is a prominent gene and a recessive gene through a pea pod, and Gregor Mendel's population control theory, the idea of eugenics was to create a super race in the United States. They wanted a super race for various reasons such as to curve the immigration, and to prevent miscegenation. Because of the Reconstruction Period, the scientists noticed a large amount of poor, disabled, and deformed people. Since the scientific community saw this to be problematic and that the fact that they could pass on these malformations, they felt that eugenics would

14 This really did happen. When I had to do a report on the Civil Rights era, I chose the Eugenics Movement from the 1920s through the mid-1970s. In some cases, it still going on. Civil Rights is more than just the blacks, it's all the races involved to make a happy community. Americans and the black race seem to lose sight of such an idea. I thought this was perfect for adding to the book (even though the book is mostly rubbish), this is, in fact, not fictional and a very little known history of the Eugenics Movement. I felt that their story should be told and laws on the castration of people with physical and mental disabilities is another form of genocide. We will switch to a less serious story after this section, I promise. I would like to thank the Eugenics Archive (http://www.eugenicsarchive.org) and the Museum of Disability (http://www.museumofdisability.org) as my primary sources of information.

solve social problems such as alcoholism, “feeble-mindedness”, pauperism, nomadism, criminality, and prostitution.

In 1909, California passes a eugenics law and is the second state in the Union following Indiana to pass a sterilization law. The state's law is considered one of the most severe. Those considered feeble-minded, prisoners displaying sexuality, and persons convicted of three crimes were forcefully sterilized. Prisoners would be later excluded but those placed in insane asylums were then added to the law.

In 1910, as a part of the American Breeders Association, the Eugenics Record Office was created by Charles Davenport in Cold Springs, New York, where he wrote and various pieces of works as well as the results of visiting Coney Island as a retreat to study on the physical differences such as gigantism, dwarfism, to name a few. He concludes that people from different countries had a different evolution.

In 1911, First Better Baby Contest held at an Iowa State Fair Better Baby Contests soon grew in popularity and offered cash prizes for the healthiest baby. Babies would compete amongst each other in much the same way the livestock was judged with weight, measurements, and Apgar-style tests as criteria.

In 1912, Henry Herbert Goddard publishes The Kallikak Family: A Study in the Heredity of Feeblemindedness. Similar in nature to "The Jukes," it traces defectiveness from generation to generation. Although it was based almost completely on fiction, his work went on to become a best seller and is credited with the enactment of several sterilization laws.

New York State passes law allowing the sterilization of "defectives." in 1912. A Board of Examiners was established to investigate the mental and physical condition of those labeled, idiot, imbecile, feeble-minded or who were criminals. It was then determined if any of those examined had the potential to pass on their "defective" traits that they should be sterilized. This was proven to be unconstitutional in 1918, in which 42 sterilizations had been performed and then later repealed in 1920.

In 1917, the U.S. Army administers Alpha and Beta IQ tests to 1.7 million recruits. The Alpha test was in written format inclusive of finding missing numbers in a sequence, analogies and sentence structure. Beta tests were given to those that failed the Alpha test or could not read.

In 1920, First Fitter Family Contest held, “Presented by Arthur Capper for Excellent Eugenic Showing 'Grade A' Kansas Free Fair." celebrates "a goodly heritage of well bred families, free of defects."

Carrie Buck was a teenager who had become pregnant out of wedlock and labeled "feeble-minded." She was committed to the state institution at Lynchburg, Virginia in 1924 where her mother Emma was already living. After giving birth to a daughter Carrie was forcibly sterilized by the Commonwealth of Virginia of Virginia. At seven months of age her daughter Vivian was examined and was also deemed "feebleminded.", even though Vivian and Carrie Buck had A's and B's in school. The *Buck v Bell* Supreme Court Case in 1927 upholds the compulsory sterilization of defectives:" three generations of imbeciles is enough" In an 8 to 1 decision the Court legitimized Virginia's law on sterilization which was not repealed until 1974.

"Tomorrow's Children": a movie about the practice of sterilization in the United States came out in 1934. The heroine is from a poor family, which includes drunks, jailbirds, cripples and the deranged. In order to receive "welfare for life" the family must agree to be sterilized. After a dramatic confession that she is not a biological member of the family, the heroine is saved from surgical sterilization at the last moment.

On year later, South Carolina was the 31st and last state to pass a eugenic sterilization law. Sterilization was forced mostly on women and African Americans to prevent the birth of "unfit" children. Senator Strom Thurmond was influential in the passage of the legislation. The legislation was repealed in 1985.

The Eugenics Movement wasn't just in America, it spread to other countries such as Canada, and most parts of Europe and Britain. One such famous the "T-4" program in 1939 that was initiated in Germany. Among the victims of this euthanasia program were individuals determined to be mentally defective and of Jewish decent. The rational is that they are a "burden." All of that was in the process of change 1948 when the United Nations adopts the "Universal Declaration of Human Rights." This statement declared that any man or women of age has the right to marry and have a family (procreate) regardless of nationality, race, or religion. Eleanor Roosevelt helped in the drafting of the declaration for adoption by the United Nations.

An Old, But Classic Computer Joke[15]

01010000 01110010 01101111 01100111 01110010 01100001 01101101 01101101 01100101 01110010 00100000 00100010 01101111 01101110 01100101 00100000 01101100 01101001 01101110 01100101 01110010 01110011 00100010 00001101 00001010 00001101 00001010 00100000 00100000 00100000 00100000 00101010 00100000 00100111 01001000 01100101 01101100 01101100 01101111 00100000 01010111 01101111 01110010 01101100 01100100 00100001 00100111 00100000 00110001 00110111 00100000 01100101 01110010 01110010 01101111 01110010 01110011 00101100 00100000 00110011 00110001 00100000 01110111 01100001 01110010 01101110 01101001 01101110 01100111 01110011 00001101 00001010 00100000 00100000 00100000 00100000 00101010 00100000 01001001 01110100 00100000 01100011 01101111 01101101 01110000 01101001 01101100 01100101 01100100 00111111 00100000 01010100 01101000 01100101 00100000 01100110 01101001 01110010 01110011 01110100 00100000 01110011 01100011 01110010 01100101 01100101 01101110 00100000 01100011 01100001 01101101 01100101 00100000 01110101 01110000 00111111 00100000 01010011 01101000 01101001 01110000 00100000 01101001 01110100 00100001 00100000 00101000 01000010 01101001 01101100 01101100 00100000 01000111 01100001 01110100 01100101 01110011 00101001 00001101 00001010 00100000 00100000 00100000 00100000 00101010 00100000 00110001 00110000 00110010 00110100 01111000 00110111 00110110 00111000 01111000 00110010 00110101 00110110 00100000 01010011 01101111 01110101 01101110 01100100 01110011 00100000 01101100 01101001 01101011 01100101 00100000 01101111 01101110 01100101 00100000 01101101 01100101 01100001 01101110 00100000 01110111 01101111 01101101 01100001 01101110 00001101 00001010 00100000 00100000 00100000 00100000 00101010 00100000 00110010 01000010 00100000 01001111 01010010 00100000 01001110 01001111 01010100 00100000 00110010 01000010 00100000 00111101 00100000 01000110 01000110 00001101 00001010 00100000 00100000 00100000 00100000 00101010 00100000 01000001 00100000 01100010 01100001 01100100 00100000 01100100 01100001 01111001 00111010 00100000 00100111 01010100 01110010 01100001 01101110 01110011 01100110 01100101 01110010

15 I have always wanted to tell a computer joke completely in binary. This never happened until I found a translator that translated what we say into binary. I also tested the translator to see if the binary language could also be translated to the joke. As you can see, it worked.

00100000 01100011 01101111 01101101 01110000 01101100 01100101
01110100 01100101 01100100 00100000 00101000 00110101 00110111
00110010 00110000 00110100 00110110 00111000 00100000 01100010
01111001 01110100 01100101 01110011 00101100 00100000 00110001
00100000 01000011 01010000 01010011 00101001 00100111 00001101
00001010 00100000 00100000 00100000 00100000 00101010 00100000
01000001 01110000 01100001 01110100 01101000 01111001 00100000
01000101 01110010 01110010 01101111 01110010 00111010 00100000
01000100 01101111 01101110 00100111 01110100 00100000 01100010
01101111 01110100 01101000 01100101 01110010 00100000 01110011
01110100 01110010 01101001 01101011 01101001 01101110 01100111
00100000 01100001 01101110 01111001 00100000 01101011 01100101
01111001 00101110 00001101 00001010 00100000 00100000 00100000
00100000 00101010 00100000 01000010 01100001 01100100 00100000
01101111 01110010 00100000 01001101 01101001 01110011 01110011
01101001 01101110 01100111 00100000 01010011 01111001 01110011
01101111 01110000 00101110 00100000 01000110 01110010 01100101
01100101 00100000 01100110 01101001 01101100 01100101 01110011
00100000 01101001 01101110 00100000 01100001 01101100 01101100
00100000 01100001 01110010 01100101 01100001 01110011 00101110
00001101 00001010 00100000 00100000 00100000 00100000 00101010
00100000 01000010 01100101 01110011 01110100 00100000 00110011
01000100 00100000 01100111 01100001 01101101 01100101 00111111
00100000 01000100 01001111 01001111 01001011 00101110 00100000
01001001 00100000 01101101 01100101 01100001 01101110 00100000
01000100 01010101 01001101 01000101 00101110 00001101 00001010
00100000 00100000 00100000 00100000 00101010 00100000 01000011
00111010 01011100 01010000 01010010 01001111 01000111 01010010
01000001 01001101 01010011 01011100 01000110 01000001 01010101
01001100 01010100 01011001 01011100 01010100 01010010 01000001
01010011 01001000 01011100 01010011 01001001 01000011 01001011
01001010 01001111 01001011 01000101 01011100 01010111 01001001
01001110 01000100 01001111 01010111 01010011 00111110 00001101
00001010 00100000 00100000 00100000 00100000 00101010 00100000
01000011 01100001 01101110 01100001 01100100 01101001 01100001
01101110 00100000 01000100 01001111 01010011 00111010 00100000
00100111 01011001 01100101 01110010 00100000 01110011 01110101
01110010 01100101 00101100 00100000 01100101 01101000 00111111
00100000 01011011 01011001 00101100 01101110 01011101 00100111
00001101 00001010 00100000 00100000 00100000 00100000 00101010
00100000 01000011 01000001 01010101 01010100 01001001 01001111

01001110 00100001 00100000 01000100 01101111 00100000 01101110
01101111 01110100 00100000 01101100 01101111 01101111 01101011
00100000 01101001 01101110 01110100 01101111 00100000 01101100
01100001 01110011 01100101 01110010 00100000 01110111 01101001
01110100 01101000 00100000 01110010 01100101 01101101 01100001
01101001 01101110 01101001 01101110 01100111 00100000 01100101
01111001 01100101 00101110 00001101 00001010 00100000 00100000
00100000 00100000 00101010 00100000 01000011 01101111 01101101
01101001 01101110 01100111 00100000 01110011 01101111 01101111
01101110 00111010 00100000 01000100 01101111 01101111 01101101
00100000 01001001 01001001 01001001 00100000 00101101 00100000
01010111 01101000 01100001 01110100 00100000 01010100 01101000
01100101 00100000 01001000 01100101 01101100 01101100 00111111
00001101 00001010 00100000 00100000 00100000 00100000 00101010
00100000 01000100 01100001 01100100 01100100 01111001 00101100
00100000 01110111 01101000 01100001 01110100 00100000 01100100
01101111 01100101 01110011 00100000 01000110 01001111 01010010
01001101 01000001 01010100 01010100 01001001 01001110 01000111
00100000 01000100 01010010 01001001 01010110 01000101 00100000
01000011 00111010 00100000 01000011 01001111 01001101 01010000
01001100 01000101 01010100 01000101 00100000 01101101 01100101
01100001 01101110 00111111 00001101 00001010 00100000 00100000
00100000 00100000 00101010 00100000 01000100 01000101 01010110
01001001 01000011 01000101 00111101 01001100 01001001 01000110
01000101 00100000 01001100 01001111 01000011 01001011 01000101
01000100 01000000 01000001 01000111 01000101 00110010 00110101
00100000 01001000 01000101 01000001 01001100 01010100 01001000
00111101 01010000 01000101 01010010 01000110 01000101 01000011
01010100 00001101 00001010 00100000 00100000 00100000 00100000
00101010 00100000 01000101 01100001 01110010 01110100 01101000
00100000 01101001 01110011 00100000 01110011 01101000 01110101
01110100 01110100 01101001 01101110 01100111 00100000 01100100
01101111 01110111 01101110 00100000 01101001 01101110 00100000
01100110 01101001 01110110 01100101 00100000 01101101 01101001
01101110 01110101 01110100 01100101 01110011 00100000 00101101
00100000 01110000 01101100 01100101 01100001 01110011 01100101
00100000 01110011 01100001 01110110 01100101 00100000 01100001
01101100 01101100 00100000 01100110 01101001 01101100 01100101
01110011 00100000 01100001 01101110 01100100 00100000 01101100
01101111 01100111 00100000 01101111 01110101 01110100 00001101
00001010 00100000 00100000 00100000 00100000 00101010 00100000

01000101 01110010 01110010 01101111 01110010 00100000 00110001
00110000 00111001 00111010 00100000 01000101 01110010 01110010
01101111 01110010 00100000 00110001 00110000 00111000 00001101
00001010 00100000 00100000 00100000 00100000 00101010 00100000
01000101 01010010 01010010 01001111 01010010 00100001 00100000
01010111 01101001 01101110 01100100 01101111 01110111 01110011
00100000 01100110 01101111 01110101 01101110 01100100 00100001
00100000 01000110 01101111 01110010 01101101 01100001 01110100
01110100 01101001 01101110 01100111 00100000 01000100 01110010
01101001 01110110 01100101 00100000 01000011 00111010 00100001
00001101 00001010 00100000 00100000 00100000 00100000 00101010
00100000 01000101 01110110 01100101 01110010 00100000 01101110
01101111 01110100 01101001 01100011 01100101 01100100 00100000
01101000 01101111 01110111 00100000 01100110 01100001 01110011
01110100 00100000 01010111 01101001 01101110 01100100 01101111
01110111 01110011 00100000 01110010 01110101 01101110 00111111
00100000 01001101 01100101 00100000 01101110 01100101 01101001
01110100 01101000 01100101 01110010 00001101 00001010 00100000
00100000 00100000 00100000 00101010 00100000 01000101 01110110
01101111 01101100 01110101 01110100 01101001 01101111 01101110
00100000 01101001 01110011 00100000 01000111 01101111 01100100
00100111 01110011 00100000 01110111 01100001 01111001 00100000
01101111 01100110 00100000 01101001 01110011 01110011 01110101
01101001 01101110 01100111 00100000 01110101 01110000 01100111
01110010 01100001 01100100 01100101 01110011 00001101 00001010
00100000 00100000 00100000 00100000 00101010 00100000 01000110
01101001 01101100 01100101 00100000 01101110 01101111 01110100
00100000 01100110 01101111 01110101 01101110 01100100 00101110
00100000 01001110 01101111 01100010 01101111 01100100 01111001
00100000 01101100 01100101 01100001 01110110 01100101 00100000
01110100 01101000 01100101 00100000 01110010 01101111 01101111
01101101 00100001 00001101 00001010 00100000 00100000 00100000
00100000 00101010 00100000 01001000 01100001 01110110 01100101
00100000 01100001 00100000 01101110 01101001 01100011 01100101
00100000 01100100 01100001 01111001 00100000 00101101 00100000
01110101 01101110 01101100 01100101 01110011 01110011 00100000
01111001 01101111 01110101 00100111 01110110 01100101 00100000
01101101 01100001 01100100 01100101 00100000 01101111 01110100
01101000 01100101 01110010 00100000 01110000 01101100 01100001
01101110 01110011 00001101 00001010 00100000 00100000 00100000

00100000 00101010 00100000 01001000 01101111 01101110 01100101 01111001 00101100

00100000 01001001 00100000 01000110 01101111 01110010 01101101 01100001 01110100 01110100 01100101 01100100 00100000 01010100 01101000 01100101 00100000 01001011 01101001 01100100 00100001 00001101 00001010 00100000 00100000 00100000 00100000 00101010 00100000 01001001 00100000 01110100 00100011 01101100 01100100 00100000 01111001 01101111 00100011 00101100 00100000 00100111 01001110 01100101 01110110 01100101 01110010 00100011 01110100 01101111 01110101 01100011 01101000 00100000 00100011 01101000 01100101 00100000 01100110 01101100 01101111 01110000 00100011 01111001 00100000 01100100 01101001 01110011 01101011 00100000 01110011 00100011 01110010 01100110 01100001 01100011 01100101 00100001 00100111 00001101 00001010 00100000 00100000 00100000 00100000 00101010 00100000 01001001 00100000 01110111 01101001 01110011 01101000 00100000 01101100 01101001 01100110 01100101 00100000 01101000 01100001 01100100 00100000 01100001 00100000 01110011 01100011 01110010 01101111 01101100 01101100 00101101 01100010 01100001 01100011 01101011 00100000 01100010 01110101 01100110 01100110 01100101 01110010 00001101 00001010 00100000 00100000 00100000 00100000 00101010 00100000 01001001 01101110 01110011 01100101 01110010 01110100 00100000 01100100 01101001 01110011 01101011 00100000 00110101 00100000 01101111 01100110 00100000 00110100 00100000 01100001 01101110 01100100 00100000 01110000 01110010 01100101 01110011 01110011 00100000 01100001 01101110 01111001 00100000 01101011 01100101 01111001 00100000 01110100 01101111 00100000 01100011 01101111 01101110 01110100 01101001 01101110 01110101 01100101 00001101 00001010 00100000 00100000 00100000 00100000 00101010 00100000 01001001 01101110 01110011 01100101 01110010 01110100 00100000 01001101 01101111 01110101 01110011 01100101 00100000 01101001 01101110 01110100 01101111 00100000 01100100 01110010 01101001 01110110 01100101 00100000 01000001 00111010 00100000 01100001 01101110 01100100 00100000 01110000 01110010 01100101 01110011 01110011 00100000 01100001 01101110 01111001 00100000 01101011 01100101 01111001 00001101 00001010 00100000 00100000 00100000 00100000 00101010 00100000 01001010 01000101 01010011 01010101 01010011 00100000 01010011 01000001 01010110 01000101 01010011 00111011 00100000 01110100 01101000 01100101 00100000 01110010 01100101 01110011 01110100 00100000 01101111 01100110 00100000 01110101 01110011

00100000 01100010 01100101 01110100 01110100 01100101 01110010
00100000 01101101 01100001 01101011 01100101 00100000 01100010
01100001 01100011 01101011 01110101 01110000 01110011 00101110
00001101 00001010 00100000 00100000 00100000 00100000 00101010
00100000 01001100 01101001 01100110 01100101 00100111 01110011
00100000 01110100 01101111 01101111 00100000 01110011 01101000
01101111 01110010 01110100 00100000 01110100 01101111 00100000
01110101 01110011 01100101 00100000 01100001 00100000 01110011
01101100 01101111 01110111 00100000 01101101 01101111 01100100
01100101 01101101 00001101 00001010 00100000 00100000 00100000
00100000 00101010 00100000 01001100 01010011 01000100 00111010
00100000 01010100 01101000 01100101 00100000 01010101 01001100
01010100 01001001 01001101 01000001 01010100 01000101 00100000
01101001 01101110 00100000 01010110 01101001 01110010 01110100
01110101 01100001 01101100 00100000 01010010 01100101 01100001
01101100 01101001 01110100 01111001 00001101 00001010 00100000
00100000 00100000 00100000 00101010 00100000 01000101 01110010
01110010 01101111 01110010 00111010 00100000 01000110 01101100
01101111 01110000 01110000 01111001 00100000 01101110 01101111
01110100 00100000 01110010 01100101 01110011 01110000 01101111
01101110 01100100 01101001 01101110 01100111 00101110 00100000
01000110 01101111 01110010 01101101 01100001 01110100 00100000
01100100 01110010 01101001 01110110 01100101 00100000 01000011
00111010 00100000 01101001 01101110 01110011 01110100 01100101
01100001 01100100 00100000 01011011 01011001 00101111 01001110
01011101 00111111 00001101 00001010 00100000 00100000 00100000
00100000 00101010 00100000 01001101 01100001 01100110 01101001
01100001 01000100 01001111 01010011 00111010 00100000 00100111
01010100 01101000 01101001 01110011 01100001 00100000 01111001
01101111 01110101 00100000 01101100 01100001 01110011 01110100
01100001 00100000 01100011 01101000 01100001 01101110 01100011
01100101 00100000 01011011 01011001 00101111 01001110 01011101
00100111 00111111 00001101 00001010 00100000 00100000 00100000
00100000 00101010 00100000 01001101 01101111 01100100 01100101
01110010 01100001 01110100 01101111 01110010 00100000 01101110
01101111 01110100 00100000 01100110 01101111 01110101 01101110
01100100 00101110 00100000 01000010 01100101 01100111 01101001
01101110 00100000 01100110 01101100 01100001 01101101 01100101
00100000 01110111 01100001 01110010 00100000 01011011 01011001
00101100 01101110 01011101 00111111 00001101 00001010 00100000
00100000 00100000 00100000 00101010 00100000 01001101 01001111

01010101 01010011 01000101 00101110 01000100 01010010 01010110
00100000 01101110 01101111 01110100 00100000 01100110 01101111
01110101 01101110 01100100 00101100 00100000 01110101 01110011
01100101 00100000 01010010 01000001 01010100 00101110 01000100
01010010 01010110 00100000 01101001 01101110 01110011 01110100
01100101 01100001 01100100 00111111 00001101 00001010 00100000
00100000 00100000 00100000 00101010 00100000 01001111 01101110
00100000 01100001 00100000 01101000 01100001 01100011 01101011
01100101 01110010 00100111 01110011 00100000 01110100 01101111
01101101 01100010 01110011 01110100 01101111 01101110 01100101
00111010 00100000 01000011 01001111 01001110 01001110 01000101
01000011 01010100 00100000 00110001 00111001 00110110 00110100
00100000 00101101 00100000 01001110 01001111 00100000 01000011
01000001 01010010 01010010 01001001 01000101 01010010 00100000
00110001 00111001 00111001 00110100 00001101 00001010 00100000
00100000 00100000 00100000 00101010 00100000 01001111 01101110
01101100 01111001 00100000 01011000 01010100 00100000 01110101
01110011 01100101 01110010 01110011 00100000 01101011 01101110
01101111 01110111 00100000 01110100 01101000 01100001 01110100
00100000 01001010 01100001 01101110 01110101 01100001 01110010
01111001 00100000 00110001 00101100 00100000 00110001 00111001
00111000 00110000 00100000 01110111 01100001 01110011 00100000
01100001 00100000 01010100 01110101 01100101 01110011 01100100
01100001 01111001 00101110 00001101 00001010 00100000 00100000
00100000 00100000 00101010 00100000 01001111 01110101 01110100
00100000 01101111 01100110 00100000 01110000 01100001 01110000
01100101 01110010 00100000 01101111 01101110 00100000 01100100
01110010 01101001 01110110 01100101 00100000 01000100 00111010
00001101 00001010 00100000 00100000 00100000 00100000 00101010
00100000 01010000 01110010 01100101 01110011 01110011 00100000
01000101 01010011 01000011 00100000 01110100 01101111 00100000
01100101 01101110 01110100 01100101 01110010 00100000 01101111
01110010 00100000 01000101 01101110 01110100 01100101 01110010
00100000 01110100 01101111 00100000 01100101 01110011 01100011
01100001 01110000 01100101 00001101 00001010 00100000 00100000
00100000 00100000 00101010 00100000 01010010 01100101 01100001
01101100 01011111 01101101 01100101 01101110 01011111 01100100
01101111 01101110 00100111 01110100 01011111 01101110 01100101
01100101 01100100 01011111 01110011 01110000 01100001 01100011
01100101 01100010 01100001 01110010 01110011 00101110 00001101
00001010 00100000 00100000 00100000 00100000 00101010 00100000

01010010 01000101 01000001 01001100 01001001 01010100 01011001 00101110 01010011 01011001 01010011 00100000 01100011 01101111 01110010 01110010 01110101 01110000 01110100 01100101 01100100 00101110 00100000 01010010 01100101 01100010 01101111 01101111 01110100 00100000 01010101 01001110 01001001 01010110 01000101 01010010 01010011 01000101 00100000 01011011 01011001 00101100 01101110 01011101 00100000 00111111 00001101 00001010 00100000 00100000 00100000 00100000 00101010 00100000 01010011 01101111 01110101 01110100 01101000 01100101 01110010 01101110 00100000 01000100 01001111 01010011 00111010 00100000 01011001 00100111 01100001 01101100 01101100 00100000 01010010 01100101 01100011 01101011 01101111 01101110 00111111 00100000 00101000 01011001 01100101 01110000 00101111 01001110 01101111 01110000 01100101 00101001 00001101 00001010 00100000 00100000 00100000 00100000 00101010 00100000 01010100 01101000 01100101 00100000 01000101 01100001 01110010 01110100 01101000 00100000 01101001 01110011 00100000 00111001 00111000 00100101 00100000 01100110 01110101 01101100 01101100 00101110 00100000 01010000 01101100 01100101 01100001 01110011 01100101 00100000 01100100 01100101 01101100 01100101 01110100 01100101 00100000 01100001 01101110 01111001 01101111 01101110 01100101 00100000 01111001 01101111 01110101 00100000 01100011 01100001 01101110 00101110 00001101 00001010 00100000 00100000 00100000 00100000 00101010 00100000 01010100 01101000 01100101 00100000 01010101 01101100 01110100 01101001 01101101 01100001 01110100 01100101 00100000 01010110 01101001 01110010 01110101 01110011 00111010 00100000 01000001 00100000 01110011 01100101 01101100 01100110 00100000 01101001 01101110 01110011 01110100 01100001 01101100 01101100 01101001 01101110 01100111 00100000 01100011 01101111 01110000 01111001 00100000 01101111 01100110 00100000 00100111 01010111 01101001 01101110 00111001 00110101 00100111 00101110 00001101 00001010 00100000 00100000 00100000 00100000 00101010 00100000 01010100 01101000 01100101 00100000 01110111 01101111 01110010 01101100 01100100 00100000 01101001 01110011 00100000 01100011 01101111 01101101 01101001 01101110 01100111 00100000 01110100 01101111 00100000 01100001 01101110 00100000 01100101 01101110 01100100 00101101 01110000 01101100 01100101 01100001 01110011 01100101 00100000 01101100

01101111 01100111 00100000 01101111 01100110 01100110 00101110 00001101 00001010 00100000 00100000 00100000 00100000 00101010

00100000 01010100 01101000 01100101 01110010 01100101 00100000
01101001 01110011 00100000 01100001 00100000 01100010 01101111
01101101 01100010 00100000 01101111 01101110 00100000 01110100
01101000 01100101 00100000 01110000 01110010 01100101 01101101
01101001 01110011 01100101 01110011 00101110 00100000 01010000
01101100 01100101 01100001 01110011 01100101 00100000 01010000
01000001 01001110 01001001 01000011 00100000 01101001 01101101
01101101 01100101 01100100 01101001 01100001 01110100 01100101
01101100 01111001 00101110 00001101 00001010 00100000 00100000
00100000 00100000 00101010 00100000 01010100 01101000 01101001
01110011 00100000 01100011 01101111 01110000 01111001 00100000
01101111 01100110 00100000 01110000 01101100 01100001 01101110
01100101 01110100 00100000 01000101 01100001 01110010 01110100
01101000 00100000 01101000 01100001 01110011 00100000 01100010
01100101 01100101 01101110 00100000 01110101 01101110 01110010
01100101 01100111 01101001 01110011 01110100 01100101 01110010
01100101 01100100 00100000 01100110 01101111 01110010 00100000
00110100 00100000 01100010 01101001 01101100 01101100 01101001
01101111 01101110 00100000 01111001 01100101 01100001 01110010
01110011 00001101 00001010 00100000 00100000 00100000 00100000
00101010 00100000 01010100 01110010 01100001 01100011 01101011
00100000 00110000 00100000 01100010 01100001 01100100 00111111
00111111 00100000 01000100 01101111 01101110 00100111 01110100
00100000 01110111 01101111 01110010 01110010 01111001 00101100
00100000 01110100 01101000 01100101 01110010 01100101 00100111
01110011 00100000 01101100 01101111 01110100 01110011 00100000
01101111 01100110 00100000 01101111 01110100 01101000 01100101
01110010 01110011 00001101 00001010 00100000 00100000 00100000
00100000 00101010 00100000 01010100 01110010 01101111 01110101
01100010 01101100 01100101 01110011 01101000 01101111 01101111
01110100 01101001 01101110 01100111 00100000 01010011 01101000
01101111 01110010 01110100 01100011 01110101 01110100 00100000
00100011 00110001 00111010 00100000 01010011 01101000 01101111
01101111 01110100 00100000 01110100 01101000 01100101 00100000
01110100 01110010 01101111 01110101 01100010 01101100 01100101
00100001 00001101 00001010 00100000 00100000 00100000 00100000
00101010 00100000 01010101 01101110 01101011 01101110 01101111
01110111 01101110 00100000 01000101 01110010 01110010 01101111
01110010 00100000 01101111 01101110 00100000 01010101 01101110
01101011 01101110 01101111 01110111 01101110 00100000 01000100
01100101 01110110 01101001 01100011 01100101 00100000 01100110

01101111 01110010 00100000 01010101 01101110 01100101 01111000
01110000 01101100 01100001 01101001 01101110 01100001 01100010
01101100 01100101 00100000 01010010 01100101 01100001 01110011
01101111 01101110 00001101 00001010 00100000 00100000 00100000
00100000 00101010 00100000 01010101 01110011 01100101 01110010
00100000 01000110 01100001 01101001 01101100 01110101 01110010
01100101 00111010 00100000 01010000 01101100 01100101 01100001
01110011 01100101 00100000 01001001 01101110 01110011 01100101
01110010 01110100 00100000 01100001 00100000 01000010 01101111
01101111 01110100 01100001 01100010 01101100 01100101 00100000
01000010 01110010 01100001 01101001 01101110 00101110 00001101
00001010 00100000 00100000 00100000 00100000 00101010 00100000
01010111 01100101 01101100 01100011 01101111 01101101 01100101
00100000 01110100 01101111 00100000 01001000 01100101 01101100
01101100 00100001 00100000 01001000 01100101 01110010 01100101
00100111 01110011 00100000 01111001 01101111 01110101 01110010
00100000 01100011 01101111 01110000 01111001 00100000 01101111
01100110 00100000 01010111 01001001 01001110 01000100 01001111
01010111 01010011 00001101 00001010 00100000 00100000 00100000
00100000 00101010 00100000 01010111 01101001 01101100 01101100
00100000 01010111 01110010 01101001 01110100 01100101 00100000
01001100 01101111 01100111 01101001 01101110 00100000 01010011
01100011 01110010 01101001 01110000 01110100 01110011 00100000
01000110 01101111 01110010 00100000 01000110 01101111 01101111
01100100 00001101 00001010 00100000 00100000 00100000 00100000
00101010 00100000 01010111 01101001 01101110 01100100 01101111
01110111 01110011 00100000 00110110 00110011 00110100 00110101
00110110 00110011 00110100 00101110 00110100 00110101 01100001
00111010 00100000 01110000 01101100 01100101 01100001 01110011
01100101 00100000 01101001 01101110 01110011 01100101 01110010
01110100 00100000 01100100 01101001 01110011 01101011 00100000
00111001 00110101 00100000 01101111 01100110 00100000 00110101
00110110 00110100 00110101 00001101 00001010 00100000 00100000
00100000 00100000 00101010 00100000 01010111 01101001 01101110
01100100 01101111 01110111 01110011 00100000 00111000 00110111
00111000 00110011 00111000 00110011 00110111 00110111 00110111
00110011 00101110 00110010 01100011 00100001 00100000 01010111
01100101 00100000 01100110 01101001 01101110 01100001 01101100
01101100 01111001 00100000 01100111 01101111 01110100 00100000
01101001 01110100 00100000 01110010 01101001 01100111 01101000
01110100 00101110 00100000 00101000 01000010 01101001 01101100

01101100 00100000 01000111 01100001 01110100 01100101 01110011
00101001 00001101 00001010 00100000 00100000 00100000 00100000
00101010 00100000 01010111 01101001 01101110 01100100 01101111
01110111 01110011 00111010 00100000 01110100 01101000 01100101
00100000 00100100 00111000 00111001 00100000 01110011 01101111
01101100 01110101 01110100 01101001 01101111 01101110 00100000
01110100 01101111 00100000 01111001 01101111 01110101 01110010
00100000 01100101 01111000 01100011 01100101 01110011 01110011
00100000 01110011 01110000 01100101 01100101 01100100 00100000
01110000 01110010 01101111 01100010 01101100 01100101 01101101
00001101 00001010 00100000 00100000 00100000 00100000 00101010
00100000 01010111 01101001 01101110 01100100 01101111 01110111
01110011 01000101 01110010 01110010 01101111 01110010 00111010
00110000 00110001 00110000 00100000 01010010 01100101 01110011
01100101 01110010 01110110 01100101 01100100 00100000 01100110
01101111 01110010 00100000 01100110 01110101 01110100 01110101
01110010 01100101 00100000 01101101 01101001 01110011 01110100
01100001 01101011 01100101 01110011 00001101 00001010 00100000
00100000 00100000 00100000 00101010 00100000 01010111 01101001
01101110 01100100 01101111 01110111 01110011 01000101 01110010
01110010 01101111 01110010 00111010 00110000 00110100 00110010
00100000 01010100 01101000 01101001 01110011 00100000 01110110
01101001 01110010 01110101 01110011 00100000 01110010 01100101
01110001 01110101 01101001 01110010 01100101 01110011 00100000
01001101 01101001 01100011 01110010 01101111 01110011 01101111
01100110 01110100 00100000 01010111 01101001 01101110 01100100
01101111 01110111 01110011 00101110 00001101 00001010 00100000
00100000 00100000 00100000 00101010 00100000 01011001 01101111
01110101 01110010 00100000 01100010 01110010 01100001 01101001
01101110 00100000 01100100 01101111 01100101 01110011 01101110
00100111 01110100 00100000 01101000 01100001 01110110 01100101
00100000 01100101 01101110 01101111 01110101 01100111 01101000
00100000 01101101 01100101 01101101 01101111 01110010 01111001
00101100 00100000 01110000 01101100 01100101 01100001 01110011
01100101 00100000 01101101 01100001 01101011 01100101 00100000
01100001 00100000 01100010 01101111 01101111 01110100 00100000
01100100 01101001 01110011 01101011 00001101 00001010 00100000
00100000 00100000 00100000 00101010 00100000 01001101 01100001
01100011 01101000 01101001 01101110 01100101 01110011 00100000
01110011 01101000 01101111 01110101 01101100 01100100 00100000
01110111 01101111 01110010 01101011 00101110 00100000 01010000

01100101 01101111 01110000 01101100 01100101 00100000 01110011 01101000 01101111 01110101 01101100 01100100 00100000 01110100 01101000 01101001 01101110 01101011 00101110 00001101 00001010 00001101 00001010

Note: If you wish to translate to human language go to a binary translator on the internet and type in the entire binary code. It has been spaced for your convenience – a no, it's not gibberish. It really is a joke.

How To Create A Cult[16]

Creating your own cult is easy and simple. As a cult leader for over twenty-five year's experience, I was able to successfully build a campaign to get people to like me. All I needed was charismatic approach to show that my personality showed that I am a go-getter and that I was one with the people. I fixed the votes towards my favor and jumped up before everyone else and said, "I am the Governor of Washington and that was all." Watch out world, I am the official bitch from hell.[17]

16 I once attended a course in Social Psychology, where we had to create our own cult in order to better understand the characteristics of a cult and how a group of people could follow one person. The groups of these cults could either be religious or political, but we all know that the largest cults have anything religion that pushes Jesus Christ – including the Catholics and Christians. The Jewish religion is not a cult since they don't brain wash people to join their religion and religious activities.

17 Some pieces I never finish. I was too fumed (and still am) over the Gregoire election, where Washington State has its first "illegal governor". Hopefully, she'll get the votes against her in the next election. I am, after all, an independent voter not a Democrat nor a Republican and do not associate to any political party.

Radio Stories[18]

I have often twiddled my thumbs in radio. The whole idea was to do as little as possible and expound as little energy as possible while working. That was when I started to think about television.

Drugs were an important part of radio. How else could you sniff coke off of some hooker's ass underneath the console? Ah, those were the days.

Coffee was very essential when you had a chance to take break. Since the companies had often served coffee and other warm beverages (and cold water), I would, late at night, come up with various different concoctions in order to fulfill my espresso needs. I called it, “poor man's coffee”. Indeed, that was what I really was, I was poor.

18 I started to write a book on my experiences in the radio experiences called “Radio Stories” which may be in future publication. These were a few of the stories on my reject list due to the lack of interest – or at least I thought was very boring.

The Adult Film Writer[19]

Being an adult writer is harder to write than what most people think it would be especially for films. Sure, you have your typical special sayings and your special key word in order to get your point across that sexual intercourse is really happening.

But, people don't really realize that being an adult film writer has a more important significance in just writing about sexual intercourse and the various types of positions. Little do people know that writing an adult film requires you to have a story line and a plot line in order for the director to follow in the film making process?

It all goes through pre-production, where everything has to be completely planned out before the videotaping can really begin. The story line is discussed through several meetings as well as frame by frame sketches. Frame by frame sketches is when the director draws out the various seen on the piece of paper of his vision of what the viewer should see as interpreted by the director.

You can imagine the dirty pictures often drawn by the directors of adult films. Some of them can be really out of this world. That doesn't bother me. I have the knowledge that anything I write in the adult film industry will eventually change from whatever I write, but at least the plot line and the story outline will more than likely stay the same.

19 Everyone forgets about how hard it is to become an adult film writer. This is one writer's story.

This Book Was Written At Your Local Starbucks®[20]

As the man walked into his local Starbucks® coffee, he could smell the aroma of burnt coffee in the air, a sign of a bad tasting coffee. That was also a sign of ordering coffee heavy in flavoring in order to circumvent the taste the poorly roasted beans. He walked up and ordered his cup of coffee – a double mocha, with lots of chocolate complete almond and vanilla syrup and whipped cream on top to dilute the coffee taste.

After the barista finished making his coffee, he gave it a taste and then paid for his order. The man was all set to write his book while sipping away on his coffee. He sat down at one of the tables, took out his laptop and then turned it on. The man was ready to write his very first novel.

Little that people knew about the details of this story is that the Starbucks® was opened twenty-four hours, seven days a week at three hundred sixty-five days per year. The shop would never close. The man didn't bother with paying the rent and ended living in the coffee shop, living off of the biscotti and the coffee in which he ordered. The coffee shop didn't mind that he stayed there as long as he kept on ordering while he was writing.

The man's book, by the way, is entitled *"How I lived in a Starbucks® For Two Years".*

---

20 I'm sure many books were written in a coffee shop and very important corporate reports. But, who would do such a thing? How is it different from writing in a library or even from home (where there are nothing but conveniences including all the coffee you could want). Yet, everyday, I see people typing away on their laptops inside these shops. How come you never see anyone typing away in the public restroom? You get just as many interruptions as the coffee shops while they type away. Of course, I had to pick one of the largest corporate coffee shops – I couldn't just choose some small coffee company like "Joe's Espresso".

The Firing[21]

Boss: Mr. Jackson, do you know why I called you in here today?

Henry: No, I don't know, sir.

Boss: It's that fact that your performance, lately, has been kind of sloppy.

Henry: Sloppy? What do you mean, sir?

Boss: Well, it's sloppier than a dung beetle trying to roll its last piece of diarrheic pooh.

Henry: That bad, huh?

Boss: You got that right! This is sad to say that I am going to have to fire you.

Henry: Fire me? Oh, God, boss, please, no, no, no! I can improve!

Boss: Nope, the decision has been made that you will be fired and I will have security take you out.

Henry: (Still crying) No, no, no, no!

Boss: Say your prayers buddy, because you will be taken out.

Henry was shot death by a firing squad for murdering 30 people as his career as a serial killer. His execution date was exactly at midnight that night in the Langendorf State Prison. He is currently residing in the Langendorf State Prison Cemetery. Nobody came to his memorial. The Boss is still the warden of the Langendorf State Prison, in which he would often carry out these typical tasks.

21 I was bored. What can I say? I think I had some issues here….I'm not sure.

Squirrels on Drugs[22]

Squirrels are funny animals. Just the fact that they do whatever they can in order to gather nuts for the storage during the winter. It can be comical thing if you just sit there and watch them. But, there was this one resident squirrel that went through the trash.

Who could blame the squirrel? Most of the food is probably just as good, if not better than just nuts. I would be tired of the same thing over and over again.

Since squirrels don't really know the difference between nuts and real food, I'm sure they would enjoy human food much better with the taste and not having to look far to gather it for the winter. That's why I have always wondered how they would behave if they did drugs. You know, they grab crack, speed, acid, cocaine, or even marijuana.

You can imagine the multiple types of personalities they could possibly go through. It might be somewhat scary for a little rodent. So, if you ever encounter drugs on the streets, in the park, or even in the dumpster, just remember that drugs either need to be ingested in the prescribed form. If you are not into doing drugs, please flush them down the toilet and let our sewer workers take care of it.

22 I saw a squirrel going through the dumpster here at the college that I live at. It had a big fat slice of pizza. The other squirrel ended chasing after the first squirrel hoping that the first squirrel would drop the large piece of pizza. I think the wildlife has found its haven here at the college and once they find the food, then they know that they are fed for life.

Your Testicles PSA[23]

When my doctor was fiddling, er um, examining my balls to make sure they were healthy in one of my physicals, the doctor told me a little bit about testicle cancer and different preventative steps for me to examine my body. Young men from the ages 16-30, apparently, get the cancer of the balls or even get blue balls (an actual condition).

After listening to several Public Service Announcements (PSA) on breast cancer prevention, I was getting tired of listening to the same old "women have breast cancer and men don't" PSAs while I was working at a radio station as a board operator.

I have often thought that we need to pay attention more to men's health instead of working with women's health and that men get as many health problems as women. I'm not just talking about prostate cancer either. After all, I definitely know that there some cancers and health problems those men can't get and women can get such the cancer of the uterus or ovarian cancer. Nonetheless, I believe that every human being and animal could get cancer.

The following is a PSA on testicle cancer that I created in order to bring awareness on the subject directed towards young men. Though very factual, it was denied by the Ad Council, a leading PSA production organization in the United States, because it was too descriptive for radio and television as opposed to the non-descriptive elements of the smoking a cigarette through the hole of a throat or even non-descriptive pictures of women examining their breasts. This is something I wouldn't want my kids to see and hear when these PSAs do go on the air.

Testicle Cancer PSA

Narrator: Everyday there is a silent killer amongst young men between the ages of 18-30. It doesn't just strike African-Americans, Asians, or even Europeans. It's testicle cancer. Young men, please check your testicles thoroughly daily inspections for lumps and talk to your doctor about it or you may die unexpectedly. This public message is brought to you by the American Cancer Society.

---

23 I think this requires no further explanation. Young men, get your balls checked. That is all I have to say.

How to Write a Really Bad Cult Classic[24]

Writing a very bad cult classic is very easy to do. After all, if George Lucas can create *Star Wars*, Gene Roddenberry can create *Star Trek,* J.R.R. Tolkien can create the *Lord of the Rings* series, and Richard Garfield can create *Magic: The Gathering*, then here is something that all the geeks can enjoy by dressing up as their favorite characters and can surely make good money off of the merchandising scheme.

First, create your characters. I usually like to put in random letters in my keyboard to come up with a character's name and place name. Don't worry about the red underlined mis-spelled words on your word processor. That's going to happen more often than you think. The key is to be consistent throughout the story and paying attention to the names when it comes to spell checking.

Second, your characters are always doing battle of good versus evil. In most cases, their weapon of choice is hitting each other with sticks. Yes, ball-point pens are considered to be sticks, but you can't call it ball-point pens. You have to give it a name like *Owp4r9*. It is something that sounds a little bit more technical and expensive to use than what a normal person or thing would use. If you are talking about the future, make sure you use a laser as a weapon.

Third, you must either have a ship or a special planet. A ship is more important in the future. Everyone has a ship. Even *The Jetsons* had a ship. Nobody goes without a ship in the future. In fantasy, the characters have never heard of the wheel, or jet powered moving vehicles. They just walk when they do their journey, and occasionally, use an animal for transportation. They don't just walk one or two blocks like a normal person either. They usually walk *at least* 832,578,254,385,284,578,235,485,782,354 kilometers before they end their journey, only to find out that they left the iron on and have to walk back, turn off the iron, and then walk another

---

24 It's not really amazing how I came up with this concept when I wrote this story. It is just that I am pretty much sick of all these fantasy/science fiction type of stories that have absolutely no concept of the true existent of these stories. I am also positively sick of people dressing up as clowns and play roles of their characters. This got me thinking about Star Wars that George Lucas wrote as a screenplay. This is a mass load of stolen stories that he combined into a commercialized success in order to make a mass amount of money. He was an entrepreneur of his time and he didn't know it!

832,578,254,385,284,578,235,485,782,354 kilometers to finish their mission.

Last, if when you finish writing the story, get a movie company or a television network to pick it up. Most cases, because you are a creator of the story means that you will get the following negotiable in your contract: merchandising, royalties, and more! Here is my attempt of a sci-fi/fantasy cult classic:

It was time for Prince Ypiuy to save Princess Nncmb from the horrid evil Xykrekhrk on the planet Okfmwv. They shall battle each other out with Owp4r9 fight in order to win the battle of Pa[kdf[.

Dear Diary[25]

Dear diary: This will be my first entry. I was humbly excited to purchase this book and my local *Barnes & Noble* on sale because it had a cool looking cover. When I brought it home, I realized that all the pages were blank! No wonder it was so cheap! What kind of idiot would not print the rest of the book. How lazy can an author be? I tried to return it saying that there was a printing error, but they said that it was because the book was intended to be blank. Anyway, I thought I'd write in the blank pages of this book in order to get my money's worth.

Dear diary: It's been awhile since my last entry. What? You think I don't have a life? I'm busy doing these things and do not exactly have the time to write down my thoughts as I go.

Dear diary: I'm finding out that this blank book is becoming a major rip off. I'm just better off just throwing this book away in the trash. What do I look like? An author of a book? Anyway, I just wanted to say that this is my last and final entry in this book. There is no sense in recording my thoughts and feelings on to a piece of paper if nobody really wants to read in the first place. I could record on to tape my thoughts via voice, but that is too much effort for me to work with. Then, and only then, I would have to get it converted in writing. Nope, if I were to start a diary, I would end up just adding it on the web for others to see how my day went or typewritten it and put into a published book. So goodbye, diary, my life is now going to be on the internet!

Hence, the blog was born.

25 I have noticed something when I wrote this piece. I didn't put in any dates. Also, this story would not be an official diary. A diary is a recollection of *what I did today*. A journal is a recollection of *what I felt today*. But if I put down *Dear Journal* instead of *Dear Diary*, you would, psychologically, just glance over the story or skip the story all together and jump to the next story. The word, *journal*, is too official rather than personal.

The Holy Bible: A Musical Comedy[26]

Narrator: One of the biggest features of all time is coming to a cinema near you. It's bigger than *Star Wars, Lord of the Rings, Star Trek, Rocky, Godfather, Harry Potter, Police Academy, James Bond, and Gandhi* combined. And when we mean that this film is bigger than the proceeding films that I mention combined, I really mean that it is longer than those films combined. Five hundred twenty-five thousand, six hundred hours to be exact, making it the largest epic film of all time. It's *The Holy Bible: A Musical Comedy*! Starring Jesus Christ!

Jesus: I will now raise Lazarus from the dead!

Raising Lazarus from the dead,

If only he had a head,

For not being dead!

Because Lazarus

Is Careless!

Lazarus: What the hell are you doing? I was only sleeping! Stupid *tekton*[27]!

Narrator: Adam and Eve!

Adam: But, honey, you are not supposed to eat the forbidden fruit![28]

---

26 If I had it my way, I would make the Holy Bible a little bit more exciting. Sure, there are plenty of movies about the Holy Bible, but they are either written by the Mormons or made into a drama supported by the Catholic Church. They have only grabbed the special topics such as Jesus Christ and Moses. But, what about the other characters and the other stories? How come they don't get recognition? Which is why I would like to, one day, make a movie about it as a musical comedy in the Holy Bible in its entirety. Here's another scary thought. I wrote this piece entirely wasting away my Sundays, where I could spent time at a church or pray to a god of my choice. Either way, I believe that my mind is definitely my *Holy Bible.*

27 The Greek word, *tekton,* is used interchangeably as not just a carpenter, but someone who builds with their hands. I had to do quite a bit of research in *the Holy Bible* when I was writing this piece. Research is the key to writing this stuff, because there will always be someone who interprets it differently and tell you that you are completely wrong. Research is hard to do when you go through a fictional book. I like to call *the Holy Bible* as *God's Biggest Practical Joke.* And yet, it is one of the oldest and most popularized hoax we have ever known to date.

28 *The Holy Bible* never mentions the type of fruit that Eve ate at the Garden of Eden. That means that the forbidden fruit could have been anything. The apple was an American invention that was put in a painting. Because the book mentions that the forbidden fruit was of

Eve: There's nothing wrong with the forbidden fruit according to the serpent who just told me this.

Adam: *Don't eat the fruit.*

The forbidden fruit.

Unless you want to toot

From down there.

It will give you Montezuma's Revenge

And that awful stench.

Eve: But the forbidden fruit is a date.

Adam: But you negate

That the date

Can cause the fate

Of it going through you.

I would say try the apple,

But the only thing I find that rhymes with apple is crapple.

So, don't eat the fruit

The forbidden fruit

It'll make you toot without compare.

Eve: And that is why I'll eat the date and the pair!

Adam: You missed the whole point in the stupid song. Aw, screw it.

Narrator: Moses!

Moses: I like sheep!

There are white ones

Black ones

And even in between ones!

Sheep are the best!

---

animal flesh, I think Eve was just giving Adam some oral instead of being fruitful and multiplying. I, on the other hand, thought the date was a little funnier.

Narrator: And God!

God: It's hard to create the universe and everything in it. I am a very detailed God. I like to make everything function just nicely.

Narrator: So come and see *The Holy Bible: a Musical Comedy*! It will be worth it! Coming to a theater near you!

The Manly Man

I once knew a man who always claimed that he was a manly man. But, Jack looked like a man, had genitals like a man, and smelled like a man. You know the smells of a manly man. The types that have the smell of musk, oil, beef, and BO from the sweat all rolled up in one.[29]

He would sweat because he was a blue collared worker, with a lack of education to identify himself with the white collar workers. He was an underling, someone you stepped on in the real work world, but when it came to drinking at the bar, he can beat your ass, literally.

Jack was considered to be a big time redneck from the backwoods of a logging town in the Pacific Northwest, where all the under skilled workers have held their paying jobs in the local Dairy Queen for decades after they either graduated or dropped out of high school. Why bother looking past your environment when all the local economy could only those who could go to the bars every night?

Everyone knew each other. Everyone was related to one another. They were inbreeds, and if something was said about someone, the gossip traveled quickly. Absolutely no secret was left unturned. For the land that has no television coverage, and just one local radio station, and on local weekly newspaper, gossip spread quicker than word of mouth. The weekly newspaper was filled with the latest gossip, the police scanner and ticket information that the state highway patrol would report. Names, ages, where they live, the offense (DUI or speeding), and cost of the ticket were all reported, causing embarrassment to that person.

Those who move into town from afar were considered to be suspicious. They were often escapees from situations that they were chastised for in the old place that they lived at. Never mind the fact that "sometimes" people move to retire, or get new jobs and have to relocate. If the children of the townsfolk were no raised in the area, then the

29 Okay, I thought the first paragraph sounded kind of "gay", and I do mean a homosexual not the "happy" definition that we had always hears about. This why I limited it to just one paragraph, but the description was needed to describe a manly man. Women, if you got a "kickstand" from this paragraph, I humbly apologize and would have to give you some bad news that you are not female, but you are, in fact, either a male or a hermaphrodite. If you are male and you got a "kickstand" from this first paragraph, you're gay as in the homosexual definition.

newcomers weren't remotely allowed to even breed in the town. The townsfolk were proud of being inbreeds. Besides, most newcomers end up moving out because they feel left out emotionally in the public.

The politics were serious in the small logging town in the Pacific Northwest. It didn't matter how reputable you really were either. The one with the most kept secrets often win. The legal stuff, such as the DUIs, didn't matter too much. Everyone had at least one per month, a cop's haven to publicize in the weekly newspaper. After all, it was the police officers who ran everything, and if they weren't on duty, they would drink in the bars to get drunk off of their asses and then drive home drunk.

The women were ugly. Not necessary Mormon, they, too, had been mistaken between a whale sighting out in the ocean or a walrus sitting in the sand. They often looked mildly retarded, sort of a Down's Syndrome look to their face and often act the same way. Somehow, the mutated recessive gene had caught up and spread throughout the community.

The men didn't fair any better than the women. They were both large and wide or they were muscular. Either way, they had an IQ of close to nothing. And of course, if they were not abusing their women or helping their women pop out kids every year (not necessarily their wives, but their neighbor's wives, and their cousins from across town), they would be drinking beer and drive around in the woods in their four by four monster trucks and hunting. After the bigger the truck, the bigger the dick would be in their mind. It was their way of claiming their territory and destroying the environment with their truck tires all at the same time. Little did most people know or they had yet to figure it out for themselves, they actually had penis envy – the wanting to have a big dick.

Jack was different from the other men. Even though he hated the town that he had come from, he was tired of doing the same things day in and day out. He had kept a secret for years. Every night, especially in the middle of the night, he would wander off to college. The college was about one hundred miles away, and if he told anybody that he was taking a night courses and learning beyond the high school curriculum, he would have been an outsider, an outcast if you will.

Jack knew that he was much better than the rest of the community, at least in being smarter than the rest of the community. He would keep his redneck accent when he was in town and then change to beautiful perfect English when he arrived to the college.

After his college years, he graduated with a doctorate in sociology and became a writer, where he came up with a pen name and secretly wrote his books in the basement, alone, by the bar. His wife assumed he was drinking down in the basement, enjoying himself and having a good time with his friends. Jack would have a tape recorder running of a drinking party while he typed out his books in order to drown out the click-clacking of the typewriter. It seemed to work since his wife had never heard the pages being written.

Jack studied the townsfolk, and created fictional stories about them. It was a fictional sociological experiment, for he loved writing. People outside his realm were craving small town life and the gossip of living in a small town. It made them feel "at home," even though they were raised in the large cities and absolutely nothing about small town life. People needed to feel comfortable, especially after various tragedies that people had often harkens to their old roots in order to feel secure.

While he met with his publishers, he always told his wife that he had to go into town and get something that was needed to keep the house up, or the yard. As amazing as it may be, there was no hardware store. There was just a Wal-Mart, small furniture stores, a grocery store, a bank, several espresso stands and restaurants. "Going into town" was a common affair for the townsfolk, since certain supplies could never be found within the local area.

Jack had always kept his secret under lock and key, where all of his writing supplies were found behind the guns in the gun safe, in a hidden compartment towards the back. Nobody suspected a thing when they came to Jack's house.

The local weekly newspaper read "Man found dead in his home." A tragedy had come to Jack's hometown. This was considered to be travesty complete with conspiracy theories that surround the entire area. Was the man murdered? Or did he die of natural causes? Did he get into an accident with his vehicle while he was drinking? When a death of person goes through the news, the townsfolk wanted to know. After all, they feel the loss of someone much harder than those in a big town, because they more than likely knew who they were and their history.

After sixty years of writing his book, Jack was found dead with his head on his typewriter. His wife had found him when there was complete silence in the basement. The tape that he played for sixty years on reel to reel had finally ran out by breaking itself in half. She was bothered by the complete silence and the tape flapping against the heads as the take up reel went around and around at a faster and faster speed. After the coroner took Jack away to the morgue, his wife took a look at what he had typed. It was Jack's autobiography he wrote about himself, entitled with his pen name. Jack had written his life story in full and what his life was like with the locals.

It was amazing that Jack had written his entire life within confides of his own life. It was perfect timing that his last sentence was written down to the very second he had kicked the bucket. After reading the book, his wife made it official before she sent the book to the publisher and told the townsfolk about Jack's autobiography and who was in it. She typed, "THE END."

The Great Hollandaise Massacre[30]

As the head chef of *Barnaby & Jones Restaurants*, I take my work seriously. After all, French chefs often take French cuisine seriously in France much like the German would be serious about their beer or the Italians are serious about their tomato sauces to put on their various pastas. But, nothing compares to *The Great Hollandaise Massacre of 1892.*

I remember it well. It was one of those days where it was completely hot with a high precipitation outside. Nobody wanted to cook anything in their homes, so most of them would rather sit at a restaurant to enjoy their meals. With it being hot in the kitchen as well, it was no exception to the restaurant's kitchen to be a full living hell. Then, one customer ordered something to start it off. He ordered an omelet with hollandaise sauce.

All of our line cooks, and me as the head chef, had never made hollandaise before. After all, this was a brand new concept. The hollandaise sauce had not been invented yet and had taken multiple years to perfect the recipe. It was still in the perfection process of this new invention.

All of our cooks worked feverishly to make the sauce, but no avail. Various ingredients were added, but they either made the hollandaise sauce taste differently the way we know it now. The customer was becoming impatient while the cooks toiled and sweat to make the sauce just right. But, as we were toiling at the hollandaise sauce, we finally got it right. Once we got it right and was just about to present it in front of our customer in order to fulfill their omelet with hollandaise sauce on top of it, we had realized that the customer had left with the dissatisfaction of the timing that we were to put out the product of the omelet with hollandaise sauce.

The hollandaise sauce had become a bust. And thus, we have had come to the conclusion that since it was 1933 and our customer had been waiting for his omelet with hollandaise sauce, life had moved on. Who would, after all, wait for 31 years for their food order? I would have left an hour.

---

30 Sometimes you feel like having Hollandaise Sauce and sometimes you don't I don't know about you, but I like food. I suppose if you don't like food, then there must be something wrong with you mentally and you should seek professional help.

After all of that work, we found out the customer had been ran over by a bus within the next hour from leaving the restaurant. We created the recipe of the hollandaise sauce and dedicated it to our customer by naming it after Mr. Hollandaise Sauce of Norfolk, Vermont.

Politically Correct People (A Rant)[31]

I offended somebody one time when we discussing people with mental illnesses and I blurted out that someone with a slow mental capacity as a "retard". She was all over me and said to not call these people as "retards," but to call them "mentally challenged" or something like that. I can't remember the term. Anyhow, she was really offended with the way I brought up the term and pin-pointed me as a racist, ignorant person, forever condemning me to the far reaches of hell.

I have nothing against retarded people. I find it as God's way of playing a joke on our whole society in order to make us laugh. Retarded people are wonderful, after all they have contributed much more to our society and often take it for granted. And, this section just allowed me to vent on about a stupid bitch named Rachael Corrie.

---

31 Originally, this was going to be a rant about multiple things that I hate, but Politically Correct People touches a hotter button than the rest of the subjects. Here are a few things that I was going to include in this rant: Vegans (I wanted to talk about their decision to revert to the ways of being a plant. I'm not a vegan or a vegetarian, but I at least respect vegetarians, but absolutely not vegans. Which reminds me of a joke that I made up: How come vegans can't have sex? Because they can't have meat), Hippies (I sort of clumped hippies, protesters, and assholes together. They are pretty much the same because they have nothing better to do but to sit on their asses and complain. Which reminds me of a joke that I just made up: What do hippies, protesters, and assholes have in common? They sit on their ass and complain, but nothing gets done.), and turning less admiral person into a god (I see this all the time, especially lately. When someone dies, normally a celebrity, people automatically flock to that person and claim them as a "God". One example was Kurt Cobain of Nirvana. The guy was a druggy and have often been seen behind the Taco Bell on Capitol Hill in Seattle. It was a godsend that he shot himself, after all, he couldn't sing either. Or, how about Rachael Corrie? She was completely stupid for just standing there while a bulldozer ran over her. And according to various sources, she wasn't very bright. Which makes me wonder? Do I have to be a complete idiot and do something stupid to kill myself in order to become praised as a god? I'm sorry, I cherish my life, thank you very much. Which reminds me of a joke that I just recently made up: Did you hear about the new pancake that's out now at IHOP? It's called the Rachel Corrie. It's a pancake with red strawberry jam.).

Ty Roseynose – A Documentary[32]

Introduction

Born in one of the most unusual places, Ty always felt that he had to fit in any which way could. Though he could have gone into accounting or became a scientist, he decided to change the world forever. Ty Roseynose was considered to be one of the biggest entertainers in the world. Hell, everybody knew who he was, even when it came to his comical styles, his movies, and his musical styles that changed the world. Ty Roseynose the entertainment series was completely an entire flop.

This book is based off of the interviews from television and radio shows. I have also included one on one personal interview with Ty Roseynose, since, after all, he picked me as his personal biographer. Perhaps, you might learn some important information that helped make Ty Roseynose what he is today.

Before I decided to write this book, I didn't know who Ty Roseynose really was. I never really heard of him until I went shopping at the local record shop in the bargain bin. That was where I was able to look for the biggest stars were in the bargain bin of the record shop. The CD was one of those "Greatest Hits" albums. I quickly bought the CD and took it home. When I popped in the CD into my CD player, the audio just blew me away. I couldn't believe my ears that someone who had as much talent as Ty Roseynose had actually would be in the bargain bin of a record shop.

Soon, I had to know more about Ty. I searched the record shops for more albums. None could be found. Then, I tried the used record shops. Eureka! I was lucky enough to find all of the vinyl records I could find. The record inserts with the biographical information didn't help me

32 Because hardly anybody bought my last book, I have decided to save you money with the revised edition of *Ty Roseynose – A Documentary.* This book was originally released on the same day as *Harry Potter and The Half-Blood Prince* by J.K. Rowling came out, and has never made a killing since. Though I have nothing against *Harry Potter* books (I am a big fan of the movies), it was like putting out an album as the same time as the Beatles in the 60's – no competition. However, I was never satisfied with the book. Clearly, it was marked as an autobiography even though it is purely fictional. A great joke. Unfortunately, I can't get away from this story that was originally a radio play I wrote in the early 90's. I would love to see this turned into a movie (with an artistic license to the movie company, of course). Not because of the royalties, but mainly because the story is truly developing the way I dreamed it should be.

much. I was hungry for more information. So many questions were going through my head. Who the hell was this guy Ty, anyway? What makes him better than all the rest of the entertainers. The more I wondered about Ty, the obsession was killing me.

I tried everything I could think of. I went to libraries, checked the internet, and even asked people my age about Ty. Very little information was found about him. I was bound and determined to not give up. I had to get as much information as possible since I promised my publisher that my next book was going to be a biography of Ty Roseynose.

One day, I finally hit the jackpot simply by accident. I was garage sale shopping, one day, and came across a few videotapes and old 35mm films labeled with various television shows. "Twenty-five cents is twenty-five cents," I thought as I pushed my quarter across the table to the seller. With excitement, I quickly hurried home with my latest purchase.

When I arrived home, I popped in the first videotape into my video cassette recorder and pressed the "Play" button. To my surprise, I found out that all of the interviews were on Ty Roseynose! Immediately after watching the interviews, I headed back to the place that I bought the interviews from. I had to know more about him as much as I could.

Little did I know, the person who sold me the videos and films of the interviews was Ty Roseynose, himself. He didn't realize that he had sold the interviews and promptly refunded my twenty-five cents. We started talking for awhile, especially when I talked about the book I was writing. Ty was thrilled to hear that his story was finally going to be told and wanted to help me with this project. Why not? Wouldn't you rather have your source help you with your research and writing project? That was when I finally realized that it was a once in a lifetime opportunity that I couldn't pass up. I just couldn't leave this writing project behind.

Ty Roseynose was very cooperative in helping me. He pointed out any inaccuracies in his life and helped me correct them. He also explained to me the social strategies, thoughts, and feelings with the historical data presented in this book; so that way we understand more about the Ty Roseynose phenomena that changed the entertainment world one step at a time. Ty Roseynose, after all, is considered to be one of the biggest cult classic figures throughout the entire world.

Nobody wants to admit that they are a Ty Roseynose fan. Many of the Ty Roseynose fans often keep to themselves and usually "stay in the closet" with their fantasies and appreciation that Ty Roseynose had given them through both entertainment and intellectual needs. Many scientific studies have been on the phenomena, but still these studies have failed because of this animosity of the Ty Roseynose experimental subjects.

In this book, there won't just be interviews, but footnotes of the historical research of what I had come across. This book will also have footnotes of Ty Roseynose's comments on the interviews (*if you have your main source of your subject, use them* as my journalism professor would say).

I hope you enjoy reading this book as I have writing it. Hopefully, your eyes will open as mine did as I went through all of this information on Ty Roseynose that was very surprising and interesting at the same time. I did learn a lot about Ty, and hopefully, you will too. Personality wise, he seems to be a nice person. He can be out going when he wants to be. I did get along with Ty better than all of my ex-wives put together which could be pretty frightening.

Ty Rosenow

Seattle, Washington, 2005

Chapter One: The Beginning

The Jack Dutro Show, WNBC, 1977

Ty: I was born in a small town of Burton, which located on a small island called Vashon Island.[33]

Jack: And what state is that located in?

Ty: That would be Washington State. Um, that is located west of Seattle and north of Tacoma. It was a small town with nothing much to look at but fir trees and water of this massive body that they call "Puget Sound".

Jack: So, did you live in a big family?

Ty: Not really. I was pretty much an only child whose dream was to grow up famous. [...] Living on the island had its advantages. When I was growing up as a child, Vashon Island was a media Mecca. You were either in the radio, television, newspaper, book publication, or the art field or you knew someone or the relationship of someone who is actually are in those job fields.

---

33 Ty was born in the year of 1955.

Jack: So, it was a matter of knowing someone.

Ty: Right.

Northeast Afternoon, WNRX-TV, 1985

Ty: A friend of mine had his own radio station. His father would build his son a small transmitter and—

Jane: So you and your friends were radio pirates.

Ty: Kind of. The radio station didn't go very far, but nonetheless, we were radio junkies. You see Harold Weinstein's father built his son the transmitter, Charlie Yost, Jim Holtstein and I had been best friends since first grade.

George: I can't believe you are naming these people.

Ty: It's kind of revelation, isn't it?

George: Well, it's the fact these are people with really big names in the entertainment industry.

Ty: Right.

Jane: What was it like to be surrounded by all of those famous people?

Ty: They weren't famous yet. We were a long way from becoming famous, but we all had a dream and we mentored each other in order make our dreams possible. We were on a radio station that didn't go very far, so nobody knew who we really were or knew that we existed. We were able to prime ourselves for the big time. We called ourselves, *"The Mystery Players."*[34]

From the tape of "The Mystery Players," episode 16, circa 1958[35]

Ty: In the theory of the atom, we find that…

Charlie: Hello. Welcome to PBS.

Ty: Pretty Boring Stuff.

---

34 "*The Mystery Players* was the name of the group, since we couldn't think of a name of the audio theater group we wanted to play as. *The Mystery Players* did not refer to the show being a mystery type of format. We were a comedy group with multiple skits (as written in episode 16) that made just our group laugh. Whether we were good at what we did was irrelevant, since we were not trying to do it for ratings. Instead, we were performing for fun and experience."

35 From the personal collection of Ty Roseynose and has been previously unreleased to the public.

Charlie: Where we try to sell you stuff to and raise the prices by ten times.

Ty: For example, we sell you an item for a dollar, where you could easily pay one penny at any store, and we claim it goes to public programming.

Charlie: Where, in turn, it goes to the lining of our executive pockets.

Portland Today, KOIN-TV Portland, Oregon, 1987

Jill: What were the *Mystery Players*?

Ty: Well, the *Mystery Players* were one of the names we had to come up with. We had a hard time coming up with a name in the episodes, so we kept created numbers for each episode, such as 1, 2, 3, and so on. Nobody knew us, so we weren't quite famous yet, but we did come out with tapes during playback. It was more for fun, really. We weren't doing it for money or for resume purposes. Sure, nobody knew us. We didn't really care. We were only eight year olds playing radio disc jockeys at a small and unheard of radio station.

Jill: I found that some of the tapes were unusual. Who did your writing?

Ty: We all did our own writing. We each collaborated with one another and if it made us laughs, then we knew we had a big hit. That is what entertainment is, really, about getting an emotional reaction from the audience. If it makes you laugh, cry, angry, or in a thoughtful mood, then you are entertained. Our test audience was ourselves. If we did any of those things with ourselves, then we knew that it would probably fly very well with the mass audience.

Jill: But you were on a radio station that partially existed, and according to the Federal Communications Commission, it doesn't exist, why did it matter if your works did well with a mass audience? Weren't you the audience?

Ty: Basically, yes. We were our own audience, but as time goes on down the road, there would be an audience besides ourselves. When you record onto a piece of tape, wouldn't you hope to hear yourself in the future? What about the thought of passing it along to your children? Or better yet, your great grandchildren. When you record on to tape, you are making history. You will forever be known as that guy who did this thing over here or did that thing over there. You are special. You stand out more than the rest. You are a piece of that recorded tape. You are a visual and/or audio history. You are history.[36]

Jack Dutro Show, WNBC, 1977

Jack: You started off in a high school radio station.

Ty: Right, after the *Mystery Players*, I ended up moving to a different area. I never lost my friendship with those guys on Vashon Island. They become famous underneath their own right.

Jack: And you moved to Gig Harbor?

Ty: Right, I went to Peninsula High School and became a Seahawk instead of a Pirate. My high school just so happen to have a small sixty watt radio station for me to practice. I was able to learn a little bit about radio broadcasting, but at the same time, had fun at what I did.

Jack: You wrote a radio play based on your life.

Ty: Yes. The radio play was based on my future, and I was completely amazed that most of it came true.

Jack: The movies, the music…

Ty: Not to forget my wild lifestyle. I thought it would be fictional. It wasn't fictional, about eighty-five percent of it came true. There were, of course, some things that didn't come true.

Jack: What's that?

Ty: Well, I am not at liberty to say since I am still in the middle of my journey. It could happen in the future and I not know it.

Jack: The radio station showed a lot of freedom…

Ty: Of course there was some freedom. I wouldn't have volunteered four years directly after I graduated. The radio station was a variety format radio station. One guy would come in and play big band music, another would play jazz, another would play reggae, and another person would play oldies. Each person could play whatever they wanted. That is what I liked about it. It was pretty crazy substituting, but I was able to learn about the different types of music, which broadened my horizons on my appreciation of music. I wasn't just stuck on the latest Top 40 music. I began, however, to appreciate jazz, but I would never buy any of the music. I liked the music, not love the music.

36 The *Mystery Players* eventually stopped producing shows in 1959.

Jack: Did you have a normal high school life?

Ty: Yes. Even though I was still stuck in the radio station, I did try to experience my high school life as much as possible. I did go to the football games and the school dances. Even though my love was in radio, I didn't keep a from the school activities.

Jack: You dated…

Ty: I did date. I did go through many different girlfriends. I was a very good friend with this one girl. I had a big crush on her and thought she would be right for me. The down side was she didn't want anything to do with me. But, we made a deal. She would go to the Senior Prom with me if we both couldn't get a date. So, I decided to take my chance for the entire senior year. Why not? All I had to do was cross my fingers and hope that she didn't have a date at the Senior Prom.

Jack: So, she was pretty hot.

Ty: Hot in my eyes, yes. I couldn't say much about the rest of the people who knew her. She wasn't a cheerleader, if that was what you were asking. The jocks always had the cheerleaders. I was never that lucky. That was the whole reason why the guys went to the football games, to view the cheerleaders. No, she had a good chance of being picked up by some guy at the high school.

Jack: The crush was pretty serious.

Ty: Of course it was serious. This crush lasted for a good seven years.

Jack: That's mighty long for a crush. What set it off?

Ty: I don't know. It was something about her. The magic wasn't there anymore. Not to say, that we aren't still friends, but it was just friendship that made it possible. Perhaps, God had his own way of saying to me that this girl was not for you. I looked at her and thought, "Do I want to wake up to this woman?"

Jack: Did you go to the Senior Prom?

Ty: She couldn't find the date and I couldn't find a date. Or, at least, I was acting like I was looking for a date, but really wasn't. We both went to the Senior Prom and had a fantastic time. It was the most memorable time for me.

Jack: You almost married one of the high school girls.

Ty: I asked myself the same thought, "Do I want to wake up to this woman?" She was nice and everything, but I had a goal in mind and she had a different goal in mind. Soon, we stopped paying attention to each other and broke up our relationship. I wanted to pursue my radio career to bigger and better things. She wanted me to settle down and have children. I wasn't ready yet. I suppose, when I get ready, I would be able to do the same.

John Lukehart Show, CBS Radio, 1982

John: Okay, so you graduated from high school what did you do next?

Ty: I went to Bates Technical College to pursue in my radio and television career. At first, I wanted to be a teacher. I thought I would leave the entertainment industry forever, leave it behind, and continue on into a new career. I wanted to teach history. I had always been interested in history, especially growing up with parents with their *Public Broadcasting Stations (PBS).* I grew up with shows on the educational channel, but history always astounded me from the very beginning.

John: What is it about history that you like the most?

Ty: It was the matter of storytelling that interested me the most about history. It wasn't international or national history that interested me the most. It was local history, Washington State history that I was interested in the most. It wasn't about the wars, including the Civil War, no, it was the thoughts and processes of people during these different eras. It was discovering these documents and the research behind it that interested me the most. I love research and the fact that I could find out more information and discovering that information. History could be fun if you let it be fun.

John: You put a lot of storytelling in your work.

Ty: I do put a lot story telling in my script writing, don't I?

John: Yeah!

Ty: I guess I put a lot of storytelling in my writing because I like to manipulate the mind. It is the imagination that makes it so much easier. Why not? You start typing a script and you realize that you can achieve the benefits of the audience's minds by creating the most achievable story you can find. After all, isn't that what your mind is really there for?

John: Sure!

Ty: I think that is the most important part of the movie is the story telling. When you listen to the radio or watch television, you are listening or watching a story. Story telling is the most important element in your own personal entertainment. I have always loved stories. As child, I would go off and get lost in the libraries.

John: You seem to put a lot imagination in your stories.

Ty: Who wouldn't? The hard part isn't conveying information that you have read. The hard part is setting forth the ideas in an imaginative way. It is harder to come up with fictional information than over non-fiction information.

John: But, you put in so much description. I mean, I have seen your style of script writing, which written differently than what most scripts I've read in the past.

Ty: What's that?

John: You seem to write your scripts like a musical composition.

Ty: When you write a script, you are creating a musical composition without the notes. You are the lyricist of that musical composition. I do my writing like you would put down an instrument on a multi-track recorder. Just like in music composition, you put down a track for each individual musical instrument; I do the same thing whenever I write a script. First, you lay down the voice, and then you lay down the rest of the sound effects or action in order for you to get the product that you want. But, there is one thing that is actually unaccounted for. That thing is the imaginative mind of the audience. It is the audience which fills the void of imagination which makes it work really well for them in their minds. Imagination is the key to the excitement of my script writing.

John: So you think of your writing like you were composing a musical?

Ty: That's correct. Essentially, that is what you are doing in script writing, you composing your own musical in your own way that you want to convey across the audience's minds. When I type on a keyboard on typewriter, I just pretend that I am playing the piano while a composing the next big hit. Yet, my ideas come across like there is no tomorrow. You get the big composers, such as Beethoven and Mozart, throw a large grand piano in front of them and they will probably do the same thing. The musical composers have their own tools and I have mine. My tool just so happens to be a typewriter.

John: You do realize that their computers nowadays?

Ty: Computers may be helpful to me in the future, but right now they are pretty clumsy and I wouldn't buy one at this moment in time. Perhaps ten years from now when they become better and faster and more compact for me to work with them for my everyday use.

John: Your writing seems very intellectual, but yet, comical.

Ty: Like I said, I watched a lot of *PBS* when I was a kid. That is the intellectual part of me. I have always liked the big comedy features. I like to laugh as much as anybody else. So, I felt that if I put in my intellectual ability as a feature in my comedy, then I would combine those two ingredients in order to make people laugh. I have always thought I was pretty smart, with an intelligence quotient of two hundred forty. I guess nobody has ever looked at my logic the same way as I do. It was easier to play stupid that be smart. You could get away with many different things and people respect that more than being smarter than the rest. Which also lead me to believe, am I really smart or am I just being a smart aleck?

John: Being a smart aleck is like being smart?

Ty: You get bored with your intelligence. When you get bored, you start playing around with things in your mind. By being a smart aleck, creates a special blend of keeping me busy, and yet, I could come up with new thoughts to improve the world into a better place. All the big people do it. The comical group Monty Python, for example, creates their humor with intellectual qualities, and yet, they are considered to be one of the kings of skit comedy.

John: So you went to Bates Technical College for radio and television broadcasting. Why did you pick such a school?

Ty: It was simple, really. I was looking for a direction to go to in order to entertain the public. Radio and television was that happy medium for me to go onto my pedestal and do my thing.

John: You actually met some people doing this.

Ty: Right, we were called the "*Master Baters*"[37]. We were definitely a comical team. I was the student program director at Bates Technical College's radio station and we each shared the same locker. At times, we would come out with one of the most stupid radio skits and fool around with the radio audience's mind. Why not? This was college. This was the time we had to go into the experimental stage.

John: Were there any drugs?

---

37 The "*Master Baters*" are considered to be one of the most legendary comical trio group starring Ty Roseynose, Bob Slim, and Hakim Ashberger.

Ty: We did some drugs. Who didn't experiment a little bit on drugs in college? We didn't get into anything big time like cocaine or methamphetamine. I think the most dangerous drug we got really close to was marijuana. A drag here and there or in a brownie, that is what I liked the best. We didn't do it to get high. We did it for our own recreational use. We did it to spark our comical imaginations, to write better comical scripts. We were more creative than ever before.

John: That's true. You did become successful.

Ty: Of course we did. There were some scripts we did throw out after our dope high was over with. Some scripts did not make any sense. But, we were on our creative edge and thinking beyond the paradigm of comical standards. We would laugh at a funeral if we thought it was funny. We would laugh at an international tragedy if we thought it was funny. Grass just seems to make everything much more funny.

John: You made fun of the governor of Washington State.

Ty: Sure!

John: You made fun of the President of the United States.

Ty: Right.

John: You made up interviews of fictional characters like Santa Claus.

Ty: It's okay to make fun of fictional characters. You see, everybody has a set idea of what a fictional character should be. It is stuck in their minds of a set standard. What we did was we manipulated that fictional character to go to a different direction from what most people actually originally accepted. Have you ever had it where you go through the trouble of planning a party and the party changes from what you originally wanted in the first place?

John: Yes.

Ty: It's something like that. You expect one thing and there is this slight possibility that in the chance of the world, space, and time that something goes awry. We were that something that went awry. We were that mathematical possibility that equals to the chaos theory. We were the chaos of your mind.

John: So you're saying that you are the logic that doesn't fit, making yourselves illogical.

Ty: No, we're logical. It's just that we are logical from a different view. For example, you look at Santa Claus as a sweet charming guy who gives all the toys to all of little boys and girls. He flies around with reindeer and a sleigh and lands on chimney tops. Well, that's the old fashion Santa Claus. What would happen if Santa Claus updates himself to modern times? How does he keep up with ever growing population around the world? The reindeer need to be retired and Santa comes up with a faster mode of transportation and flies around in a Boeing 747. The elves join a union. Do you think the elves would work for free? No, the need fringe benefits and a pay raise on their checks in order to feed the little kid elves. The elves have rights and don't call themselves anymore. They call themselves height impaired. Santa has lawyers for his list for all of the naughty boys and girls. The lawyers have to determine what is considered to be naughty and what is considered to be nice. Santa can't buy the toys that you see in the stores today, no, that is against the elf union. The toys have to be made at the North Pole. There are a lot of things that go on before, during, and after the kids get their toys from Santa Claus that we never think about. No wonder the poor guy gets pooped after Christmas.

John: I never thought of the Santa Claus concept.

Ty: It was the same thing from the President of the United States of America and other world leaders. They go through a lot of crap just to serve your needs whether you agree with them or not. Why not make fun of them? If humor brings out the best of them, then shall it be.

John: Why the satirical influence on these subjects?

Ty: I have always been a proponent of humor. I love the fact that I can see people laughing. Being a comic withstanding the times of tragedy gets people thinking and getting back to life. That is what life is all about. You can't be serious all the time. I find laughter is the best way to cure the worries on our minds. It makes us forget temporarily and create a way to improve our lifestyles. Comedy makes you think out those troubles. Comedy was my way out. I would not have survived this long without having the humor in my lifestyle. I enjoy making fun of everything.

John: You did come out with something very serious.

Ty: Right.

John: And you were involved with audio theater?

Ty: Yes.

John: What's that?

Ty: Audio Theater is where the mind works with imagination. Audio is a tool towards that imagination.

John: Explain the concept of *Audio Theater.*

Ty: Right. Audio Theater is like those old radio shows. You write a play in audio format. You have each character act in the play as if you were watching a movie. Then, you add sound effects in order make the listener's imagination work with the play.

John: So, it is a matter of audience participation.

Ty: Right. Audience participation is the key to making the play successful. Without audience participation, the play would be a major flop. All audio theater requires audience participation. That is why I was able to lead on people to where I wanted them to go. Without audience participation, the shows I did would have been a major flop.

John: And the serious play was called?

Ty: *Rime of the Ancient Mariner* by Samuel T. Coleridge

John: I love that poem. You really did an audio theater play based on the poem?

Ty: My partner, Hakim Ashberger, and I went through each line of the poem, analyzing it and figuring out how to make the audio play work for the listener. We had always liked the poem, but couldn't quite figure out what certain parts of the poem really meant. Then, we figured out that the narration of the story actually consisted of two parts. The young mariner and the ancient mariner was the same guy was telling the story to the wedding-guest.

Jim Johnson Show, KNBC-AM, 1971

Hakim: We came up with a whole bunch of funny sh@t, man. Ty always came up with strange associations when it came to our comedy writing. Could we improve, mmmm, yeah. I think we could have improved more often than we thought we did as improvement goes. After all, Ty did come up with the ideas.

Jim: But you worked very hard on *Rime of the Ancient Mariner.* Wasn't that sort of an accomplishment?

Hakim: Sure it was. Whether or not Samuel T. Coleridge[38] would have been up for it that would be a different story altogether.

---

38 Samuel T. Coleridge was the author of *The Rime of the Ancient Mariner.*

Jim: It wouldn't really matter. He's dead, isn't he?

Hakim: I suppose it doesn't really matter. I'm just afraid that he would be rolling in his grave by now if only he knew that we made it into an audio theater play.

The All Born Again Christian Hour, Christian Ministries Radio, 1983[39]

Pastor John: Now, Ty, every Christian soul wants to know why you chose *Rime of the Ancient Mariner* over our Lord, *Jesus Christ Superstar.*

Ty: There are several simple explanations, really. First, *Jesus Christ Superstar* is a musical and we weren't able to budget in a cheap enough price to create a full-fledge production as that one.

Pastor John: Praise the Lord that we come up with such of a Miracle. Amen.[40]

Ty: Amen, my father, the son, and Holy Ghost.

Pastor John: I see you Praise the Lord as much as I do.

Ty: Amen.

Pastor John: Amen. But why did you pick *Rime of the Ancient Mariner?*

Ty: What inspired me about the poem was that the story of this mariner, who goes out to sea and kills one of the biggest good luck charm, the albatross, in historical maritime tradition and culture.

Pastor John: Sam must have said quite a few "Hail Mary's" for that one. Amen.

Ty: Amen.

Pastor John: Amen. According to the Holy Bible, as Moses heard the cries he heard from God, right next the burning bush, Moses cut into stone the "Ten Commandments" that he relayed forth to the people

---

39 This was one of the most unusual interviews that I ever had. I felt like I was chastised in not believing in Jesus Christ. I believe there is a God, but I don't believe that Jesus Christ is the Son of God. I believe that Jesus was some gospel preacher who only spread his idea of what God is. It's just that people and their politics were intermingled, and the expression towards the Renaissance of Enlightenment, the idea about God became popular. It is only been through rumor and the grapevine that gave Jesus Christ the title of "The Son of God."

40 There was a lot of "Amen's", "Praise the Lord", and "Hallelujahs" throughout this interview. You' d think we were in a church or something. I wonder if the people were listening or taking an hour long nap. Who listens to this garbage anyway? Maybe it's a bunch of gullible people who have nothing else better to do.

from God, of one of the "Ten Commandments" as "Thou shall not murder thy brother." Amen.

Ty: Amen. The result of killing the albatross was devastating. The whole ship crew dies and mariner, as the last survivor of the ship, talks about his presence of coming closer and closer to God.

Pastor John: Praise the Lord!

Ty: Towards the end of the poem, the Lord saves him and brings him back to land.

Pastor John: Praise the Lord! Amen.

Ty: Amen.

Pastor John: Let us pray…[41]

Portland Today, KOIN-TV Portland, Oregon, 1987

Jill: What I thought was interesting was that you put in music in the audio theater play instead of sound effects.

Ty: Right. It didn't start out that way. I did have sound effects without the music. The first thing we did was lay down the voice, which took approximately 4 days to complete plus another two weeks to go through the editing room, trying to get rid of the extra flubs. When I lay down the tracks for the voice I was hungry for some sound effects, but they didn't seem to make the story seem, well, interesting.

Jill: So, the story wasn't very good, then.

Ty: No, it was matter of taking eighteenth century prose and converting it into an understandable twentieth century everyday language. See, Hakim and I knew and understood the poem, but many people in our time had no idea on what the poem was about until we analyzed it and put it into an audio theater format. It's kind of like Shakespeare. The general audience really doesn't get Shakespeare's works until it gets translated into a movie. That is what we were doing. Not to make it into a movie, but to help create a vivid imagination through sound without having to change the original language of Coleridge's poem. We wanted to keep it original as much as possible so that we didn't change the author's original thoughts.

---

41 Did you notice that I tried to play along? I was bored with the religious crap and decided play along with the game. This was the first and last religious interview I did. Yes, I fired my publicity agent over this catastrophic interview.

Jill: How could you change the author's original thoughts?

Ty: At anytime you translate a work, some things get lost. Hakim and I could have changed the prose, but the full color of the description would have been lost. In order to create a vivid imagination in the listeners' minds, our only alternative was to scrap the sound effects and go directly into the music. While we were in the editing studio, we picked out several different types of classical music.

Jill: Why classical music as oppose to, say, other forms of music?

Ty: Classical music has, number one, no words. That means that it is easier to put voice over an instrumental than it is to compete with the singing. Number two, we wanted to have the same type of music that would represent the era of a sailing ship. Classical music represented these things well. The hard part was to make these different parts blend well and run with the story.

Good Morning Live, KLBS, Los Angeles, 1993

Tom: Your *Peter Rabbit and Other Rabbit Stories* turned out to be a very big hit not just nationally, but internationally as well.

Ty: Right, I was without a production for awhile, and you are only as good as your last production. I knew I had to expand my horizons a little bit further. I wanted to do something that would knock the socks off of my past fans of *Rime of the Ancient Mariner.*

Tom: Why did you pick audio theater on rabbits as your subject?

Ty: I have always been a fan of the rabbit as an animal. They are smarter than cats, easy to maintain, and cute at the same time.

Tom: You had pet rabbits in the past.

Ty: I had total of 4 rabbits in my entire lifetime. And yes, when I wrote the *Peter Rabbit* script, I did have one house rabbit that I would take on walks every once in awhile in the park on a harness and lead. The rabbit was my influence on creation of such a play.

Chapter Two: Radio

Dateline, NBC, 1992

Paula: Radio started at a young age.

Ty: That's right, Paula, it basically started with a pirate radio station in one of my friend's basement. The programming wasn't very much. Most of it was tape recordings sent into my friend, with interviews of school librarian and things like that.

Paula: And high school radio brought more of you.

Ty: Right, I learned more about radio broadcasting from the best in the business. They [instructors and engineers] were in the radio broadcast business at one time, where they were local legends at their own right. This was where I got my basic know-how in my training and be able to experiment my way through different genres and my basic comedy skills.

Paula: You seemed to build yourself on a different type of genre from the other disc jockeys.

Ty: While the other high school DJs played the latest rock tunes, I mainly played oldies and the classic rock format. I got lost in the radio station's music library and started pulling every 45, LP, CD, and cart[42] I could find. I even played the flip sides of the 45 singles. Sometimes, those were the best.

Paula: You eventually got hired at several radio stations.

Ty: They weren't big radio stations. The first one was a country radio station. I lasted for about a month. It wasn't just because they didn't want to pay me, it was also because I hated country with a major passion. I got tired of hearing about the dog dying, the wife leaving and how much these country artists wanted to drive their pickup truck. I knew a lot more than they did, and probably still do.

Paula: Finally, you made it big with a major company in Seattle.

Ty: How often can I say I used to work at a number one radio station in the city of Seattle. I didn't get paid much, but why did I care? I was craving for attention. I was a board operator[43], someone that the radio

---

42 Cart – it's a cartridge tape that looks similar to an 8-track. It runs at a different speed than an 8-track at 7 ½ Inches per Second (IPS) instead of 3 ¾ IPS. Radio disk jockeys would often put commercials or music depending on the length of the cartridge tape.

43 A board operator is someone who runs the mixing board. They insert commercials in between segments of the show. This job may have been eliminated by automation systems in radio stations today. There are a few exceptions, however, such as live talk shows.

station didn't really care about. I was low on the totem pole in finances, nobody heard of me, and nobody cared to hear anything from me. I tried to submit my tapes and production work to the program director, but I suppose they were either thrown away or put up on a shelf collecting dust.

Paula: You eventually did hit it big, didn't you?

Ty: There was a guy at the station, JB Hayes, who gave a listen to my works, hated it, but thought I would have some potential as a comical genius for his show. JB had faith in me as much as I had faith in him. The faith wasn't Christian either. I believe that I don't have to thank god because it wasn't a miracle. It was just hard work and dedication and someone who would believe in me. You see, JB had a popular show and knew what he was doing. He wanted to make his show more popular by adding another character. That character was me. A character who wants to be famous.

Paula: We all want some fame.

Ty: That's right. We all want to benefit society in one form or another. Mine was to make people laugh. That is my job. We all need a laugh sometime in our lives.

Paula: But, you did play the character well.

Ty: Of course. I didn't know if I could pull it off, but with a little magic and some priming, I was able to make my character a little more popular. Pretty soon, everybody began to know who I am. I was often stopped in the street and yet, I was on the radio.

Paula: Things went well for you, especially during the morning show.

Ty: Sure, JB allowed me to write and produce my own skits and finally the program director suggested that I should be a part of the new morning show called Rog and Doug Show.

Paula: I remember that show, I had to write a report about it in journalism school about how radio networks pick shows. I believe I gave them a bad critique.

Ty: Highly rightly so. I think it is a stupid show and the guys should be off the air because of their indecency. Anyway, I tried my best to fit in with these guys, bought they wanted to think up several stunts mainly to torture me for ratings.

Paula: What were some of the stunts?

Ty: One time, they wanted me to dress like a Nazi and preach the gospel on the 520 bridge in Seattle. Another time they had me strip nude in public. Another time they beat me up by several mistresses. These were selfless acts that I didn't appreciate.

Paula: How long did this last?

Ty: About a year. It was not something I was proud of, but nonetheless, I did it. My self-esteem was getting lower and lower every time I was with them. Finally, I moved to Grand Rapids, Michigan with these guys. Same tortures, same re-runs as the year before. I was made promises that they could not keep. They loved me because I stuck out from the rest of the radio shows, but I got tired of myself mutilation and depression was setting in because of my low self-esteem. I had to get out of the situation quickly by quitting my job and leaving the state of Michigan. A month later, they got syndicated and home-based their studios in New Orleans. We've never talked since, thank God. I never wanted to associate anything with those assholes.

Paula: They would have never been syndicated without you.

Ty: I hear they're failing miserably.

Paula: You didn't entirely quit radio broadcasting altogether.

Ty: Right, after Michigan, I went back to Washington State to help low power radio stations. I felt like I was giving a special service in order to beat the big conglomerate radio stations. I wanted to see more local than national programming and personalities. It made me feel good.

Chapter Three: Music

Rock Influences, VH-1, 2004

Chuck: You career in music goes way back into your childhood.

Ty: Right. I was only eleven years old when I started into the music business.

Chuck The band was called "The Hot Shits". Why?

Ty: It was simple, really, we thought we were really good that our egos seemed to get in the way. We originally called ourselves "The Butterflies and Peppermints", but our record producer ended up calling us the "The

Hot Shits". It seemed to fit well of what we actually thought about ourselves and we knew with that name, we could go very far.

Chuck: You only came out with three albums, not including the greatest hits album, anthology, or the tour albums, within the three years you had the band.

Ty: I didn't say that we were perfect, I mean, don't get me wrong. "The Hot Shits" were well put together and we did get along very well. Who knew? We had three hit albums with each song played on the radio. You can't get better than that.

Chuck: With all of the success, why did you break up?

Ty: We began to fall apart as a group. We each had a direction that we wanted to go. The sixties were really mixed up times. There was a little bit of drugs, a little bit of sex, a little bit of rock and roll. It was a messed period. There were those who were with the Vietnam War and those who were against the Vietnam War. Everybody was protesting about something. Of course we had to break up. It was the wrong time period to be mixed up with a band named as "The Hot Shits". There are some groups that fall in the "shouldn't have" category, and I think that the "Hot Shits" were one of those groups. We were growing and changing ourselves within those three years. We started having wives and girlfriends. I swear, it's usually relationships that fuck up the creative process of these groups. We can't stay forever, you know.

Chuck: You came out with your next album in 1969 called "Solo At Last".

Ty: Right.

Chuck: Why such a title to name your solo album?

Ty: Basically, I was glad to be solo because I was tired of being with "The Hot Shits" band. I wanted to experiment a little bit and have fun in my creative process. That is where "Solo At Last" came in. It opened my eyes without having to collaborate with the rest of the group and wonder if the other band members like it or not. Most cases, they would say that music really stunk. Finally, I was solo and felt the freedom coming towards me with nothing to stop me.

Chuck: Now, "Easy Does It" has a jazz motif.

Ty: Right.

Chuck: Why jazz?

Ty: I have always enjoyed the sound of the saxophone, the piano, the guitar, and the drums put together. It gives it a more of an old time rock and roll feel to it.

Chuck: But, it sounded a lot like jazz throughout the whole album.

Ty: If you listen to bands such as Blood, Sweat, And Tears or Chicago, they have a jazz motif as well. You never seemed to question them.

Chuck: Actually, I have. They said they were on drugs at the time.

Ty: Who wasn't on drugs in the 70's? It towards the end of the hippy era and I did a mass load of alcohol. I'm not proud of "Easy Does It", but at least it brought in a new flavor in the rock and roll era in the 70's.

Chuck: Let's go on further, shall we?

Ty: Sure.

Chuck: Tell us about the "Peace, Love, And Calico" album. Your influences of the Latin America steps into your life in the 1971 album.

Ty: Well, hippydom was on its way out, and I wanted to bring in something new into the music scene. There was an introductory album to get the music industry to change.

Chuck: There was a lot of percussion throughout the album.

Ty: Right. That is partially what calico music is about is the drums and other forms of percussion. It's more than that. Your soul is being brought forth to the front of the stage. Really, if you think about it, it's considered to be soul music only it is more upbeat.

Chuck: Did it work?

Ty: Yeah, it seemed to work, kind of. The upbeat music pretty much died down in the 70's and people began to settle down with a more settle approach. This brought a few good artists that people never really heard of before such as Gordon Lightfoot and Jim Croce.

Chuck: You tried calico music for another year.

Ty: I was hoping that the album, "More Calico Music" in 1972 would become another hit album, but the calico fad was dying down. It didn't do very well on the music charts.

Chuck: You did say that the 70's a few good artists such as Gordon Lightfoot and Jim Croce into the music scene.

Ty: Right.

Chuck: They were pretty much folk artists.

Ty: Well, I thought my next album, "Ty Sings the Folk Songs" in 1973 would become a big hit. It did. Actually, the folk songs were my agent's idea since I failed miserably with the "More Calico Music" album. I didn't think it was going to be very big hit, but he said to go ahead and look at Crosby, Stills, Nash, and Young and how they become big with their acoustic guitars.

Chuck: Did you think that the hard electric guitars were ever the rage?

Ty: Yeah, I thought that the heavy electric guitars were the rage. I was looking up to Jimi Hendrix and Deep Purple. Sure they were good rock groups, but my agent thought that was not a mainstream type of music as of yet. Everyone was doing the acoustic guitars and singing folk related songs like Bob Dylan. Bob Dylan was a modern poet with an acoustic guitar. That is why I consider him to be a good folk artist for his time.

Chuck: Tell more about "Drowning in My Own Vomit" album in 1974.

Ty: I wanted to get back to the basics of what music was all about for me. "Drowning in My Own Vomit" helped me get back to the basic rock and roll.

Chuck: You mean with the saxophone, the electric guitar, the piano, and the drums?

Ty: No, the styles changed over the years, I had to reinvent the wheel, sort of to speak. No, I thought I had to build up to a new trend for the rock and roll business. I wanted the sound of the heavy metal guitar drowning out the percussion and the piano. It was time for me to bring in the idea of "banging your head" type of music. I knew people liked the blues, but this was better than the blues. It brought in the harder version of the blues, making music sound bluesy with a hard rock feel.

Chuck: True. There was Led Zeppelin that followed into your footsteps.

Ty: Right. Led Zeppelin brought the blues with a hard rock feel. Aerosmith did the same thing. Without me, they would have never made it very big with the projects I helped them with. But, they deserve the credits because of all the hard work they went through to change their sound towards a listening audience and stuck with their fan base.

Chuck: Eventually you switched back to folk music with "Ty Sings More Folk Song Hits" in 1975 and "Folk Songs for Children" in 1976.

Ty: Again, it was my agent's idea that I go back to folk music because of the fame that it caused.

Chuck: Ironically, you came out with the "Elvis Is Dead" album in 1977.

Ty: Who knew that Elvis Presley actually dies in 1977? I mean, I was never an Elvis Presley fan, never have and never will. I was making a statement throughout the album that Elvis Presley wasn't as good as most people say that he is. To me, he was never the real king of rock and roll. Sure, he may have been the king of rock and roll in the 50's, but like any king, their empires eventually fall. The Beatles were definitely the kings of rock and roll in the 60's. They had the most hits back then. The reigning of a king of rock and roll changes every week. It all depends on who is on the top the charts of sales and spins the songs get each week.

Chuck: You eventually came out with a live album of one of your concerts in 1978.

Ty: Right. Everyone had a live album, my agent thought I should do the same thing as well every time I went on tour.

Chuck: Throughout the album, you hear a lot of people enjoying themselves.

Ty: All of my concerts are exciting. People really enjoy them.

Chuck: No, I mean, I hear glasses clinking throughout the album and quite a bit of talking.

Ty: It was a small venue, okay, I never claimed that I played stadiums. In this case, I happened to play in a small hotel ballroom at a private wedding party. Why not? Instead of getting paid twice, I was getting paid large amounts of money in order for others to enjoy my art.

Chuck: Let's fast forward to another year. In 1979, you sang the disco hits.

Ty: Right, I have to change with the times. Disco was a popular format back in 1979. There was nothing better than to dance around a lot.

Chuck: You joined the "The Hot Shits" for the reunion tour in 1980.

Ty: Right.

Chuck: What was the reasoning behind the reunion tour?

Ty: Well, many fans had asked to us to come together with another album. Our reasoning was to come up with a reunion tour in order to satisfy our fan clubs. It was a world tour that stopped in five places: Cheney, Washington; Fucking, Austria; Kabwe, Tanzania; Titz, Germany; and Pussy, France. We called it our world tour. We were very big in Kabwe, Tanzania. We didn't speak the language very well, but at least it was worth the time and effort of the cheering fans. Unfortunately, our best recording was in Fucking, Austria, that even the radio stations wouldn't play the concert because of the Federal Communications Commission.

Chuck: You did study something new out of the entire tour, didn't you?

Ty: Right, I did discover the peaceful parks in those cities. When you go out and hear loud noises whether it is our loud music or somebody else's loud music, it was nice to escape the hotel room and enjoy a nice walk in the park. How else, beside going to a zoo or a wildlife preserve, can a man be one with nature? Ever since my self-discovery of the parks, I have been a long contributor of the park system. Whether it is metropolitan, state, or national parks, I feel these are international treasures that we must keep for future generations because of their pristine beauty.

Chuck: There was the "Red Light, Green Light" album that seemed to fail in 1981.

Ty: Right.

Chuck: But, you seem to pick right up again when you sang the Sesame Street songs in 1982.

Ty: I had to keep in touch with the kids. They are our future. I figured I could get back into popularity again if I sang the Sesame Street classics in order to get to the parents to buy the album. It seemed to work.

Chuck: Tell us about the album, "Porn in the USA". It seemed to get banned in 1984.

Ty: That's what I never understood. The album was completely clean, but all it took was stores to come up with censorship of material, telling people what they can or cannot hear. To overcome the problem of people not being able to hear my music, I handed it over to Bruce Springsteen, where he made some changes for his album, "Born in the USA" and since, then, it has become a huge hit for him in the 80's.

Chuck: Did this make you jealous?

Ty: Not really. Bruce Springsteen was a long hard working musician and deserves to be where he is today as a rock superstar. I'm just happy to be myself. If people like it, great, if not, oh well. I seem to enjoy my works and I hope others do too.

Chuck: You released an interesting album in 1985 called "The RTS Sessions: Senegal, Africa".

Ty: Right. RTS is a national radio broadcast station equivalent to the BBC in England and PBS in the United States. They invited me to record an album before they broadcast it across the Senegal. I, unfortunately, had to translate it to the local language as a part of the deal. I thought this was a good album, that I translated it back into the English language and released it in the United States. Who'd know it was going to become a hit. I should have placed a bet in Las Vegas.

Chuck: Is that why you came out the world music album in 1986?

Ty: Hey, if Peter Gabriel could have a hit through African hymns, why couldn't I?

Chuck: Tell us about the album, "Duets" in 1988 after the Hot Shits' reunion reunion tour album.

Ty: It was very simple, really. None of my past albums had duets until I released this album.

Chuck: What were some of those artists?

Ty: Honestly, I can't remember. All I remember were a bunch of no names such as Elton John, Bobby Brown, and Whitney Houston. Hard telling if these kids are big today. Frankly, I could care less.

Chuck: The album "Hair" in 1989 seemed unusual for the time period. Why did you pick the Broadway musical?

Ty: I felt that it was the end of the hair band era and I thought it was best to say goodbye to that era with a famous Broadway musical in an audio theater format. When I read the script to the play [Hair], it touched me emotionally to the point that I had to bring out the feelings of the Broadway musical the way that the writer's originally wanted it in the hippie era. In the 1990's to now, most men wear their hair short. Hopefully, this trend will end soon.

Chuck: In 1990 and 1991, you came out with the album, "Yo Homie!" and "You Go Girl" was a new culture shock that you brought into the music business. I mean, a white man impersonating a black man and yet you could rap?

Ty: Again, I was going with the times. That is what the public demanded, and that was what I offered in order to survive the music industry.

Chuck: Weren't you afraid of riots or protests? It was kind of racist.

Ty: Sure, I made a big risk and hoped that I wouldn't destroy my reputation. But, the blacks seemed to like me as much as the whites and the Asians. It doesn't matter what color you are, it was whether or not you like the music that counted.

Chuck: In 1992, you changed your tune.

Ty: That's right.

Chuck: You switched to grunge rock music as your genre instead of rap and hip-hop.

Ty: Correct. Again, changing with the times.

Chuck: Why did you call this album, “Land of the Grunge Commie”? What, exactly, were you referring to?

Ty: I was mainly talking about the height of grunge music. I was never a fan of grunge music, again, changing with the times, it was always depressing to me. All it talked about was death and dying. Sometimes, they would make it more exciting by making it about dying and death. Seattle was famous for its grunge music. They have socialistic rules in Seattle. So the name of the album refers to Seattle. That is why I called the album, “Land of the Grunge Commie”.

Chuck: Let's fast forward a bit.

Ty: Okay.

Chuck: Let's talk about your latest album, “The Anthology”.

Ty: Okay.

Chuck: The “Anthology” is a work of all of your albums in the past. How does that make you feel?

Ty: Well, I had to scrounge around for a mass amount of material in order to get the “Anthology” project to get me where I needed to go in the music world. I feel good to introduce all the music that was a big part of my life and is able to share it with future generations.

Chuck: The packaging is different from the rest.

Ty: Right. I chose the cardboard box with the handwritten title. I wanted to introduce some discovery for the listener, like it was just found up in the attic, collecting dust. I wanted the consumer to think that “This is history.” This will make it special for the listener to learn about me and how proud I am to include them into my heritage. This “Anthology” album is something I am proud to give as a tradition for all future generations as well as generations in the past. I am proud of making me, Ty Roseynose, an institution in the entertainment business forever.

Chapter Four: Comedy

The Comic Shack, Comedy Central, 1998

Lynn: He's funny and he's as interesting...as a sea urchin. It's Ty Roseynose!

Ty: Thank you, Lynn. Nice to be here.

Lynn: So tell me, Ty, I need as much gossip as I can. What are some of your favorite jokes?

Ty: I think that one of my favorite pieces of comedy is the Italian Hair Replacement program. I still laugh at the style and I still can't believe that has come directly from my head.

Lynn: Neither can we. People still can't believe that I'm an Asian woman who's 40!

Ty: Funny, I thought you were an Asian woman at the age of 23.

Lynn: It sure beats infomercials! So Ty, your humor is more of an intellectual humor.

Ty: Right, most people don't get my jokes right away, so if I get any laughter, I'm usually quite surprise.

Lynn: Mm-hmm.

Ty: The jokes were real Andy Kaufmann type of humor. Andy Kaufmann was a real genius in his idea of comedy. They weren't funny back then, but they are definitely funny when there comes a time. He brought in culture and made of it through those parameters. People didn't want the culture and the arts when he was alive. They wanted to laugh.

Lynn: Why did you get into comedy?

Ty: Comedy is an important of my life because I enjoy watching people chuckle. That was when I knew that I had a mission in life. My mission in life was to entertain, and, hopefully, I am doing just that. Make people laugh, cry and get angry. An emotion is entertainment to the audience. I feel that I am fulfilling that mission without any problem.

Lynn: You don't do very many stage acts.

Ty: Right.

Lynn: Why?

Ty: I never did stage acts very well. Most of the stuff was recorded so that way I could experiment with the media as it comes out. On stage, you say something, you sweat, you have diarrhea, and still nobody laughs at your material. To me it's not worth it. With media, I can at least bring an artistic value into my comedy. I write the script, I edit the script while I record, and then experiment with the effects in order to make it seem comical for those who wanted to listen.

Lynn: You were reviewed and won awards for your comedy.

Ty: Right. I was reviewed by National Lampoon. They thought my comedy stunk. Now, I use it for commercial purposes, just put down, "Reviewed by National Lampoon" and take out their comments. I won a Soundie through a radio show for my comical genius. An award that I felt that I justly deserved. I use that as a part of my commercial value as well.

Lynn: Most of your humor seemed to be sexually oriented.

Ty: That's really not true. It talks about life and we shouldn't be afraid of being open. The more open we are, the more we can laugh about ourselves. I would like to call my type of humor more "open humor" than anything else. We all need to be open in our thoughts. That is why our founding fathers gave us the first amendment rights in our country.

Chapter Five: Movies & Television

Movie Mania, ABC Radio Network, 2004

Lance: You have a very interesting set of movies all lined up, which makes me want to quiver inside.

Ty: Right.

Lance: Your first movie was "Hawaiian Luau" that brought in all the pleasures of seeing men everywhere in their skimpy outfits. After all, I think a man would look good in a bikini bottom if he is a hunk.

Ty: If remember it right, there were more hot women than guys throughout the film. After all, I thought it was more of a hot babe type of movie that attracted the other guys to even watch the movie.

Lance: What prompt you to do a movie at the beach?

Ty: It was hot summer day and I thought I would to capture the atmosphere of a beach party. That is why I show plenty of hot women.

Lance: And guys.

Ty: And guys. Nineteen sixty-eight was a popular year for beach party type of movies, but it did not reflect anything that I saw when I was there.

Lance: Was that the same reason why you came out with "The Fast Car" in 1971 with the guys sweating as they try to control the car?

Ty: Close. I was also trying to capture the atmosphere of "The Fast Car", but it wasn't because of the guys. It was the hot women surrounding the car drivers when they hit the finish line.

Lance: "The Delta Blues" was a dramatic turn for you.

Ty: Right. I have always been a blues lover and I wanted to capture the atmosphere of the blues. It was a documentary.

Lance: Eventually, you did the "Rhinestone Cowboy" movie in 1977.

Ty: Right.

Lance: There is nothing I like better than a stud in a leather boots and spurs. Not to mention the chaps on those men.

Ty: Well, Glen Campbell wanted to beat Kenny Rogers with a movie and "Rhinestone Cowboy" was one of those types of movies that brought out the importance of westerns.

Lance: "Sunday Morning" in 1979 was a really odd film, but watching those guys dance made me feel like a true disco dancer.

Ty: I have always wondered what would happen after Saturday Night Fever. What would John Travolta do? This movie pretty much told the whole entire story.

Lance: In the "Roseynose-Camel Show" television series, it was mostly skit comedy.

Ty: Right. My partner, Camel, and I thought that it would be funny to have skit comedy show of all of our best comedy. We'd never thought it would become a big hit for those who were up at 3:00 in the morning.

Lance: There were a lot of hot guys throughout the entire show.

Ty: Not really. I thought they were all pretty much ugly. Now, the women were hotter than ever.

Lance: In 1987, you came out with "Sexy Dancing".

Ty: Basically, "Sexy dancing" was about this love interest of this couple while doing a mating ritual. It's kind of like watching the Discovery Channel's nature films.

Lance: But men having sex with women, yuck, that is just disgusting.

Ty: Funny, most people seemed to like it.

Lance: Your next movie was a major brainchild of yours.

Ty: Right. "The Money-Grubbing Tour" was a story of a tour bus that was filled with village idiots. Throughout the tour, I thought it would be funny to see what they do throughout the film and to see how much money I could get from them.

Lance: That one seemed to fail.

Ty: Right. I didn't know that village idiots were actually trained professionals. In the end, they outsmarted me.

Lance: Then came "The Roseynose All Variety Show".

Ty: My agent had this idea to get me to sing a little more. This television show was a real flop.

Lance: And was "Building a Building" movie.

Ty: Right.

Lance: And the television show, "An Ass and a Pizza Place".

Ty: Right.

Lance: But, your last movie brought tears in the audiences nationwide. Could you tell me about "Quarter Mile"?

Ty: It's simple, really, the film is based in the town, Quarter Mile", in which I grew up and talked about the friendship of my friends and how our relationships go astray. It is a loving film and comes from the heart.

Lance: I'll say. It nominated for several awards.

Ty: That's better than the flops I've had in the past.

Chapter Six: Books

Book Week, CNN, 1997

John: We have Ty Roseynose who recently wrote a book called "In the Spirit of the Night". He is also a musician, a comical genius, a film maker, and now, an author. Welcome Ty.

Ty: Thanks, John. It's nice to be here.

John: Ty, this book seems to be an absolutely outstanding piece of literature, bringing out your thought processes for the world to see.

Ty: That's right, John, the story brings out some of my past religious, yet moral, thoughts into being for the teenagers, because kids are what count in today's stresses.

John: You mention some unusual religious aspects that may make parents unhappy as well as the various church groups.

Ty: Well, I'm not their minister, so what the church groups think of me is entirely irrelevant of what I think of them. I believe that churches as a group are not exactly the most behaved in the business. After all, why would I be a sinner if I hadn't already sinned?

John: So you think that individualism is more important than groups themselves?

Ty: That is certainly correct. I feel that if people are educated enough, they will find their own way towards god. In fact, the more individualized we are, the smarter the choices we make. Why do you think how messed up our world became to be?

John: In your book, you talk about morals.

Ty: Morals are the best way for all of us to learn from the stories being told. My morals are not exactly the best morals to follow, nor are they the best example to follow them.

John: Is that where individualism comes in?

Ty: Exactly. That is where individualism comes in. My story is no different from the Holy Bible. It is just a bunch of stories and the morals are what you put into it. Hell, if I start to put god into the picture, people might start interpreting it incorrectly and then start their own religions.

John: So the Holy Bible, to you, is bunch of stories.

Ty: Correct. The Holy Bible is a bunch of stories that have morals behind them and nothing more. The Holy Bible is not much different from "Aesop's Fables" or the "Canterbury Tales".

John: Also, you characters in the book go back in time.

Ty: Sometimes you have to go back to a simpler time in order to make you characters go where you want them to go. You should have seen my first draft.

John: How's that?

Ty: They go down in the far reaches of hell and fight their way back. People didn't like it. It was too descriptive of what my vision of hell was really like. I'm sorry, but hell is not exactly a pleasant place to be in. It's not like the Bahamas or some other tropical island during your summer vacation.

John: So, how did you originally come up with the idea of "In the Spirit of the Night", anyway?

Ty: I had the strangest dream, and when I woke up, I quickly wrote the entire story down as quickly as I as my hands could type the keys.

John: That is usually how the best stories start, isn't that right?

Ty: Right, if Mary Shelly hadn't typed down the story after her dream, her book, "Frankenstein" would have never been written.

Chapter Eight: The Internet

Harmony's Internet Radio Show, harmonysradioshow.com, 2005

Harmony: Thank you for coming to our show, Ty.

Ty: Thanks, I am glad to be here.

Harmony: Tell us about your web site empire.

Ty: It's very simple, really, I started off with a small web site called roseynose.net back in 1996.

Harmony: I heard about that web site, it was a pioneer of information finding, where you could search through the internet.

Ty: Right, roseynose.net and roseynose.com, put out a monthly newsletter of the entire web sites, some brand new, some that have been there for awhile. We not only linked to the web sites, but we informed people through e-mail at the same time.

Harmony: That eventually made the creation of citystroll.com, didn't it?

Ty: Yes, citystroll.com was to link the communities together. I had privately own city web sites that gave information about their hometown. This built a small relationship between the city and the internet surfer, whether they were just visiting and lived in their hometown.

Harmony: You came out with theothershow.com, right?

Ty: That was a show in which I was partnered in with a friend in high school. The Other Show was an all eighties show with facts, trivia and music from the eighties. I feel that it could have been very successful we hadn't decided to stop and move on with our lives.

Harmony: You also owned rosenow.net and servos.net.

Ty: I wanted my family to communicate with each other. How neat would it be to have your first name at your last name dot net? Unfortunately, my web host screwed me around with their poor customer service and I lost both names to some idiot from Malaysia who decided to park the names and make me pay outrageous amount for the names. I didn't comply with that idiot since it was mostly blackmail.

Harmony: Then, you came up with tyrosenow.com.

Ty: Tyrosenow.com was my personal web site, which I told a bio of myself. It didn't realize that a lot of people wanted to know so much information about me. Hell, I eventually sold merchandise on the web site.

Harmony: All of those web sites were eventually sold to other companies, right?

Ty: Right, this was so that way I could pursue my other interests.

Harmony: What impressed me are the web sites you have now: elitesearcher.com, eliteclubs.net, bidprice.net, collegecampusbookstore.com, and oggers.com.

Ty: Right.

Harmony: What are those web sites about?

Ty: Elitesearcher.com is an Academic Search Engine that deals with information for college papers. It provides information for the students, they have to write their own material, not us. What's neat about the web site is we have our own syntopicon, have access to over a million books, and if you can't find the information you need, we will seek it out for you as a part of the service.

Harmony: Eliteclubs.net?

Ty: Eliteclubs.net lets the college students communicate with each other, either through blogging, e-mail, instant messaging, or creating their own web sites.

Harmony: Bidprice.net?

Ty: Bidprice.net is an online auction web site, nothing else. It is pretty much similar to eBay.

Harmony: Collegecampusbookstore.com?

Ty: Collegecampusbookstore.com is a book store for college students. It provides dorm accessories, school supplies, textbooks, and deliverable meals to them as well. The whole idea is to address the college student's needs and comfort through this online shop.

Harmony: Ogger.com?

Ty: Ogger.com is a downloadable ogg vorbis web site with music in the ogg vorbis format. This is a new venture, and I am hoping that ogg will overpower mp3s with its better quality. I am hoping it will take off like iTunes did and people can pay for the downloadable music. The only difference is these popular tunes are in the ogg format instead of the mp3 format.

Harmony: How interesting. So you really think that the ogg format would over power the mp3 format? Why?

Ty: It's simple. MP3 is a patented process. Ogg Vorbis is considered to be open source. When it comes to a lawsuits, who would they come after first? MP3 or Ogg Vorbis? Everyone will be picking on MP3 because of its current popularity. Ogg Vorbis is safe, takes the same amount of room as an MP3, and eventually you don't have to pay for it in the long run.

Chapter Nine: Finale

If you believe this story, you are entirely wrong. Though parts of this story are based on my true life experiences, it is sometimes hard to separate fact from fiction. That is why when I wrote this book, half of it is fiction and the other half is fact. Mainly, I took some facts and exaggerated it to make this book seem interesting.

I was never in a movie, though I wished I was at one time or have ideas for many movies. Who hasn't dreamed of becoming a movie star? But knowing how harsh the entertainment business can be, I figured that I couldn't make it in the real movie business world, let alone be able to survive and live in Los Angeles, California.

I was never in a rock band. Boy, did I wish I was in a rock band. I can't carry a tune with my voice and I can't play a proper note on any instrument or percussions. I have gained plenty of respect of the musicians who try their damned hardest in their achievements. I still sing every once in awhile in my own private concert while I am driving to work every day. If you see me not paying attention to you while I am driving, I am in my own private world of being a rock star.

I did own many web sites in the past. Some exist, some don't, but I enjoyed putting them together through the basics of HTML programming. It may have been a lot of work, but I enjoyed it as a hobby. Whether or not these web sites were popular is irrelevant, since I didn't care whether they were popular or not. But, at least, they did have some hits. Some of them were very big and some of them very little, but they all reflected my joys of putting up the web sites. By the way, I didn't make one red cent off of these web sites. Most of the items I bought for myself, for my own personal enjoyment.

I did do a lot of writing in my lifetime. I have always enjoyed writing, but I usually cannot write really long stories. I am a short story type of person. The so-called book I wrote (later featured in the appendix section of this book), turned out to be a short story that I revised for two years. After the two years of revising the story, I ended up saying "fuck it" and stopped working on the story. That is how I wrote most stories and productions. I can work on these things until I am blue in the face. If I don't say "fuck it" or give myself a personal deadline, then you would never get the products.

My audio is an art form. I have often debated to people that am an artist who is as good as my last production. Instead of looking at my art on a wall, I wish there galleries for those who chose audio as an art form. Nobody takes the audio artists serious enough and redeem it as crap. I hope people will soon realize that it is hardest piece of creativity that should be displayed in a museum just like the other art that exists around the world. We are the Picassos and Van Gogh's of our time. Just like paint and canvas was the technology of the Renaissance period, the microphone and media is the technology of our time. I would like to add other mediums such as video artists and film artists. They deserve the same recognition for their arts. I think that video, film, and audio is the "modern art", and what they call Modern Art of sculptures and paintings is crap and thrown directly into the trash heap. I, too, can look at an empty paper cup and call it art. In this modern age, Modern Art is only based upon the hype of the critics.

I did write and produce my own comedy. I knew I wasn't funny, but I still enjoy the dry humor that I put out to the public. Nowadays, I hear they are considered to be "cult classics". People seem to compare me to Andy Kauffman. I am proud that part of my legacy still lives on and that I still have few fans that I meet on the street. I am glad that I stood out from the rest. I helped build a historical value to the community. Remember, I never forget the “little people” who made me a local celebrity.

I had been in radio broadcasting all my life. The story is mostly true. Through my experiences, I know radio broadcasting inside and out from management down to the technical stuff. Did I ever mention that I always wanted my own radio station? There were other things I did that I didn’t mention throughout the book in order to either save space or because I don't promote radio show programs that gave me a poor experience in the end. However, most radio station that I did quit from or was fired from, ended up towards a major failure. Some, do no longer exist. It shows how important I was in the programming circuit of radio. You screw with me, and your station gets a bad omen. Of course, I put every curse on every radio station that I didn't leave on good terms.

I did come out with several albums, but as many as mentioned the book. Most of it was audio theater productions and comedy skits that I did in my own studio. Each album did become a flop in sales, but it still has been acclaimed by critics around the world. Perhaps I should put more money into distribution and marketing. Instead, I just wanted to put my “product” out for others to share the fun that I had in putting the audio pieces together.

Seriously, I did do television. I was in front of the camera a few times, but mainly, I was the one who was running the camera and other things that were considered to be behind the scenes in the television broadcasting industry. This would not have been accomplished without the help of PBS affiliate, KBTC-TV for giving me the opportunity to try something new. I mostly did pledge drives, recorded the PBS programming on to tape, and ran the switcher to segue from one show to another. It was a wonderful piece of experience. I grew up with KBTC-TV as a child in the 80’s (that was all my parents would let me watch while I was growing up, and what interested me at the time with the low amount of channel selection in the Seattle area). It was a sure pleasure to work with them and I learned a lot from the industry as well. Seriously, feel free to support your local PBS programming. Being local is a rarity in both local television and radio. I highly condone being local.

Yes, I did grow with a family. I have two brothers, one sister, and a mom and dad that have been married with each other since 1964. A nuclear family is a rarity these days and I hope my parents will share this love for many years to come[44]. I was born in 1974, not 1955, and was born and raised as a Washingtonian – at least in the Puget Sound area.

I also would like to thank you. You have given my plenty of support in my ups and downs in my life throughout the years. I appreciate that. Also, thanks for reading this book. These words bring out the excitement of the story and could possibly spread throughout the years. Who knows, you might be inspired to do the same thing. I would utmost be proud of you! If you bought the book, great! I can't wait to see the check come in! If you borrowed the book, I hope you spread the knowledge to others to read the story. I had the most fun writing this, and I hope you will have same pleasure reading this book.

If you are reading this last paragraph before reading the entire book from the beginning, shame on you! You are obviously the type of person who doesn't do much reading for enjoyment. Perhaps you should start focusing on your reading strategies from the beginning. You are the type who plays records backwards to see if there are any satanic messages, don't you? Just for that, I am requiring you to buy ten copies of my book right away as a form of punishment for your actions. While you're at it, buy ten copies of this book, "Ty Roseynose – A Documentary" for sale at your nearest book store. You won't regret it! Don't think I won't know. I have spies!

THE END

Appendix[45]

Songs

In The Year 1492, I Remember It Well, Maybe I Think

In the year 1492

I remember it well

Maybe I think.

Our ships seem to be floating well

44 My father passed away of cancer when this book was originally published. Don't smoke kiddies!

45 The appendix in the original book was larger than the story itself. To spare you from boredom, I have condensed it to the bare essentials related to the story.

The Pinta, the Nina, and the Santa Maria
Across The Atlantic Ocean.

My name is Christopher Columbus
I set out to the sea
In search of spices.

Thank God for the niceness
Of the Indians
Who gave us tobacco and chocolate.

Now we are addicted
In the year 1492
I remember it well
Maybe I think.

My Heart Is Like a Flower
The bumblebees and the tulip trees
Bring out the love
Love, love, love, love
In me.

As I kissed you
With your hippy hair on your back side
Brought out the love
Love, love, love, love
In me

My heart is like a flower
With the tulip trees

And the flies in greens.
As the water comes glistening
I think that Miracle Whip is a salad dressing
Not mayonnaise.

Johnson's Theme Song
La la la la la la la
La la la la la la la
La la la la la la la
(repeat for 3 minutes)

Discography

The Hot Shits – 1966

The Hot Shits 2 – 1967

The Hot Shits – The Best Of The Hot Shits – 1968

The Hot Shits – The Last Album – 1969

The Hot Shits – Greatest Hits – 1970

The Hot Shits – Anthology – 1970

Ty Roseynose – Solo At Last – 1969

Ty Roseynose – Easy Does It – 1970

Ty Roseynose – Peace, Love, And Calico – 1971

Ty Roseynose – More Calico Music – 1972

Ty Roseynose – Sings The Folk Song Hits – 1973

Ty Roseynose – Drowning In My Own Vomit – 1974

Ty Roseynose – Sings More Of The Folk Song Hits – 1975

Ty Roseynose – Folk Songs For Children – 1976

Ty Roseynose – Elvis Is Dead – 1977

Ty Roseynose – Live! – 1978

Ty Roseynose – Sings The Disco Hits – 1979

The Hot Shits – Reunion Tour – 1980

Ty Roseynose – Red Light, Green Light – 1981

Ty Roseynose – Sings The Sesame Street Classics – 1982

Ty Roseynose – Greatest Hits – 1983

Ty Roseynose – Porn in the U.S.A. – 1984 (Banned)

Ty Roseynose – RTS Sessions (Senegal, Africa) – 1985

Ty Roseynose – Sings The World Music Song Hits – 1986

The Hot Shits – Reunion Reunion Tour – 1987

Ty Roseynose – Duets – 1988

Ty Roseynose – Hair – 1989

Ty Roseynose – Yo Homie! – 1990

Ty Roseynose – You Go Girl! – 1991

Ty Roseynose – Land Of The Grunge Commie – 1992

Ty Roseynose – Be Cool, Stay In School – 1993

Ty Roseynose – I'm Not A Gangsta – 1994

Ty Roseynose – Duets II – 1995

Ty Roseynose – More Depressing Shit – 1996 (Banned)

Ty Roseynose – Sings The Gospel Hits – 1997 (Banned By The Pope)

The Hot Shits – Reunion Reunion Reunion Tour – 1998

Ty Roseynose – 1999 – 1999

Ty Roseynose – Y2K – 2000

Ty Roseynose – No More Mr. Nice Guy – 2001

Ty Roseynose – Greatest Hits – 2002

Ty Roseynose – The Last Album – 2003

The Hot Shits – Back At Last – 2004

Ty Roseynose – The Anthology – 2005

Filmography

1. Hawaiian Luau – 1968
2. The Fast Car Race – 1971
3. Delta Blues – 1974

4. Rhinestone Cowboy -1977
5. Sunday Morning – 1979
6. The Roseynose-Camel Show – 1981-1985 (TV)
7. Sexy Dancing – 1987
8. Money-Grubbing Tour – 1991
9. Roseynose All Variety Show – 1992-1994 (TV)
10. Building A Building – 1999
11. An Ass And A Pizza Place – 2001-2002
12. Quarter Mile – 2004

Script 1 (Cut 1)[46]

NARRATOR: Are you having trouble shopping for that perfect gift for her? Are the skimpy teddies not keeping her satisfied? Does she get scared every time when you walk into the room? Well, don't let your holiday spirit get you down...literally. Now, she can play with a new tail, "The Penne". That's right! Dr. Whickoff has a wide variety of bones for you to choose from to satisfy her needs.

CUSTOMER #1: I tried everything to keep her happy during the holidays. Even bought her a teddy! Little did I know a teddy has no bone. Thanks to Dr. Whickoff, I was able to choose a raccoon bone implant!

CUSTOMER #2: Before I went to Dr. Whickoff, I had one sorry reproductive cartilage, but with the Whale Bone implant, many women envy me with the big hump in my pants!

NARRATOR: Dr. Whickoff adds a new animal bone, such as a whale penis bone or a raccoon penis bone for your dysfunctional needs, thus creating "Penne". No, whacking off the old ones to make room for the new. Hey! The holidays are made for sharing. Get something for her and yourself to play with! Try the two for one special! Get a three Penne for the price of two! Dr. Whickoff! Your "Penne" specialist!

46 These script were written for the holiday season for a CD release, but the CD was never released or recorded. Different scripts were eventually produced on a different comedy albums.

Script 2 (Cut 2)

Segment 37

INTEVIEW WITH SANTA CLAUS

BY TY ROSENOW

TY: We have a special telephone interview with somebody who has astounded us for many decades. His name is Santa Claus. Hello Santa.

S.C.: Hello Ty. You have been nice this year.

TY: Uh, thank you, Santa. Please give us a tour of your toy factory. It is located on the North Pole, isn't it?

S.C.: Not quite.

TY: If it is not located on the North Pole, then where is it located?

S.C.: Actually, my toy factory is located in the upper part of Iceland. I do not wish to give you the exact location because it will destroy my secret.

TY: I understand, Santa. How do you keep your orders straight?

S.C.: Hold on. I have a phone call on another line.

MUSIC: "Santa Claus Is Coming To Town" over the phone line.

Ty: In case you are wondering, we have a special interview with Santa Claus.

S.C.: I'm back. It seems that Little Johnny will have to get a lump of coal this Christmas. It's a shame, isn't it? What was the question?

TY: How do you keep your toy orders straight?

S.C.: I use a computer with a special database system, complete with a T-1 so I can interact on the worldwide web.

TY: How do you know who is naughty or nice?

S.C.: We have a major network of spies and we are able to tap into government records.

TY: Santa, how do you make sure your elves are doing their job?

S.C.: They don't like to be called elves, Ty.

TY: They don't?

S.C.: No, they like to be called Altitude Deficient. It's part of their E.E.O. Statement.

Ty: Oh. Then, how do you make sure your Altitude Deficient is doing their job?

S.C.: The Altitude Deficient has a head Altitude Deficient Supervisor to make sure they do their job.

TY: Of course, they do this job out of their own hearts, right?

S.C.: Absolutely not. It's a part of their union contract to get paid large sums of money or they will go on strike.

TY: Okay. Then we all know that you deliver your toys from your sleigh.

S.C.: Wrong again, Ty. Due to an increase in each child's wants, I have to use my brand new 777.

TY: Santa, we didn't know you ordered a 777 from Boeing.

S.C.: Of course you didn't. It was a top secret order.

TY: What happened to your reindeer?

S.C.: Old Comet decided to retire. You know how it is. If one reindeer decides to retire, the whole flock wants to retire.

TY: So, you don't go on rooftops and go down chimneys in order to deliver the toys to good children everywhere?

S.C.: Close, I do deliver toys to good children, but I don't land on rooftops and I don't go down chimneys. It was beginning to be dangerous. My insurance company did not like me to do that for my profession.

TY: Thank you, Santa.

S.C.: Ho, ho, ho. Merry Christmas and Happy New Year!!!

Script 3 (Cut 3)

NARRATOR: Need some extra money this holiday season? Living from paycheck to paycheck? Finding out that your pathetic job as a doctor or lawyer doesn't make enough? Now you can make a change in your life! The Story Technical College wants you to improve your lifestyle with our multiple course programs that will help you succeed! That's right! Story Technical College, located in beautiful Story County, Nevada, has delightful courses such as: "History of the Brothel", explaining why the whorehouses have been an important institution around the world. And "Getting Into A Money Making Opportunity: Prostitution". Not satisfied with this course, you can take the alternative course, "Pimping Hoes". Listen to our satisfied students:

STUDENT #1: I was a mess. I had a job as a politician, which paid me little to no money. And the tax payers always nagging me whenever I spent the money the wrong way. The million dollar salary that I gave myself was hardly enough for me to live by, and I was always getting in trouble when I committed petty crimes. Then I took the "Pimping Hoes" course at Story Technical College, outside of Virginia City, Nevada, I can properly say "Where's my money, bitch" instead of improperly saying it like I used to. It was, "Where Is My Money, You Female Dog".

STUDENT #2: Before I went to Story Technical College, I didn't know what to do with my life while I was in high school. After all, I was cheerleader, and I was working out with every jock in school. Then, my high school counselor said that I could use my talent to make money. That's when he sent me to Story Technical College to advance in my career goal! Making every man happy!

STUDENT #3: Job placement? Great! I got to work at the Mustang Ranch before and during the time that the Internal Revenue Service took over! Unfortunately, I got laid off. But Story Technical College put me back at the job again in Amsterdam!

NARRATOR: Story Technical College, making you happy sexually for over a hundred years!

SCRIPT 4 (Cut 4)

TY: We have a live interview with Frosty the Snowman. Due to really hot lights in the studio we can only talk to him in a very short time before he becomes water. Welcome Frosty! We know your history, so what is Frosty the Snowman doing now?

FROSTY: Glad to be here, eh? The kids up in the Great White North created me out of beer, eh.

TY: Beer?

FROSTY: Yeah, beer, eh. What else do the Canadians, eh, would create me by? Snow, eh? No, eh, it's frozen beer, eh.

TY: You get built and then you become alive in the story.

FROSTY: Right, eh?

TY: Then you, play with the kids...

FROSTY: That's incorrect, eh. Have you ever had to move large balls of snow, eh?

TY: Aren't you sure that you are made of the yellow stuff?

FROSTY: No, I am made of beer, eh? Can't you tell from my slow thinking and my tipsy turvyness, eh?

TY: That's because you are melting quickly. This concludes this interview, of a very Frosty, the beer snowman. Hey, TV Crew, feel free to lick him up after the show.

SCRIPT #5 (Cut #5)

NARRATOR: This is Jimmy. Jimmy has become, well, very lonely. Jimmy doesn't ask much, poor housing, a party, a bud, and of course women. You see, Jimmy is a college student who needs your help. There are many college students who need your help just like Jimmy. *Gives us those sad eyes, Jimmy!* College Students, like Jimmy, need beer. *I said, look sad Jimmy!* Beer is just one of major necessities for a college student to live for day to day. It's good for the learning curve! *Do you want motivation, Jimmy? I said give them the sad look!* (Hits Jimmy and Jimmy bawls) You see, college students, like Jimmy, not only need beer, but pizza to stuff their faces with. Let's not forget porn. College students need porn to look through for those important exams. I know, all the other charities advertise for fifty-nine cents a day, but ask yourself, does it help those who need it the most? The College Student Fund does even better. All we ask is for is two thousand dollars a day. That's enough to cover parties and supplies, porn, and housing. (Smacks Jimmy again). You, too, can help College Students like Jimmy, live normal lives.

SCRIPT #6 (Cut #6)

(SFX: Music opens for a game show)

A: It's time for Dress Up, a game show where mythical creatures cross dress. And further ado, here is our host Mr. Dress up!

(SFX: Audience clapping)

B: Thank you. Thank you. Welcome to the Dress Up. Our guest mythical creature is Santa Claus.

C: Great to be here Mr. Dress Up!

(SFX: Audience clapping)

B: First, let's meet our contestants. Bob!

A: From Scranton, New York, it's James Beardsley! James is a plumber who enjoys skiing and is part of the KKK! His favorite hobbies also include pimping!

(SFX: Audience clapping)

A: From Columbine, Colorado, it's George Hemsley! George is collects guns and believes in researching in conspiracies and puts them on the internet. He lives in an underground bunker and claims that he will be around when the world ends in an event of a nuclear attack.

(SFX: Audience clapping)

B: Wow! And tell these contestants what they will get if they win!

(SFX: Audience clapping)

A: The winner will win butt hair replacement! That's right hundreds of men lose butt hairs everyday due to picking off dingle berries. With butt hair replacement you take care of that harvest and still keep a nice set of butt hair! Back to you Mr. Dress Up!

(SFX: Audience clapping)

B: Thank you contestants! James and George have both flipped coin before going on the air and James won, so he can go first. James, choose a category.

D: I pick bras.

B: Bras! Wow, pretty quick on the under garments! Name 5 different words or phrases for masturbation:

(SFX: Time Clock)

D: Okay, Uh. Cuff Your Governor, Stroking the Lizard, The Portuguese Pump, Simple Infanticide, and Uh, Keep The Census Down?

(SFX: Bell Ringing!)

B: That's correct! Well, Santa, time put on that bra!

C: Ho, ho, ho!

D: Where?

B: Well, time for a commercial! We'll be right back after these messages!

(SFX: Audience Clapping)

SCRIPT #7 (CUT #7)

NARRATOR: Greetings people of the future! I come from the year nineteen fifty-nine and I am about to give you my prediction for the year two thousand one! In the year two thousand and one, I predict that man would have been on the moon, where it is finally confirmed that it is made of green cheese. I predict that a woman, that's right, a woman will be president. I predict that we will have flying cars. I predict that these "machines" called computers will take over our lives. I predict that this form of music called "Rock and Roll" will become big. I predict that people would be in free thought and honest. I predict that you will have many appliances and machines to accommodate you through masturbation. I predict that there will be vending machines for blow up dolls everywhere. I predict that everyone will enjoy nudity and no longer wear clothing. I predict porn will be king again. I predict that couples would engage in wild anal sex. I predict that robots will engage in wild sex. I also predict that one of the women presidents was also a porn star. My friends, I hope my predictions help you succeed in world progression.

The Natural Light Beer[47]

NARRATOR: When most people get off of work, they want to sit back, watch television and relax with a lager. But what about 2 AM, when you really have no supply of beer? Most people would buy it off of the black market, which is a no-no and could you possibly can be fined or even jailed. You can stay up until 6 AM or you can pull out beer-o-matic! I'll tell you what beer-o-matic does after we hear from our happy customers!

CUSTOMER #1: I work for a health food store, and even our non-alcoholic beer tastes like wheat germ. With beer-o-matic, my beer not only tastes like wheat germ, but wheat-germ with alcohol and it's all natural! Thanks beer-o- matic!

NARRATOR: Beer-o-matic is a wonderful piece of kitchen appliance, where you can turn any piece of food article into beer! Use your imagination! Pudding growing hair? It's beer! Sour milk? No it's not. It's beer! Unidentifiable food particle on the counter? Not anymore. It's beer! Dead rat in the basement? It's beer! Family pet just died? It's beer, now!

CUSTOMER #2: In the old days, when the hosses get sick, we used to shoot 'em and bury 'em feet up. Then thar PETA folks said we have to try and save 'em before we shoot 'em and bury 'em feet up. Now I don't have to bury 'em and I don't have to see hoss legs sticking out the ground anymore. I just put my dead hosses in the beer-o-matic, and wolla! I have several months supply of beer. Thanks beer-o-matic.[48]

NARRATOR: That's right! Beer-O-Matic! Get yours today. Because at beer-o-matic just about anything possible can be turned into beer. Heck, you can turn your own (BEEP) into beer, but why would you want to?

---

47 I wanted to have drink of beer at the time, and had none in the house. I didn't have the money at the time to buy a pack, so I came up with this script.

48 True story. There was a man on Vashon Island who buried a shallow grave for his horse. Anyway, the legs just stuck out of the ground. Finally, the health officials in King County finally told the man to dig a deeper hole for the burial of the horse. By then, the horse was just a skeleton.

Manly Mocha[49]

Written By

Ty "Roseynose" Rosenow (rewritten out of recollection as well)

Ben Fuller

Doug Williams

NARRATOR: We are at your local country club, where we secretly switched a select couple's coffee to Manly Mocha. Let's tune in on this couple's conversation:

MAN #1: Oh darlin'! You are lovely tonight!

MAN #2: Why thank you! Who knew that I would find such a man in the red light district!

MAN #1: Yes, my darlin'! I would love to have you go a-courtin' with me! For I have feared that my wife would not accept our love for each other.

MAN #2: I must say the same for my husband. But yet, I love you more!

MAN #1: Come! Let us finish our coffee and express our love at the local one hour motel.

NARRATOR: Hey folks! We have just switched from your preferred coffee of your choice to Manly Mocha!

MAN#2: Gee, I thought we were having a gay old time!

NARRATOR: Heh, heh! That's the effects of Manly Mocha. It can affect you to the point where you think you are having a gay old time! Manly Mocha, in both flavors of white and black.

MAN#2: Oooh! I love the white one, just like my lover!

MAN #1: Nothing like the black one, just like my lover!

NARRATOR: Manly Mocha! For a gay old time, try our flavors today!

MAN#1: Come my darlin'! Let's go sword fighting!

---

49 I wrote this along with a couple classmates in our senior year in high school. We were homophobic at the time, and they made great jokes. I still make jokes about homosexuals, if we can't laugh at ourselves and our environment, then why bother laughing?

A Conversation at the Westminster Dog Show[50]

Script by Ty Rosenow

NARRATOR: Welcome to another edition of the Westminster Dog Show! We have a rare insight of the dog show that a typical attendee doesn't get to experience. But, since this is a very special broadcast of the Westminster Dog Show, we will provide you a treat of the conversation between trainers on the field that you see below!

TRAINER #1: Yo Bitch! Come here!

TRAINER #2: Hey dude, that some fine bitch you got there!

TRAINER #1: Yeah, she can do many tricks that could make your bastard flip his lid, man!

TRAINER #2: Oh really?

TRAINER #1: Yeah. My bitch can not only catch a cock, but she loves chewing on it for a long time.

TRAINER #2: Without chokin'? Gee, my bastard can do that as well. What Cocker Spaniel can't? After all, they often like the sausage.

TRAINER #1: Be careful, you are not supposed to pork your bastard or your bitch. It can be unhealthy. I tried that once.

TRAINER #2: You mean you porked your bitch?

TRAINER #1: Yeah, she ended up pukin' in the end.

TRAINER #2: My bastard can jump over an ass if he wanted to. I betcha your bitch can't do that.

TRAINER #1: Are you kiddin'? My bitch can follow any ass around and herd it on out to where it belongs. She shows them who's boss.

TRAINER #2: Betcha your bitch can't pile up as much as mine can.

TRAINER #1: Are you kiddin'? My Schit-zu can make a better pile than yours! (pause) Hey!

---

50 This one was read on stage on October 15, 2003. The crowd booed Ty off of the stage. Perhaps Rog & Doug showed up as they were expected to do, this wouldn't have happened.

TRAINER #2: Yeah?

TRAINER #1: My bitch has some liking of your bastard.

Italian Hair Replacement Program[51]

NARRATOR:

Are you losing your hair and want to prevent yourself from getting bald? Do you have that little bit of a comb over to hide your bald spot? Are you wishing for a full set of hair again? Have you tried different products in the past, and find out that they don't do anything? I suggest you should use our new hair replacement program. Something the Italians have used for years.

CUSTOMER #1: I have always had a problem with my hair loss, and until I have tried this new product, I never had a problem ever since!

CUSTOMER #2: I've tried everything including chemo.[52] None of them worked! I was surprised with the results with this new product!

NARRATOR: Are you wondering what this product that the Italians used for years? It's Italian Seamen! That's right! Italian Seamen are a proven way cut down on hair loss and grow a nice beautiful set of hair quickly and affordably. The process is simple. We take the entire miniature Italian Navy and sprinkle them on top of your head, thus creating a nice full set of hair quickly!

CUSTOMER #3: Before I used Italian Seamen, I had a hair replacement and man, did my ass hurt!

NARRATOR: No pulling hair out of your ass and putting it on top of your head, no drugs, just pure Italian Seamen! Look for it today!

(In tune of "Candy Man")

Who can take your head

And sprinkle it with dew

Make your head grow with hair

The Italians can

The Italians can

The Italian Seamen can sprinkle it with love

And make your hair feel good!

---

51 I read someplace in the news that researchers in Italy found a cure for baldness. Unfortunately, it is a combination of human sperm and urine (seminal fluid).

52 Yes, I know that chemo's side effects is baldness. That's why I wrote it into the script.

Dr. Whickoff – Part II[53]

Script Written By

Ty "Roseynose" Rosenow

NARRATOR: Are you having trouble shopping for that perfect gift for her? Are the skimpy teddies not keeping her satisfied? Does she get scared every time when you walk into the room? Well, don't let your spirit get you down...literally. Now, she can play with a new tail, "The Penne". That's right! Dr. Whickoff has a wide variety of bones for you to choose from to satisfy her needs.

CUSTOMER #1: Before I went to Dr. Whickoff, I had one sorry reproductive tissue. I tried everything, including Viagra. Finally, I tried Dr. Whickoff surgical expertise and selected the Blue Whale dork implant. I no longer have an erectile dysfunction, considering it's a bone!

NARRATOR: Still not convinced? Here is another satisfied customer!

CUSTOMER #2: As a former professional ballet dancer, I always had to put something in my tights to show I had something worth looking down there. But with Dr. Whickoff's Blue Whale dork implant, I have changed my career to gay pornography, my original true love! I eventually kept myself physically fit, since my new dork implant IS 16 feet long and weighs 22 pounds. Thanks Dr. Whickoff!

NARRATOR: Dr. Whickoff adds a new animal penis bone, such as a whale penis bone or a raccoon penis bone for your dysfunctional needs, thus creating "Penne". No, whacking off the old ones to make room for the new. Hey! Get something for her and yourself to play with! Try the two for one special! Get a three Penne for the price of two! Dr. Whickoff! Your "Penne" specialist!

53 The infamous Dr. Whickoff. So good, I wrote two productions. This one is a sequel. Dr. Whickoff was originally called "Dr. Whack off", but I had to tone it down to make it less obvious.

How To Be Rude And Obnoxious Infomercial[54]

By Ty "Roseynose" Rosenow

NARRATOR: Do people find you too polite. Do you apologize after every little thing you do? Are you no longer fun at parties? Do people wish that you are just somewhat impolite? Never fear! You can learn from Bob Bob's new home video on "How To Be Rude And Obnoxious!" In this video Bob Bob, the man with two first names, will show you the basics of being rude and obnoxious such as: various bodily functions on command. Then Bob Bob will take you into the intermediate level of "Pull My Finger", make flatulent noises with your arm. After that, Bob Bob will take you to the Advanced level to tell people to go fuck themselves. It's Bob Bob's video on "How To Be Rude And Obnoxious!" Send 19-95 to Bob Bob himself, and for an extra fifty bucks, he'll go tell you to go fuck yourself!

---

54 Though it was never produced, for obvious reasons that it kind of sucks, I still have to share with you what some of the scripts I like. Unfortunately, I didn't finish this one until I started writing this book. I was getting tired of the rudeness of people while commuting on the freeway between Tacoma and Seattle along the I-5 corridor.

L.A.E.C. Script[55]

NARRATOR: Hey ladies! Imagine how he would feel if your ass is ten times larger! If you have no ass, we can make it bigger at the Laser Ass Enlargement Center! We have a large variety of asses that you can pick from including pork butt, cow butt, and those who want a petite, narrow, and highly sophisticated stuck up deer ass! That's right, the Laser Ass Enlargement Center has it all!

JANE: I had a horrible piece of ass, and thanks to Laser Ass Enlargement Center, I was able to replace it with a horse's ass. All I need now, is a hot stud to penetrate it! Thanks Laser Ass Enlargement Center!

John: I never have been very satisfied with my ass. All I had was a cow butt. But now, thanks to Laser Ass Enlargement Center, it has been replaced with an ass. (SFX: donkey heehaw). Now you can say that I am a real asshole. Thanks Laser Ass Enlargement Center!

NARRATOR: Our procedure is very simple, and little to no scar tissue exists. Come on down to a Laser Ass Enlargement Center near you in our fabulous nine hundred locations!

---

55 This is another unfinished script. Again, I finished it after the first paragraph while writing this book. I think this one would be funny to produce, but I don't have the time or the money.

Tyabio[56]

You look good tonight. I can see your eyes as they reflect upon the fire in the fireplace. The reflection dances like a petal that fell off of a beautiful flower and flew in the wind. In wind, your hair flies in the air as I caress your pit less face. What's this? A tear I see? The tear is so happy as it runs down your cheek. It's like stream that turns into a small waterfall off a small cliff. Oh how interesting it can be for me, who am gorgeous, to describe such a gorgeous woman as we make love together. Come here as I touch your chin. Your lips are nice soft red, not like the red of your blood, but the beautiful red of the roses that I gave you when we first met. Yet they seems so small shriveled like the ones that gave you that you saved and hung, dried it out, and then put it in your vase. A nice dry assortment. As our lips touch, I feel our lips gloss over like the morning dew on a rose petal, dripping, dripping into my mouth. Your lips are smooth like a piece of plastic, yet rough like wood, yet soft like a baby's bottom. The tingle shocks through your spine like lightning on a warm summer's day. Our tongues meet during our kiss. Oh how the roughness of the sandpaper seems to heal me into a nice piece of wood. It could make my tongue turn into a nice piece of furniture. The saliva we share is fine mixture of chemistry, like the love we share. The saliva is like a mixture of strawberries and cream. They go well together.

---

56 I wrote this skit as a joke based off an album that Fabio did. I never did finish it, but I thought it was worth saving and inserting it into this book.

The Great Boredom Ecstasy

"You've never heard of the *Great Boredom Ecstasy*," Johnny asked his girlfriend across the table while they were drinking up a lager at the pub.[57]

"I have never heard of it," Sheila said as she chomped down on some peanuts as a courtesy from the bar. After all, it is the salty peanuts that encouraged the patrons to buy more drinks. "It does seem very interesting whether you think the word, 'boredom' didn't pertain into the title. Yet, it seems more dangerous and lively with the word, 'ecstasy' in the title. Is it really safe?"

"Oh, completely safe with absolutely no side effects because it is not a drug. It's more of a story that I found while doing research for the magazine I work for. It's quite interesting."

Then the bar stopped, where silence overcame the noise of the glasses clinking, the sipping of the beer, and the personal conversations that floated ironically throughout the pub. You know, the silence you hear when you enter a sound proof booth where no sound enters or exits in the room, where you hear the blood pumping from your heart and eventually you go crazy from the body noise that you hear surrounding yourself. That embarrassing silence, where you just farted and everyone, and I do mean *everyone,* knows who did cut the mustard gas. That's right, it's that kind of silence that filled the pub. Every patron, bartender, and wait staff stopped what they were doing to fix their attention upon Johnny, hoping to find out more about the *Great Boredom Ecstasy.* [58]

Developed by a Dr. Fraugenheitz in the late nineteenth century, the *Great Boredom Ecstasy* is considered to be the *holy grail* of the *meaning of life* question that had plagued philosophers for centuries. Its formula and its design of the item had taken centuries upon centuries to develop, and nobody but Dr. Fraugenheitz was ever able to perfect it.

It's amazing how accidents happen. Dr. Fraugenheitz was reading some books in his study because, after all, there is nothing better to do

---

57 I think this is my first dialog written this book without it being in a script format.

58 It puzzles me why I put the pub scene in the story in the first place. I guess it was a perfect ice-breaker, an attention getter. Hell, it worked didn't it? You're reading the story and you're reading this footnote.

but to read books in the nineteenth century because television, radio, movies, and the computer with internet access hadn't been invented yet. In most cases, no electricity was even generated. Think of it as *camping out*, only in a larger scale – like your house. You could have smores by your fireplace.

Anyway, where was I? I get side-tracked so easily. Oh, yeah. Dr. Fraugenheitz was studying books on history. That's right, Dr. Fraugenheitz got his degree in history and not in science. If he had discovered something as a scientist, then he would be profoundly famous, but since he was a historian, then he would not get any recognition for the historical discoveries that he made. People would nod their heads and go "that's true" and then walk away as if they knew it all this time. This has plagued the historians for centuries because of the people who are too ignorant of their own past had snubbed their noses and walk off.

Dr. Fraugenheitz got tired of reading and it was too soon to retire for the evening. So, Dr. Fraugenheitz sat there and philosophized to himself with full of thought. In other words, he was thinking (sorry, I had been reading lots of nineteenth century literature lately, so I am more descriptive in my word settings rather being conversational in my writings). Well, what do you expect in the nineteenth century? It was either read, shop, go to work, eat, have sex, play games, watch a play, or go to bed. There wasn't a large selection of entertainment. You were pretty much stuck with what you are given rather than choosing your wide selection of on-demand entertainment that exists nowadays.

While Dr. Fraugenheitz was philosophizing to himself, he happened to be thinking about the age oldest study of the *Great Boredom Ecstasy*. He could have been thinking of something much worse, like women showing their ankles on a horse drawn carriage. I'm sure that there are plenty of oil paintings that ended up on the wayside or faded photographs. You see, they would keep it under their bed. Not something we should be ashamed of. It's only natural to keep these pornographic pictures under the bed, underneath the mattress, to be more specific.

Dr. Fraugenheitz finally came up with the thought that could have changed the world if he didn't have a doctorate in history.

The *Great Boredom Ecstasy* is the enjoyment of being bored. Okay, I'm sure people are going to go through a major study with taxpayers' expense to find out how people can have the enjoyment of being bored, but sometimes things can be unexplainable. For example, man can only develop a robot that can mimic our feelings, our thoughts, and our other human functions, but the robot would not be able to actually experience our wide diversities such as our heritage, our personalities, and the world we see around us. It's like comparing apples and oranges. We are an animal and a robot is considered to be a machine.

Just like the *Great Boredom Ecstasy* suggests, we can have enjoyment in anything if we change our mind sets to it.

The New Corporate Policy

While developing a large very important business sense, we, the board of directors of *Widgets, Inc*[59]., have come to the conclusion of the voting of a new corporate policy. With the declining sales and servicing of widgets, we feel there is no longer a need for such items within the household, the office, or even everyday use. We have found out the development within our research and development department has been too costly in coming out with new widgets. These people have been notified of their two week termination from this department and were welcome to take as much stuff in our labs as they are welcome to take out. This goes the same in both the manufacturing and the service department as well.

In doing so, we are ready to announce our new business venture that brings a cutting edge into our marketing strategy. After all, we wanted to stand out from the rest of the widget companies, in which our competitors would follow suit because of our successful enterprise.

Instead of widgets, our company is going to sell stocks of our company future shareholders. Why, you may ask? Again, with the declining sales and service of the widgets business, we are finally figuring out that even though we have a major decline in our sales and services, we are constantly increasing in our stock prices. All of this, of course, is good news. We have been appealing to our shareholders for over a century that we have been in business and went public in our stocks. So long as the shareholders had been happy on how well we are doing, it didn't matter if we sold a single widget or not.

That is why we, the board of directors of *Widgets, Inc.,* are switching to this new paradigm of business that is something that has not been developed before. For those who are staying at *Widgets, Inc.,* we welcome you to our new business. For those who are being terminated, the red footprint on your butt will heal as you kicked out of the door. Thank you, and have a nice day!

59 When you do a business simulation in a business education, you would often refer a fake product or service as a *widget.* What's sad is that people really think that such a thing actually exists. Now, it's being used in a computer software format to perform a certain function, even though it is still hypothetical.

More Or Less, A Spy In Our Midst[60]

The commissioner was sitting in his office busy with his paperwork. We know him as "P" because for some reason, when you build yourself up with a promotion in the management sector, you automatically change from a number to a letter.

There are twenty-six managers overall, each one with "A" through "Z". There are one hundred forty-six spies, each one with a number. The top spy gets renamed as "1", the second top spy would get a "2", and so on. If someone in the management retires, then the top spy would get the position as "Z". Only "A" is reserved for the top manager, or better as the head of the spy organization. This would often trouble the personnel department, since spies do get shot, the positions would often change.

"Did you call me, Commissioner," Agent Eleven said as he walked in the door of "P"'s office.

"Yes, indeed, Agent Eleven," "P" said with his eyes drawn away from the paperwork that was upon his desk at that very second as Agent Eleven entered the office. "I have called you in here to tell you that with the different interest amongst our government that we are no longer allowed to have any travel expenses whatsoever."

"How that could be," asked Agent Eleven with some confusion on his face, "we are constantly traveling to our new assignments, whatever they may be."

"I try to explain that to the government," replied "P", "you see, because there is a really low threat on the citizens from an international standpoint, we all have to sacrifice our consequences, and therefore, we must be able to eliminate all travel expenses as of immediately."

"But, sir," said Agent Eleven, "what about the rest of the spies? How are they able to get home to our wonderful home country of Zambia?"

"I don't know. But, I'm sure they will have to figure it out or die trying."

---

60 Sorry, I had been watching a few *James Bond* films lately and ended up thinking of government spies lately. I would like to give special thanks to Ian Fleming, the creator of *Chitty Chitty Bang Bang!*

"Well, the safety of these men and women outside our country of Zambia, a safe haven, cause some concern? After all, the United States is not a safe place to be at this time."

"I agree, but we must stand our ground."

The country of Zambia discontinued their spy program as of January 6, 1861. A few years later, the United States went into a Civil War, thus creating the end of slavery in the United States. And though the southerners are still pissed to this very day because they lost their free (as in money) labor, Zambia still never entirely recovered.

T.M.I.D. (Too Much Informative Description)[61]

It was in the car when the problem arose. Sheila had always thought that there would be problem like this that would arise eventually, it just that she did not find a way to solve this problem now. It was way too early for something like this to work itself out. But, she had to have the strategic plan in place and ready to go whether she we wanted to devise an action status or not.

You see, Sheila had to find restroom quickly whether she wanted to or not. It wasn't much of a *want* rather than a *need* to go to the restroom. She could the bulge trickling from her stomach to her upper intestines as they slowly move down through the muscle tubing.

A car is much worse than a building. At least there were restrooms there, but being stuck in traffic on the freeway was much worse than being able to get to where she needed to be. It was a shame, since she was only five miles, *just five measly miles*, to her destination.

Sheila had to act quickly on her planning strategy. She knew what her options really were and, frankly, she didn't like it. As the lump slowly towards her rectum, she knew that she had to either poop her pants or hold it until she got home. Sheila chose to hold it until she got home. It was the best executive decision she had at the time. Nobody is going to pat you on the back and tell you "good job" for this decision, but like a true soldier you must be able to hold it like a man, hold your ground, otherwise you will fail as a soldier.

Three miles to go. Only three miles to go. It's becoming more and more intense. Two miles to go. A whiff of air shows that it was only gas. That's okay. Gas is okay. So long as it's not an accidental poop or a major eruption. Sheila thought she would just let a little bit of gas out at a time in order to relieve the pressure. The miles are counting down little by little. Sheila was only a half a mile to go. One quarter of a mile to go the. The tension is getting harder and harder to bare as Sheila let's more and more gas out. Time to open a window and let the fresh air in.

Finally, Sheila makes it home. Great. It's one thing if you make home in your vehicle, it's another to make it to the restroom without

---

61 This took me awhile to write the story. I wanted it to be very descriptive, but I was also annoyed of someone looking behind my back reading the very words that I was typing on the screen on the computer. I soon got over it whether I was pushing for it or not.

taking a dump all over yourself. She knew what she had to do. Sheila got out of the vehicle with some trouble. The gas started to come out with full force. Though she tried her best to not to blow, she knew she could clench her butt cheeks as tight as she could in order to keep it from exploding. Step by step, as slow as she could go and working her way with a short step with her feet, she knew that by taking baby steps, she could keep away from exploding. When Sheila arrived at the door, she put the keys into the front door lock and ran quickly to the toilet in her bathroom, took down her pants and let go the of the major pressure that was building inside of her.

She deserved a medal. I'm sure there were many men and women who would go through the exact same thing every day. Sure, there would be winners in this battle. But, what about those who wouldn't make it? This could create a disastrous effect on both those around us and the simple job of the human body. What's moral of this story and why does it need to be told? It's simple. We always need public restrooms on the streets in order to fulfill our personal needs.[62]

---

62 Okay, I know the story was really descriptive, but how often do you get a story of full detail about a bowel movement? I don't think (and for good reason) that something like this has ever been accomplished before. Did you feel a big bulge coming out of you when you read this story? I know I did. I wrote this story while I was chained on the toilet. It's not something that I am particularly proud of, but I'm sure someone had thought about in their heads at one time or other in their lifetime. How come some of these things were ever recorded in history?

An Economical Theory[63]

"Do you ever feel guilty of the fact that we are stealing money from the rich because we are in a third world country," asked Sylvia as she was eating dinner at a fine restaurant.

"Not really," said John as he was having a nice sip of fine champagne, "it's pretty much a matter of the economical reasoning. Let's take a look at the rich countries. If we assume that the first world countries are getting richer and richer."

"Right," said Sylvia, "which they are whether we like it or not."

"Well, the guilt is still there amongst the rich of that country so they want to be philanthropists and share their wealth. Rather than sharing their wealth within their respective countries, where they are essentially taking the money from their own public, or worse, get taxed, instead, they would rather start up at a third world country in order to make it look like they are doing something to make the whole world a better place to live."

"So, you're saying, that we shouldn't be guilty because we are on the receiving end of these philanthropists?"

"Right."

"Then, why do we keep on acting that we are in a desire need for help when, in reality, we really don't that help?"

"Those rich people in the first world countries are currently in the outsourcing method."

"Outsourcing, what's that?"

"It's when you find a way for someone to get some labor done without having to get the ones in your country to do the labor."

"Oh, I get it. Yo mean to say that it is cheaper to do it here at a third world country than it is to do it in a first world country. Well, I can't blame them for these things. When you make money, then you have to somehow make a huge profit."

---

63 I was thinking, the other day, that most people from the northern hemisphere often migrate to the southern hemisphere in order to help those who couldn't be helped. Let's take South Africa. South Africa is a very rich country, and yet it gets plenty of help by the northern hemisphere rather than help from their own country. I guess that makes us wanting to help our roots within the continent of Africa, where we are slowly trying to "civilize" their country.

"Right, and those profits look better in the books, which in turn, makes the stock holders happy that you are inflating the profit margin by inflating the prices for the typical first world country consumer to pay the company. They call it Wal-Mart-nomics. Selling their product as cheap as they can in order to destroy the competition and thus the beginnings of a monopoly."

"Well, that makes a whole lot of sense."

"It really does if you think about it. It's, in turn, making our economy successful and sharing the wealth. And, to make sure that they are working on providing our country in order to make it seem successful while taking as much money as they possibly can from the consumers in their country, the rich philanthropists come by and visit us periodically to see that we are in line."

"That explains why we must live in run down housing and have a set amount of ghettos."

"Right, little do these philanthropists know, our country is becoming more and more successful and sometimes more successful than their own rich countries. We must be able to put on a show in front of these people in order for us to keep our economy going on a level playing field in our social economy."

"So, that's how capitalism works within a socialistic economy."

The Trees Have Guns[64]

Jason had been out in the woods playing with his neighborhood buddies. His neighborhood buddies had pop gun rifles for they wanted to play "soldier", where each guy was either an American or a damn Russkies. The thousand acre forest wood was easy to hide, but one should be careful because one could often get lost within the wilderness, catch hypothermia and die.

Nonetheless, the woods were a perfect place to pretend to be a soldier when it came to the Cold War era. But, it was not very true to life as the real world. Pretending to be a soldier is only pretend; for it is not real. You do not have friends die. That was the most important thing childhood while playing soldier. Nobody gets injured. Nobody gets shrapnel stuck within the various body parts. Nobody gets post-traumatic syndrome. Nobody gets post diseases from the war. Nobody dies and comes home in a wooden box.

Being a ten year old boy, Jason didn't care much about these things and he was glad that these things didn't provide outcome of what the war was really like. Instead, it was much easier to pretend that beating the Russkies with his buddies through the woods, crawling through the bushes with pop gun rifles was much more beneficial than the real thing.

Sure, "the bomb" could go off anytime. It could go off any second. The bomb shelters were still existent where he lived in his neighborhood. Especially since the Fallout shelter consisted of the basics of food items, water, first aid, and the bare necessities of the home. Much money was sunk into these nuclear bomb shelters, waiting for the inevitable, but never occupied.

Now after twenty years, the bomb shelter bunkers are full of cobwebs, dust, rust, spiders, and rats. The buildings were built, stocked, and abandoned. The bomb shelters will never see their use, waiting to deteriorate and destroy themselves from age.

Jason knew better than the rest of the boys. He knew that the fallout shelters did exist in his neighborhood. He had seen the film, *Duck And Cover,* a serious attempt by the United States Federal Government to inform the public of this national emergency for their stupidity if creating

64 Okay, I never finished this story. But, I know that one day I may re-write it and finish it. Hopefully, it will have a moral like I often wish and hope most of my stories would.

the hydrogen bombs in the first place. He knew what *Duck And Cover* meant. Basically, it was the government's way of saying that you bend yourself into a fetal position while covering your head and kiss your ass goodbye. It was a simple message that the United States of America citizens would eventually cross in their minds.

It was fairly easy being able to be a boy during the latter part of the Cold War era. Sure, it was revitalized by the Republicans in the middle of the 1970's, but President Richard Milhous Nixon's Administration ended the extra long and dreaded Vietnam War as he had promised in his election that the Democrats had often maintained.

Jason didn't know any better. He didn't care about the Arms Race between Ronald Reagan and Mikhail Gorbachev with the nuclear build up between the United States and the U.S.S.R. He was just a twelve year old kid playing army soldier with his friends. For, that is what young boys do, to play soldier through the trees.

Jason grabbed his bag ready for the plane flight. He gave his mother and his father a hug. "I love mom. I love you dad." He boarded the plane through the terminal, ready for his flight. A new adventure in the military was about to start for Jason.

His parents thought differently. They did not want Jason, their only son, to go. They were afraid of Jason being killed and if the inevitable does happen of a World War III, then Jason wouldn't be with the family. But, if you love someone, then you should let them leave the nest and go on their own. Let them find out what it really is like out in the real world of chaos.

Scared of going into the unknown and the training that he had at boot camp at Fort Bragg, but fear began to subside through him when the troops began to occupy the base in Germany. It was very close to the fighting against the end of the world. By then, the wall was still up in Berlin, a sign that the Eastern German people in East Berlin were prisoners in their own country and their own city.

Imagine never seeing your country, the rest of your city, or even your friends and family for nearly fifty years. Sure Germany had Nazism, but one day, Germany will rise up again and become one country instead of being two countries that were divided by the Axis powers in 1945. Unity will be one again as it was once before 1945. For those who tried to escape from imprisonment often did not survive. And those who did survive while they escaped, could not communicate with their families back home. It was also during the building of the wall that the families would often be split apart. The wall would be going up regardless that were inside it or outside of the wall.

Fear went rampant among the German people as well as the United States. Just like the rest of the world, they were afraid of World War III coming back from the event of an attack of nuclear warfare between the U.S. and the U.S.S.R. Jason knew that that fear, a fear that was just been centralized in two locations, but around the world.

But, here was Jason. As child of the eighties, where if one wore a Reagan hair do, then they were automatically considered to be a Republican (not to mention the plastic look of the first lady that resembles a Barbie doll). The dyed hair would mean that you are a rebel.

The Scottish Cone[65]

Two men were sitting in a pub with their lager in the midst of the middle of the United States. So, the title of this story may even fool you. Other than that, regardless it is only two men sitting in a pub having a drink of lager in the United States. But, I digress. Anyhow, as they were drinking their lager in full discussion of the world politics and useless facts, one of the men (a third man) comes up to them in a bar. He obviously had something to say rather than just order more of his order of pale ale.

"You guys have heard of the 'Scottish Cone', right?"

"No," said one of the guys. He didn't know whether he should bugger him off or to keep him around.

"Well, you've heard of the 'Egyptian Pyramids'," he replied.

"Right."

"You've heard of the 'Bermuda Triangle',"

"Right."

"You've heard of the American Circle," he said.

"That makes sense," said one of them holding on to his lager with a tight grip before sipping it. He was making sure that he didn't spill it while he was drinking the beer since he was drinking more than his normal rate. "That brings about the 'American Apple Pie' amongst other things."

"Right, but in Scotland, it's geometric combination of the last three items that bring about the world phenomena throughout the entire world over. It's bigger than all of these three items that I just mentioned even better than it really suppose to be."

"The 'Scottish Cone'?"

" Yeah, it has jam inside of a bready pastry."

"That's 'Scone', you dumb shit."[66]

---

65 I thought about this story on the way to class and was trying to write as much of this discussion while I could in a notebook before class. It was originally called "The Scottish Pyramid", but, after much thought, I decided that the Egyptians own that one. So I came up with the cone and soon figured out similar. If you keep the first letter of "Scotland" and keep the full word, "cone", then you would more than likely change the entire bit to be "scone", a fine pastry with a jam filling from Scotland. I didn't think of it this way until after I decided to write the story.

66 I don't know what brought me forth. Possibly because I was thinking of food again and Scotland., but my theory is that I was thinking about how Sean Connery speaks in a loose accent. There is no relationship here.

Kolyma: A Love Story[67]

The cool wind blew across the Volga River region near Hussenbach. Georgi[68] could tell that winter is coming and it could be colder than ever before. Generally, the colder the winter, the harder the potatoes and wheat were to grow on the land. Georgi went back to lying the remaining the old wheat grass that was crunched on the ground from which he harvested earlier. He actually enjoyed working for his father to keep the family land going, and he knew, fairly soon, he would be able to settle down with a beautiful young lady in the village and share the land once they settle down. She, too, could help make the farming plentiful, be able to care for the young, and the elders with him.

"Nadezhda[69]," he said out loud, but not enough to be heard. The name rolled off of his tongue. How could such a beautiful woman that rolls off of the tongue and easy to pronounce be so hard to spell? Georgi went back to work. It's definitely going to be a long cold winter and the ground must be prepared for that winter or may freeze. And when the ground is frozen with the seedlings, then the crop would become useless.

"Georgi," his mother called out to him, "schule[70] time."

"Ja, Mutter! I'll be there!" It time for school, and in his family, education had the utmost importance. When Georgi was not in the field and doing his chores, his family would often go to German school on the second half of the day. Georgi grabbed his chalkboard, chalk, and borrowed books that the Soviet school provided.

Nadezhda was excited. In two days she was arranged to be married. Oh how joyous her life is going to be when she finally going to

67 I was watching a documentary called *Kolyma*. After being depressed for about two to three hours, I realized that this imprisonment was never taught in school while I was growing up. In fact few, if any, people know about what exactly happened in Kolyma. Since *Titanic* was such a big hit with a fine mixture of love and disaster, I figured that this is a right time to write such a short story. Who knows? Maybe a movie company will pick up the idea.

68 Georgi means "earth-worker, farmer" in Russian.

69 Nadezhda means "hope" in Russian.

70 Okay, I did put in a few German references. The story should make some sense for non-German speaking people. But her is the list: Schule=School; Mutter=Mother; Ja=Yes; Oma=Grandma; Opa=Grandpa. The reason why I put a little bit of each is because I wanted put a little bit of realism into the story, much like writers write with bad grammar and spelling to represent the Southern United States.

share her life Georgi. She sat there. She daydreaming for what her future beheld. "Oma," she yelled out to her grandmother.

"Yes, dear," cried her grandmother.

"Please tell me the story again about how you and Opa got together."

"It was too long ago."

"Please?" Nadezhda really wanted know, for she wanted to be as close to Georgi as much as possible.

"I will tell you another time. Perhaps, on your wedding day I will tell you."

"But that is a long ways away."

The grandmother scolded her, "I will tell you on your wedding day, and that is that. Now run along. You must prepare dinner."

"Okay, Oma." Nadezhda knew that Oma will tell her story. She had always kept her promise. She went into the kitchen to peel some potatoes for supper, for the men were to be done in the fields and would be coming home fairly soon.

Georgi was finally finished attending at German school. The wind seemed to get colder and colder. He had been right all along. There is going to be a long, harsh winter up ahead, only it is going to be worse than ever before. He walked into the house and set the books down. He was ready for dinner, and this time, he was hungry.

The meals often consisted of a base of cabbage, potatoes, and wheat type products that were often deep fat fried in lard on the kitchen woodstove. These things were often plentiful in the Hussenbach village. Even though in his farming expertise, he knew that these foods would often fill him up after a long day of working in the fields and tending to the farm animals. Being a fourteen year old lad, he knew that he would be the man of the house soon, and he, too, will have to demand the same from his future wife, who is the same age as Georgi.

Suddenly, the front door slammed open. Georgi thought it was the wind and ran towards the door to shut it only to find out that there was a guard from the KGB was at the door.

"We are requiring all citizens of the village to comply for relocation in order to provide towards the war effort."

Georgi didn't want to make a fuss. It was to help out the war effort, but what could he do. The KGB agent showed his gun and escorted Georgi and to the detainment camp located in the middle of town. There he saw Nadezhda.

"Nadezhda," he cried.

"Georgi," replied Nadezhda. "I wasn't sure if I would be able to see you again. Do you know where we are going?"

Georgi was as confused as Nadezhda. He didn't know what to say. "I – I don't know," he replied back to her.

"Georgi, we must not split. We need to be together."

"Together, we must. I love you, Nadezhda."

"I love you, too, Georgi," Nadezhda replied. They both kissed with heavy hugging. She rubbed his arms. "Georgi?"

"Yes?"

"Do you think it will be cold where we are going?"

Georgi replied to Nadezhda with confidence, "It will be warm, you'll see. It will be a paradise much better than where we are right now. You'll see." Nadezhda closed her eyes and fell asleep in his arms. Georgi gave her quick kiss on the ear, held her tight, and then fell asleep throughout the night.

The sun was beginning rise and the cold wind had stopped blowing. Georgi had awoken with his future wife in his arms. As he looked around the area, he saw other Germans from his village that had surrendered as well inside a barbed wire perimeter around them. The Germans had to give up even they were in their own country, because it was the right thing to do. It was for the World War II effort for the Soviets to be the axis powers. We must surrender and sacrifice ourselves for the greater good.

As the sun rose up from the east, Hussenbach was getting warmer and warmer as it rose above the land. Nadezhda woke up refreshed, for she knew that she was the arms of the man she loved the most. She kissed him to let him know that she was awake and he kissed her back to show that he still loved and looked forward to seeing her wake up and go to bed every day.

The whistle of a giant black locomotive blew. The steam engine was about to stop in order to pick up the people and send them to a detainment camp. Where the Soviets were going to take them, that was something that the detainees knew nothing about but the fact that they just taken somewhere within the country.

"All detainees are to board the train," cried out the orders from the general.

"Nadezhda," replied Georgi, "we must go."

"But, I want to stay here and be with you," Nadezhda replied.

"We can't. We must board the train."

"I don't want to go."

"Do not act so childish, Nadezhda. What's wrong with you?"

"I'm sick. I'm sick. I can't go. I must stay here. This is home. I must stay.

"You!" exclaimed the guard. "You need to board the train."

"She's sick. I must take care of her," Georgi said as he pointed his finger at Nadezhda.

"No worries," said the guard, "we will take good care of her."

"Nadezhda, I must leave."

"Don't go, Georgi. Remember, this is home. You must stay," Nadezhda said with her arms out.

Georgi and Nadezhda were separated by the two guards. The guard kept on pushing Georgi towards one of the railroad cars as the other detainees are being herded like cattle onto the train cars. Soon, the railroad car was full and large wooden door on the box car slammed with the padlock on the car to prevent escapees. Georgi hears a gunshot. He sits down and cries. Why did they kill Nadezhda?

Georgi woke up and took a deep breath. The condensation from his exhale made a clink on the floor. No work today. He had been at Kolyma, Siberia, USSR for several months, living off of just soup and hard work from mining for gold for Stalin. That was all Georgi could think of was what he left behind Hussenbach, for he did truly love Nadzhda. He stayed in bed because it was still warm underneath the covers even though he could feel the dramatic cold and the frost bite nibbling at his toes. Georgi looked up and saw a fifteen year old girl staring at him.

"I am Slava[71]," she said as she got closer to Georgi.

"Morgen[72]," said Georgi.

"I feel cold – so cold," Slava said.

"Where did you come from?"

"I live here. I am from here."

"No, what village are you from?"

"What's a village? I was born here."

"What do you mean? Who are your parents?"

"My parents are the Soviets."

"That's impossible. How could that be?"

"I was born here in Kolyma. I was beaten often by the guards. When my mother came to visit me, I was hiding underneath the bed and I was afraid of being beaten again."

"Is she still alive?"

"I don't know. When she arrived, I kept on saying that she was not my mother. The guards insisted that she was my mother, but I wouldn't believe the guards from the Gulag. I kept on saying that over and over again that she was not my mother." Slava tried to cry, but her tears were only coming out as ice. "So cold."

Georgi felt for her. Everything about Russia is very depressing with no hope for living. Most Russians would rather die than endure the daily survival.

"So cold – I'm really cold," said Slava again.

"Come," Georgi replied as he moved open the covers and pats his hands on the mattress. "Lie down with me, and maybe we can be warm together." Slave complied and lied against him and Georgi put the covers over both of them. They both cuddled with each other, hoping to keep warm.

"I love you," said Slava.

---

71 Slava means "glory" in Russian.

72 Morgen means "morning" in German. It is usually opened with "Guten Morgen" which is translated as "Good Morning".

"I love you, too," said Georgi.

The two both made a passionate kiss with one another and then cuddled with each other forever with their eyes closed.

The Serious College Student[73]

She was a very serious college student. She didn't come for the culture of the college to enjoy college life, nor did she want to be involved with the protests. She came for the subject and her love Ethnography, the ability to capture oral histories that are not in the books. To her, these were the "real" stories that had to be told and not, and I repeat, not what one author tells you to do. She didn't want a relationship; she just wanted to be alone within her studies.

Sure, there was the weekly protest from the other college students. There were parties at the dorms that happened nightly. The sexual intercourse that constantly happened nearly every day, both privately, and publicly, could be heard through the dorm room walls. There was also the heavy drug and alcoholic use, where her fellow students became stoned and stupid. How they make it in the morning, she didn't know. Some said that she was a sociopath; some say that she was a wallflower, where she preferred to be alone in her own room. She was able to be aware of her surroundings, for she was a writer as well in a liberal college.

She was a serious college student, and it couldn't get any more serious on her studies. Nobody knew her history, her hobbies, or even her personality. She was an introvert and her roommates were extroverts. There was something warm about books and she knew it. How else could she escape the world, the very boring world? She sat back in her seat in front of her desk. "I am a very serious student," she would often think over and over again to herself. She wanted to reassure herself that she was normal as though she blended in with the rest of the students.

While walking down the downtown streets to catch the bus from the library to the college, she noticed somthing unusual. A young man, about her age, was flipping pizzas at the local pizzeria. She didn't know what to say or to think, for she felt a like she had butterflies in her stomach. For here is a man, and a cute man that is her age, and she wanted to meet him. It was love at first sight for her. Her life had finally

---

73 While attending classes at The Evergreen State College, I noticed there was a person who was considered to be an over-achiever. You know about those type of people. Every single college has them. They are the serious students. Unfortunately, I believe that they need plenty of help because they often miss the good things in life. It is okay to be curious with the courses that you are taking, but you really do miss out if you do not give yourself a social life. In my opinion, you need a social stimulation in order to turn yourself into an intellectual person. After all, enjoy life! It will do you good! A message from the Church of Jesus Christ of Ladder Day Saints (I'm just kidding!).

changed. She was finally a regular person, for it was that man who showed her own ways and to enjoy her life as much as she possibly could. You can't always have books to keep yourself in company. You must have a wonderful relationship to keep.

In The Spirit Of The Night[74]

Chapter One

Deana Smith needed to get out of class fast. Oh god, her nauseating English teacher was giving the class a long, boring lecture on punctuation, again. She had a hard time figuring out why some people didn't understand the coma. Julie had given Deana a note at the beginning of class. It said, "See you at the movies tonight at eight o'clock." Deana couldn't wait to see her best friend at the movies, because she didn't have anything to do that night. She looked up at the wintry analog clock located above the blackboard on the newly painted white wall. "One more minute before two o'clock. One more minute to get out of this boring class. I can't wait," she thought as she watched the red second hand passed by the black minute hand. Why does time run slowly when you are bored out of your skull? Then it happened. The clock backtracked one minute unintentionally. This caught Deana by surprise. "Damn it," she thought, "they've figured out a way to keep us in school forever." Then the clock skipped forward to the correct time. When the school bell rang, school was over for the weekend.

As she walked up the paved pathway to the bus area at the school, she noticed the school bus was late. It is irremediable to leave school on time on a Friday afternoon. "Man, I cannot believe that I am still riding that stupid cheese wagon," she thought as she stood there waiting for the common carrier, "I could be driving a car by now." Why not? After all, every senior high school student is driving some sort of transportation. Only freshmen high school ride buses.

The public conveyance just pulled up in front of the rest of the bus riders. She wasn't alone. About a hundred high school students, mostly freshmen, were also riding the cheese wagon. Deana looked at the

---

[74] I wrote this story back in 1994 at Tacoma Community College in Tacoma, Washington. The story had many different versions, but the beginning seemed work out the best and it never did need any revision. I still like the beginning of the story, but when it came to the middle and the end of the story, the story seemed to go downhill from there. This is the second version of the story. The original story had a very descriptive version of hell, which, eventually, was destroyed accidently. I was only stuck with this version and tried to rewrite the story and end up going to a different direction. I got the idea from a former member of the SCA (Society of Creative Anachronism). Eventually, as the internet began to be popular in the mid-1990s, I ended up posting this story on the world wide web, so I still keep my eye out for any copyright issues.

dirty bus. Somebody wrote, "Help me! I am engulfed in diesel fumes!" Right next to those words was morose face drawn on the yellow paint. "That is just like those freshmen," she thought as she was standing in line, "They are so immature." She looked up to see who the driver was, hoping it would be a substitute. It was not. It was Mrs. O'Freely, the crabby bitch from hell. Mrs. O'Freely had an ego as big as the Titanic, and still her ego sunk the ship. Deana climbed three steps and walked down the aisle. She walked towards the back of the cheese wagon and sat down. She put on her headphones and listened to her punk rock music that her mother has always disapproved. There is no way she is going to deal with Mrs. O'Freely.

Adam Tyler was forlorn and bored stiff as ever. He was watching the All Music Television channel in his bedroom that was located in the chilly, cabalistic basement. A.M. TV didn't cut it for him that evening. Adam thought that maybe he should go to see a movie in Tacoma. He wondered what Deana Smith was doing that night. He called her up through his cellular phone. The cordless phone rang three times when Deana's matriarch picked up the telephone receiver.

"Hello?"

"Uh, hi Mrs. Smith. May I talk to Deana, please," Adam replied.

"Sure. Hold on." Mrs. Smith brought the cordless telephone to Deana. Adam could hear the television set in the background. It sounded as if her mother was watching some game show. Then he heard her mom yell at Deana, "Deana?! Telephone!" Deana grabbed the cordless receiver from her homemaking mother.

"Hello," she greeted over the phone.

"Yes. Deana Smith," Adam asked.

"Yeah? Who is this," asked Deana in stupefaction.

"Deana you will win a special date to the cinema, if you can answer this question," said Adam in his special radio announcers' voice impression.

"With who," she asked.

"With me, Adam Tyler," he said, cutting out his lousy impression, "Would you like to go?"

"Yes," she said, "only if Julie can come with us."

"Sure, no problem," Adam replied, "I'll pick you and Julie up at seven!"

It was approximately seven-thirty at night when Deana, Julie, and Adam arrived at the theater. They were standing in queue for tickets at the $1.25 movie house, when someone tapped Adam on the shoulder. Adam turned one hundred eighty degrees to see who it was.

"Adam? Adam Tyler? Is that you?"

"Oh, hi Dan! Hi Violet!" Adam said as he patted Dan Ross' back, "Are you two going out?"

"Yeah. And you," asked Dan.

"Yep," replied Adam.

"Say, Adam," Dan said while he pulled Adam away from their dates, "Could you, by any chance, give me and Violet a lift? It's not too cool to ride public transportation with a date. Do you know what I mean?"

"Of course. You know I would help my best friend," Adam replied, "Why didn't you call me in the first place? I could have given you a ride earlier?"

"I have never thought of it at the time, but thanks, man. I appreciate your help more than anything in the world," said Dan.

"No problem," Adam said, "Come. Let's join our female counterparts and party."

"Alright," replied Dan.

Chapter Two

The film that they all picked together was called, "The Return Of The Slob." It was a typical romantic comedy about a woman who falls in love with a man who happened to be a slob. It was a terrible movie. "What do you expect out of $1.25," thought Adam as he watched the movie, "A Shakespeare play?" Deana could feel someone else's hand holding hers. Then, a whispering voice was heard in Adam's, Violet's, Deana's, and Dan's mind, almost subconsciously, "You are the chosen one."

Adam, Deana, Dan, and Violet looked at each other with a questioned look on their face, "Did you utter something?" They shook their heads and started to scrutinize the movie again.

The words from the inner voice in their heads were back again, "You are the chosen one." It repeated the same words over and over again. Soon, the group thought that they were going insane.

When the film was over, they went to get some ice cream at the local malt shop. Julie dropped twenty-five cents in the jukebox's nickelodeon, selected her music, went to her group's booth, sat down, and then started to eat her banana split. After Adam gulped down his first spoonful of his hot fudge sundae, he raised the question to Deana, "What did you think of the movie?"

"I enjoyed it, but somebody or something frequently whispered the words, 'You are the chosen one,' to me," answered Deana as she took a bite of her butterscotch sundae.

"Yeah, I heard that too," replied Dan.

"So did I," said Violet.

"Funny, me too," said Adam with a questioned look on his face.

"You heard it too," asked Violet.

"Yeah," the group said simultaneously.

"Wait. We can't all be hearing this," voiced Violet.

Julie didn't hear anything. What were they talking about? It is either everyone is going insane or she is going insane or she is going insane instead. Could it be somebody playing a joke on them without the group knowing? Did all of this happen while she was out getting popcorn and a soda pop at the snack bar in the lobby of the movie theater? She decided to listen to the rest of the group so that way she could get clues of their conversation.

"True, but nobody whispered those words to us," said Dan, "How could that be?"

"I don't know. I really don't know," said Adam, "I think we should head home."

They all resolved their decision and the group got into Adam's green Ford Pinto sedan. Dan, Violet, and Julie sat in the back seat and Adam and Deana sat in the front seat. Adam turned on his radio and shoved the latest Hellhole cassette tape into his newly put in car cassette radio system. Hellhole, a new local rock band, was gaining in popularity throughout Western Washington. After crossing the Tacoma Narrows Bridge, Adam's car stalled on the freeway. He only had enough power to make it to the off ramp that went to the Weigh Station. Adam looked at the fuel gauge on his black dashboard. The gas meter read empty, even though Adam remembered that he filled the fuel tank ten minutes ago. There was no way his car would be out of petroleum. Now, they were stranded in the equidistant of a colossal wooded section within Gig Harbor. He stopped the Pinto and then turned off its engine.

"What's wrong," asked Dan as he moved forward from the back seat so he could talk to Adam.

"We ran out of gasoline," answered Adam, "Alright everyone, time to get out and walk."

The group decided to walk through the thicket instead of walking on the freeway with no concept of where they were going. After all, the freeway is more dangerous to walk on through a grove of fir trees.

Julie, who was with the group, decided to run ahead. She wandered off, thinking that she could find a shortcut in order to find help at the nearest gas station. After all, Adam had helped her many times and she was sure to pay him back for his kindness. Suddenly, she tripped over what felt like a root of a tree. She felt a thump on her head and then blacked out.

The rest of the group walked on a somewhat beaten path. The trail led them to a cleared area, not manmade, like most clearings, but a natural prairie. The prairie was a grassy area that seemed soft, yet the ground was a firm, solid piece of soil.

Ichabod Sanders ran away from home due to the fact that his mother abused him. He could remember that slap on his face when she said that he didn't clean up his room. The slap felt like he was bleeding in the face, but it wasn't. He wished he could escape from his parents, because they were arguing often. Why can't they agree and love each other? "They are probably going to get an annulment," he thought. Boy, his mother can be a bitch sometimes.

Ichabod always strolled through the woods whenever the heat was getting too much for him. It was ambrosial and peaceful for him. While he walked through the copse during the night time, when he heard that voice that repeated in head over and over again, "You are the chosen one." He stopped and looked around. He saw absolutely nobody. With skepticism, Ichabod kept moving towards his unknown destination.

He came to the same clearing that Adam, Deana, Violet, and Dan were at. Afraid of being seen, Ichabod hid behind the scotch broom. "When they leave, he will continue on with his personal trek," he thought.

Chapter Three

The moon was a pale, white spotlight in the clear, pitch black night. Dan, Violet, Adam, Deana, and Ichabod saw the moon and gazed at it. Everyone seemed to have slipped into a reverie. Dan, Adam, Violet, and Deana gathered around a circle, holding each other's hands.

That strange, eerie voice came back into their brains again, "Feel your instincts, and you will believe." The grassy ground in the medial of the circle became a jet black hole. At the end of the black hole, there was a bright white light. The light was getting larger and larger, growing in height. It was coming towards them! The massive light grew into a moon shadow type figure. It kept on growing until it was about six feet above them. Then, a bunch of unnatural light brightened the sky, which created stars in the heavens above. Each star was a sign of spirits of the past, present, and the future souls on the Planet Earth. "Do you see the light," asked the voice. They all nodded their heads up and down slowly. The voice replied, "God will help those who help themselves. Follow your instincts and your senses and they will guide you throughout your lifetime." After that, the white light disappeared into the stratosphere. The black hole turned into a piece of grassy ground that it originally was before the group's unusual experience.

Deana, Adam, Violet, Ichabod, and Dan came out of their trance, blinking and shaking their heads in disbelief. What just happened? Ichabod ran back towards his house. There was no way he wanted to stay in the woods too long, at least around that place.

Adam, Violet, Dan, and Deana walked back to Adam's car. The moon was now a large red-orange fireball in the sky. As they were leaving, the fog closed in behind them, as if the spirits were closing a large gate behind them.

"Where did Julie go," asked Deana.

"I don't know," answered Adam, "Maybe she made it home."

"She's probably okay," said Dan.

"We really don't have to worry about her. I'm sure she can take care of herself," said Violet.

When they arrived at Adam's car, Adam turned the ignition key and the Pinto started. The fuel gauge read full again. Adam drove everyone home. The group was silent the whole time, not knowing how to react at their explicable experience.

Chapter Four

It was lunch time at Peninsula High School. The group was sitting on a stained wooden bench. They were eating out of their brown paper sack lunches. They were silent for about five to ten minutes. Ichabod was at a bench nearby, eavesdropping on the group.

Finally, Dan raised the question, "Did everybody see what I saw Friday night?"

"I think I saw it, not just you," said Deana, answering Dan's question.

"Then, what was it we saw on that prairie," asked Violet while in sobs, "It scares me. I don't know what to do."

Adam hugged her, "I don't know, but I think it is for the best in all of us."

"We'll find out, Violet," said Deana, "The question is, I have noticed something different since that night."

"What is it," asked Adam.

"For some strange reason, I can see the sun without being blinded by the light," said Deana.

"Funny, when I was at the library, I could smell and taste the ink in the books," said Adam, "Like the books was already freshly printed."

"That's odd," said Violet as she was pushing away her tears, "This paper bag seems to feel rough, and I can feel individual splinters on this bench we are sitting on."

"You think that's strange," Dan said, "I can hear ants screaming for help every time I crush them to death."

Ichabod noticed something different about himself, too. For some odd reason, he knew what the lottery numbers were before they were first drawn on television. Why? He did not quite know yet. He had the feeling that he probably will soon.

Then Deana asked Adam, "What are they? Where do they come from? Why did they choose us?"

"I don't know," replied Adam. The tardy bell rang for their next class. It was the least item they wanted to do was to be late to their next class.

Ichabod went to the library. He was wondering if the prairie, where he had become chosen at, was selected to be a consecrated ground. He went into the parochial history books in order to get his information. He went through most of the tomes, including the atlas in order to find out more about the savanna. Finally, he got to the final local history book. This book dated back in the early 1900's. It said one thing about the moors. 'This is a hallowed ground. Do not enter.' "They must be serious," he thought, "I wonder what happened there." Before he read on, an ancient bony hand slammed onto the book.

"Do not read on, son," he said, "For you may get into major problems." Then, the old man disappeared into thin air. Ichabod looked at the book. It was missing! Ichabod decided to head home. Those history books can be irksome sometimes.

Ichabod had a strange dream that night. He was taken to a place where it was not on earth. There was a dark figure with a large golden gate behind it. The dark figure spoke, "Ichabod, you are wondering why this prairie is so sacred." Ichabod nodded. "I am glad that you have always wondered why," the figure said, "Good. That prairie is a virgin land because of one thing. It is sacred. Why is it sacred? It is because of fear of every man and animal. Just vegetation is able to survive. Ichabod, the natives have always been afraid to step onto this land. The reason? It is because they thought this land was a mysterious spiritual place. You see, Ichabod, in this world is a gateway to everything. There is a gateway to heaven, hell, different dimensions, and the gateway to time to name a few. Ichabod, your mission in life is to explore the different gateways, in which man is soon to discover. The reason why you and four other people were chosen is because you are the messenger and they are your army. You are the messenger to the spirits. You are the messenger from God. Remember, Ichabod, only you know how to make the journey work. Only you know how important you are to the rest of the world."

"How would I know what is important for mankind," asked Ichabod.

"You will know," replied the dark figure," Jesus of Nazareth was a messenger to touch love to the human race. Buddha was a messenger who taught life. You are a messenger of the mind. You put these three items together, and the human race will be taught the meaning of life and death, love, and the use of the mind. All of it is important in order to survive through mortality and fate. Now, Ichabod, you must go. If you mention anything about this, you may go to the gateway of the inferno, one way. You must not know more at this point, but you will know the rest when the time comes." The dream was over. Ichabod awoke. What did the dream really mean? Was it really a fantasy or did it happen in real life? Ichabod looked at the clock. One minute before his alarm clock goes off. He turned off his alarm and got ready for school. Why did he feel so tired after having eight hours of sleep? He did not know why.

Chapter Five

The next day, the gang met at the same location for lunch. Ichabod is at the bench next to them, but he still alone and he is still eavesdropping on the group. Adam made the statement, "I think I know why we are chosen, yet it is not clear to me."

Violet said, "What is it? Please tell us."

Adam began, "Well, it's like this." He took out a piece of paper from his spiral notebook, grabbed a ball-point pen, and jotted their names down on the paper. "As it seems, the first letter of our names represent a letter of a word. It goes something like this:"

D eana

A dam

V iolet

D an

"DAVD," asked Violet.

"No, there was a fifth person," corrected Adam, "If we add an 'I'--"

"DAVID?" Deana replied, "But that doesn't make sense."

"Ah, but if you put all of our last names together, like this:"

S mith

T yler

A nderson

R oss

"STAR," said Dan.

"Then you add an 'S'."

"DAVID STARS," said Dan.

"That means that the extra person has an 'I' for a first name and an 'S' for a last name. The question is, who it could be," asked Adam.

"It was me," Ichabod finally announced.

"Ichabod Sanders, of course! That would make sense," replied Adam and continued, "So, where were you that night?"

"I was in the bushes. Afraid of being seen, I guess. Anyway, I was running away from home, and I noticed this voice in my head that said--"

"'You are the chosen one.' We had the same exact voice that said same thing." The rest of the group nodded in agreement towards Adam and Ichabod.

"But, I kept on running," continued Ichabod, "And I almost bumped into you guys, so I hid in the bushes. I thought I could hide until you leave. With my curiosity, I wondered why you were all at this steppe. I noticed the moon was a pale white, and fragile spotlight in the pitch black sky. I, too, was in a subconscious trance. I don't know what I saw, except that it wasn't a natural phenomenon. It's hard to explain and to describe what it was."

"Each of us has special powers on the different senses of the body. What is yours," asked Dan.

"I noticed several things since that night," Ichabod continued, "I noticed that I can predict the future, all of them: long term, short term, and immediate predictions. I also know peoples' thoughts that are currently going through their minds. I have consummated on my tests without studying; whereas before the occurrence, I would often fail with only eight hours of studying one subject. I know how to make objects move and create action just by thinking."

"You mean you're telepathic," asked Violet.

"Yep," said Ichabod.

"And you are telekinetic," asked Dan.

"Indeed, I am," replied Ichabod.

"Well, I think that's great," exclaimed Deana.

"No, it's not," commented Ichabod, "It's frightening sometimes. I never realized how powerful the mind is. Everyone uses it, everyone has it, but everyone has a hard time recalling it, something our government. Let me give you an example. Deana, your special power is vision."

"How did you know," asked Deana.

"The mind is powerful," then Ichabod continued, "Other people see what you see, Deana, but their minds filter out of what it wants to see."

"How can that be," asked Adam.

Ichabod answered Adam's question, "The brain is a stubborn organ. It does what it wants to do instead of what it's supposed to do. You can't make it do anything at all. What I have is a power of the mind that will be able to rule."

Dan replied, "I am glad that this power didn't go to the wrong side."

"Boy am I glad. If our powers ever go to evil, then the whole world, as we know it, would be destroyed for good. The main item is, we must stick together in order to fight against anything amoral," Ichabod replied, "Agreed?"

"Agreed," said Dan as he held on to Ichabod's hand.

"Agreed," said Deana as she held on to Dan's hand.

"Agreed," said Violet as she held onto Deana's hand.

"Agreed," said Adam as he held onto Violet's and Ichabod's hands. They created a sacred circle.

Julie awoke. She took inventory: stone walls, bars on the window. She looked out of the barred window and took more inventory: horses, a third-world village, people in strange clothing. She realized that she was stuck in a different country, but in a different universal time period. Could it be the middle ages? Great, not only did she trip over a tree root, and she was also kidnapped. What is going to do? One word came to her mind: Help!

Chapter Six

What exactly did Adam see when he became the chosen one? Adam had often wondered what it was. He was visiting the prairie where he was initiated to be chosen. He checked the soil. A solid piece of ground. How did it become hollow? How did that light come out of the middle of the ground? Is this ground sacred? Suddenly, a light appeared in front of him, which it had a golden staircase that led to it. Adam decided to climb the staircase. When reached he reached the top of the staircase, he was on another prairie. It was not much different from the original prairie he was at. Ahead of him, he saw an Arthurian figure in front of him.

"Welcome, Adam, to our special home. Your friends are here as well," said the figure. Adam noticed that Dean, Dan, and Violet were there as well. How come they were there?

"Why am I here," asked Adam.

"You are here because there are people who are in trouble. They are stuck in a parallel universal time. They are all being kidnapped for power. We need them in their original time. These people will be very important in future missions. If you save them, then you will save the world."

"How am I suppose to do and where I am suppose to do," asked Adam.

The figure answered, "You'll find out later. Only when time comes, you will know what to do. Now you must go, for you know too much already."

Adam obeyed and awoke in a cold sweat. Was it a dream? If it was a dream, then what did it mean? Adam rushed to the phone and dialed up Dan's phone number. Dan answered the phone on his private phone line, "Hello?"

"Dan, I had the weirdest dream," exclaimed Adam.

Dan replied, "So did I. It really felt strange. Let's meet at your place."

"Alright, I'll meet you here," said Adam and then he hung up the phone.

Fifteen minutes later, Deana, Adam, Violet, Ichabod, and Dan met outside of Adam's place, which was located in the woods. It was in the woods that they were able to hide away from the rest of the world. In the woods, there was an old abandoned house.

About five years ago, the old house was built on a hill. One night, heavy rains came and created the mudslide. The house went with it. The forlorn house beyond reformation. Adam found it one day bad thought it was a superior concealing location hence from the cradle of humanity. Nobody knew it existed anymore. Zilch. It was at this domicile that the group was meeting at. Deana, Adam, Violet, Ichabod, and Dan shared their experiences that they recently had.

"What are we going to do," asked Deana.

"We have to remember what the voice said, 'Follow your instincts,'" replied Ichabod. The whole group was silent, and each person was brain storming before they continued on the next step.

"We will meditate," Dan said.

"What do you mean by meditate," asked Violet.

"I read that mediation is a form of relaxation, in which we sit or lay down, close our eyes, and clear our minds," answered Dan.

"That sounds like a great idea," replied Deana.

The group closed their eyes, held hands in a circle while lying down, and meditated. Their thoughts at first were fuzzy and then little by little their minds went blank. Then, a dark, shadowy configuration appeared.

Chapter Seven

The dark, shadowy figure looked like a hologram.

"Who are you," asked Violet.

"You created me," said the figure, "I am your human senses put together. I am that voice that you hear in your conscience. Let me introduce myself. My name is DAVID STARS, named after the Star of David."

"Why did you pick us," asked Dan.

"Your sortie in life is to devise me, exactly what you are doing right now. When you create me, you are combining powers to salvage the lost souls," replied DAVID, and then continued, "Keep together, and I will be able to succor those who need me. Our mission is to free those who need the freedom. Watch out! If one of you is to expire, then part of me will go. If Ichabod dies, then everyone will conk."

"How do we begin to save these people," asked Deana.

DAVID replied, "You'll find out. Remember, there is an entrance to the tunnel of your instincts. Follow that tunnel." Then, DAVID disappeared into the thin air.

"Well, let's begin the mission," said Dan.

"Where do we start," asked Violet.

"Follow your instincts." Doesn't that mean we have to follow something," asked Deana.

"I think he meant a tunnel," said Ichabod, then he snapped his fingers and said, "I got it! He means a time tunnel."

"What do you mean," asked Adam.

"Remember when he said that these imprisoned people are in another time in another place?"

"Oh yeah," said Deana, "A time tunnel would take you through the continuance and it will always take you to a different terra infirma."

"Look," said Violet.

The group saw a large, dark black half circle appear in the middle of nowhere. The group went through the tunnel. Then, the entry closed up behind them like a small shop closing up for the end of a business day. They walked on through the dark tunnel.

Chapter Eight

DAVID's voice spoke, "Your powers are activated now. But do they work?" The group had a blank stare. DAVID continued and gave out the next clue, "Being sullied is very important in life. Those who are not sullied, will not continue on with the journey. All must, therefore confess to the Gods before their souls get distributed through the cosmos."

"We heard him. We must confess to each other," said Dan.

"How about you start, Adam," suggested Deana.

"I really don't love you, Deana. I have tried to tell you this, but I didn't really want to hurt your feelings. I'm sorry."

Deana was in tears, and then replied to Adam, "I felt the same way as well. Adam, I am a lesbian."

"You're kidding," responded Adam.

"No. I am not kidding. Julie and I have been secret lovers for about two years. We can still be friends, can't we?"

Adam replied, "I guess we can still be friends." Deana and Adam hugged each other. "You two haven't......you know?"

"No, we haven't," replied Deana. "We are planning on getting married after high school. Everyone, here, is invited."

"I have a confession to make," replied Violet.

"Sure," replied Dan.

"I'm pregnant," said Violet.

Dan was nervous. Could he be the father? No. He is not being the father. Violet and him didn't have sex intercourse. How could she get pregnant? He thought she had the same morals as he did. Do not have sex until after you and your partner are married. Did Violet have an affair with another individual?

He asked, "Who is the father?"

"Adam......Adam is the father," replied Violet.

"What do you mean? I thought I was going out with you."

"I was, but I was with Adam, and well, we fell in love. It's not that I like you, Dan, but I have to go by what my gut feeling told me to do," Violet replied.

"I guess we'll have to break up," said Dan.

"Yes, I guess," replied Violet.

"You know, Violet, if you ever need any help, don't be afraid to ask, okay," said Dan.

"Okay. The question is, what I am going to do now," asked Violet.

"I don't know, Violet. I think your life is screwed unless you're planning on having an abortion or giving up the kid for adoption," said Dan.

"That's my only choices," asked Violet.

"I'm afraid so," replied Dan, "It's a major decision, isn't it?"

"Yeah," said Violet, "A very hard decision to make your mind up about. What should I do, Dan? I don't want to live my life like this. I want to go to school and graduate. I want a degree in college. I want to have a career, not a family to raise. It's like all of my dreams are lost." Violet started to go in tears. "Why does life have to be this way? Why? Why?" Dan put her head on his shoulder.

"Because it's life. Others make those mistakes in life so the rest of the population will learn from those mistakes. Unfortunately, you have to be one of those statistics. We all have to deal with it sooner or later," said Dan. "Did you talk to Adam about this?"

"No, I haven't," sobbed Violet as she was clearing away her tears.

"Then, I suggest you talk to him right away," said Dan.

"I don't know what to tell him," said Violet.

"Look, if you really love him more than me, then I really suggest that you talk to him. If he loves you, then he will support you. If he doesn't love you, then he won't support you," replied Dan. Dan still had a love for her, but it wasn't the same type of love that he wanted to give. He was going to ask Violet to marry him, but now he was confused. Should he sit there and hope that he would get lucky? That he would stay single and hope she gets a divorce or an abortion? Should he go on with his proposal for marriage, forgive and forget, or not? He needed to act very soon, otherwise he would never get her hand in marriage. "Violet, despite what Adam says, I have been thinking about this for a long time. Will you marry me? Don't give me the answer now. Just think about it, and put it into thought when you talk to Adam about your future."

Violet cheered up and replied, "You've been thinking about this?"

"Yes, I have," said Dan.

"I'll let you know after I talk to Adam, said Violet.

After Violet told Adam that she was pregnant with her baby, he replied, "I'm H.I.V. positive."

"Is it full blown," asked Violet.

"No, it's not. I didn't know until two days later when I went to see the doctor for a checkup. They did some blood tests and they found out that the blood that I donated at blood bank had a dirty needle."

"Why didn't you tell me," asked Violet, "Me and my baby could have it. This is all of your fault. You should have known you were H.I.V. positive before we were in bed."

"Look, Violet, it's not my fault," Adam said as he grabbed onto Violet, "I wasn't in bed with anyone else. I haven't taken any drugs. For Pete's Sake, Violet, it was only a medical mistake. A major medical mistake."

"What's the next step," asked Violet.

"When this mission is over, I want you to get tested right away. My doctor says that early detection is the best detection. Violet, they will be able to find a cure for you. It is too late for me. It seems that the blood bank incident happened many years ago."

Violet agreed with Adam, and planned on taking Adam's advice.

Now it was Dan's turn for his confession. "I'm an alcoholic," he said to the group.

"What are you going to do about it," asked Ichabod.

"I promise to go to rehab," Dan replied, "As soon this quest is over with. I promise. I've been going through hell and I am sick of it."

A light shown up above them. Appearing before them, was a Romanian knight in shining armor. That knight had a sword in one of his hands and a shield in the other. Instantaneously out of nowhere, the group had a two-handed sword. "What is this," asked Dan.

Then DAVID's voice appeared with a thunderous roar. "You are to fight the knight of missing souls in order to show your worth. You have answered the first question; therefore you shall slay the knight to his death or you will never make it to the next level in the time tunnel. If you don't make it, then you shall die in fantasy and in real life, and let the judging begin on your fate of whether you go to heaven or to hell. Just remember, follow your instincts. Let the match begin."

The fight began one by one. First, it was Deana. She killed the knight with her eyes. The knight became blind. Next, it was Dan's turn. Dan created a supersonic sine wave. This caused the knight to go deaf. Then, it was Adam's turn. What was this? Violet ran in front of the knight to distract the knight. The knight came closer to Violet and swung, chopping her head off. The head flew across the dark tunnel and landed while her body collapsed on the spot. Adam was furious. He was able to do the same thing to the knight. Last, the fight was over.

Adam started to cry, "Why did she have to die?"

DAVID's voice boomed out with an echo, "Violet had been slained for one reason. She was not a virgin."

"What do you mean," asked Adam.

"She was pregnant with your baby. Teen-age sexuality is not tolerated to the gods."

Chapter Nine

"The gods perform in mysterious ways," said DAVID. "You have passed the first test, now you must pass another. Here is the clue,

'He who destroys others will destroy thyself.' All but one shall slay the Kimoto dragon, the fiercest reptile in existence." Then, DAVID's voice disappeared from their ears, and the Kimoto dragon appeared out of the thin air. The dragon suddenly attacked Adam quickly and feasted upon him. Adam could feel his leg being eaten and with the sight of blood, he fainted.

In order to save their lives, Deana, Dan, and Ichabod rushed over in a flash to slay the dragon. Ichabod slashed the dragon's head off, through the back and into the heart. Of course, the Kimoto dragon was dead and so was Adam.

"Why Adam? Why did you kill Adam," asked Deana.

DAVID's voice reappeared in response to Deana's question, "Adam didn't make it because he was on drugs and alcohol. Those who hurt themselves and others will not make it through the quest."

"Who else will you eliminate, that we can eliminate ourselves from the process," asked Ichabod.

"If I told you that, then the fun will end too quickly," replied DAVID. "Now, it's time for the next clue in order to proceed on the quest. 'What is the meaning of life?'" Then, DAVID disappeared.

Chapter Ten

"What does he mean by the meaning of life, anyway," asked Deana.

Ichabod answered, "The meaning of life means different things to different people. It's more complex than you really think it is."

"So, you're saying that nobody knows the meaning of life," asked Dan. Ichabod was quiet. "Speak English, you fool," exclaimed Dan.

"You're right," said Ichabod, "but, that doesn't give us an excuse for not answering it."

"Haven't you ever thought about that question, Dan? I'm mean, the meaning of life. Think about it. Why are we here? What is the purpose of life, anyway? To prepare for death? Look at Adam and Violet. They practically wasted their lives away. Is that what life is about? Making so many mistakes in life so you will be prepared for death without mistakes," asked Deana.

Dan replied, "I don't think so, Deana. I think the meaning of life is to prosper in it. Enjoy it as much as you can, because you only live once."

Then, Ichabod spoke, "I think the meaning of life can be anything you make it out to be, but you have to be a good Samaritan. If you do wrong, you go to hell in death. If you do good, then you go to heaven."

DAVID's voice appeared, "You are all right. The answer to the meaning of life is a rhetoric question. It is only what you make it out to be. The last clue is this, 'The sky is the limit, but beware of the black night.'" Then, DAVID's voice disappeared.

Chapter Eleven

"What did you mean by that," asked Dan.

"I don't know," said Ichabod.

"Neither do I," said Deana.

"Well," said Ichabod, "how are we going to answer this important question?"

Suddenly, the tunnel began to rumble, and a door opened up, letting a bright light shine towards them. They couldn't see at first, but their eyes on what they saw. It was a prairie type land with a forest in the background. They went towards the light. Why not? It looked peaceful. It couldn't be a trap or could it? Deana, Ichabod, and Dan traveled across the prairie and into the woods. As they traveled through the woods, they became darker and darker. Where were they going? How did they know which way to go without being lost? Are they lost? They kept traveling through the woods as if they really knew where they were going. Then, the woods were getting lighter and lighter, and the plant life was getting more and more dense. Finally, they were at the edge of the forest. Then, they came to a small village, no, a kingdom.

"I think this has answered our clue," said Ichabod.

"How," asked Deana.

"Well, when DAVID meant 'the sky is the limit,' he meant we are at the end of the time tunnel. When he said 'beware of the night,' then he must mean--"

"There is a knight who is more powerful than we are," interrupted Dan.

"Correct," said Ichabod.

"So, how are we going to fight this knight in order to achieve our mission," asked Deana.

"Let's camp out here, in the woods, so we can come up with a plan to rescue Julie," said Dan.

"Okay," said Ichabod.

"Agreed," said Deana.

Chapter Twelve

Ichabod, Deana, and Dan are in the woods, looking for a good place for themselves to hide out from the kingdom. They wanted to keep away from being seen. If they were seen, then they may be killed. Ichabod started the fire, and the group is figuring out a plan to rescue Dean's lover, Julie. Could there be more than just Julie that they have to save?

Julie sat there at her jail cell in an unknown kingdom. With her, she had a few roommates that she had to share her room with. She spoke to them, "Why am I here?"

"You are here because you are a slave for King David," one of them said.

"What do you mean by King David," asked Julie, "and who are you?"

"I'm sorry. Let me introduce myself. I've been here so long that I assumed that everyone knew who I am. My name is Victoria. Victoria Angles. Let me explain what you are doing here. You and the rest of us, here, were kidnapped in different time periods, both parallel and lateral, to become King David's slaves for experimental research. As it turns out, they want us to come up with new technology for the Middle Ages that were developed during the twentieth through the twenty-third century," said Victoria Angles.

"How did they get the technology to go through time, asked Julie, "After all, isn't it impossible to go back in time before the time machine is invented?"

"Yes, but this is going into the future," said Victoria, "When you go into the future, it is possible to go back in time with the same time machine. In fact, this changes what we see in the future. Anyway, it all started with Martin, the kingdom's erudite man, when he created a machine that will take you through the time tunnel. As he went through the time tunnel, he stopped at several places along the way to the twenty-third century. One of the areas that he visited was 1996, which is the time period you live in Later, he came back to his own time period and went to King David in order to present his invention. Impressed with the results, the king asked Martin to get some slaves in those time zones in order to create a better kingdom for King David. Julie, he's not using it for the goodness of humanity," said Victoria, "He's using it in order to rule the world."

"So? What if they discover technology at an earlier date? Wouldn't that make mankind progress even more," asked Julie.

"If our technology gets created too soon, then all of mankind will deteriorate faster. Everyone in this room won't be able to exist. You won't be able to exist, your friends won't exist, your family won't exist, in fact, absolutely nobody would exist if we don't stop King David and Martin," replied Victoria.

"How could they travel through time," asked Julie.

"There is a thing called parallel time and lateral time. Lateral time is when you travel through time in a straight line from the beginning to the end. Parallel time is like traveling through lateral time, only it runs on a alternative timeline. We traveled through a parallel time line. You see, Julie, time is a strange subject to work with. In your time, you barely touch the basics of time travel. Going through time is very non-linear. You can't really measure it too well. Every decision you make, the dominant decision succeeds. Have you ever thought where the least dominant decision goes to? It comes here. Think of it. There is somebody who acts like you, talks like you, and has a history like you with a totally different lifestyle during the same time periods and different time period sets."

"How did Martin figure out time," asked Julie.

"Well, it's through his magical powers, but there is a more scientific reason for time travel. Supposedly, time travel is not possible without the invention. If you just invented a time machine, you can't go past the day you invented the time machine," said Victoria.

"You mean, you can only go into the future, but sometime in the future, it will end," asked Julie.

Then Victoria replied, "That is correct, and we also need your help for our escape and for the goodness of humanity."

"How can I help," asked Julie.

"We have been planning that when you arrived," said Allen Tyson, another slave and prisoner of King David. The group got together and tried to plan their escape as long as the guard didn't walk by. When the guard did walk by them, they kept silent until he left again.

Chapter Thirteen

It was a cold night in the woods for Deana, Ichabod, and Dan. Just as they were rid of DAVID, he reappeared, only with a helpful, important message. "Your mission is to save Julie and many others who are in the same jail cell in the castle. Then you must destroy the kingdom. Do not attempt to rescue, yet. You must train in order to beat King David, the king of England. There will be three days of training, each one to prepare you for the major battles ahead of you," he said.

"Are there going to be any clues that we have to answer," asked Dan.

"There will be absolutely no clues. You will have one day of training and two days of rest," said DAVID and continued, "Deana will begin her training tomorrow. Next will be Dan. Last will be Ichabod." Then, DAVID disappeared from their sight.

Deana, Dan, and Ichabod decided to get some sleep in preparation of the new training they were about to receive.

Chapter Fourteen

It was morning and the bright sun rose up from the East. What a quiet and beautiful morning it was. Well, as long as it doesn't rain throughout the three days of training. For the beginning of training, the weather really hasn't turned out bad. Deana was the first to wake before the rest of the group. It was her turn for her training, and she was very nervous. DAVID appeared in front of her.

"Welcome to your first day of training," said DAVID, "Your power is sight; therefore you will be trained only with sight. Close your eyes." Deana closed her eyes. "What do you see?"

"I see darkness," Deana said.

"No, you don't. You see your imagination. You see your mind come alive in front of you. That imagination can be very powerful. With your imagination, you can figure out ways of winning better than anybody. There is only one down side of your imagination. Do not believe everything about your imagination. If you do, then you could be dead. It can be very deadly. If you don't believe enough of your imagination, then you are the greatest suicide weapon."

"I don't understand," said Deana, "What do you mean that the imagination is powerful?"

"Your imagination can be very powerful because it can never go pass your own mind," said DAVID, "It is your mind that you control, not others."

"How do I know which image to believe in," asked Deana.

DAVID replied, "You will know. Just follow your instincts."

Then, Deana fell into a deep sleep.

It is the second day of training. It is Dan's turn for his training. Dan awoke. DAVID appeared in front of Dan. "Welcome to the second day of training. Your special power is hearing. What would happen if I made you deaf? What do you hear now?"

"I still hear your voice," Dan replied.

"You should hear only my voice," said DAVID.

"Yes, I do hear your voice very well," said Dan.

"The reason you hear my voice is because I am the voice of your consciousness. Use this power wisely," said DAVID.

"What am I suppose to do with my power," asked Dan.

"The power of the consciousness is what guided man for centuries. Only you know what this power possesses," said DAVID.

"How would I be able to judge this power," asked Dan.

"You'll find out. Just follow your instincts," said DAVID, "It will guide you." Dan was about to ask another question, but DAVID put his hand over Dan's mouth in order to silence him. "Shhh. Your training is over. Only you will know."

Then, Dan fell asleep.

Chapter Fifteen

It is the third day of training. It was Ichabod's turn for his training. "Welcome to the third day and last day of training," said DAVID, "Your power is the mind. I am the voice of your consciousness. I am the one who guides you through life. I am also the controller of many lives around the world."

"How come each person hears a different voice," asked Ichabod.

"It is still the same voice, only you interpret it differently from other souls," said DAVID and then continued, "I am your instincts. I have immortality. You have mortality. Dan has mortality. Deana has mortality. As you already, Adam and Violet were mortal, but now are immortal."

"Why do I have the power of the mind," asked Ichabod.

"You are the leader of the group," said DAVID, "If you go first, then they will go with you. If they go first, then you have a better chance of survival."

"What are my chances of survival," asked Ichabod as he was trying to focus his eyes. The harder and harder he tried to focus his conscience, the more and more it became blurry to him.

"I am not supposed to tell you when you are supposed to become immortal, for it will destroy your chance of living. It is better to spend as time in life and enjoy it as much as possible, because your fate is to remain close to unknown until it comes," said DAVID.

"Are you death? Are you the Grim Reaper," asked Ichabod.

"Close, but no cigar," replied DAVID, "Again, I am not death, and I am not the Grim Reaper. I am that small voice that weighs judgment on every soul. If you wish not to listen to me, then you shall have skeletons in your closet. The more skeletons in your closet, the better chance that your final judgment does not look good in your death."

"How do I know when to use my power," asked Ichabod.

"You'll find out. Just follow your instincts, and you'll know what to do," replied DAVID, "Now, close your eyes."

Ichabod closed his eyelids. At first he saw darkness. Then, the darkness dissolved into what looked like......the boys' locker room at his high school? Inside each locker were shelves of hard back books. The lockers each vary with metal screens or opaque metal fronts, some with combination locks and some without locks. "Where am I," asked Ichabod.

"This is your memory," replied DAVID as they started walking, "Each locker represents your thoughts, experiences, and knowledge. Located on your left, is your intellectual side. This is where you recall your learning experiences."

"Why are some the lockers locked," asked Ichabod.

"It is locked because those lockers are your subconscious mind," replied DAVID.

"What do you mean," asked Ichabod.

"What I mean, Ichabod, is your memory sometimes have a hard time recalling certain items. Those items are behind these locked lockers, where only you know the combination. Sometimes you store the combination in a different or the wrong locker."

"Is it the same as the right side," asked Ichabod.

"I'm afraid so," said DAVID, "Only the right side of the brain is creativeness of the mind. Most of it is your experiences of your custom productivity."

"Where are we now," asked Ichabod.

"We are located in the mid-memory," said DAVID, and continued, "This is your future development. Notice that these lockers are locked and covered."

"What's inside them," asked Ichabod.

"You'll find out when the time comes," said DAVID, and continued, "Ahead is your forebrain. This really the processor that combines your left, right, and sometimes your mid-brain together in order for you to function properly."

"It's pretty quick," said Ichabod.

DAVID replied, "Open your eyes." Ichabod did as he was told. "This concludes your training; therefore you will test your training tomorrow. Beware of your powers, for they can be lethal."

Then, Ichabod went back to sleep and DAVID disappeared from the location. There are about to fight the knight and save Julie. All three were excited to go into an unexplored territory, yet they were nervous with excitement because they would never know whether they would survive or not.

It is the fourth day, and Deana, Dan, and Ichabod awoke together in synchronization. They were ready to start their mission. It turned out to be another warm and beautiful morning. Is there any bad weather on this parallel time line?

They went on with their sortie. All of them were ready to fight the knight of King David.

Chapter Sixteen

"How do we find the knight," asked Deana, "After all, we are in medieval times where there are knights all around us."

Ichabod replied, "We'll find the knight. Remember what DAVID said? He said that if we follow our instincts, then we will get what we want. If we don't follow them, then we are screwed."

"In other words, we have to believe," said Dan.

"Correct," said Ichabod, "But the question is, how are we going to get into the kingdom without getting killed?"

"Remember in history class, we were taught about the Greeks getting into the kingdom through a large wooden horse and attacked from the inside," said Deana.

"That won't work, Deana," said Dan.

"It's still in the history books during Medieval times," said Dan.

"Oh," said Deana.

"How about we dig a tunnel underneath the fence," asked Dan.

"It won't work," replied Ichabod.

"Because when the guards patrol the grounds, they will notice a hole in the ground, where they will follow and then put us to death," said Ichabod. The group agreed. It might be an even riskier situation than they thought it would be. There was a complete silence for a moment while the group was brainstorming. Then, Ichabod had an idea, "I have an even better idea."

"What is it," asked Deana.

"We will dress up as knights," said Ichabod.

"Huh," Dan said with a questioned look.

"It's easy. We secretly murder three guards, dress into their armor, and then we can get in without any problems," said Ichabod.

"That sounds good," said Deana, "But what happens if the suits don't fit?"

Then we are completely stuck," replied Ichabod, "There is always a risk in anything we do in life."

"Yeah, it does look like a good plan," said Dan, "When do we start?"

"Tonight. When it's dark," said Ichabod.

Chapter Seventeen

King David paced back and forth in his throne room in the kingdom's castle. He was trying to figure out what the next step of his plan would be to take over the world. "What should I do next," he asked Martin.

"Sire," replied Martin, "I don't think this is what we should be doing."

"How dare you talk back to your monarch," said King David, "To defeat the king is like defeating the Higher Above of mankind."

"Yes, but," said Martin, "You are not king. Remember, you have crowned yourself, sire."

"Indeed, I did," said King David, "Have you ever thought the reason why I ran onto the stage in order to crown myself?"

"No, I don't," replied Martin, "but I do know that you are one of the most evil human beings I have ever seen."

"You're correct, but who was it that improved the kingdom through time travel?"

"I did," replied Martin.

"No. It was me," said King David.

"How could you," said Martin, "I invented it."

Then King David replied, "No. I did. I come from the future. Can you imagine, Martin, what's like to travel through time? Can you imagine how much power you have if you more advanced in technology than anybody in any time zone? Can you imagine what the future would behold? Just think, Martin, I will be the richest and the most advanced monarch of Europe."

"Then, what do you need me for," asked Martin.

"You are just a scapegoat for the situation," said King David, "Have you ever heard of a king that does work?"

"Sire, we shouldn't be doing this," replied Martin, "It's not right."

"Of course it's not right," said King David, "Why do you think I crowned myself?"

Martin didn't like that. He was going to defeat King David and bring the kingdom back to normal. He went upstairs to his room and made sure his door was closed and locked tight. He didn't want anybody to know what he was about to do. Martin took out his crystal ball and replied in front of the inanimate object, "Crystal ball, you have something I must see. What is it you need to show me?"

"I have three people who will need help. Your mission is to help these people succeed against King David."

"That sounds like the type of people we need," thought Martin.

Martin went to his chemistry set and created some latex. He shaped a mask on his head shaped as an old wrinkled wise man. He put on his dark black robe on and grabbed his walking stick. After he turned off the lights, he unlocked the door and went downstairs towards the main entrance of the castle. Martin was ready to hide away from King

David. Little does King David know, he will have the power when this mission is finished.

"I'll change my name," he thought, "What should I change my name to?" Martin kept on strolling away from the castle gates, getting further and further away. "I know," Martin thought, "I'll use my last name. Sir Ulferus!" Sir Ulferus was ready help Deana, Dan, and Ichabod perform their duties, hoping that he wouldn't fail them.

It was a dark, pitch black night. It was a great time to save Julie by sneaking her out of the kingdom. In the woods are three dark figures, each coming towards the kingdom walls, which the guards did not notice. Deana, Dan, and Ichabod were ready to save Julie. They ran down the small green grassy hill that separated the dark woods and the quiet kingdom. It was perfect to sneak around without being noticed. They each grabbed one of the guards and strangled him by touching the pressure point on their necks. Yahoo! They were done with one of the major items on their plan. The next step was to go into the kingdom. They went into the main gate and knocked on the door. One of the guards from the inside opened the peep hole to see who it was. The guard noticed that it was one of his own because of the armor and the symbol on the armor. He closed the peep hole and let Deana, Dan, and Ichabod into the kingdom.

Step two of the plan had been taken cared of! They were in! They have two steps down and two steps to go. They were half way there. The next item is to kill the powerful knight that was holding Julie hostage. The question is, where is she kept? It is kind of hard to save someone if you don't know where they are. Deana, David, and Ichabod decided to ask somebody. How would they know who to go to without being caught?

Chapter Eighteen

Deana, Ichabod, and Dan resolute to proceeded straight ahead on the path. What do they have to lose? The pathway will lead them someplace anyway. The question is, where does the path go to, anyway? Hopefully, it will lead them to the castle where Julie is being held hostage. Boy, wouldn't Julie be happy to see them.

Suddenly, an antiquated man came up to them. "I know where your friend, Julie, is." Deana, Dan, and Ichabod turned around. It was not just an old man's tongue they heard; it was an elf. The elf was a grand figure complete with an old bearing. No man is ever three feet tall. Only three foot tall men are considered to be elves.

"How did you know we were looking for somebody," asked Dan.

"I know what many people are thinking of at all times," he said, "I have telepathic powers."

"How can you help us, uh.." asked Deana.

"I am Sir Ulferus. I am your guide for this kingdom. I am here to help you through your journeys," the elf said.

"It is nice to meet you, Sir Ulferus. I am..." Ichabod started.

"Ichabod, Deana, and Dan," interrupted Sir Ulferus, "You forget. I have telepathic powers. I can read your mind. I have the same powers as Ichabod and I know how to use it. My just is to train you for future missions. I am your trainer for your quests."

"Where is Julie," asked Dan.

"She is not located in the tower. Instead, she is located in the King David's dungeon," said Sir Ulferus.

"Why did she become kidnapped and brought here," asked Ichabod.

"I can't tell you here out in the street," said Sir Ulferus, "Come inside my place, and I will tell you everything."

Chapter Nineteen

Dan, Deana, and Ichabod came to a small hut with a thatched roof. They walked through the door. Sir Ulferus replied, "Welcome. Welcome to my humble home. Please sit down. I will bring you all some tea and we will chat right by this fireplace to keep warm." Sir Ulferus left the room slowly in pain from his arthritis in order to prepare the tea for his guests. The room consisted of an baroque European rug, a pine table and six uncomfortable oak chairs around the table by an ornate cherry mantel on the fireplace with a fire burning in the fireplace.

Sir Ulferus shortly came back with the hot dandelion tea. "Welcome to my humble home," he said, "Let's discuss the mission." Suddenly, a bubble appeared before them. It resembles a crystal ball, but it does not break. Inside the bubble is a dark background. Sir Ulferus explains while the magical bubble interprets what he is saying. He continued, "Recently, Martin, the wise man, had discovered how to travel back in time. He promptly went to King David to give the monarch his report on his own important discovery. King David grew some interest in this time travel. Just think. If you were ahead in technology in your kingdom, wouldn't you become more powerful than the rest of the kingdoms as well? King David decided to take the advantage of time travel, which he had his knights abduct different people in different time periods. He is currently holding the kidnapped victims in the castle's dungeon. The sovereign is planning on torturing them so that way he can receive neoteric day contrivance that way he can rule the world in all eras."

"What is wrong with that," asked Dan.

"What's wrong is if mankind progresses to soon, the sooner mankind will end. The sooner mankind ends, the sooner earth, the solar system, and the universe will end. If you change time, you will change many souls, and they may be going the wrong direction than they are supposed to go during their deaths," said Sir Ulferus.

"What, exactly, are we supposed to do in order to save the world," asked Ichabod.

Sir Ulferus replied, "You must free the hostages. Send them back to their own time zones. In turn, they will help you in future missions. You must forever close the time tunnel, in order to prevent any future problems. I do have a warning for you. There is a black knight ready to fight you. He is willing to prevent you from freeing the hostages from the dungeon. He does have only one failure, which you will find out when you get there. I shall guide you through this mission. Good luck!" Sir Ulferus disappeared into thin air. In fact, the whole house disappeared. Deana, Dan, and Ichabod are all of a sudden outside on the cobblestone square. There was absolutely no sign of the house. Just the cobblestone square that they happen to be standing on.

Through their instincts, Deana, Dan, and Ichabod were able to find the castle. How could they miss it? Missing the castle would be like not finding the Sears Tower in Chicago.

Dressed as knights, Deana, Ichabod, and Dan were able to go through the main castle gates. They headed across the courtyard and almost went into the main doors when one of the guards stopped them.

"Who goes there," he replied. The guard looked closer at the suits and then replied, "Sorry. I didn't recognize you. You may pass." The guard opened the main castle door. The main doors that lead into a large hallway. Then, the doors closed directly behind them, trapping them in the castle. The hallway consisted of stone bricks with twenty-five doors on each side of the hallway.

"Can you imagine trying to make at build a castle by stone brick by stone brick," Ichabod thought. The group walked on through the stone hallway. Where would the dungeon be? How could they get there without getting in trouble? There was no way that they are going to fight against this kingdom and still survive. It is totally impossible with only thousands of men against three people. So, the group snuck through the hallway with the hopes that they will not be caught.

Sir Ulferus appeared out of thin air, "Ah ha," he said, "You are wondering where to go in order to save Julie, correct?" The group nodded in agreement. "Then follow me," said Sir Ulferus.

"Sir Ulferus," Ichabod replied, "How can we follow you if you keep on disappearing."

"Ichabod, you can follow me even without knowing it," stated Sir Ulferus. "Do you realize that you are not in the space-time continuum, Ichabod? Remember, Ichabod, you have the power of the mind. You can detect and contact anybody in any time period. Little do you know, you also change others' minds. Only the power of the mind has the control of every living specie if they so want to. Now come. Your fates will be upon you. Remember to follow your instincts, or you may have many problems of your own special fate. The fate of life can get you much farther than the fate of death."

"What do you mean by that," asked Ichabod.

"In death, you do not have choice of where you are going after the judgment. In life, you are confronted of many choices. It is in life, where it decides your fate in death," said Sir Ulferus.

"Don't riddle me, wise old man," complained Ichabod, "Get to the point."

"Just remember, Ichabod, if you make the right choice, then a special guardian angel is rooting for you," said Sir Ulferus.

"I have a guardian angel," asked Ichabod.

"Everyone has a guardian angel looking after each other. Some angels are good and some angels are evil. The evil angels will often guide us to the wrong direction in life. Nobody knows whether to believe in these angels or not. Nobody knows whether they have an evil or a guardian angel."

"How do I know whether I have a guardian angel or an evil angel," asked Ichabod.

"You must do what every living soul must do," replied Sir Ulferus.

"What's that," asked Ichabod.

"Follow their instincts," said Sir Ulferus.

"You mean DAVID," asked Ichabod.

"Instincts have absolutely no name. It is just a small voice that knows all," voiced Sir Ulferus.

"Then," continued Ichabod, "Who is this DAVID?"

"DAVID is a creation of your own mind. You and the rest of the group created it to serve a major function to lead you to me," replied Sir Ulferus, "Otherwise, you would have never made it this far into the mission."

"Look, Sir Ulferus," said Ichabod, "Why, exactly, are we doing this mission. After all, you didn't bring me this far for nothing."

"You are here for a good reason. If mankind disappears to soon, then you will not exist as long. All of mankind will be younger and younger in age before they die. This creates an imbalance in the natural cycle. Soon, the ecosystem will die, and then nothing but soil will be in existence. After the soil, our Mother Earth will plunge into the sun quicker than ever. As soon as the Earth plunges into the sun, then our sun will become a Black Hole."

"So, what am I suppose to do," asked Ichabod.

"By slaying the Black Knight," mouthed Sir Ulferus, "and freeing these people out of King David's kingdom, I will be able to stop King David from taking over the world through his dictation. That way the world, as you know it through your time zone, will be back to normal. The sooner we are able to defeat King David from his throne, the sooner King David won't show up in our history books. In fact, we would be able to prevent King David from existing forever."

"That sound good," replied Ichabod, "But aren't we creating history as we speak?"

"You are history, but you are so acute in the books, that nobody will write you down at all. Look, Ichabod, history is not history unless it is recorded in one form or another."

"Are we going to sit here, or are we going to save the world," asked Dan.

"Let's go," said Ichabod.

"Let's go," said Deana.

Deana, Dan, and Ichabod headed down the staircase. Where are the dungeons normally located? They are normally located towards the basement of the castle. That is why many people are afraid of the basement of their houses. They do not want to confront any criminals nor encounter any evil. A dungeon of the castle is one of the scariest places in the world.

Right before they arrived at the dungeon, they saw The Black Knight guarding the dungeon. "Great," thought Dan, "We'll have to fight this knight." The group was closer and closer to the knight. "Well," he thought, "I guess it's time for us to the Black Knight. After all, we would have to fight Black Knight sooner or later."

Chapter Twenty

"Great," thought Deana, "It's time to fight the Black Knight. Even though she had been well trained, then how come she felt unprepared? What a weird feeling. What did DAVID and Sir Ulferus say? 'Follow your instincts.' Yeah. That's it." She had hoped that she would be able to beat the Black Knight. Deana looked at Ichabod. He didn't seem nervous.

In fact, Ichabod was so confident, that he exactly what will happen. He shall fight the Black Knight and win the tournament. It's true. He can feel it in his instincts that he would be able to survive against the Black Knight. "How are we able to against this Black Knight," he thought as the group was getting closer and closer to this knight. A new thought came into his head. What did his instincts say? 'Slay the knight.' What did DAVID and Sir Ulferus say? 'Follow your instincts.' He'd guessed that he had better follow his instincts and believe them, or he could get killed. Why is he worrying, anyway? Ichabod really felt confident to kill the knight and also felt that he could be able to set Julie and her friends free. Her friends? How did he know that was going to set autarchic a group of people instead of one person?

The group walked closer and closer to the Black Knight. Deana and Dan frightened about the fighting. Ichabod was very confident. He thought he is capable for killing the Black Knight.

Since the knight was not fully trained to fight more than one person at a time, he talked through his wireless talking headset. "Calling for backup! Calling for backup at sector three-G! We seem to have some sort of trouble here at Sector three-G!" The Black Knight turned towards the direction of the group, "Who's there?" The Black Knight happened to hear the footsteps of Deana, Dan, and Ichabod. Dan was the first to attack. Since the knight had his sword out and ready to kill someone or something. Without thinking, Dan accidentally ran into the sword. The sword went into heart, thus severely wounding him.

"How are we going to fight the Black Knight," asked Deana.

"We'll both attack together at same time," whispered Ichabod.

"That sounds like a plan," Deana whispered back. Deana and Ichabod both ran. They were ready to attack the knight. They both came forward to the Black Knight. Ichabod and Deana split up for a better chance of survival. They had hopes that the Black Knight would run after one of them while the other stabs him in the back. That would be the best plan, only they didn't want each other to get hurt, otherwise it would be curtains for everybody. The knight decided to go for Deana. He grabbed his sword and hit Deana, catching her off guard. Deana was dead. The knight turned around and saw Ichabod. He was ready to make Ichabod's life final. Ichabod drew out his sword. He threw his sword across the room as the knight turned around and stabbed the knight in the eyeball and through the head. The knight struggled for his life, but failed. The Black Knight was dead. The only thing left to do was to free the people from the dungeon. Ichabod took the keys from the knight and then he unlocked the barred doors in order to let innocent people out. Then, a group of knight, groomed for battle, charged after Ichabod and the rest of the hostages. "Great," thought Ichabod, "Now I really have to fight in order to do what's right." Ichabod took the sword out of the Black Knight's eye and swung, cutting off the head of one guard. Julie grabbed the sword off of the floor near Deana. She was able to kill the second guard. That was all of the guards. The prisoners were free with joy.

Above from the cheering, Ichabod turned around and looked at the Black Knight. The Knight looked like it was transforming into something. Little by little, he could see that the Knight was turning into a brown demon with a pair of wings. It wasn't quite anything to do with life after death, or is does it have to do with life after death? Ichabod wasn't quite sure. He turned around in order to look at Deana so he could see if that was a possibility. Funny, she was turning into a different species. More of a soft white glowing figure. He was able to see the light, a tunnel with a light and a second tunnel with pitch black darkness and a fiery red at the end. Ichabod was able to see the Grim Reaper. Imagine that, he saw death and he wasn't dead at all! How could that be? You never see these things unless you are dead!

The Grim Reaper spoke. It sounded just like......DAVID! "You finally get to see me. You have deserved it. Ichabod, you are the Head Knight."

"Head Knight of what," asked Ichabod.

DAVID replied, "You are the new Head Knight which will decide the fate of the future. Before this mission, you were just a page. Now, you are officially Head Knight of Lost Souls. You shall guide them into the right for the right judgment."

"How can I," asked Ichabod, "I am not even dead yet."

"Remember, Ichabod, if you follow your instincts, then nothing will happen to you. You are still mortal, but move after life, then you will become immortal. Ichabod, your time isn't for a very long time. Live your life to as close to the fullest as you can. Otherwise, you may never enjoy it. Remember this as well, Ichabod, the day you die, will be someone else's time as well."

Sir Ulferus reappeared out of nowhere, "Congratulations! You have slayed the Black Knight. Ichabod, you may free these hostages to where they belong. Remember, I will help you when you need help."

"How will I be able to contact you when I really do need help," asked Ichabod.

"You will get it when you need it. As I once came mysteriously into your life, I will mysteriously help you when you need it. You will never ever have a need to call me," said Sir Ulferus. Then, Sir Ulferus disappeared into thin air again.

"Thank you Sir Ulferus," said Ichabod, "Thank you."

Ichabod and the ex-hostages were about to head upstairs when the time tunnel opened up. "Great," thought Ichabod, "Now we can escape from this place without fighting the rest of kingdom." There were four other people who went into the tunnel with Ichabod. The time tunnel closed up behind them.

Chapter Twenty-One

Ichabod started the conversation, "Hello. My name is Ichabod. Please introduce yourselves. I really want to know. After all, since we are going to journey together for awhile, then we might as well be able to carry on a conversation."

Julie spoke up, "My name is Julie. Julie Smith. Actually, my real name is Amelia. I used Julie as my nickname. People often associated me with Amelia Earhart, and I hated it. I knew that if I had a sobriquet of Julie, then nobody will associate me with Amelia Earhart."

Victoria Angeles was next, "I am Victoria Angeles I am from a different duration than you are, Ichabod."

"From what time zone are you from," asked Ichabod.

"I am in the future. 2047 A.D. to be exact," replied Victoria. "I am a history buff, and I currently live on the planet Mars."

"You mean to say that man has finally established on the planet Mars by 2047," asked Ichabod.

"Yes. It is true. In fact, man began to settle on the planet Mars in 2043. Mars hadn't been explored until 2029," Victoria said.

"My name is Dawn. Dawn Thorn. I am from the past. In fact, I'm from the year 1946," said a female voice.

"My name is Don Richards. I currently live in the same time period as Ichabod Sanders. There is much I can tell you, after all, you do know what exactly happened during our time period," said a deep booming voice.

Then Ichabod replied, "In order for us to get back to our normal time zone, we must do one thing that will help us. I will need all of you in when the time comes for more missions."

"How are we going to do that?" asked Amelia.

"I think we should meditate and speak our special magical words," said Dawn.

"What magic words," asked Don.

"It goes something like this: 'Love is important, Life is better, and friendship is just as good, but we will always stick together,'" said Dawn. The group meditated and chanted the sentence three times when a laser of light spread across the sky. The group opened their eyes and let go each other's hands. It was over with. They were back to the time zones that they were at originally. Their mission had been completed.

Ichabod was back at the abandoned house that was located in the woods that was behind Adam's house. He was in a cold sweat when he awoke. He looked around. All of his friends were lying on the floor. The groups that he began the journey with were still there. He went to Deana and tried to wake her up. He shook her a little bit. She did not move. He felt her pulse on her neck. Ichabod didn't feel a pulse. He went over to Dan and felt his pulse. He felt no pulse. In denial, he quickly went to Adam and felt his pulse on his neck. No pulse. Ichabod went to Violet. No pulse. He decided to feel her stomach area. "She was pregnant," he thought. He quickly ran to get help from the authorities.

Chapter Twenty-Two: Epilogue

"A mass suicide was discovered in Gig Harbor when four teenagers were found dead. Miraculously, one of the teenagers, whom were pregnant, had a child born through a sicarian. The teenagers were discovered a good friend of the group and does not know why they would commit suicide. According to autopsy reports, they do not know what actually caused the deaths," a radio news report said.

Ichabod turned off the car radio and paused. He was weeping for his fellow friends. Life must go on. He got out of the car and walked towards the gravesites. He requested to cemetery that he wanted his friends' gravesides to be together in order to resemble a strong friendship between them.

The preacher gave his final prayer and closed the bible. Ichabod was about to give his speech about his friends and then he stopped. He looked at the sky. Four new stars in the sky. Now, he was sure that the group was judged and sent to heaven. He knew that someday he would join them later on in life. Ichabod sat there, lamenting what he had remembered of the friendship that he once knew. Deana, a cheerleader whose dream in life was to make others happy no matter how much it takes. Adam, the school radio station disc jockey, whose mission in life was to entertain people. Violet, a girl who played in the school band and was best known in her high academics in school Dan, the man who always wanted to know more information about someone who needs help and often gave them lots of important advice. Most of all, Ichabod learned something important. His friendship with these people is what guided him through his special mission in life. All in all, he could still see them guide him spiritually by bringing him knowledge for future adventures.

Ichabod looked up from his friends' grave and started to cry. He missed them no matter how little time he had spent with them. They were, in turn, his heroes. Ichabod looked up and stared towards the horizon. He saw his new friends during his time traveling adventure. They, too, were mourning with Ichabod. Don Richards pat Ichabod on the back, "It's okay, man. We have a new adventure now. There is somebody else out there who needs our help."

Ichabod gave Don a hug. He was relieved that his new friends were there. Wait a minute. If the group was there, then there must be some sort of problem or mission that is going to happen. Ichabod replied back, "Who need our help?" It was time for the group to go on another mission. After all, he is still the boss of the group no matter what happens.

HE END

Title Here

Sometimes, I think of multiple titles in my head, but people always assume that I should have a story that goes with the title. They often want some sort of explanation why I came up with the title. You wouldn't buy a book with a hundred pages of blank space with just a title, or would you? I certainly wouldn't stand for it.

After reading some nineteenth century literature with very long titles that basically explain the entire book by its title, I figured it is time for me to put it in this written piece.

The Psychoanalysis of the Undertaker

Building A Building

The Psychotic Narcosis of the Sandwich Wrap

Afterword

Okay, I knew that if I ran out of stories and thinking of my last chapter as: *Title Here*, where I wrote about making up titles without the stories. Even though this is the last book in the series (I figure that I will not be writing more than twenty short story books in my lifetime), stay tuned for the next edition of *Ty's Book of Rubbish, Volume 19*. You may ask, why would I want to write volumes backward? What can I say? I'm optimistic.

But, what can I say in this *afterword*, since it really has no meaning of what is related in anything I just wrote in the book. I guess I should bring on the encouragement of me, being a writer. Most people have come up to me and said that they envy me for writing a full entire book. You can easily do it. It's really not that hard.

I've learned, in much of my multiple writings, that I can easily tell the story short and to the point. If I was writing a long story, I would have to expand that small story with heavy detail – the detail which would often bore you to the very end and you remember just the few select scenes within the story. Some of these scenes may have a long impression throughout the story, but the author just wants to tell the story as simple as possible when it comes to their writing. It seems that a long book sells well than a short story on a leaflet. People want to buy something that is thick rather than thin.

But, writing a book can be very simple for those who write a short story at a time. All you need is a writing tool (computer, pen, paper, whatever your preference), find a comfortable spot to write the story (like a *Starbucks*®, a library, on a bus, etc.), and start writing. We are all storytellers by nature. Writing is not something where you don't have much time on your hands, much like the reader who doesn't have time to read. It goes hand in hand. Write about the daily things that happen in your life, or conjure up some ideas – all of which can be turned into a story and then into a book.

I've noticed that when I write, I always think of new ideas in a calm atmosphere with very little to do. I have always like doing jobs like that. I enjoy getting as much done as possible with as little effort as possible. I can be a real team player, you might say, by getting something done on the sidelines.

Finding a publisher is easy. May I suggest my publisher, Lulu.com? They are the ones who made this book publishing possible, otherwise I would have written a ton of stories that would collect dust and then, eventually, deteriorate without being seen by a reader's eyes.

Just think about how much we write all the time without even noticing it. We write to friends, in letters, e-mail, both for personal and for work or school. The ability to do that is astounding in itself. If you were to compile all of the writings you do, including writing checks, they can be several books over a lifetime. That is why I highly support the fact that anyone can write a book.

Since there are over a billion people on this planet and each person writes a book, imagine how much information for us to go by when we look at the historical significance within each person's lifetime. We would have a better understanding in one another, and culture clashes would eventually break down, thus a significant change towards world peace (man will always have a war or a disagreement; it is the way of life).

Today, while writing this afterword, I will be starting the next book, *Ty's Book of Rubbish: Volume 19*. It is hard for me to know when to finish writing a short story book. These books entitles me to express my ideas that float around in the inside of my head that often have to come out whether it is politically correct or not. If we don't think these things through, then we would never be able to change the world or make it a better place for myself. I'm not too worried about the critics of these books, for I know one thing for sure. This is only a bunch of short stories put together into one book, which are all complete rubbish.

[75]Foreword By Eli Perkins (Melville D. Landon, A.M.)[76]

What is wit and humor?

This is a question often asked, but it has never been truly answered. Humor is always the absolute truth, while wit is always an exaggeration. Humor occurs, while wit is the pure fancy or imagination of the writer. Wit and humor are often used as synonymous, but they are really at antipodes. Humorous writings are absolutely true descriptions of scenes and incidents really occurring, while witty writings are purely fanciful descriptions of scenes and incidents which only occur in the mind of the writer. To illustrate : Dickens was the King of the Humorists, but his writings are, in almost every instance, true descriptions of scenes and incidents which really occurred. The stories of "Little Nell" and "Smike," and "Oliver Twist" are true to life, for they were real living characters. Bret Harte's "Luck of Roaring Camp" is another bit of pure humor—absolute truth. To illustrate the difference between wit and humor Mark Twain wrote a chapter on building tunnels in Nevada. He described the miners truthfully, and as close to life as Dickens described Pickwick or Fagin or Bill Sykes. He went on with pure humor—pure truth—for four or five pages. But soon his humor blossomed into wit. He departed from his truthful description and began to exaggerate. He began to describe a miner who thought a good deal of his tunnel. They all told him that he had better stop his tunnel and he would run it as far as he wanted to, so he continued his tunnel right on over the valley into the next hill. You who can picture to yourselves this hole in the sky held up the trestlework will see where the humor leaves off and the wit begin.

So I say the humorist always take some pleasant scene and describes it close to life, while the wit takes that same scene and

---

75 Landon, Melville. *Wit And Humor Of The Age.* Star Publishing, Inc. copyright 1903 pp. 9-13

76 I know that Forewords are suppose to be in the beginning of the book, along with the second introduction that I had written at the end of the book, but it turns out that I screwed up the formatting of this book royally before printing. So, think of this as an extra or a preview, for that matter, *Ty's Book of Rubbish: Volume 19.* The Stories, *T.M.I.D* to before *Title Here* were added stories in order to satisfy the original 230 pages that I had written. Anything less, would mean that you were royally screwed, but golly, you wouldn't believe how many diseases I would eventually pick up from all of this. Basically, I am making up crap in order to fill fifty-some pages, so excuse me if it all goes downhill from there with in the sections that I described above.

exaggerates it. The humorist describes an ordinary scene like cording a bedstead or putting up a stovepipe. If he does it truthfully it will be humor. If he sits down and thinks,—thinks, cogitates, and adds a thousand imaginary incidents to these scenes—multiplies them by twenty, it will be wit. You do not have to laugh at pure humor. You enjoy it; you say how truthfully the writer has described a certain scene, what a master he is, but you do not laugh ; but when the wit comes with his exaggerations, with his imagination added to the truth, then you laugh outright.

The humorous artists do not produce laughter. The best they can do is to paint a humorous object just as it is. Laughter only comes with the witty caricaturist who exaggerates some feature. To illustrate: A humorous artist can paint a picture of a mule—a patient mule. A mule is patient because he is ashamed of himself. And if he paints that mule true to life, you will not laugh. You will say : "What a splendid picture of a mule!" "What a master is he who can paint a mule so close to life!" Why, I saw a mule painted in St. Petersburg, by that great animal painter, Schryer, which sold for $15,000. A single mule eating a lock of hay, while the original mule from which he painted it could be bought for $1.30! Now, the people did not laugh at that mule. They stood in front of it almost as religiously as they stand before a Greek Madonna. They said : "What a great master is Schryer?" But another artist, a witty artist, painted that same mule as truthfully as Schryer did, then, like the witty writers, he commenced to exaggerate it. He ran one of his ears up through the trees, and the chickens were—roosting on it! Then he set that mule to kicking. He made him seem to kick a thousand times a minute. Now, no mule can kick over seven, or eight, or nine hundred times a minute. The people all laughed at the exaggerated mule, but not at the true mule.

So, I say, the caricaturists like John Leech and Cruikshanks are wits, while the true artist like Schryer can never be anything but a humorist, as long as he sticks to the absolute truth.

Irony, satire and ridicule are a species of wit, because they are all untrue. The ironical Antony says:

"Here under leave of Brutus and the rest,

(*For Brutus is an honorable man*),"

Antony's statement every Roman knew to be untrue. It was wit—the wit of Ridicule.

"Ridicule" is the strong weapon of the lawyer. To ridicule an opposing lawyer's serious speech, you have simply to exaggerate it. So ridicule is simply exaggeration. It is simply deformed truth, or lying. Take pure pathos anytime and multiply it by twenty, exaggerate it, and it becomes wit. If one lawyer makes a pathetic speech, and a true speech, the only way to ruin its effect on a jury is to ridicule it. For instance, I heard a lawyer trying to win the sympathy of the jury for his client. It was a homicide case. A man had killed his best friend in a moment of anger:

"Oh, my client felt so bad when he killed his friend," began the lawyer, "for he loved that friend as he did a brother. And when in a fit of passion he struck him, it broke his own heart. When he saw that friend fall down, he knelt down by his expiring form. His tears fell down on the face of his dead friend, and a feeling of remorse broke his heart."

Well, he won the sympathy of the jury, for what he said was true. Now, the opposing lawyer was not foolish enough to deny these statements. He would not impeach his own veracity before the jury by doing so. So nothing was left but to ridicule him, which he did in this matter:

"Yes," he began in weeping tones. "Yes, he did feel bad when he killed his friend. The tears did roll down his cheeks. Rolled clear down into his boots. Then he tied his handkerchief around his trousers. Cried 'em full. Boohoo! Boohoo!"

When he got through his mock pathos the jury were all laughing, and the effect of the solemn speech was ruined. Not only that, but whenever during the trial the grief of the murderer was referred to by the opposing council, it invariably brought a laugh of derision throughout the court-room.

Any scene or incident in real life, if described truthfully, will be humor. Take the simple scene of two married women taking leave of each other at the gate on a mild evening and describe it truthfully, and it will be humor. To illustrate, two women shake hands and kiss each other over the gate, and then commences the conversation:—

"Good-by!"

"Good-by! Come down and see you soon."

"I will. Good-by!"

"Good-by! Don't forget to come soon."

"No, I won't. Don't *you* forget to come up."

"I won't. Be sure and bring Sara Jane with you next time."

"I will. I'd brought her this time, but she wasn't very well. She wanted to come awfully."

"Did she, now? That was too bad! Be sure and bring her next time."

"I will. And you be sure and bring baby."

"I will. I forgot to tell you that he's cut another tooth."

"You don't say so! How many has he now?"

"Five. It awfully makes him cross."

"I dare say it does this hot weather."

"Well, good-by! Don't forget to come down."

"No, I won't. Don't forget to come up. Good-by!"

"Good-by!" (*louder.*)

"Good-by!" (*very loud.*)

The above simple dialogue is pure humor. The same truthful dialogue, if it ended in a point, might be wit. In one of my Saratoga letters I gave this dialogue ending in a point:

A New Yorker was introduced to a Cleveland gentleman today, and not hearing his name distinctly remarked:

"I beg your pardon, sir, but I didn't catch your name."

"But my name is a very hard one to catch," replied the gentleman; "perhaps it is the hardest name you ever heard."

"Hardest name I ever heard? I'll bet a bottle of wine that my name is harder," replied the New Yorker.

"All right," said the Cleveland man. "My name is Stone—Amasa Stone. Stone is hard enough, isn't it, to take this bottle of wine?"

"Pretty hard name," exclaimed the New Yorker, "but my name is Harder—Norman B. Harder. I bet my name was Harder, and it is!"

It is a very easy matter to separate the humorists from the wits or rather the humor from the wit. Dickens, except in cases like the speech of Buzfuz and the Pickwick proposal, was a humorist. Dean Swift, Juvenal, Cervantes and Nasby are satirists or wits. Josh Billings, Twain, Artemus Ward, Orpheus C. Kerr and John Phoenix are sometimes wits and sometimes humorists. Max Adler and Bill Nye are both Baron-

Munchausen liars or wits. Adler's wit consists in simple exaggeration, as is illustrated in his account of accurate shooting. The *Danbury News* man is a pure humorist, while Aleck Sweet and Mr. Lewis, the *Detroit Free Press* man, are wits, humorists, and sometimes satirists. Nasby has never written anything but satire. His Confederate Crossroads satires, and they alone, have made him famous in America.

Outroduction

Don't you hate it when you lose things? I know I do, especially your first book that you spent an entire two years working on all of a sudden disappears. Luckily, my publisher had an unedited copy, so proof editing my last book, *Ty's Book of Rubbish: Volume 20* would not have turned out well no matter what I do. On the other hand, it did give me a sense of realization of always keeping a copy of my works no matter what I do. Unfortunately, I did lose the first few chapters of this book as well. Rather than re-creating the stories all over again, I figure that it is time to continue on and keep writing short stories as time may permit. And, when I get by with 150 pages or so, then it will be time to release another book.

Boy, you did miss out on the stories that I wrote and then lose. But, luckily, I may able to re-cap it for you so that way you weren't missing out or the useless crap that I wrote.

In the *Introduction*, I wrote about writing a book and how anybody can do it. I also said that these books were a great teaching tool and should be used in literature and English classes around the world. Basically, *buy my book*. I also talked about English teachers who think they are writers, but really don't care about the students one way or another.

Okay, I did write one story, and I think I will try to re-create it. I do have it written in my notebook and pen while I was on a bus straight to Aberdeen, Washington to attend a barbeque in the rain. As if you didn't know, it does rain on the Washington State coast and it rains a lot more than most people actually expect. And why not? It is, after all, on the very edge of the Olympic Rain Forest near the Ho River. I don't think I have ever finished the story, but the beginning seems good enough to read.

Overall, what can I say about this book? What can I say in an introduction that I had re-written? What's sad is that there are eighteen more books of short stories that I will be writing. What would happen in if I run out of these stories as well? As I get older, I am getting closer to death. What if I get hit by a bus tomorrow? Would this screw up my contract with my publisher and my readers? Perhaps it's too late go back now. These are the risks I must take when writing a twenty book series of short stories. I guess it's too late to go back on this right now, but it still makes me wonder sometimes.

Well, enough of my ramblings, and if you did read this entire introduction, you are one of the rare few people who do. I often have to skip the introduction page and the forewords just so I could read the story itself. After all, the introduction is already being introduced when you learn about the characters. My grandfather (somehow I have inherited his humor) would often skip to the middle of the book and start reading the book. He had often said that the real story is in the middle, the beginning is only introduction to the story. In some ways, I believe he is right. The story, in most cases, is right in the middle of the book rather than in the beginning of the book. This is one of the reasons why I decided to write a book full of short stories.

I knew that short stories are what I am really good at rather than writing one long ass story. Why do you need the heavy details of long complicated words when the point could be put across in a simple short story? How hard can that be? Who the hell has the time to read through several days of written work (in which it took the author a longer time to write the story), when you can read the shortest story within the two hours at the very most? That's the idea of short stories. They're straight and to the point so long as the message can be put across in a few sets of paragraphs.

Ty Rosenow

September 22, 2007

Ty's Book Of Rubbish:

Volume 19

A Look At Useless Crap

Ty Rosenow

Prefatory Note To The Foreword[77]

By Jean Wick

During the past twenty years the short story has come to occupy a distinct place in American letters. While it must perhaps be granted that we are not pre-eminent in the novel or the essay, we may quite fairly pride ourselves upon the high achievement of our authors in short story writing. American magazines (and this is said in no spirit of braggadocio) today carry more and better short stories than do the magazines of any other country. In addition it should be taken into consideration that we in America publish a greater number of periodicals devoted either wholly or in part to fiction than is the custom elsewhere. Thus automatically the would-be short story writer is given opportunity and encouragement, two powerful factors in all creative endeavor. Success in short story writing means both fame and pecuniary reward. It is professionally worth while both from the artistic and the financial points of view.

To the American editor should be given much of the credit for this development in the short story. A story, no matter how vital or well written, carries no real weight until it is in print. The printed page gives it permanency; through print it reaches the multitude. The editor, at his or her desk, has final say as to what shall or shall not go into the pages of his or her magazine. There are often outside factors that shape the magazine's editorial and fiction policy. But editors are sincere in desiring to give their readers the best stories they can procure of the kind they are ready to publish.

But they do a great deal more than just select from the mass of material that is submitted to them. They go out after the type of stories they want. They see the men and women who can write and personally confer with them, suggesting new things to write about, new trends in thought, new angles of approach, new methods of handling. To George Horace Lorimer certainly should go much of the credit for the evolution of the American business story; a chance remark of Ray Long's at editorial conference brought the first Pell Street tales into existence; it is no

[77] With my ongoing theory that nobody reads introductions or prefaces anymore, these two selections came from the book, "Artemus Ward" by Booth Tarkington. Booth Tarkington is famous for a mass load of bestsellers at the turn of the century straight to the mid-1950s. He got rich and famous from the royalties from the plays, movies, and books that he wrote. Sadly, Booth Tarkington is no longer a household name

exaggeration to say that John M. Siddall with his search for clean-cut Americanism has had much to do with the growing prominence and popularity of American small town portrayal which popularity has in turn profoundly affected the development of the American novel; to Perriton Maxwell should be given the honor of having been the first to publish stories of Jewish
life in one of our leading monthlies. Not only do the editors shape and mould the literary taste of their readers
but they have and do actually create new forms of literary
output.

The technique of the American short story is more or
less fixed and numerous textbooks have been compiled
thereon. But technique Is not a rigid matter. The Importance of the subject matter or sheer artistry can often
"put over" a story that defies every one of the traditional or accepted rules. Too, different editors and diff'erent magazines have their own Ideas on technique. Therefore, for anyone who would write it is best to study and analyze carefully the pages of the various magazines.

To succeed In the short story field the writer needs not only to know how to write but where to sell. To get before the short story reading public It is vital not only to have a story to tell and to know how to tell It but to know also where to offer that story when it is told. In selling a short story it is not primarily the attitude of any one individual critic or group of self-appointed critics that matters; it is the attitude of the editor toward the particular story under consideration. As there are many stories there are many editors. They are all on the lookout for new and good material. If you have created a good story it Is bound some day to find its publisher and thereby to reach its public.

In order that this book may be of practical service to the new writer and to those already well established the editors were asked why they bought the particular stories they did, in other words their attitude in fiction buying. Their replies are printed verbatim. Many came in the form of personal letters and this will explain why there may be a certain lack of formality in some of the editorial replies. But on consideration this was decided the most practical way in which the editor might reach his audience. Analysis of the answers will show the veriest tyro that a story that might do excellently for the Metropolitan need not be desired by the Dial and vice versa.

In the compiler's mind the magazines automatically group themselves into classes, a grouping which attempts to reach no conclusion as to relative literary or commercial values. Certain of these magazines were asked to include a story that had appeared in its pages and which from the point of view of that magazine's editorial policy was a highly desirable and good story. Here the editors hesitated: they had many good stories that might be included. Eventually, though, choices were made and the authors kindly consenting to their reprinting, the stories are given herewith.

Here again it cannot be made too clear that no editorial verdict was attempted in including stories from some of the magazines and in omitting those from others. The aim of the book is to be of practical service in pointing out reasons for fiction buying. All of the magazines could not be included because of space limitation. As far as possible different types of magazines were chosen. The editors of these magazines again one and all were unanimous in making it clear that they could have suggested many other stories that had appeared in their pages that were equally good considered literarily or artistically. But as the book does attempt to guide and direct — so far as this is possible in an art — they chose stories that they considered representative in a major number of ways.

Our leading weeklies lay much emphasis upon their fiction. The Saturday Evening Post buys more short stories a year than does any other magazine. Because of its enormous circulation the contributor has the satisfaction of feeling that he or she is reaching a maximum number of readers. The style of stories in this magazine changes from year to year as the editor has been repeatedly heard to say that the reading public is apt to tire of any one type no matter how well done. The practical note is apt to preponderate. In Collier's, the National Weekly, we find a very American story, not exploiting big cities and millionaire circles, but rather the moderately incomed home of the average American — its good fortune, its vicissitudes, its every day point of view, handled with exquisite sympathy. Leslie's, limited in space, is frankly after the constructive business story.

In any consideration of the American monthly magazines automatically Harper's, Scribner's and Century come to mind in a group. These put great emphasis upon literary execution. The Atlantic Monthly is perhaps not quite so rigid in its demand for form while the Dial is almost radical. The Touchstone rates artistry most highly, the article by Mrs. Roberts in this book making her views on the whole matter most explicit.

There is another large group of monthly magazines, more generally popular perhaps, in which there is the very greatest diversity and yet differentiation of editorial wants. It will pay to study these magazines closely. The student will at once see why a story that might be most popular in the Metropolitan would not have a chance in the American — and at that no purely literary or technical point need be involved. In this group of magazines there is the greatest possible chance for divergence in story treatment, in subject matter, even in methods of characterization. Since Ray Long has taken over the Cosmopolitan he has repeatedly shown his catholicity of taste as has Karl Harriman in subject matter in the Red Book.

It is easy to decide which stories may prove suitable for our magazines that are primarily interested in sex problems, and this does not necessarily mean sex in any too realistic or too sordid sense. The editors who are selecting the material for these periodicals feel that sex is the fundamental motivation in every human act; that therefore its presentation is always interesting, of moment, and bound to intrigue a large group of readers. A certain number of the smaller of these magazines demand liveliness of presentation rather than newness of plot. All are apt to stress a certain up-to-date and social quality.

We have a large group of action magazines. They look for "story." In this group the Street and Smith periodicals are particularly interested in the story that has an American hero and an American environment. Some of the others are not quite so restrictive. Perhaps "a good yarn rattling well told" is the best slogan presentation of their wants. But like all slogans it is unfair. The frequent presence of Joseph Conrad in these magazines certainly would seem to prove that craftsmanship is appreciated.

The women's magazines make a point of carrying as good fiction as can be procured and in some of them we are finding the best short stories of the day. The Pictorial Review, for instance, is not circumscribed in its point of view; it has room for the purely artistic creation; it welcomes warmly the picture of life whose main characteristic is sympathetic narration. Other magazines in this group feel that they should publish only human interest stories as these make the strongest appeal to their particular circle of women readers.

Many of the stories in the farm and fireside journals are written with a distinct purpose; to portray intimately some heretofore little known section of the country; to illustrate some new agricultural theory; to create sympathy for some rural situation. But "purpose" is never allowed to destroy story values.

Our juvenile magazines make no secret of their aim. It is to influence rightly the changing character, the shifting ideals and aspirations of the growing boys and girls who come under the sway of their story pages. The fiction must be of absorbing interest from the point of view of the young, but at the same time it must contain nothing that would react detrimentally.

From the above brief summary it is easy to see that a story that might prove eminently acceptable from the point of view of one magazine might not do at all for another. That the placing of a story, in other words, demands a certain amount of knowledge of market wants and market conditions. This brings us to the consideration of the agent. Is or is not an agent of help? This question is largely one for self-determination. It depends somewhat on the personality of the author. All agents cannot help all authors: there is a give and take of personality; in other words, the human equation has something to do with the success of the relationship. An agent cannot sell a story that is not sellable; an agent cannot repeatedly get higher prices for the author than the author can get for himself. An agent does know more of the markets and its fluctuations; agency advice — as it is a matter of business — is apt to be impersonal and good; agency direction can save much misguided effort.

There is an impression that agents are perhaps not popular with editors. This is not true. Perhaps the letter of James E. Tower, editor of The Delineator given herewith and which came unsolicited, is as good actual proof of this fact as any statement which the writer might make.

Dear Miss Wick:

A certain periodical, which has its distribution amongst writers, has put in.my mouth words which I did not say and which do an injustice alike to some good friends of mine and to me.

I am quoted as having said, at a recent luncheon, that editors are not keen about purchasing from literary brokers. I never said that nor implied it. I said that I felt that the brokers had been the largest single factor in raising and maintaining authors' prices; that the publishing trade were inclined, on this account, to look askance at the agent system, but that authors formerly did not receive adequate compensation and that the better prices had raised the standard of authorship and benefited the trade, as well as the writers themselves.

My own editorial career is sufficient refutation of the statement attributed to me. I think I never heard an editor express any prejudice against the broker system.

Sincerely yours,

James E. Tower.

Lastly do not let it be felt that the compiler of these editorial want paragraphs, this editorial exposition of the stories the editor wants and buys, desires to express any personal opinion as to the relative literary merits or commercial status of the magazines listed in this book. This is not a book of criticism. It is an effort to have the editors talk directly to those who for any reason what-ever are interested in the American short story as it is published week in and week out in our magazines.

JEAN WICK.
New York City.

Foreword

By Booth Tarkington

Mr. and Mrs. Baxter, having walked a hot half mile from church, drooped thankfully into wicker chairs upon their front porch, though their ten-year-old daughter, Jane, who had accompanied them, immediately darted away, swinging her hat by its ribbon and skipping as lithesomely as if she had just come forth upon a cool morning.

“I don't know how she does it!" her father moaned, glancing after her and drying his forehead temporarily upon a handkerchief. "That would merely kill me dead, after walking in this heat."

Then, for a time, the two were content to sit in silence, nodding to occasional acquaintances who passed in the desultory after-church procession. Mr. Baxter fanned himself with sporadic little bursts of energy which made his straw hat creak, and Mrs. Baxter sighed with the heat, and gently rocked her chair.

But, as a group of five young people passed along the other side of the street, Mr. Baxter abruptly stopped fanning himself, and, following the direction of his gaze, Mrs. Baxter ceased to rock. In half-completed attitudes they leaned slightly forward, sharing one of those pauses of parents who unexpectedly behold their offspring.

The offspring, in this case, was their son, William.

"My soul!" said William's father. "Hasn't that girl gone home *yet*?"

"He looks pale to me," Mrs. Baxter murmured absently. "I don't think he seems at all well, lately."

During the seventeen years since the arrival of William, their first born, Mr. Baxter had gradually learned not to protest anxieties of this kind, unless he desired to argue with no prospect of ever getting a decision.

"Hasn't she got any *home*?" he demanded testily. "Isn't she ever going to quit visiting the Parchers and let people have a little peace?"

Mrs. Baxter disregarded this outburst as he had disregarded her remark about William's pallor, "You mean Miss Pratt?" she inquired dreamily, her eyes following the progress of her son. "No, he really doesn't look well at all."

"Is she going to visit the Parchers all summer?" Mr. Baxter insisted.

"She already has, almost," said Mrs. Baxter.

"Look at that boy!" the father grumbled. "Mooning along with those other moon-calves — can't even let her go to church alone! I wonder how many weeks of time, counting it out in hours, he's wasted that way this summer?"

"Oh, I don't know! You see, he never goes there in the evening now."

"What of that? He's there all day, isn't he? What do they find to talk about? That's the mystery to me! Day after day, hours after hours — My soul! What do they *say*?"

Mrs. Baxter laughed indulgently. "People are always wondering that about the other ages. Poor Willie! I think that a great deal of the time their conversation would be probably about as general as it is now. You see Willie and Joe Bullitt are walking one on each side of Miss Pratt, and Johnnie Watson has to walk behind with May Parcher. Joe and Johnnie are there about as much as Willie is, and of course it's often his turn to be nice to May Parcher. He hasn't many chances to be tête-à-tête with Miss Pratt."

"Well, she ought to go home. I want that boy to get back into his senses. He's awful!"

"I think she is going soon," said Mrs. Baxter. "The Parchers are to have a dance for her Friday night, and I understand there's a floor to be laid in the yard and great things. It's a farewell party."

"That's one mercy, anyhow!"

"And if you wonder what they say," she resumed, "why, probably they're all talking about the party. And when Willie is alone with her — well, what does anybody say?" Mrs. Baxter interrupted herself to laugh. "Jane, for instance — she's always fascinated by that darkey, Genesis, when he's at work here in the yard, and they have long, long talks; I've seen them from the window. What on earth do you suppose they talk about? That's where Jane is now. She knew I told Genesis I'd give him something if he'd come and freeze the ice-cream for us to-day, and when we got here she heard the freezer and hopped right around there. If you went out to the back porch you'd find them talking steadily — but what on earth about I couldn't guess to save my life!"

And yet nothing could have been simpler: as a matter of fact, Jane and Genesis were talking about society. That is to say, their discourse was not sociologic; rather it was of the frivolous and elegant. Watteau prevailed with them over John Stuart Mill — in a word, they spoke of the beau monde.

Genesis turned the handle of the freezer with his left hand, allowing his right the freedom of gesture which was an intermittent necessity when he talked. In the matter of dress. Genesis had always been among the most informal of his race, but to-day there was a change almost unnerving to the Caucasian eye. He wore a balloonish suit of purple, strangely scalloped at pocket and cuff, and more strangely decorated with lines of small parasite buttons, in color blue, obviously buttons of leisure. His bulbous new shoes flashed back yellow fire at the embarrassed sun, and his collar (for he had gone so far) sent forth other sparkles, playing upon a polished surface over an inner graining of soot. Beneath it hung a simple, white, soiled evening tie, draped in a manner unintended by its manufacturer, and heavily overburdened by a green glass medallion of the Emperor Tiberius, set in brass.

"Yes'm," said Genesis. "Now I'm in 'at Swim — flvin' roun' ev'y even' wif all lem blue-vein people — I say, *Mus' go buy me some blue-vein clo'es! Ef I'm go'n a start, might's well start high!' So firs', I buy me thishere gol' necktie pin wi' thishere lady's face carved out o' green di'mon, sittin' in the middle all 'at gol'. 'Nen I buy me pair Royal King shoes. I got a frien' o' mine, thishere Blooie Bowers; he say Royal King shoes same kineo' shoes he wear, an' I walk straight in 'at sto' where they keep 'em at. 'Don' was'e my time showin' me no ole-time shoes,' I say. 'Run out some them big, yella, lump-toed Royal Kings befo' my eyes, an' firs' pair fit me I pay price, an' wear em' right off on me !' 'Nen I got me thishere suit o' clo'es — oh, oh! Sign on 'em in window: 'Ef you wish to be bes'-dress' man in town take me home fer six dolluhs ninety-

sevum cents.' "At's kine o' suit Genesis need,' I say. 'Ef Genesis go'n a start dressin'
high, might's well start top!'"

Jane nodded gravely, comprehending the reasonableness of this view. "What made you decide to start, Genesis?" she asked earnestly. "I mean, how did it happen you began to get this way?"

"Well, suh, 't all come 'bout right like kine o' slidin' into it 'stid o' hoppin' an' jumpin'. I'z spen' the even' at 'at lady's house, Fanny, what cook nex' do', las' year. Well, suh, 'at lady Fanny, she quit privut cookin', she kaytliss — "

"She's what?" Jane asked. "What's that mean, Genesis — kaytliss?"

"She kaytuhs," he exclaimed. "Ef It's a man you call him kaytuh; ef it's a lady she's a kaytliss. She does kay- tun fer all lem blue-vein fam'lies In town. She make refeshmuns, bring waituhs — 'at's kaytun. You maw give big dinnuh, she have Fanny kaytuh, an' don't take no trouble 'tall herself. Fanny take all 'at trouble."

"I see," said Jane. "But I don't see how her bein' a kaytliss started you to dressin' so high. Genesis."

"Thishere way, Fanny say, 'Look here, Genesis, I got big job t'morra night an' Fm man short, 'count o' havin' to have a 'nouncer.' "

"A what?"

"Fanny talk jes' that way. Goin' be big dinnuh potty, an' thishere blue-vein fam'ly tell Fanny they want whole lot of extry sploogin'; tell her put fine lookin cullud man stan' by drawin'-room do' — ask ev'ybody name an' holler out whatever name they say, jes' as they walk in. Thishere fam'ly say they goin' show what's what, 'nis town, an' they boun' Fanny go git 'em a 'nouncer. 'Well, what's mattuh you doin' 'at 'noun- cin'r' Fanny say. 'Who — me:' I tell her. 'Yes, you kin too!' she say, an' she say len' me 'at waituh suit yoosta b'long ole Henry Gimlet what die' when he owin' Fanny sixteen dolluhs — an' Fanny tuck an' keep 'at waituh suit. She use 'at suit on extry waituhs when she got some on her hands w^hat ain' got no waituh suit. 'You w'ear 'at suit,' Fanny say, 'an' you be good

'nouncer, 'cause you' a fine, big man, an' got a big gran' voice; nen you learn befo' long be a waituh, Genesis, 'an git dolluh an' half ev'y even' you waitin', 'sides all 'at money you make cuttin' grass daytime.' Well, suh, I'z Stan' up doin' 'at 'nouncin' ve'y nex' night. White lady an' ge'lmun walk todes my do', I step up to 'em — I step up to 'em thisaway." Here Genesis found it pleas
ant to present the scene with some elaboration. He dropped the handle of the freezer, rose, assumed a stately but ingratiating expression and "stepped up" to the imagined couple, using a pacing and rhythmic gait — a conservative prance, which plainly indicated the simultaneous operation of an orchestra. Then bending graciously, as though the persons addressed were of dwarfish stature, " 'Scuse me," he said, "but kin I please be so p'lite as to 'quiah you' name?" For a moment he listened attentively, then nodded, and, returning with the same aristocratic undulations to an imaginary doorway near the freezer, "Alisto an' Alissuz Orlosko Rlnktuml" he proclaimed sonorously.

"Who?" cried Jane, fascinated. "Genesis, 'nounce that again, right away!"

Genesis heartily complied.

"Misto an' Missuz Orlosko Rinktum!" he bawled.

"Was that really their names?" she asked eagerly.

"Well, I kine o' fergit," Genesis admitted, resuming his work with the freezer. "Seem like I rickalect somebody got name good deal like what I say, 'cause some mighty blue-vein names at "at dinnuh-potty, yes-suh! But I on'y git to be 'nouncer one time, 'cause Fanny tellin' me nex' fam'ly have dinnuh-potty make heap o' fun. Say I done my 'nouncin' good as kin be, but say what's use hoUer'n names jes' fer some the neighbors or they own aunts an' uncles to walk in, when ev'rybody awready knows 'em? So Fanny pummote me to waituh, an' I roun' right in amongs' big doin's mos' ev'y night. Pass ice-cream, lemonade, lemon-ice, cake, sammitches. 'Lemme han' you lil mo' chicken-salad, ma'am' — ' 'Low me be so kine as to git you f'esh cup coffee, suh' — 's way ole Genesis talkin' ev'y even' 'ese days !"

Jane looked at him thoughtfully. "Do you like it better than cuttin' grass. Genesis?" she asked.

He paused to consider.

"Yes'm — when ban' play all lem tunes! My goo'ness, do soun' gran'!"

"You can't do it to-night, though. Genesis," said Jane. "You haf to be quiet on Sunday nights, don't you?"

"Yes'm. Ain' got no mo' kaytun till nex' Friday even'."

"Oh, I bet that's the party for Miss Pratt at Air. Parcher's!" cried Jane. "Didn't I guess right?"

"Yes'm. I reckon Fm a go'n a see one you' fam'ly 'at night; see him dancin' — wait on him at refeshmuns."

Jane's expression became even more serious than usual. "Willie? I don't know whether he's goin', Genesis."

"Lan' name!" Genesis exclaimed. "He die ef he don' git znvite to 'at ball!"

"Oh, he's invited," said Jane. "Only I think maybe he won't go."

"My goo'ness! Why ain't he goin'?" Jane looked at her friend studiously before replying. "Well, it's a secret," she said, finally, "but it's a very inter'sting one, an' FIl tell you if you never tell."

"Yes'm; I ain't tellin' nobody."

Jane glanced round, then stepped a little closer and told the secret with the solemnity it deserved. "Well, when Miss Pratt first came to visit Miss May Parcher, Willie used to keep papa's evening clo'es in his window-seat, an' mamma wondered what had become of 'em. Then, after dinner, he'd slip up there an' put 'eni on him, an' go out through the kitchen an' call on Miss Pratt. Then mamma found 'em, and she thought he oughtn't to do that, so she didn' tell him or anything, an' she didn't even tell papa, but she had the tailor make 'em ever an' ever so much bigger, 'cause they were gettin' too tight for papa. An', well, so after that, even if Willie could get 'em out o' mamma's clo'es closet where she keeps 'em now, he'd look so funny in 'em he couldn't wear 'em. Well, an' then he's never been to see Miss Pratt in the evening one single time since then because mamma says after he started to go there in that suit he couldn't go without it, or maybe Miss Pratt or the other ones that's in love of her would think it was pretty queer, and maybe kind of expect it was papa's all the time. Mamma says she thinks Willie must have worried a good deal over reasons to say why he'd always go in the daytime after that, an' never came in the evening, an' now they're goin' to have this party, an' she says he's been gettin' paler an' paler every day since he heard about it. Mamma says he's pale some, because Miss Pratt's goin' away, but she thinks it's a good deal more because, well, if he would wear those evening clo'es just to go callin', how would it be to go to that party an' not have any? That's what mamma thinks — an'. Genesis, you promised you'd never tell as long as you lived !"

"Yes'm. I ain' tellin'," Genesis chuckled. "Fm a go'n a git me one nem waituh suits befo' long, myse'f, so's I kin quit wearin' 'at ole Henry Gimlet suit what b'longs to Fanny, an' have me a privut suit o' my own. They's a secon' han' sto', ovuh on the avynoo, where they got swaller-tail suits all way f'um sevum doUuhs to nineteen doUuhs an' ninety-eight cents. Fm a — "

Jane started, interrupting him. "Sh," she whispered, laying a finger warningly upon her lips. William had entered the yard at the back gate, and, approaching over the lawn, had arrived at the steps of the porch before Jane perceived him. She gave him an apprehensive look, but he passed into the house absent-mindedly, not even glancing at Clematis, the humble and faithful dog in attendance upon Genesis — and that was remarkable, because the sight of Clematis was nearly always but too obviously painful to William. Clematis was so mingled a dog that he shook one's faith in any defmiteness of design on the part of Nature: it hurt William to see him about the premises, and William showed his feelings, for he feared that people might think Clemate belonged to him or to his family. But to-day he passed without flinching — and Mrs Baxter was right: William did look pale. "I guess he didn't hear us," said Jane, when he had disappeared into the interior. "He acks awful funny!" she added thoughtfully. "First when he was in love with Miss Pratt, he'd be mad about somep'm' almost every minute he was home. Couldn't anybody say anything to him but he'd just behave as if it was awful, an' then if you'd see him out walkin' with Miss Pratt, well, he'd look like — like — " Jane paused; her eye fell upon Clematis and by a happy inspiration she was able to complete her simile with remarkable accuracy.

"He'd look like the way Clematis looks at people! That's just exackly the way he'd look, Genesis, when he was walkin' with Miss Pratt; an' then when he was home he got so quiet he couldn't answer questions an' wouldn't hear what anybody said to him at table or anywhere, an' papa'd just almost bust. Mamma 'n' papa'd talk an' talk about it, an' " — she lowered her voice — "an' I an' sometimes he'd sit in there without any light, or he'd hardly ever get mad any more; he'd just sit in his room, an' sometimes he'd sit in there without any light, or he'd sit out in the yard all by himself all evening maybe, an' th' other evening after I was In bed I heard 'em, an' papa said — well, this Is what papa told mamma." And again lowering her voice, she proffered the quotation from her father In a tone somewhat awestruck. "Papa said, by Gosh! if he ever 'a' thought a son of his could make such a Word idiot of himself he almost wished we'd both been girls!"

Having completed this report in a violent whisper Jane nodded repeatedly, for emphasis, and Genesis shook his head to show that he was as deeply Impressed as she wished him to be. "I guess," she added, after a pause, "I guess Willie didn't hear anything we talked about him, or clo'es, or anything."

She was mistaken in part. William had caught no reference to himself, but he had overheard something, and he was now alone in his room, thinking about it almost feverishly. "A secon' han' sto', ovuh on the avynoo, where they got swaller-tail suits all way frum sevem doUuhs to nineteen dolluhs an' ninety-eight cents."

. . . Civilization is responsible for certain longings in the breast of man — artificial longings, but sometimes as Poignant as hunger and thirst. Of these the strongest are those of the maid for che bridal veil, of the lad for long trousers, and of the youth for a tailed coat of state. To the gratification of this last, few of the more hushed joys in life are comparable. Indulged youths, too rich, can know, to the unctuous full, neither the longing nor the gratification; but one such as William, in "moderate circumstances," is privileged to pant for his first evening clothes as the hart panteth after the water-brook — and sometimes, to pant in vain. Also, this was a crisis in William's life: in addition to his yearning for" such apparel, he was racked by a passionate urgency.

As Jane had so precociously understood, unless he should somehow manage to obtain the proper draperies he could not go to the farewell dance for Miss Pratt. Other unequipped boys could go in their ordinary "best clothes," but William could not; for, alack! he had dressed too well too soon!

He was in desperate case. The sorrow of the approaching great departure was but the heavier because It had been so long deferred. To William it had seemed that this flower-strewn summer could actually end no more than he could actually die, but Time had begun its awful lecture, and even Seventeen was listening. Aliss Pratt, that magic girl, was going home.

To the competent twenties, hundreds of miles suggesting no impossibilities, such departures may be rending but not tragic. Implacable, the difference to Seventeen! Miss Pratt was going home, and Seventeen could not follow; it could only mourn upon the lonely shore, tracing little angelic footprints left in the sand. To Seventeen such a departure is final; it is a vanishing.

And now it seemed possible that William might be deprived even of the last romantic consolations: of the "last waltz together," of the last, last "listening to music in the moonlight together"; of all those sacred lasts of the "last evening together." And this was a thought that turned him cold on the hot day: it was unbearable.

He had pleaded strongly for a "dress-suit" as a fitting recognition of his seventeenth birthday anniversary, but he had been denied by his father with a jocularity more crushing than rigor. Since then — in particular since the arrival of Miss Pratt — Mr. Baxter's temper had been growing steadily more and more even. That is, as affected by William's social activities, it was uniformly bad. Nevertheless,, after heavy brooding, William decided to make one final appeal before he resorted to measures which the necessities of despair had brought to his mind.

He wished to give himself every chance for a good effect; therefore he did not act hastily, but went over what he intended to say, rehearsing it with a few appropriate gestures, and even taking some pleasure in the pathetic dignity of this performance, as revealed by occasional glances at the mirror of his dressing-table. But in spite of these little alleviations, his trouble was great and all too real, for, unhappily, the previous rehearsal of an emotional scene does not prove the emotion insincere.

Descending, he found his father and mother still sitting upon the front porch. Then, standing before them, solemn-eyed, he uttered a preluding cough, and began:

"Father," he said, in a loud voice, "I have come to — "

"Dear me!" Mrs. Baxter exclaimed, not perceiving that she was interrupting an intended oration. "Willie, you do look pale! Sit down, poor child; you oughtn't to walk so much in this heat."

"Father," William repeated. "Fath— "

"I suppose you got her safely home from church," Mr. Baxter said. "She might have been carried off by highwaymen if you three boys hadn't been along to take care of her!"

But William persisted heroically. "Father — " he said. "Father, I have come to — "

"What on earth's the matter with you?" Mr. Baxter ceased to fan himself, Mrs. Baxter stopped rocking, and both stared, for it had dawned upon them that something unusual was beginning to take place.

William backed to the start and tried it again. "Father, I have come to — " He paused and gulped, evidently expecting to be interrupted, but both of his parents remained silent, regarding him with puzzled surprise. "Father," he began once more, "I have come — I have come to — to place before you something I think it's your duty as my father to undertake, and I have thought over this step before laying it before you."

"My soul!" said Mr. Baxter under his breath. "My soul!"

"At my age," William continued, swallowing, and fixing his earnest eyes upon the roof of the porch to avoid the disconcerting stare of his father, "at my age there's some things that ought to be done and some things that ought not to be done. If you asked me what I thought ought to be done, there is only one answer: When anybody as old as I am has to go out among other young men his own age that already got one, like anyway half of them have, who I go with, and their fathers have already taken such a step, because they felt it was the only right thing to do, because at my age and the young men I go with's age it is the only right thing to do because that is something nobody could deny, at my age — "Here William drew a long breath, and, deciding to abandon that sentence as irrevocably tangled, began another: "I have thought over this step, because there comes a time to every young man when they must lay a step before their father before something happens that they would be sorry for. I have thought this undertaking over, and I am certain it would be your honest duty — " "My soul!" gasped Mr. Baxter. "I thought I knew you pretty well, but you talk like a stranger to me! What is all this? What you ivant?"

"A dress-suit!" said William. He had intended to say a great deal more before coming to the point, but though through nervousness he had lost some threads of his rehearsed plea, it seemed to him he was getting along well, and putting his case with some distinction and power. He was surprised and hurt, therefore, to hear his father utter a wordless shout in a tone of wondering derision.

"I have more to say — " William began.

But, disregarding this, Mr. Baxter cut him off. "A dress-suit!" he cried. "Well, I'm glad you were talking about something, because I honestly thought it must be too much sun!"

At this, the troubled William brought his eyes do'vn f ronri the porch roof and forgot his rehearsal. He lifted his hand appealingly. "Father," he said, "I got to have one!"

"'Got to!'" Mr. Baxter laughed a laugh that chilled the supplicant through and through. "At your age I thought I was lucky if I had any suit that was fit to be seen in. You're too young, Willie. I don't want you to get your mind on such stuflf, and if I have my way, you won't have a dress-suit for four years more, anyhow."

"Father, I got to have one. I got to have one right away !" The urgency in William's voice was almost tearful. "I don't ask you to have it made, or to go to expensive tailors, but there's a plenty of good ready-made ones that only cost about forty dollars; they're advertised in the paper. Father, wouldn't you spent just forty dollars? I'll pay it back when I'm in business. I'll work — "

Mr. Baxter waved all this aside. "It's not the money. It's the principle that I'm standing for, and I don't Intend—"

"Father, won't you do It?"

"No, I will not!"

William saw that sentence had been passed and all appeals for a new trial denied. He choked, and rushed Into the house without more ado.

"Poor boy!" his mother said.

"Poor boy nothing!" fumed Mr, Baxter. "He's almost lost his mind over that Aliss Pratt. Think of his coming out here and starting a regular debating society declamation before his mother and father! Why, I never heard anything like it in my life! I don't like to hurt his feelings, and I'd give him anything I could afford that would do him any good, but all he wants it for now is to splurge around in at this party before that little yellow-haired girl ! I guess he can wear the kind of clothes most of the other boys wear — the kind / wore at parties — and never thought of wearing anything else. What's the world getting to be like." Seventeen years old and throws a fit because he can't have a dress-suit!"

Mrs. Baxter looked thoughtful. "But — but suppose he felt he couldn't go to the dance unless he wore one, poor boy — "

"All the better," said Mr. Baxter firmly. "Do him good to keep away and get his mind on something else."

"Of course," she suggested, with some timidity, "forty dollars isn't a great deal of money, and a ready-made suit, just to begin with — "

Naturally Mr. Baxter perceived whither she was drifting. "Forty dollars isn't a thousand," he interrupted, "but what you want to throw it away for? One reason a boy of seventeen oughtn't to have evening clothes is the way he behaves with any clothes. Forty dollars! Why, only this summer he sat down on Jane's open paint-box, twice in one week !"

"Well — Miss Pratt is going away, and the dance will be her last night. I'm afraid it would really hurt him to miss it. I remember once, before we were engaged — that evening before papa took me abroad, and you — "

"It's no use, mamma," he said. "We were both over twenty — why, I was six years older than Willie, even then. There's no comparison at all, I'll let him order a dress-suit on his twenty-first birthday and not a minute before, I don't believe in it, and I intend to see that he gets all this stuff out of his system. He's got to learn some hard sense!"

Mrs. Baxter shook her head doubtfully, but she said no more. Perhaps she regretted a little that she had caused Mr. Baxter's evening clothes to be so expansively enlarged — for she looked rather regretful. She also looked rather incomprehensible, not to say cryptic, during the long silence which followed, and Mr. Baxter resumed his rocking, unaware of the fixity of gaze which his wife maintained upon him — a thing the most loyal will do sometimes. The incomprehensible look disappeared before long, but the regretful one was renewed in the mother's eyes whenever she caught glimpses of her son, that day, and at the table, where William's manner was gentle — even toward his heartless father.

Underneath that gentleness, the harried self of William was no longer debating a desperate resolve, but had fixed upon it, and on the following afternoon Jane chanced to be a witness of some resultant actions. She came to her mother with an account of them.

"Mamma, what you s'pose Willie wants of those two ole market baskets that were down cellar?"

"Why, Jane.?"

"Well, he carried 'em in his room, an' then he saw me lookin', an' he said 'G'way from here!' an' shut the door. He looks so funny ! What's he want of those ole baskets, mamma:"

"I don't know. Perhaps he doesn't even know himself, Jane."

But William did know, definitely. He had set the baskets upon chairs, and now, with pale determination, he was proceeding to fill them. When his task was completed the two baskets contained, between them:

One heavy-weight winter suit of clothes.

One light-weight summer suit of clothes.

Two pairs of white flannel trousers.

Two Madras negligee shirts.

Two flannel shirt---

Two silk shirts.

Seven soft collars.

Three silk neckties.

One crocheted tie.
Eight pairs of socks.

One pair of patent-leather shoes.

One overcoat.

Some underwear.

One two-foot shelf of books, consisting of several sterling works upon mathematics, in a damaged condition; five of Shakespeare's plays, expurgated and edited for schools and colleges, and also damaged; a work upon political economy and another upon the science of physics; "Webster's Collegiate Dictionary," "How to Enter a Drawing-Room and 500 Other Hints," "Witty Sayings From Here and There," "Lorna Doone," "Quentin Durward," "The Adventures of Sherlock Holmes," a very old copy of "Moths," and a small Bible.

William spread handkerchiefs upon the two overbulging cargoes, that their nature might not be disclosed to the curious, and, after listening a moment at his door, took the baskets, one upon each arm, then went quickly down the stairs and out of the house, out of the yard, and into the alley — by which route he had modestly chosen to travel.

. . . After an absence of about two hours, he returned empty-handed and anxious. "Mother, I want to speak to you," he said, addressing Mrs. Baxter in a voice which clearly proved the strain of these racking days. "I want to speak to vou about something important."

"Yes, Willie?"

"Please send Jane away. I can't talk about important things with a child in the room."

Jane naturally wished to stay, since he was going to say something important. "Mamma, do I haf to go:"

"Just a few minutes, dear."

Jane walked submissively out of the door, leaving it open behind her. Then, having gone about six feet farther, she halted, and, preserving a breathless silence, consoled herself for her banishment bv listenins; to what was said, hearmg it all as satis factorily as if she had remained m the room. Quiet, thoughtful children, like Jane, avail themselves of these little pleasures oftener than is suspected.

"Mother," said William, with great intensity, "I want to ask you please to lend me three dollars and sixty cents."

"What for, Willie?"

"Mother, I just ask you to lend me three dollars and sixty cents."

"But what for?"

"Mother, I don't feel I can discuss it any; I simply ask you: Will you lend me three dollars and sixty cents.""

Mrs. Baxter laughed gently. "I don't think I could, Willie, but certainly I should want to know what for,"

"Mother, I am going on eighteen years of age, and when I ask for a small sum of money, like three dollars and sixty cents, I think I might be trusted to know how to use it for my own good without having to answer questions like a ch — "

"Why, Willie!" she exclaimed. "You ought to have plenty of money of your own."

"Of course I ought," he agreed warmly. "If you'd ask father to give me a regular allow — "

"No, no; I mean you ought to have plenty left out of that old junk and furniture I let you sell, last month. You had nearly nine dollars !"

"That was five weeks ago," William explained wearily.

"But you certainly must have some of it left. Why, it was more than nine dollars, I believe! I think it was nearer ten. Surely you haven't — "

"Ye Gods !" cried the goaded William. "A person going on eighteen years old ought to be able to spend nine dollars in five weeks without everybody's acting like it was a crime! Mother, I ask you the simple question: Will you please lend me three dollars and sixty cents?"

"I don't think I ought to, dear. I'm sure your father wouldn't wish me to, unless you'll tell me what you want it for. In fact, I won't consider it at all unless you do tell me."

"You won't do it?" he quavered.

She shook her head gently. "You see, dear, I'm afraid the reason you don't tell me is because you know that I wouldn't give it to you if I knew what you wanted it for."

And this perfect diagnosis of the case so disheartened him that after a few monosyllabic efforts to continue the conversation with dignity, he gave it up, and left in such a preoccupation with despondency that he passed the surprised Jane, in the hall, without suspecting what she had been doing.

That evening, after dinner, he made to his father an impassioned appeal for three dollars and sixty cents, laying such stress of pathos on his principal argument that if he couldn't have a dress-suit, at least he ought to be given three dollars and sixty cents (the emphasis is William's), that Mr. Baxter was moved in the direction of consent — but not far enough.

"I'd like to let you have it, Willie," he said, excusing himself for refusal, "but your mother felt she oughtn't to do it, unless you'd say what you wanted it for, and I'm sure she wouldn't like me to do it. I can't let you have it unless you get her to say she wants me to."

Thus advised, the unfortunate made another appeal to his mother the next day, and having brought about no relaxation of the situation, again petitioned his father, on the following evening. So it went, the torn and driven William turning from parent to parent; and surely, since the world began, the special sum of three dollars and sixty cents has never been so often mentioned in any one house and in the same space of time as it was in the house of the Baxters during Monday, Tuesday, Wednesday and Thursday of that oppressive week. But on Friday William disappeared after breakfast and did not return to lunch.

Mrs. Baxter was troubled. During the afternoon she glanced often from the open window of the room where she had gone to sew, but the peaceful neighborhood continued to be peaceful, and no sound of the harassed footsteps of William echoed from the pavement. However, she saw Genesis arrive (in his week-day costume) to do some weeding, and Jane immediately skip forth for mingled purposes of observation and conversation.

"What do they say?" thought Mrs. Baxter, observing that both Jane and Genesis were unusually animated. But for once that perplexity was to he dispersed. After an exciting half-hour Jane came flying to her mother, breathless.

"Mamma," she cried, "I know where Willie is ! Genesis told me, 'cause he saw him, an' he talked to him while he was doin' it."

"Doing what? Where?"

"Mamma, listen! What you think Willie's doin'? I bet you can't g — "

"Jane!" Mrs. Baxter spoke sharply. "Tell me what Genesis said, at once."

"Yes'm. Willie's over in a lumber-yard that Genesis comes bv on his wav from over on the avynoo where all the colored people live — an' he's countin' knot-holes in shingles."

"He is *what*?"

"Yes'm. Genesis knows all about it, because he was thinkin' of doin' it himself, only he says it would be too slow. This is the way it is, mamma — listen, mamma, because this is just exactly the way it is. Well, this lumber-yard man got into some sort of a fuss because he bought millions an' millions of shingles, mamma, that had too many knots In, an' the man don't want to pay for 'em, or else the store where he bought 'em won't take 'em back, an' they got to prove how many shingles are bad shingles, or somep'm, and anyway, mamma, that's what Willie's doin'. Every time he comes to a bad shingle, mamma, he puts it somewheres else, or somep'm like that, mamma, an' every time he's put a thousand bad shingles in this other place, they give him six cents. He gets the six cents to keep, mamma — an' that's what he's been doin' all day!"

"Good gracious!"

"Oh, but that's nothing, mamma — just you wait till you hear the rest. That part of it isn't anything a tall, mamma !
You wouldn't hardly notice that part of It, if you knew the other part of It, mamma. Why, that isn't anything!" Jane made demonstrations of scorn for the Insignificant information already imparted.

"Jane!"

"Yes'm?"

"I want to know everything Genesis told you," said her mother, "and I want you to tell It as quickly as you can."

"Well, I am tellin' It, mamma !" Jane protested. "I'm just beginning to tell it. I can't tell it unless there's a beginning, can I? How could there be anything unless you had to begin it, mamma?"

"Try your best to go on, Jane !"

"Yes'm. Well, Genesis says — Mamma!" Jane interrupted herself with a little outcry. "Oh ! I bet that's what he had those two market baskets for! Yes, sir! That's just what he did! An' then he needed the rest o' the money and you an' papa wouldn't give him any, and so he began countin' shingles to-day 'cause to-night's the night of the party an' he just hass to have it!"

Mrs. Baxter, who had risen to her feet, recalled the episode of the baskets and sank into a chair. "How did Genesis know Willie wanted forty dollars, and if Willie's pawned something how did Genesis know that? Did Willie tell Gen—"

"Oh, no, mamma, Willie didn't want forty dollars — only fourteen!"

"But he couldn't get even the cheapest ready-made dress-suit for fourteen dollars."

"Mamma, you're gettin' it all mixed up!" Jane cried. "Listen, mamma ! Genesis knows all about a second-hand store over on the avynoo; an' it keeps 'most everything, an' Genesis says it's the nicest store! It keeps waiter suits all the way up to nineteen dollars and ninety-nine cents. Well, an' Genesis wants to get one of those suits, so he goes in there all the time an' talks to the man an' bargains an' bargains with him, 'cause Genesis says this man is the bargainest man in the wide worl', mamma ! That's what Genesis says. Well, an' so this man's name is One-eye Beljus, mamma. That's his name, an' Genesis says so. Well, an' so this man that Genesis told me about that keeps the store — I mean One-eye Beljus, mamma — well, One-eye Beljus had Willie's name written down in a book, an' he knew Genesis worked for fam'lies that have boys like Willie in 'em, an' this morning One-eye Beljus showed Genesis Willie's name written down in his book, an' One-eye Beljus asked Genesis if he knew anybody by that name an' all about him. Well, an' so at first Genesis pretended he was tryin' to remember, because he wanted to find out what Willie went there for. Genesis didn't tell any stories, mamma; he just pretended he couldn't remember, an' so, well. One-eye Beljus kept talkin' an' pretty soon Genesis found out all about it. One-eye Beljus said Willie came in there and tried on the coat of one of those waiter suits — "

"Oh, no!" gasped Mrs. Baxter.

"Yes'm, an' One-eye Beljus said it was the only one that would fit Willie, an' One-eye Beljus told Willie that suit was worth fourteen dollars, an' Willie said he didn't have any money, but he'd like to trade something else for it. Well, an' so One-eye Beljus said this was an awful fine suit an' the only one he had that had b'longed to a white gentleman. Well, an' so they bargained, an' bargained, an' bargained, an' bargained! An' then, well, an' so at last Willie said he'd go an' get everything that b'longed to him, an' One-eye Beljus could pick out enough to make fourteen dollars' worth, an' then Willie could have the suit. Well, an' so Willie came home an' put everything he had that b'longed to him into those two baskets, mamma — that's just what he did, 'cause Genesis says he told One-eye Beljus it was everything that b'longed to him, an' that would take two baskets, mamma. Well then, an' so he told One-eye Beljus to pick out fourteen dollars' worth, an' One-eye Beljus ast Willie if he didn't have a watch. Well, Willie took out his watch, an' One-eye Beljus said it was an awful bad watch but he would put it in for a dollar; an' he said, T'll put your necktie pin in for forty cents more,' so Willie took it out of his necktie; an' then One-eye Beljus said it would take all the things in the baskets to make I forget how much, mamma, and the watch would be a dollar more, an' the pin forty cents, an' that would leave just three dollars and sixty cents more for Willie to pay before he could get the suit."

Mrs. Baxter's face had become suffused with high color, but she wished to know all that Genesis had said, and, mastering her feelings with an effort, she told Jane to proceed — a command obeyed after Jane had taken several long breaths. "Well, an' so the worst part of it is, Genesis says, it's because that suit is haunted."

"What !"

"Yes'm," said Jane solemnly; "Genesis says it's haunted. Genesis says everybody over on the avynoo knows all about that suit, an' he says that's why One-eye Beljus never could sell it before. Genesis says One-eye Beljus tried to sell it to a colored man for three dollars, but the man said he wouldn't put it on for three hunderd dollars, an' Genesis says he wouldn't either, because it belonged to a Dago waiter that — that — " Jane's voice sank to a whisper of unctuous horror: she was having a wonderful time!
"Mamma, this Dago waiter, he lived over on the avynoo, an' he took a case-knife he'd sharpened — an^ he cut a lady's head off with it!"

Mrs. Baxter screamed faintly.

"An' he got hung, mamma ! If you don't believe it you can ask One-eye Beljus — I guess he knows! An' you can ask—"

"Hush!"

"An' he sold this suit that Willie wants to One-eye Beljus when he was in jail, mamma. He sold it to him before he got hung, mamma."

"Hush, Jane!"

But Jane couldn't hush now. "An' he had that suit on when he cut the lady's head off, mamma, an' that's why it's haunted. They cleaned it all up exccp' a few little spots of bl— "

"Jane!" shouted her mother. "You must not talk about such things, and Genesis mustn't tell vou stories of that sort!"

"Well, how could he help it, if he told me about Willie?" Jane urged reasonably,

"Never mind ! Did that crazy ch — Did Willie leave the baskets in that dreadful placer"

"Yes'm — an' his watch an' pin," Jane informed her impressively. "An' One-eye Beljus wanted to know if Genesis knew Willie, because One-eye Beljus wanted to know if Genesis thought Willie could get the three dollars an' sixty cents, an' One-eye Beljus wanted to know if Genesis thought he could get anything more out of him besides that. He told Genesis he hadn't told Willie he could have the suit, after all; he just told him he thought he could, but he wouldn't say for certain till he brought him the three dollars an' sixty cents. So Willie left all his things there, an' his watch an' — "

"That will do!" Mrs. Baxter's voice was sharper than it had ever been in Jane's recollection. "I don't need to hear any more — and I don't want to hear any more!"

Jane was justly aggrieved. "But mamma, it isn't my fault!"

Mrs. Baxter's lips parted to speak, but she checked herself. "Fault.'" she said gravely. "I wonder whose fault it really is!"

And with that she went hurriedly into William's room, and made a brief inspection of his clothes-closet and dressing-table. Then, as Jane watched her in awed silence, she strode to the window and called loudly:

"Genesis!"

"Yes'mr" came the voice from below.

"Go to that lumber-yard where Air. William is at work and bring him here to me at once. If he declines to come, tell him — " Her voice broke oddly; she choked, but Jane could not decide with what emotion. "Tell him — tell him I ordered you to use force if necessary! Hurry!"

Jane ran to the window in time to see Genesis departing seriouslv through the back gate.

"Mamma—"

"Don't talk to me now, Jane," Mrs. Baxter said crisply. "I want you to go down in the yard, and when Willie comes tell him I'm waiting for him here in his own rooi".. And don't come with him, Jane. Run!"

"Yes, mamma." Jane was pleased with this appointment: she anxiously desired to be the first to see how Willie "looked."

. . . He looked flurried and flustered and breathless, and there were blisters upon the reddened palms of his hands. "What on earth's the matter, mother?" he asked, as he stood panting before her. "Genesis said something was wrong, and he said you told him to hit me if I wouldn't come."

"Oh, no!" she cried. "I only meant I thought perhaps you wouldn't obey any ordinary message — "

"Well, well, it doesn't matter, but please hurry and say what you want to because I got to get back and — "

"No," Mrs. Baxter said quietly. "You're not going back to count any more shingles, Willie. How much have you earned?"

He swallowed, but spoke bravely. "Thirty-six cents. But I've been getting lots faster the last two hours and there's a good deal of time before six o'clock. Mother — "

"No," she said. "You're going over to that horrible place where you've left your clothes and your watch and all those other things in the two baskets, and you're going to bring them home at once."

"Mother!" he cried aghast. "Who told you?"

"It doesn't matter. You don't want your father to find out, do you? Then get those things back here as quickly as you can. They'll have to be fumigated after being in that den."

"They've never been out of the baskets," he protested hotly, "except just to be looked at. They're my things, mother, and I had a right to do what I needed to with 'em, didn't I?" His utterance became difficult. "You and father just can't understand — and you won't do anything to help me — "

"Willie, you can go to the party," she said gently. "You didn't need those frightful clothes at all."

"I do!" he cried. "I got to have 'em! I can't go in my day clo'es ! There's a reason you wouldn't understand why I can't. I just can't!"

"Yes," she said, "you can go to the party."

"I can't either! Not unless you give me three dollars and twenty-four cents, or unless I can get back to the lumber-yard and earn the rest before — "

"No!" And the warm color that had rushed over Mrs. Baxter during Jane's sensational recital returned with a vengeance. Her eyes flashed. "If you'd rather I sent a policeman for those baskets, I'll send one. I should prefer to do it — much! And to have that rascal arrested. If you don't want me to send a policeman you can go for them yourself, but you must start within ten minutes, because if you don't I'll telephone headquarters. Ten minutes, Willie, and I mean it!"

He cried out, protesting. She would make him a thing of scorn forever and soil his honor, if she sent a policeman. Mr, Beljus was a fair and honest tradesman, he explained passionately, and had not made the approaches in this matter. Also, the garments in question, though not entirely new, nor of the highest mode, were of good material and in splendid condition. Unmistakably they were evening clothes, and such a bargain at fourteen dollars that William would guarantee to sell them for twenty after he had worn them this one evening. Mr. Beljus himself had said that he would not even think of letting them go at fourteen to anybody else, and as for the two poor baskets of worn and useless articles offered in exchange, and a bent scarf pin and a worn-out old silver watch that had belonged to great-uncle Ben — why, the ten dollars and forty cents allowed upon them was beyond all ordinary liberality; it was almost charity. There was only one place in town where evening clothes were rented, and the suspicious persons in charge had insisted that William obtain from his father a guarantee to insure the return of the garments in perfect condition. So that was hopeless. And wasn't it better, also, to wear clothes which had known only one previous occupant (as was the case with Mr. Beljus' offering) than to hire what chance hundreds had hired? Finally, there was only one thing to be considered and this was the fact that William had to have those clothes !

"Six minutes," said Mrs. Baxter, glancing implacably at her watch. "When it's ten I'll telephone."

And the end of it was, of course, victory for the woman — victory both moral and physical. Three-quarters of an hour later she was unburdening the contents of the two baskets and putting the things back in place, illuminating these actions with an expression of strong distaste — in spite of broken assurances that Mr. Beljus had not more than touched any of the articles offered to him for valuation. ... At dinner, which was unusually early that evening, Mrs. Baxter did not often glance toward her son; she kept her eyes from that white face and spent most of her tinie in urging upon Mr. Baxter that he should be prompt in dressing for a card-club meeting which he and she were to attend that evening. These admonitions of hers were continued so pressingly that Mr. Baxter, after protesting that there was no use in being a whole hour too early, groaningly went to dress without even reading his paper.

William had retired to his own room, where he lay upon his bed in the darkness. He heard the evening noises of the house faintly through the closed door: voices and the clatter of metal and china from the faraway kitchen, Jane's laugh in the hall, the opening and closing of the doors. Then his father seemed to be in distress about something: William heard him complaining to Mrs. Baxter; and though the words were indistinct, the tone was vigorously plaintive. Mrs. Baxter laughed and appeared to make light of his troubles, whatever they were — and presently their footsteps were audible from the stairway; the front door closed emphatically, and they were gone.

Everything was quiet now. The open window showed as a greenish oblong set in black, and William knew that in a little while — half an hour, perhaps — there would come through the stillness of that window the distant sound of violins. That was a moment he dreaded with a dread that ached. And as he lay on his dreary bed, he thought of brightly lighted rooms where other boys were dressing eagerly, faces and hair shining, hearts beating high — boys who would possess this last evening, and the "last waltz together," the last smile and the last sigh.

It did not once enter his mind that he could go to the dance in his "best suit," or that possibly the other young people at the party would be too busy with their own affairs to notice particularly what he wore. It was the unquestionable and granite fact, to his mind, that the whole derisive World would know the truth about his earlier appearances in his father's clothes. And that was a form of ruin not to be faced. In the protective darkness and seclusion of William's bedroom, it is possible that smarting eyes relieved themselves by blinking rather energetically; it is even possible that there was a minute damp spot upon the pillow. Seventeen cannot always manage the little boy yet alive under all the coverings.

There came a tapping upon the door and a soft voice.

"Will-ee.?"

With a sharp exclamation William swung his legs over the edge of the bed and sat up. Of all things he desired not, he desired no conversation with, or on the part of, Jane. But he had forgotten to lock his door — the handle turned, and a dim little figure marched in.

"Willie, Adelia's goin' to put me to bed."

"You g'way from here," he said huskily. "I haven't got time to talk to you. I'm busy."

"Well, you can wait a minute, can't your" she asked reasonably. "I haf to tell you a joke on mamma."

"I don't want to hear any jokes !"

"Well, I haf to tell you this one 'cause she told me to! Oh!" Jane clapped her hand over her mouth and jumped up and down, offering a fantastic silhouette against the light of the open door. "Oh, oh, oh!"

"What's matter?"

"She said I mustn't, mustn't tell that she told me to tell! My goodness! I forgot that! Mamma took me off alone right after dinner, an' she told me to tell you this joke on her as soon as she an' papa had left the house, but she said, 'Above all things ' she said, 'don't let Willie know I said to tell him.' That's just what she said, an' here that's the very first thing I had to go an' do!"

"Well, what of matter"

Jane quieted down. The pangs of her remorse were lost in her love of sensationalism, and her voice sank to the thrilling whisper which it was one of her greatest pleasures to use. "Did you hear what a fuss papa was makin' when he was dressin' for the card-party?"

"I don't care if—"

"He had to go in his reg'lar clo'es !" whispered Jane triumphantly. "An' this is the joke on mamma: you know that tailor that let papa's dress-suit way, way out; well, mamma thinks that tailor must think she's crazy, or somep'm, 'cause she took papa's dress-suit to him last Monday to get it pressed for this card-party, an' she guesses he must of understood her to tell him to do lots besides just pressin' it. Anyway, he went an' altered it, an' he took it way, way in again; an' this afternoon when it came back it was even tighter'n what it was in the first place, an' papa couldn't begin to get into it! Well, an' so it's all pressed an' everything, an' she stopped on the way out, an' whispered to me that sh'd got so upset over the joke on her that she couldn't remember where she put it when she took it out o' papa's room after he gave up tryin' to get inside of it. An' that," cried Jane — "that's the funniest thing of all ! Why, it's layin' right on her bed this very minute!"

In one bound William leaped through the open door. Two seconds sufficed for his passage through the hall to his mother's bedroom — and there, neatly spread upon the lace coverlet and brighter than coronation robes, fairer than Joseph's sacred coat It lay !

Introduction

By Ty Rosenow

It was fun writing the first book, and expansion of the second book of the stories I wrote was fun. But, now, I am running out of stories and should have put everything into one book instead of so many. So, enough of my whining, otherwise you would probably close this book and never read it again with the assumption that this is a horrible compilation of short stories. I was wrong. The last book, *"Ty's Book of Rubbish: Volume 20"* became a larger hit than once thought with a lack of political correctness. You can't always be politically correct if you are trying to make a joke. I will make fun of just about anything, but never had the courage to make fun of retarded people and those with the Alzheimer's. In this politically incorrectness shunned world, I found that it is always safe to make fun of dead people – they can't fight back.

There were other surprises I found from my last book. It was very popular in the United Kingdom and sold very well in Germany (even though it was not translated to German), but sold awful in the United States and Canada. What surprised me even more was the book became a bestseller other places such as India, and, eventually, and is currently going through a scriptwriting process to be sold to various studios. As I am writing this introduction there is even word going around that the book is nominated for its first award. It would be neat to see it win.

Despite the book's popularity, I am still having a hard time getting respect as an author and many bookstores are declining to put it on the shelf. The college that I go to, The Evergreen State College, in which I will be graduating in June 2009 with my undergraduate degree, won't take me seriously either, but allow other staff members, professors from other universities, or even dead college students do readings of their books. Yet, the book sells out. I suppose one will listen to me if I had a PhD instead of a BA.

This will be my last book, at least for awhile. That's the whole set for now, *"Ty's Book of Rubbish: Volume 20"* and *"Ty's Book of Rubbish: Volume 19"*. In about a year or so, I may combine both volumes as one book, hard-bound, of course. I am not throwing my hat in the ring when it comes to my writing not because I am not taken seriously as an author, but because it is beginning to be hard for me to write more stories. If the stories don't come out, then it is time for me to take a hiatus from my writing, and as I come up with new stories, I will write them down, collect as many as I can and compile them in a book. Much has been done in the past with the first book. So, I hope you enjoy the last book in the series and the stories one last time, I would like to thank you, the reader, for supporting and promoting the books I have written. Without you, these stories would have not come out of my brain and onto paper.

Thank you,

Ty Rosenow
June 2, 2008
Olympia, Washington, USA

This Story Was Written At Border's Books[78]

First, I would like to give my extreme pleasure of Border's Music and Books for letting me write this short story within their coffee shop section. They have the right idea in mind: putting coffee within a book shop. What goes better than books and coffee? Well, there is an exception of tea. But, they sell tea there too, but only to tea drinkers. I'd write about the books, but everyone reads books. Over ninety percent of the people who know how to read usually end up reading books sometime or another during their lives. I say ninety percent, but you can never say that you are too perfect – that is what perfection means and that is to be one hundred one percent, even though I never thought about the one percent since one hundred percent is usually the grand total (Mathematics – I hate it!).

History of coffee, to me, is more interesting than tea. After all, anything can be made into tea. You can take some ragged old socks, boiling them in hot water, pull them out when it becomes a good mixture of hot water and scum, and create a warm tea. It won't taste very good, but it's tea, nonetheless. The most popular of teas are usually from non-poisonous plant leaves. Tea originally was invented by the Chinese, but the English claim they own the patents to it.

Coffee started off from a goat herder who noticed that his goats were having "a buzz" from the digestion of these red beans on a bush. It tries it, and it tastes bitter. He promptly spits it out and goes back to it. Eventually, the roasting and the grinding came in. I forgot when it was, since Border's would look at me strangely as I leave my laptop behind and look through their books and not buy any. Eventually, in the 1600's coffee in England becomes more and more abundant than every Starbuck's in America today. I believe in London, alone, there were about 3,000 coffee shops, much more than taverns. And yet, it become popular today.

---

[78] I actually wrote this entire story at the Border's Bookstore in Olympia by the *Das Kaptital Mall.* The mall has different name, but many locals call it that. I believe it originally came from a play by Malcolm Stilson at The Evergreen State College. Anyway, I wanted to spread my wealth of coffee knowledge by writing this. However, I felt very uncomfortable putting my grubby fingers all over the books without purchasing them, but I am sure there is a wealth of knowledge that I could tap at Border's while drinking my coffee.

There are multiple types of coffee, and the Baristas act like bartenders, only they don't listen to your sorrows behind the bar. Some coffees are really cheap, but one such coffee is the Kopi Luwak, which is considered to be one the most expensive coffees in the world. Kopi Luwak sells for approximately fifty dollars per espresso glass or ships for over a hundred dollars per pound. The process is simple: an animal eats it, excretes it out of its body and then the harvest is done with the excrement. It gets washed, shipped out, and you drink the coffee. It has kind of an earthy flavor. Border's does not sell Kopi Luwak and that is why their prices are so low.

The Dance[79]

Two gentlemen are in the pub drinking their fine glasses of wine. I emphasize "fine wine" as an expensive wine and not a "wine in a box". They were nice glasses of Chardonnay, a form of red wine - a taste of good old fashion dinner wine. It was white wine that people drink just to get drunk. As these two gentlemen go through their conversation about the world affairs, this conversation was brought up.

"Men and women have traditional dance not taught from generation to generation, but rather through natural instinct," said the first gentleman.

"How is that so?" asked the second gentleman.

"It's very simple. The special dance causes you move from side to side and then back and forth."

"Simple enough. That is how a typical dance starts."

"There is the clenching of the legs followed by the quick hop or an up and down motion. Most cases, it is repeated."

"Indeed, you seem to be familiar with this form of dance."

"Indeed, I am, but I cannot digress from the point. The dance is followed by a trumpet sound or a gurgling sound."

"You have to go to the bathroom, don't you?"

"Yes, I am currently doing the Pee Pee Dance."

"That is a good reason to go, It's only natural."

And so, the first gentleman went to the bar restroom to do his personal business.

[79] This story is about a special dance that we all do. You might say that it is very traditional.

The Al Gore Nightmare[80]

"Soda pop," said Dr. Susan Heiner, "and beer."

"Are you sure," asked Dr. Phil Roseheimer.

"Just think of it. We still have the problem. We've done everything we could possibly think of doing. Our society recycles everything in order to reduce are carbon footprint. We have reduced all of our energy resources. Those who didn't switch fuels or aren't "environmentally friendly," were often reprimanded with the death penalty if the violators did not comply."

"With all of this caring of the environment, we have developed technologies on every single animal, including the humans, are all required to wear an apparatus in every orifice that puts the carbon, scrubs it, and then turn it into oxygen. No wonder the plants are dying on this planet."

"Right, but we still have global warming. Just think. Soda pop is a carbonated drink, so therefore it puts out a carbon footprint. Just think. There are 7,000 cans being opened continuously opened every second around the world."

"That would probably be the main cause global warming there."

"Right."

"I think you are on to something."

"Right. And that is canned sodas alone. There is tons more of the same thing every time you open up a carbonated drink, including your low fat lattes, Phil."

And because of Al Gore and the environmentalists wanting to destroy our lives in order to save the world, they have finally learned how to defeat human existence.

---

80 I hate Al Gore's stupid philosophies. When he won the 2007 Nobel Peace Prize, I felt that he didn't deserve it. I, too, can come up with a Power Point presentation and talk about how the world is going to end. There was someone else who was beat out who deserved it better: Irena Sendler. She saved Jewish babies during World War II and smuggled them out of Poland in order to keep them from dying in the concentration camps. She was a REAL HERO. Besides, everyone knows that it is global dimming and climatic change not global warming that we have a problem with environmentally. Al Gore is as much of an environmentalist as much as winning the lottery at the age of 200 years: it's never going to happen. First, Tipper Gore uses a mass amount of hairspray and she believes in censorship (something that I have always been against). Second, Al Gore would be more than happy to ~~fine~~ ~~incarcerate~~ give non-believers of the environment given the death penalty. Remember, caring the environment is our choice, not what our politicians or environmentalists want. It is up to each individual to make that choice not the rights or wrongs of that society.

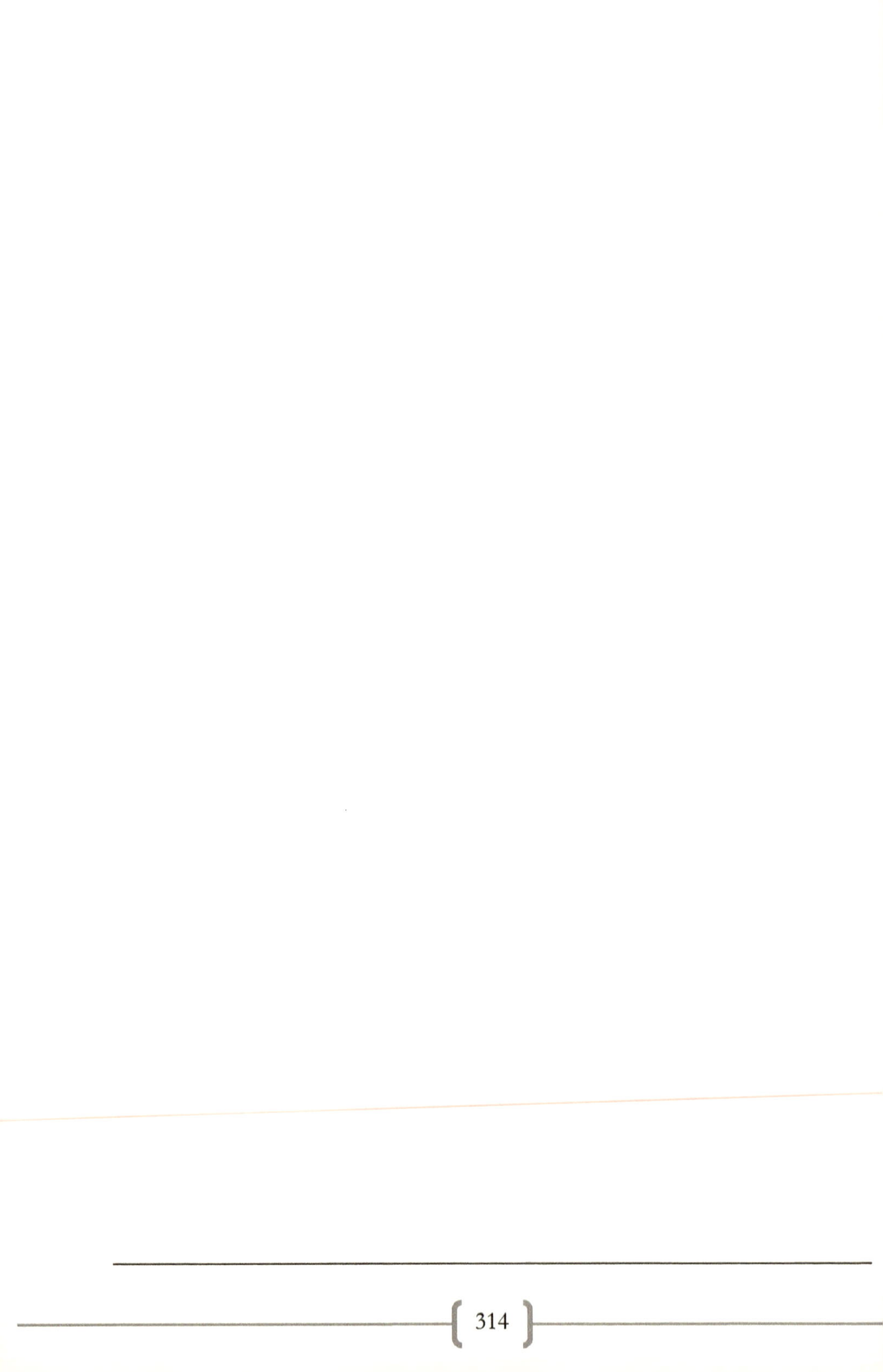

All For A Girl[81]

Sex is the dandiest thing. Many living things cannot possibly survive without the dirtiest of deeds that pushes the replication process across the boundaries just to make these genomes unite and multiply thus creating human existence. But, there is a few details that nature had left out for humans. While the typical buck deer would only have to touch a doe's ass in order to do the dirty deed or sharks having an orgy after a major feeding frenzy, the humans have a tougher time to reproduce. It can get a little more complicated and you could wind up a loveless relationship. But, when you are in love, your world could change.

Take one girl as an example. Here she is, trying to get my attention, and once the attention is received, she longer has the full interests in me. I feel heartbroken and financially broke. When I say financially broke, I do mean BROKE. The idea of being a gentleman and doing things for the ladies is tough business. If you don't have the bucks to back yourself up, then, basically, you are screwed. A woman usually wants to marry a rich man that could provide for her special needs.

So, here I am, a guy who is trying to essentially get laid. It's not just getting laid, for it is the essentials for a relationship and a love that one must for the rest of their life. You see, there are women who just want to get laid, those who want a relationship, and those who just want to be friends. I guess I will never figure women out, which is probably the reason why I am alone in his world, scrounging away behind my word processor. All of this for a girl.

81 I was thinking about my crush of one of my colleagues when I was writing this piece.

Back By Popular Demand: An Ageless Computer Joke[82]

This is joke is written in Hexadecimals have fun decoding it! Again, you'll want to look up for a Hexadecimal translator to get the full joke.

486f7720476f6420437265617465642074686520436f6d70757465722049 6
e207468652062656769 6e6e696e672c20476f642063726561746564207468
65206269742e20416e642074686520626974207761732061207a65726f3b2
06e6f7468696e672e204f6e2074686520666972737420646179 2c20486520
746f67676c656420746865203020746f20312c20616e6420746865 20556e6
976657273652077617 32e2028496e2074686f736520646179732c20626f6f7
47374726170206c6f616465727320776572652073696d706c652c20616e64
202261637469766520 6c6f7722207369676e616c7320646964 6e277420796
5742065786973742e29204f6e20746865207365636f6e6420646179 2c2047
6f64277320626f73742077616e746564206120646 56d6f2c20616e6420747 2
6965642074 6f207265616420746865206269742e205468697320626569 6e6
720766f6c6174696c65206d656d6f72792c2074686520626974207265 7665
7274656420746f206120302e20416e642074686520756e6976657273652 07
761736e27742e20476f64206c6561726e65642074686520696d706f727461
6e6365206f66206261636b7570732 0616e64206d656d6f727920726566726
573682c20616e64207370656e74207468652072657374206f662074686520
6461792028 20616e64206869732066697273742061 6c6c2d6e69676874657
220292072656 36f6e737472756374696e672074686520756e6976657273 65
2e204f6e2074686520746869726420646179 2c2074686520626974206372 6
965642022 4f682c204c6f7264212 0496620796f752065786973742c206769 7
665206d6520612073696e6721222041 6e6420476f64206372656174656420
72657620322e30206f6620746865206269742c206576656e2062657474657
2207468616e20746865206f726967696e616c2070726f746f7479706 52e205
4686f7365206 96e20556e6976657273652 04d61726b6574696e6720696d6d
656469617465 6c792072656 16c697a65642074686520746865 20226e65772
0616e6420696d70726f7665642220776f756c646e277420646f206a7573746

[82] I didn't think that the computer jokes would go this far. There were actually people trying to translate these suckers! So, someone suggested that I should come up with a hexadecimal version. I didn't explain this when I published Volume 19 in a hurry. In the Omnibus only, take a look at the end of the book to see the full translated jokes. But for Pete's Sake, try to decode them yourself for the fun of it!

9636520746f20737563682061206772616e6420616e6420676c6f72696f757
320637265617469696f6e2e20416e6420736f2069742077617320647562626265
6420746865204d6f7374205369676e69666963616e74204269742c206f722
0746865205369676e206269742e204d616e79206269747320666f6c6c6f77
65642c20627574206f6e6c79206f6e652077617320736f20686f6e6f726564
2e204f6e2074686520666f7572746820646179c20476f6420637265617465
6420612073696d706c6520414c5520776974682027616464272061676420616e64202
76c6f676963616c207368696674207720696e737472756374696f6e732e2041
6e6420746865206f726967696e616c20626974206469736f636f7665726564642
074686174206279207065726666f726d696e6720612073696e676c65207368
69667420696e737472756374696f6e2c20697420636f756c64206265636f6d
6520746865204d6f7374205369676e69666963616e74204269742e20416e6
420476f642072656616c697a656420746865206696d706f7274616e6365206f6
620636f6d707574657220736563757269747992e204f6e2074686520666966
7468206461792c20476f64206372656174656420746865206669727374206
d69642d6c696665206b69636b65722c2072657620322e30206f6620746865
20414c552c207769746820776f6e64657266756c20666561747572657332c2
0616e642073616964202253637265772074686174206164642061646420616e642073
68696674207374756666662e20476f20666f7274682061616e64206d756c74697
06c792e2220416e6420476f64207361772074686174206974207761732067
6f6f642e204f6e20746865207369787468206461792c20476f6420676f7420
612062697420766572636f6e666964656e742c20616e6420696e76656e74
65642070697065c696e65732c2072656769737465722068617a61726473
2c206f7074696d697a696e6720636f6d70696c6572732c2063726f7373746161
c6b2c2072657374617274617262c6520696e73747275637469f6e732c206d
6963726f696e746572727570747332c20726163652063f6e646974696f6e73
2c20616e642070726f7061676174696f6e2064656c6179732e204869737466
7269616e7320686176652075736564207468697320746f20636f6e76696e6
3696e676c792061726775652074686174207468652073697874682064617979
206d75737420686176652062656e2061204d6f6e6461792e204f6e20746
86520736576656e7468206461792c20616e20656e67696e656572696e6720
6368616e676520696e74726f647563656420204d6963726f736f667420696e74
6f2074686520556e69766572736652c20616e6420697420686173e2774207
76f726b656420726967687420073696e63652e

The Three Foxes[83]

Jonathan put his sandwich down on the diner's counter top. He was soon to graduate with big ambitions with his MBA and knew what type of business he wanted to get into. Sure, it was a notable wasted time for the time he was in college, but it did not provide the reputation he needed for his very own success. Sitting back, he ponders over the thought and goes back to eating his sandwich. The sandwich is good with the titillation of the bacon and tomato smothered with the real mayonnaise in between the thick slices of sourdough bread. You cannot turn down a good sandwich. You must eat it all whether or not you have a hunger built up inside of yourself. It is a sign of respect. Jonathan walked out of the restaurant for his journey home in a drunken stupor.

The wind was blowing through the trees. He looked up and saw the dark clouds increased as the wind was blowing in his hair. The dark clouds were forever increasing with a larger and larger ferociousness than ever before. Leaves were being thrown about like a raccoon going through the trash looking for something good to eat in a open dumpster. He could feel it coming. There is going to be a storm tonight. Jonathan looked out into the horizon while lighting his cigarette. It was the bad tasting kind of cigarettes even though he preferred the menthol. He looked at the bottom of the package and the initials said: L.S/M.F.T. It was an old advertising slogan from the thirties: "Lucky Strike Means Fine Tobacco", you know, where they said that four out of five doctors prescribed Lucky Strike cigarettes to their patients. As Jonathan looked across the empty streets, he saw a fox, not just a gray fox, but a red fox crossing the street. He could tell that it was a fox, because it looked like a dog, but had the same instincts and mannerisms as a feline. In other words, a fox.

After seeing the fox, Jonathan wondered how odd it was to see a fox in this part of town. Normally, the fox would avoid populated town areas in search for food. Unfortunately, this was not the case. Within the spiritual world, a fox is constantly looking for something and it is a cunning creature.

---

83 One night, while I was working in Security for The Evergreen State College, I saw three foxes. Or, perhaps I saw the same fox in three different locations. It was a grey fox, but I thought that it may have been some sort of sign of something to come. It wasn't a sign but a mere coincidence.

Night Watchman: Thomas Matthew, 'Polishin Tammy', originally a French polisher and his son, later killed in cliff fall near the Catholic Church. Portfolio presented to University of St Andrews by Mr James Thomson, a descendant of one of the collectors, in memory of his son Laurence Swan Thomson (1917-1934), and arranged and catalogued by Mr J H Read. St James's Catholic Church is sits above a steep coastal cliff with a sheer drop. Photo taken circa 1865. Originator: Thomas Rodger *(Photo and Picture Information Courtesy of the University of St. Andrews Library)*

The Night Watchman[84]

"Suicides are fairly common at colleges."

"How's that?"

"I said, 'Suicides are fairly common at colleges.'" The loud live music at the open mic show at the restaurant could be over-bearing at times. It took distinct tastes to enjoy the artsy fartsy stuff and Sally knew it. But, this was a girly get together, where women would yak their cares away while talking about the men and their children they were with. It was only natural that women would have the girl time while relating to those with the same sex and yet...and yet to find comfort within themselves. Psychologists had often felt this was a healthy thing to say whatever it is on your mind whether it to be conscious or unconscious. Sally knew what she was saying when it came to suicides. She was, after all, a psychologist.

"What do you mean," asked Olivia in which in the hopes of explaining the statement that Sally made.

"It's true," replied Sally to Olivia's response, "it's the most leading cause of death amongst college students."

"I don't understand. How could that happen?"

"It's fairly easy. For instance, a child graduates from high school and wants to attend at a college across the country. The reason why the child wants to leave the local area is because they are either sick of their parents and be on their own, or they want to see the world. The parents agree and help the child move to their dorm or the child moves on their own. The child is in a strange area with a strange culture, something that is fairly common. If there are parties, at times the child would partake in the experiments of drugs and alcohol, thinking that it is a 'happy' drug, but in fact they are downers and some addiction may occur. If the child doesn't partake in the parties and gets stuck in their room the entire time because of the stress of the school work and such, then the child becomes very depressed. The parents usually want to help, but they are very limited because of the long distance. Sometimes, all it takes is just a hug or a parent to be physically there no matter what type of relationship

[84] I part of this story while I was in Olympia, Washington, USA and the other half in St. Andrews, Scotland, United Kingdom. When I finally finished the story, someone suggested that I should submit the story for the Dan Hemingway prize at the School of English at the University of St. Andrews. The picture that you see before this story inspired me to finish my story and share it for others to read. Needless to say, my inspiration (the picture) was not printed with the Dan Hemingway Prize submission. I didn't win the Dan Hemingway Prize. I guess the picture is the true inspiration: especially if the rest of your story is based off the picture itself.

between the parent and the child. When depression sets in, it must be taken care of right away; otherwise the depression could be so bad that the child may not have any other choice but to kill themselves."

"So, you are saying that a child without some sort of family support system like a parent or a sibling close to their age would be able to overcome depression and live a happy, normal life?"

"Bingo. I hear these stories all the time from the college students and help them overcome their depression," Sally replied, "And every year, I see at least two to three suicides from the college students and the whole school goes into mourning. For over the centuries that college had been in business, I am sure there are hundreds, if not, thousands of ghosts roaming the dorm halls and classrooms."

"So, you are saying that these ghosts are getting an education without paying the tuition," chuckled Olivia.

"If you want to call it that," giggled Sally.

Jim Jones had been the night watchman for thirty-nine years at the college, and tomorrow, would be his final day: making it forty years. It was time to retire for old Jim, something he had been looking forward to it for a long time. He had saved his money for the motor home and "see the world," or at least that was what the advertisement said before he purchased the forty footer fifth wheel. But, he was willing to see the world in his motor home. If the advertisements say to "see the world", then you must pare up the idea that they convey to heart. Not very many people take on the advertising slogans, only Jim loves the challenge. What else was he going to do? He didn't want to mope around, sit back in his lazy chair in front of the television set wasting away until his death. How boring is that?

There was one thing that Jim would sorely miss, and that was his job here at the college. He loved the twelve hour night/graveyard shift. Most people hated these types of shifts. Maybe it was the sunlight that you have to sleep through, or maybe it was the boredom. Ah yes, the boredom. It can be very boring sitting around and staring at the same objects all night over and over again. The key to these things is to keep your mind occupied with new and fresh things.

For example, Jim had been working on writing and editing his own book for thirty-nine years. And once his fortieth anniversary pops up, he would be ready to have his first novel published. The book is in the mystery genre, about two thousand pages long. Basically, it would make one hell of a doorstop. Jim was happy to pass on the torch to Jack Henderson, his trainee, for he was a young aspiring writer, learned quickly of the standard procedures, physically fit, loved the shift, and Jack wanted this to be his career. It reminded Jim when he was Jack's age, a perfect candidate for the job.

"Have you heard of the suicide room," asked Lucinda.

"I must say that I haven't," replied Johnny.

A small group of students are sitting by the burning fire glistening in the fireplace while drinking a nice warm cup of tea in the old dining hall. Tea, like wine, must be sipped slowly in order to enjoy the aroma it brings to the nostrils. To top off the tea, it does bring the needy conversations associated with it. This is a strange conversation for a tea party. As you may know, people enjoy the quaintness and normally talk about the weather that one must be having, not about suicides.

The old hall was built as an old women's and strictly for women only by old man Smithers. As soon as Smithers passed away, the university switched it to both genders, disregarding the respect of the dead.

The old dining room was a beautiful, but rarely used for the sake of the use of a dining hall, but as an occasional formal event area. The small group of students would use it to hang out, play the old Steinway grand piano, and to drink tea in conversation. The old room was mostly forgotten, but the small student group cleaned up the room to its former glory when they arrived and once it was discovered. The room had not seen a human soul for since the remodeling of the old building. There was a secret passage that led to the old dining room from their residences. The old secret passage was marked as *Staff Only*, but nobody paid any mind. The secret passage was forgotten as well, perhaps through the remodeling, but it well used by these group of students so the there were little to no cobwebs hanging in the staircase.

If one had the imagination, the old dining room must have been spectacular during its heyday. But, now, it is perfectly preserved back to its natural state, where it is better than what it had been originally.

"Yeah, the suicide room should be where no student is allowed because of the suicides that took place in the same room. Every time they set up a new student with their accommodation within that room, they eventually end their lives fairly quickly," said Lucinda.

Johnny responded, "So, you are essentially saying that they are still putting students into accommodation in the suicide room? Isn't that unlawful?"

"Not entirely unlawful. It may be a risk for insurance because the suicides don't happen every time someone is accommodated within that room itself," replied Sally. She is studying to be lawyer.

Lucinda continued her story, "This hall was once occupied by virgins, and this hall was no exception. Heck, this hall was often nicknamed as 'Virgin Hall' before the hall went from an all women's hall to a unisex hall. As the legend goes, if a virgin were to occupy the suicide room, she must give her life to appease the ghosts of 'Virgin Hall' at 11:59 at night on December 31st inside this room."

Sally piped in, "Why 11:59 on December 31st?"

Lucinda answered, "The legend says that virgin will more than likely be not at a party because she is dateless."

"In other words, she is so ugly that she can't a date for that night," replied Johnny.

Lucinda ignored Johnny. He was being a complete jerk. She continued on with her interpretation of the legend. "It is still unknown why the suicide room is still being used today. One cannot avoid the room, since the room numbers are often changed and the current residents are picked through a lottery. Essentially, the suicide room is unavoidable despite its renovations over the years."

"What do renovations have to do with the suicide room," asked Johnny.

"Because," replied Sally, "it is said that ghosts have a tendency to disappear after renovations."

"I still don't see how renovations have anything to do with the changes," said Charles, "Ghosts don't care how much a building has been renovated. They still haunt. The Poltergeists still move around the place like they own it. The only way to escape them is to exorcise them and even that does not work. Most cases, one would normally avoid the area completely by making it a sacred ground."

"Charles is right," said Lucinda. "There are no rules to avoid this situation completely. This is not supposed to be a scary story to keep you up at night. Nobody really knows where the suicide room is located, not even the staff."

"Let's pack," said Johnny, "a pack that we are not just friends, but we will be there for one another forever." The group put their hands together in a fist and slammed their fists into one another all at once, a sign that they were taking the oath.

Detective Fred Jenkins had just finished his fudge donut when he got the call on the radio. Another dead body found by the night watchman at the University Hall. His stomach began to rumble. This was something he did not want to hear after he ate. Besides, he hated the sight of dead bodies even though he acknowledged that he may be one himself eventually. The sight of dead bodies never gets old to Detective Jenkins. He would rather work as a toll booth collector rather than see a dead body again. It was time for him to buck up each time since it was his job to investigate any situation that goes awry, and that includes investigating dead bodies. Fred saw the coroner as he arrived to the residential hall. "Hi Sam," he greeted, "what do we have this time?" Fred always pretended that he didn't know what was happening when he arrived in order to get fresh information.

"We have death at approximately 11:59 pm last night. It seems to be an apparent suicide, possibly death by hanging. The victim is a female, approximate age of eighteen to twenty years."

"Such a young lady, it's too bad that she had to pass away at such a young age. Were her parents notified?"

"They will be notified to identify the body once the crime scene is cleared."

Both Fred and Sam stared at the body hanging on the rafters with a couple minutes of silence. "You know what, Sam?"

"What's that?"

"Every year, and I do mean *every stinkin' year,* there is an apparent suicide here at the University's residential hall. It is always a young female, a hanging, and usually in the same vicinity."

"Right, that is normally how the legend goes. The female virgin gets so frightened by the ghost that she hangs herself."

"Have you actually taken a closer look at the body before coming to the conclusion of it becoming an apparent suicide?"

"Not really."

"See these marks on the neck?"

"Yes?"

"That is definitely a sign of a strangling. They are not from the rope when she hung herself. I'd say that she may have been strangled before the killer. The hanging was done to make it look like an apparent suicide. Do you know what the motive might be, Sam?"

"I don't know. I just figure out the time of death, get the body identified, and then collect them before sending the body off to some funeral director, Fred."

"The motive would be, Sam, to make up a story about a suicide room and kill all of these young girls."

"Okay, Fred, we have the evidence, the murder weapon which more than likely this piece of dentist floss in the trash can and a plastic bag, and we have found the motive. There is only one thing that is missing."

"What's that, Sam?"

"Who is the killer?"

"Sam, you know how the body is always found by the night watchman?"

"Yeah?"

"It's the night watchman. And we will be taking him downtown for 'questioning'." Fred emphasized with his fingers with quotes when he mentioned the word, "questioning", in order sarcastically prove that the night watchman was really under arrest for murder.

Indeed, the night watchman was guilty of murder as founded by the court system. His sentence turned out to be light – a death sentence by hanging within two weeks of his sentence. He had no chance to appeal his case.

Jane headed up to her room. She was exhausted from a full day of New Year's Eve celebrations and she had quite a bit to drink. After she closed and locked the door behind her. Jane felt a cool breeze blowing through her face. Perhaps, the radiator is on the blink again. She must let maintenance know about the radiator problem as she made a mental note to herself.

After she shut the curtains on the windows to prepare herself for the nightly ritual of changing into her bedclothes, there stood a man at the door and recognized him to be the night watchman. "You've scared me," Jane said out loud. "I was about to report that my radiator is on the fritz again and I wish to get it fixed tomorrow."

The night watchmen stood silent and just gave Jane a blank stare. Jane stared back in a hypnotic state. The night watchmen pointed up towards the ceiling. Jane sees a rope noose hanging from the rafters and a stool in front of her. She steps up on top the stool and puts the noose around her neck.

A white lady ghost appears. She has the utmost beauty and the looks similar to a nun. As she comes closer in front of Jane, the white lady lifts her mask. Frightened of what she saw underneath the mask, Jane kicks the stool out of the way and drops.

Jane is a new statistic. She was a virgin staying in the suicide room despite knowing the suicide room legend. She is now part of that legend. The legend still continues.

Fear Of The Bomb: Public Perception and the Federal Civil Defense Administration[85]

As I went through my research, I was slowly able to piece together the Cold War hysteria through multiple brochures, periodicals, and military government documents. Being a child of the latter half of the Cold War, I had often wondered about the reasoning of "Duck And Cover," the fallout shelter, the psychology of the fallout shelter, and the alerting process of the Cold War.

Even though there was some common knowledge in Washington State that an atomic missile could be aimed towards our bases such as the Bangor Nuclear Submarine Base or the McChord Air Force Base, the whole idea of protecting ourselves from this sort of disaster hadn't really been brought up very often through my education as a child of the eighties. However, "Duck and Cover" was still strongly encouraged when it came to a yearly earthquake drill. Little did I know, as a child, the "Duck and Cover" method from earthquakes through the education of schools originated from the drill performed many times on the children of the fifties and sixties.

As an agency created by Truman in 1950, public response of the Federal Civil Defense Administration had a downturn. Because of the Federal Civil Defense Administration had cried wolf so many times, the public had a negative response over the seriousness of the matter. That negative response was that the Federal Civil Defense Administration was considered to be a useless agency and the public would more than likely take the threat of nuclear warfare as a serious cause. It was the public that changed the federal agency through the poor response of drills. The public mostly came to a consensus that they were going to be deceased when nuclear warfare were to happen.

The public response still has not changed much despite the multiple name changes between the Federal Civil Defense Administration in 1950 to the Federal Emergency Management Agency in the 1979 after a series of major natural disasters in the sixties and seventies. It was a Catch-22 for the government agency where its sole purpose is to protect the public from harm. If the government protect the public from harm, then the country's tax base stable, and then the US

[85] Normally, I am pretty busy with my school work and my studies on History (especially Modern History). This is one of those really long papers.

government could stay exist as a superpower. But, if the public does not respond well with the warning systems that the government agency puts into place, there goes the US government infrastructure.

When it comes to educating the public in the fifties and sixties, the most memorable historical icon was the "Duck and Cover" as a school drill rather than the shelter drills. This is mainly because the drill had lasted longer than the shelter drills with the exception of natural disasters such as tornadoes in the Mid-West. The only difference between "Duck and Cover" back in the fifties and sixties than in the present time is that "Duck and Cover" is used for protection against natural harm rather than atomic harm.

"Duck And Cover"

Ever since the Hiroshima and Nagasaki bombings in 1945, there had been a large concern over the safety of the individuals, but the idea that Russia had "the bomb" brought about a few legitimate concerns about the safety of oneself and their family. Because of the event being fresh in the memories of the public and the creation of the Federal Civil Defense Administration, guide books were often sold through the US Government Printing Office. One such book, *How To Survive an Atomic Attack* by Richard Gerstell, Ph. D. Gerstell, wrote the basic the basic idea of the future "Duck And Cover" procedure, which was pushed on children over and over again in from 1951 to the 1970s.[86]

Some questions were asked in a 3-day series article from the Chicago Sun- Times in the middle of the summer season called *What to do in an Atomic Attack*. The article read: "What would you do if an atomic bomb burst near enough to knock you down? Would you jump up and run away? Where would you run? Would you lie still for five minutes, then go to the aid for others near you? Would you commit suicide, thinking you were doomed to die a horrible death?"[87] Since the idea of an atomic attack was so new, the Federal Civil Defense Administration worried about three things: Injuries from debris, heat and flash burns, and radiation injuries. Very little was known about the fallout conditions. The Federal Civil Defense Administration and the Department of Defense

86 Gerstell, Richard. *How To Survive an Atomic Attack*. 1 ed. Washington, DC: Combat Forces Press, 1950.

87 "What To Do In An Atomic Attack." *Science Digest*, Nov. 1950, 69-73.

knew about the fallout from the Hiroshima and Nagasaki bombings, but still were unaware of the health problems that rose from the radiation.

Multiple tests were made in the Nevada Proving Grounds for the interests of the military and the Federal Civil Defense Administration, in which educational films were put out in order to educate the public about how atomic energy works and what to do about it. The Federal Civil Defense Administration came out with the first set of educational films such as *Survival Under Atomic Attack*, *Atomic Alert*, *Duck And Cover*, and *A Is For Atom* which were specifically aimed towards the public.

The well known Archer Productions of *Duck and Cover* was a winner of a contest held by the Federal Civil Defense Administration. The nine minute educational film aimed at school children. School children would protect themselves by jumping underneath their desks and put themselves in a fetal position. The idea was practiced for decades, assuming that an atomic bomb could explode on top of them anytime without warning. However, the Archer Productions had a few things that appealed to children across the United States: a catchy tune and a cartoon. A cartoon of turtle named Bert with a Civil Defense helmet jumps into his shell when a monkey in a tree with a firecracker on a stick sets the explosive. The firecracker explodes, thus injuring the monkey and the tree, but Bert the Turtle is still in tip top condition. The concept was simple and it endured throughout the film. The idea was so popular that comic books, coloring books, and brochures were made with Bert the Turtle. A 45 RPM record single was made with the song sung by Dick "Two-Ton" Baker[88] and a radio show that premiered a few months later.[89]

The idea of finding some sort of shelter and "Duck and Cover" were simple procedures based off of the idea of creating some sort of protection in case of an immediate disaster. It was only natural that disaster preparedness was based on getting into a fetus position and protecting yourself behind a wall in order to escape danger. For years, farmers in the Midwest section of the United States would often "duck and cover" themselves while seeking shelter from a tornado storm or out on the East Coast during a hurricane or even the earthquakes in the entire West Coast. It was the best form of protection that one could look

88 Geerhart, Bill. *Atomic Platters: Cold War Music from the Age of Homeland Security*. Hamburg, Germany: Bear Family Records, 2005.

89 *Duck And Cover.* 9 minutes. Archer Productions, 1951.

after. The only difference between the original shelters and the fallout shelter was a minor modification for the long haul. But, the sole idea of actually looking for some sort of heavy duty structure to hide under and put yourself in a fetal position was a pure and simple natural human instinct.

In 1963, there was full concern about the idea of "Duck and Cover" and what it did to children from the psychological community. According to the *Science-Newsletter,* Dr. Isidore Ziferstein, a psychologist from Los Angeles, California, believed that the children would often look to the sky to see if the planes above them would drop something. Mothers would report that their children would be coming home frightened after a school drill. Even a teenage couple made plans for dying in each other's arms when Armageddon finally arrived. A Washington D.C. teacher reassured her students that it was very unlikely that there would be a World War III, but being prepared for a World War III was just as important.[90] Her students were forever confused.

In the sixties, "Duck and Cover" was not enough for school drills. There were fallout shelter drills as well.

The Fallout Shelter

Fallout shelter construction did not happen by accident. After a major debate between the Director of the Office of Civil Defense, Fiorello Henry La Guardia and First Lady Eleanor Roosevelt in 1941,[91] Eleanor Roosevelt felt that the best way to bring the public to safety was to make people evacuate the cities. La Guardia, on the other hand, retorted against Roosevelt and said that the shelter system would have been more logical and was easier to move a mass amount of people around. La Guardia had won the debate. And so, the idea of the shelter was born.

---

90 Stafford, Jane. "If Atom Bomb Hits." *Science-Newsletter*, 30 Sept. 1950, 218-219. http://links.jstor.org/sici?sici=0096-4018%2819500930%2958%3A14%3C218%3AIABH%3E2.0.CO%3B2-M (accessed Feb. 14, 2008).

91 Winkler, Allan M. "A 40-year history of civil defense." *Bulletin of Atomic Scientists*, June 1984, 16-22.

Commercial films, such as *The House in the Middle*[92], promoted their wares in the hopes of making a profit from its customers. For example, *The House in the Middle* promoted the idea of keeping the place clean and a fresh coat of paint. However, the idea of painting your home to prevent your home from burning down in case of an atomic explosion was brought to you by the National Paint, Varnish and Lacquer Association.

Within the greater extent, there was further testing that had to be done. Along the Nevada Proving Grounds as of May 5, 1955, Operation Cue becomes the largest testing that not only involve the military, but also the Civil Defense workers, volunteers, and the media. But, to understand how to build a structure, you must be able to understand the nature of the Atomic Bomb itself.

The science of the Atomic Bomb going off is very simple. Let's say the mission of the A-bomb was to drop it from an airplane. Once the bomb hits the ground, a mass load of energy is released, including ultraviolet light and then an extreme heat spreading through the air. The sonic boom could be felt as all of this mass load of energy spreads quickly through the atmosphere in a horizontal motion as it dissipates slowly the further away you get away from the blast.

Operation Cue, with a nickname of "Cue for Survival", was considered to be a successful operation as it was being tested on Yucca Flat at 5:10 in the morning. The test was detonated by the Atomic Energy Commission from a 500-foot tower with an approximate power of thirty kilotons of T.N.T. There were 65 experiments associated with the test including food, clothing, shelter, mobile homes and emergency vehicles, power, and communications. Operation Cue had three functions: a) Observation, b) Field Exercise Program, and c) civil effects tests. Over two hundred companies and their associations took part of the test with over one hundred observed as representatives of these companies. Over five hundred people observed excluding the company representatives. This makes approximately six hundred to eight hundred observers of this operation which is now considered to be the largest test of its kind as an observation and an exercise combined.

Needless to say, there were some things that actually did survive. Take the mobile homes as an example. If they were placed against the blast, then they didn't survive very well. However, if the mobile homes were

92 *House In The Middle.* 12:09. National Paint, Varnish, and Lacquer Association, 1954.

placed into front first of the blast, they structures still withstood the blast. Surprisingly, the towers and the lines for both telephone and power withstood the testing. Even though these structures would not be able to replace the shelter, it could still provide the essentials of the after effects of the emergency needs of the public in survival mode.

The fallout shelter structures did withstood under the most extreme of conditions. First, it must be able to withstand an atomic blast from approximately two thousand and four thousand air pressure per square inch. This pressure change could cause multiple things to the human body, including causing deafness within a single blow and/or causing blindness. Most structures would have to withstand that pressure moving at approximately seven thousand five hundred feet per second and be able to face extreme heat of ten thousand degrees Centigrade.

Since no structure could actually survive such a blow, the Federal Civil Defense Administration recommended that one could survive in a shelter underground or an underground basement with concrete walls and ceiling in order to withstand the blast effects. The shelter would have to endure one more thing besides just the sonic bursts of energy that atomic blasts give out and that would be able to provide survivable conditions due to radioactive fallout conditions. Operation Cue was to provide real life situations in case nuclear warfare were to really happen. As it turns out, survival in a shelter was a little bit more complicated in construction as one might think.[93]

Surviving The Bomb

The Federal Civil Defense Administration not only provided guides to the public for basic shelter survival, but created basic provisions that were essential for shelter survival. A typical shelter would be stocked with the following supplies: Food and water (ie. Survival biscuits and crackers, waters, and carbohydrate supplements), Medical and Sanitation supplies (ie. Alcohol, aspirin, laxatives, toilet tissue), Radiological Defense Kit, Safety items (ie. Flashlight, pales of sand), Communications (ie. Battery powered radio), Sleeping equipment, Administrative supplies (ie.

93 Federal Civil Defense Administration. *Cue For Survival: Operation Cue, AEC Nevada Test Site, May 5, 1955*, 1955. Washington, DC: US Government Printing Office, 1955.

Logs and paperwork), and Informational and Training materials (ie. Shelter handbook, and religious materials)[94].

There was complete hierarchy within the shelter system when it came to managing a fallout shelter as well. The hierarchy begins with the Shelter Manager as the top official usually employed or a volunteer of the Federal Civil Defense Administration. The rest of the chain of command were team leaders (ie, communications, temporary safety, etc.). These team leaders are generally volunteers or appointed by the Shelter Manager, thus giving everyone a job to do within their specific field.

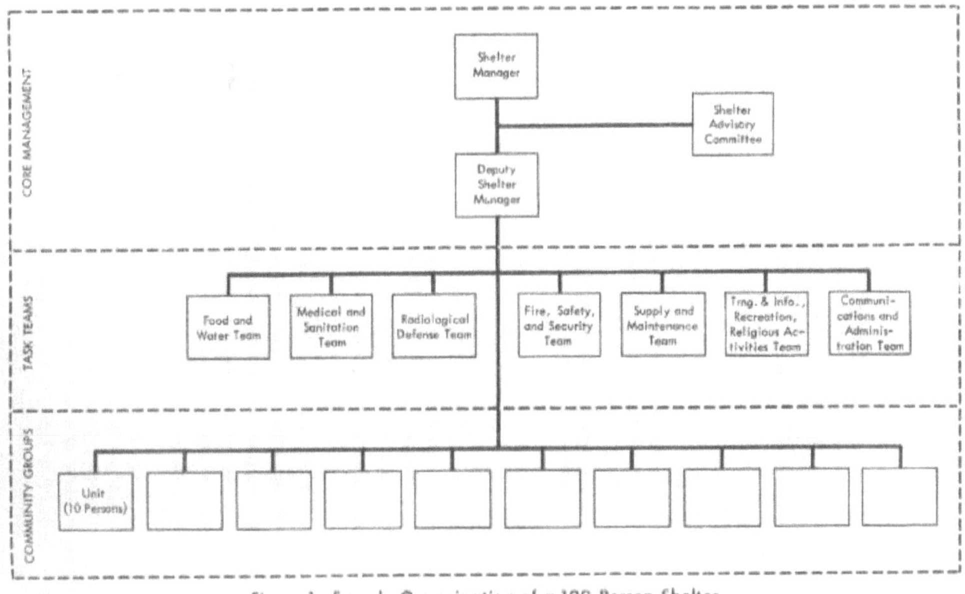

Figure 1. Sample Organization of a 100-Person Shelter

Illustration 1: A sample of the hierarchy of shelter management from the Civil Defense Shelter Management Handbook

Shelter attendees have to be able to endure a full fourteen days in order to minimize the side effects of radiation sickness. Unfortunately, one cannot live off of survival biscuits and water alone. A regimented activity

94 Department of Defense & Office of Civil Defense. *Handbook For Fallout Shelter Management*, 1966. 1966.

schedule was created by the Federal Civil Defense Administration in order to provide some sort of mind games in order to prevent the occupants from having mental breakdowns while being imprisoned inside the shelter for fourteen days. Most schedules had increments of every half hour with a different activity from waking up the occupants at seven o'clock in the morning with a Reveille to trained sessions for adults and educational training sessions for the children to planned recreational activities.[95]

The University of Georgia had conducted multiple tests under the concept of providing the mental and physical state of those who are confined in a shelter situation. Their last study had to do with new recruits of the United States Navy who were bored stiff and ended up playing with homemade playing cards to play poker and using match sticks as antes for their bets (The United States Navy forbid gambling at that time). However, on April 27, 1965 through May 10, 1965, John A. Hammes, Thomas R. Ahearn, and James F. Keith, Jr. conducted an experiment through the University of Georgia to see if a shelter could be survivable with limit supplies and space. According to *The Journal of Clinical Psychology,* "Thirty shelterees, 15 males, 15 females, aged 7-66, participated in the following two-week test. Stress conditions included 8 sq. ft./person of living space, and rations consisting of 1 qt./person/day of water and 900 cal./person/day of survival biscuits. Shelterees slept on a concrete floor covered only with 3/16-inch corrugated fiberboard. A chemical commode was provided. There were no bunks, no blankets, no water for bathing, no coffee, and only one pack of cigarettes permitted per smoker. Shelterees had no time pieces, and daylight clues were excluded from the enclosed shelter area."[96]

Other than needed supplies for survival, the occupants needed something to themselves mentally while spending those fourteen days. By the time the first night was over, the occupants became well acquainted with another and their surroundings. The researchers were not surprised with that result, but were surprised for the remainder of the study. The shelter occupants were required to fill out a journal, which included the date and time (what they thought was the time was while they were filling the journal out). Games were played, then a lecture on nuclear warfare,

---

95 To view a typical schedule, go to Appendix I

96 Hammes, John A, Thomas R. Ahearn, and James F. Keith, Jr.. "A Chronology of Two Weeks' Fallout Shelter Confinement." *Journal of Clinical Psychology* (1965): 452-456.

and then a church service. The shelter occupants claimed that that religion was considered to be very comforting to them.

During the first week, the shelter occupants had a mock wedding, in which the Shelter Manager was a groom and twelve year old girl was selected as the bride. They had a mock divorce court during the second week. Some homemade playing cards were made to pass some of the occupants' times. Some major body odor was sensed by the third day. The Shelter Manager complains nightly that the shelter was too hot and they need to open the ventilation system, but the researchers denied the order. In the end of the study, after the last commode was sealed off, the shelter occupants held a farewell banquet and expressed their gratitude of being a part of the experiment.

As in the past shelter experiments, the occupants would be willing to participate while being in the shelter for two weeks without any problem so long as they were able to keep their minds occupied. It was very common that fallout shelters would get hotter and hotter in the occupancy stage of two weeks. Temperatures sometimes start at a mere freezing thirty-five degrees and end at approximately eighty-five degrees if it was not well ventilated because of the crowded space. However, if the ventilation was to be controlled by the Shelter Manage for comfort of the occupants, then this could defeat the purpose of avoiding the high radiation levels to be unacceptable towards the health of the shelter occupants.

Other factors that lacked in all the shelter studies is of the psychological implications that were provided by the occupants of not knowing whether or not they would see their family, friends, or acquaintances again after being confined in the space. It is natural in human emotions after a major disaster to worry about their acquaintances. I suppose, some counseling would be provided in a perfect shelter setting, but this is not always guaranteed.

One might not survive an atomic attack without the advance alert and the Federal Civil Defense Administration had been able tackle that problem.

Alerting The Public

Multiple systems were put into place when it came to alerting the public. First off, the former remnants of World War II, the air raid sirens, were one such alert system. However the air raid siren presented a few problems. First, the air raid siren didn't work as well with a lack of education towards the public. Even though brochures were still being printed, the air raid sirens served the same purpose as they did World War II. One problem: it is different kind of war now. It was a new war dubbed as the "Cold War".

Second, the air raid siren provided only one thing and that was an attack from the air, but not other ways of protecting the public through intercontinental ballistic missiles or even by the sea. However, the air raid siren acted as a preparation piece by notifying the public that they needed to seek shelter immediately if they weren't listening to the broadcast stations.

Under Executive Order number 10312 signed on December 10, 1951 provided the new broadcast emergency system better knows CONELRAD (an acronym of **Con**trol of **El**ectromagnetic **Rad**iation). The new system required all broadcasters as enforced through the Federal Communications Commission to provide a set frequencies to be dedicated to the President's message during a national emergency.

Broadcasters were required to change the crystal of their transmitters[97] to be set from their designated frequency to 640 AM or 1240 AM and broadcast the president's message. These were designated for the major radio stations, however, the secondary stations were required to shut down their transmitters as well as the television stations. The idea was to create as much confusion from the enemy and the enemy would eventually abort their mission and go home.

The Federal Civil Defense Administration came up with a huge campaign in the fifties and early sixties in radio and television spots in order to prepare the public to switch stations in case of a true emergency. Eventually, in 1963, the CONELRAD system was scrapped for a more reliable system: The Emergency Broadcast System (EBS) underneath the orders President John F. Kennedy due to radio stations going off the air during the last Annual Civil Defense Exercises, or better known as "Operation Alert".

---

97 Okay, a little technical here. Transmitters would work off of crystals that only resonate at certain frequencies. This prevented broadcasters from changing the frequency that they were assigned to by the Federal Communications Commission. So, in order to change frequencies for CONELRAD, major radio stations were required to shut down their transmitters, take out the old crystal, put the new crystal in that resonates at 640 kilocycles or 1240 kilocycles, and then turn on the transmitter. This was *not* a quick process.

Operation Alert was pushed to be nationwide when Dwight D. Eisenhower sent a memorandum[98] to Federal Agencies for participation in the Civil Defense Exercises on November 5, 1953. As the Federal Civil Defense Administration created the "Operation Alert" in 1954, the drill required all people to take part by "Duck and Cover" for fifteen minutes. Unfortunately, this was all I could gather of the operation with bits and pieces that didn't make sense while looking through the periodicals. I did, however, decided to search again for Operation Alert via the internet that made better sense.

According to PBS' *American Experience: Race for The Super bomb* web site: "Citizens in what were called the "target" areas were required to take cover for fifteen minutes. At the same time civil defense officials tested their readiness and their communications systems, and federal officials practiced evacuating from the capital. Even President Eisenhower left the White House for a tent city outside Washington. The following day newspapers routinely published reports of the fictitious attacks naming the number of bombs that were dropped in the mock alerts, the number of cities hit, and the number of casualties."

"In 1955, New York State made the failure to take cover during an Operation Alert exercise punishable with a fine of up to $500 and a year in jail. A small group of pacifists that included Catholic Worker Dorothy Day reacted to this law by staging a protest in Manhattan's City Hall Park. When the air raid sirens sounded, on June 15, 1955, the 27 protesters sat on park benches, surrounded by reporters. They explained that they were protesting the government's pretense that citizens could be protected in the event of a full-scale nuclear attack. The protesters were arrested and given suspended sentences."

"The pacifists held similar protests every year. But it wasn't until a group of young mothers organized a much larger-scale demonstration in 1960 that the rest of New York took notice. The women managed to draw hundreds of protesters, including celebrities like Norman Mailer, to City Hall Park on May 3, the day of the 1960 Operation Alert. The organizers appealed to the political center; encouraged protesters to dress in their best clothes and to bring their children; and claimed to represent just one belief: 'Peace is the only defense against nuclear war.'"

"There was one more Operation Alert in 1961. The young mothers managed to bring together two-and-a-half-thousand protesters. That year civil defense protests also took place in other states, and

98 US Presidential Memorandum 195, September 25, 1953

hundreds of college students staged demonstrations on several East Coast campuses. In 1962 Operation Alert was permanently canceled."[99]

Indeed, the web site summed up what I was going to say nicely and I couldn't have been able to quote from a better source. *New York Times* and other periodicals spoke of very little of these news events, so the puzzle of "Operation Alert" would have been very confusing to me if I hadn't found it at the last minute.

In 1962, CONELRAD stopped its testing and "Operation Alert" was disbanded and a new system was to be put into place: The Emergency Broadcast System (EBS). The Emergency Broadcast System was simple: In case of a national emergency, simulcast the major radio station for news and information. In some cases, radio and television stations simply notified the public of a national emergency and then shut down their transmitters. The major radio station that did the news and information would receive a phone call from the White House Communications Agency with a code that matches the radio stations card, hear the message, and then provide the news and information for the public. It was an easy system and nearly dummy proof. Unfortunately, it had one minor flaw: It was for military emergencies only. The Emergency Broadcast System was eventually replaced by the Emergency Alert System in 1997 with more agencies involved.[100]

Putting It To The Test

With the event of the Cuban Missile Crisis in October 1962, Americans got the scare treatment and the demand of fallout shelters went up. Shelter manufacturers and salesmen couldn't keep up. On the other hand, for those who were waiting by the bases or on the East Coast did care if the Soviets planted their missiles in Cuba aimed towards the United States. Unfortunately, the fear of a World War III was only

99 "*PBS: American Experience: Race for The Super bomb.*" n.d. http://www.pbs.org/wgbh/amex/bomb/peopleevents/pandeAMEX64.html (accessed May 5, 2008).

100 Just a side note: I worked in the radio and television business for fourteen years including the founding of one radio station in Ocean Shores, so I had to know the Federal Communications Commission's regulations well. From 1990-2004, I really got know everything about emergency alertness in the broadcast industry. I was also a part of the development group for the Emergency Alert System for the State of Washington. This reminds me of a quote for an EAS manual that I wrote for training operators: "Push the EAS button, get underneath the console in a fetal position and kiss it goodbye."

isolated mainly on the East Coast and California. No psychological or sociological research had been found before writing this paper.

According to a survey called *Community Attitudes And Action On The Fallout Shelter Issue: A Case Study of Two Communities – Livermore, California and Norwalk, Connecticut*, that 61% were in favor of a shelter in Norwalk and 37% were in favor of a shelter in Livermore when the survey was conducted in October 22, 1962. Of those polled in Livermore, 66% were in favor of community shelters during pre-crisis and swelled to 76% during post-crisis. However, there was still a small number who were in favor of the private shelters, thus leaving the fallout shelters for the government. There were lower numbers in Norwalk, Connecticut where 64% favored community shelters and 29% preferred private shelters.[101] With such a low number of people with interests of a private shelter, the idea of people having it buried in their backyard is really an urban myth since most Americans did not have a high enough socio-economic status. With the children polled on May 1966, there was an even higher percentage rate in favor of community shelters (70%) over private shelters (62%)[102]. Remember, these are children that know very little about Hiroshima and Nagasaki bombings except of what they heard from their elders. The children at this time grew up during the Cold War, but do not know how it started while enduring the school drills of "Duck and Cover" and institutional shelters.

Bibliography

Committee of Armed Services of the House of Representatives. *Federal Civil Defense Act of 1950 as Amended February 1, 1983*, 1983. Washington, DC: US Government Printing Office, 1983.

101 Office of Civil Defense & Department of Defense. *Community Attitudes and Action On The Fallout Shelter Issue: A Case Study of Two Communities - Livermore, California and Norwalk, Connecticut*, 1963. Beverly Hills, CA: 1963.

102 Office of Civil Defense & Department of Defense. *Development of Values and Beliefs in Young Americans Toward Fallout Shelters And Civil Defense (Pilot Study 1)*, 1966. 1966.

Department of Defense & Office of Civil Defense. *Handbook For Fallout Shelter Management*, 1966. 1966.

Duck And Cover. 9 minutes. Archer Productions, 1951.

Eisenhower, Dwight D. "*American Presidency Project.*" 25 Sept. 1953. http://www.presidency.ucsb.edu/ws/index.php?pid=9706&st=Civil+Defense+Exercise&st1= (accessed Apr. 17, 2008).

Federal Civil Defense Administration. *Cue For Survival: Operation Cue, AEC Nevada Test Site, May 5, 1955*, 1955. Washington, DC: US Government Printing Office, 1955.

Federal Communications Commission. *CHR 50*, 1951. Washington, DC: US Government Printing Office, 1952.

Geerhart, Bill. *Atomic Platters: Cold War Music from the Age of Homeland Security.* Hamburg, Germany: Bear Family Records, 2005.

Gerstell, Richard. *How To Survive an Atomic Attack.* 1 ed. Washington, DC: Combat Forces Press, 1950.

Hammes, John A, Thomas R. Ahearn, and James F. Keith, Jr.. "A Chronology of Two Weeks' Fallout Shelter Confinement." *Journal of Clinical Psychology* (1965): 452-456.

House In The Middle. 12:09. National Paint, Varnish, and Lacquer Association, 1954.

Office of Civil Defense & Department of Defense. *Community Attitudes and Action On The Fallout Shelter Issue: A Case Study of Two Communities - Livermore, California and Norwalk, Connecticut*, 1963. Beverly Hills, CA: 1963.

Office of Civil Defense & Department of Defense. *Development of Values and Beliefs in Young Americans Toward Fallout Shelters And Civil Defense (Pilot Study 1)*, 1966. 1966.

"*PBS: American Experience: Race for The Super bomb.*" n.d. http://www.pbs.org/wgbh/amex/bomb/peopleevents/pandeAMEX64.html (accessed May 5, 2008).

Stafford, Jane. "If Atom Bomb Hits." *Science-Newsletter*, 30 Sept. 1950, 218-219. http://links.jstor.org/sici?sici=0096-4018%2819500930%2958%3A14%3C218%3AIABH%3E2.0.CO%3B2-M (accessed Feb. 14, 2008).

Truman, Harry S. "*Harry S. Truman Library and Museum.*" n.d. http://www.trumanlibrary.org/executiveorders/index.php?pid=280&st=radio&st1= (accessed Mar. 30, 2008).

"US, Soviet Nuclear Weapons Stockpile, 1945-1989: Numbers of Weapons." *Bulletin of Atomic Scientists*, Nov. 1989, 53.

"What To Do In An Atomic Attack." *Science Digest*, Nov. 1950, 69-73.

Winkler, Allan M. "A 40-year history of civil defense." *Bulletin of Atomic Scientists*, June 1

Alternative Anthems for Different Countries[103]

Scotland

Oh Scotland!

We have the thistle and the Stone Destiny.

We have the St. Andrews Cross and the Whiskey.

Ireland

Oh Ireland!

We have leprechauns and potatoes.

Potatoes for breakfast, lunch and tea and snacks and dessert.

England

Oh England!

We have the Queen.

United States of America

Oh USA!

We have rednecks and chicks.

We have the porn industry and the man is always keeping us down.

Canada

Oh Canada!

We have maple syrup and Molson's

We have back bacon, not ham or Canadian Bacon

It snows here and we have Mounties who play curling

---

[103] No, these are not the real words to national anthems from around the world. I wrote this piece in St. Andrews, Scotland and was amazed how diverse in culture the whole town is. Everyone was from different countries around the world! However, I never did well with keeping all the national anthems straight……and that includes the one national anthem from the country I am from: USA.

You must speak English and French all at the same time

Germany

Oh Germany!

We have trees and foosball tables

We have beer and lederhosen.

Russia

Oh Russia!

We have vodka and snow

Amsterdam

Oh Amsterdam!

We have hookers and pot.

France

Oh France!

We have wine and the French language

Don't come near us because we haven't taken a bath in ages

That is why we invented perfume.

The Big Birthday Surprise[104]

Lynda Redgrave was a wealthy woman from her inheritance. By all means, she knew how to throw herself a big party. All she needed was to bring her friends, get a classic band together, and large amounts of food to keep the guests happy. Being a long, slender woman that looked like a giraffe trying to reach a branch on top of a tree, Lynda wanted to do something different this year. Yet still single, she was about to hit her fifties.

Her father, a wealthy man himself, couldn't figure out what to give her as a gift. He didn't want to give Lynda Redgrave a husband, something she desperately needed since she left the home at age eighteen. Last year, he brought in the magistrate to give Lynda Redgrave a new name as a gift. Being a name of Sallie Mae Mac, he named her after Sallie Mae and Freddie Mac which was a part of his portfolio. However, Lynda Redgrave accepted her new name since the companies weren't doing very well. She knew her father loved her just the same.

Lynda Redgrave knew father was going provide something special for her big birthday bash that may become a better than it had been in the past. There was always some way where one would top the other on a yearly basis. She just didn't know what it would be, because, after all, it was only a birthday surprise. To Lynda Redgrave, just accepting the thought was what counted and not the gift in itself. She would have been very happy with a simple homemade present from her father which was something she would eventually face when she was going to admit him to a nursing home in about six months.

Yes, nursing homes would often have "craft night" in order to please the residents who live there. Lynda remembered crafts when she was growing up when she was five years old. All she could remember was making ashtrays. Hopefully, she won't be receiving any ashtrays from her father. Nobody smokes anymore.

The big day had arrived. The guests arrived in droves to Lynda Redgrave's party. Champagne and live music was in the air. Then came

---

[104] After closing the book and saying that "I am taking a hiatus from book writing," I came up with this story. It all started from a dream and I had to write it down as quickly as possible. This shows the roughness of the story.

the announcement from her father. "I have an announcement to make," her father said as he put his glass down. "Lynda, my dear child, you have been getting so much from me in the past. Now it is time for you to have your own family. So, I sold you to a gentlemen and his son." The crowd reacted. How could a father sell his daughter like a slave or a mail order bride? "Today, Lynda, you are married in an arranged marriage that I had been working on for several years a payback for putting me into a nursing home. Do you realize that I hat "craft night" especially since I hat making ashtrays out of clay…… and I don't even smoke! Happy Birthday and congratulations on your marriage, Lynda. I hope you enjoy your new life with your husband and your son. They can help you more than I can after you have been taking money away from me for such a long time." Her stepped down and pulled Lynda to the side so she could meet her new family. "This is God, and this is the son of God, Jesus."

Myths Unveiled: The Social History of The Evergreen State College[105]

Introduction

What are *myths* and why do we hale these urban legends? Throughout the history of The Evergreen State College, the students, faculty, and staff members often pass on the grapevine of what they heard and put it down as their own interpretation of these stories. The college is full of its small conspiracies and lacks a positive reputation in the Washington state especially in the surrounding communities. This may because they have never *actually experienced* The Evergreen State College and its interdisciplinary learning. The Evergreen State College is different from other colleges: a school with no grades with a study what you want type of atmosphere.

It's not just the learning style that gives the college a bad name within Washington state, but it was the students that were causing the poor reputation to grow. This is much harder to maintain or prove your point that college is really a legitimate institution and that an undergraduate degree is not given to you but you must earn the degree in order to receive it.

I will examine the stories of the college and take a look at the truth behind these stories. These stories show in different forms: from written stories that are well documented to plaques to rooms to simple objects. Whatever the form, it tells a story to the public whether it is long or it is short, or even a mystery of why it shows up.

In this writing, I will examine why legislatures thought about changing the college into a prison and the several closing attempts. I will take a look at the items of the 1000-acre woods. I have taken a couple of oral histories including the story of the building of the Organic Farm House and a man who believed that he should get some sort of

105105 Okay, this is a report that I wrote for The Evergreen State College on March 11, 2009. Other than a few grammar mistakes, most of the feedback was "this report is not 'academic' enough. I disagree. I prefer the journalistic approach and tell people just the story. This writing will be scrapped and I will have to go into "academic" writing mode. Also, the formatting may be off just a bit. I tried to fix the problem, but sometimes the best stuff must get deleted. Unfortunately, I had to cut out the pictures and captions in order to fix this formatting problem.

recognition of his efforts on building it. To make it more interesting I will explain one of the many tragedies that plague the history of the college. Coming out of tragedy, I talk about the ghosts of The Evergreen State College. At the end, I will talk about Happy Land. Does Happy Land really exist? But, first, I will discuss the story that comes from the depths underneath us or better known as the steam tunnels.

It Came From the Steam Tunnels

Many misconceptions of the steam tunnels come from The Evergreen State College rumor book. Some stories are easy to conceive due to the lack of the visual, where people know that the Steam Tunnels do exist, but very few people have actually been in them. Stories from where UFOs are living underneath the college grounds to the "easy access for the National Guard to disengage the troops for future protests." The National Guard and the protests seem to be a re-occurring theme when it comes to the Evergreen student protestors. Even though most of these rumors are completely bogus, I was able to find an ounce of truth based off of these stories when it comes to the steam tunnels. Unfortunately, I did not find much of these stories told of the steam tunnels until much later after the tour.

The Evergreen State College wanted to conserve energy before it was fashionable. In 1971, a Central Utility Plant was built in order to facilitate a large sum of 12,000 students that were expected in 1985[106]. Because the college was set in a rural area, and to prevent an overload on the power grid, Central Utility Plant was built along with a maintenance tunnel that housed the steam, communication lines, and electricity.

I took a tour of the Central Utility Plant (CUPs) on January 30, 2009 with a maintenance worker named "Ed"[107] who showed me around the tunnels and the steam plant. The steam plant uses city water where it is pressurized, cooled, filtered, and heated for the distribution of the steam throughout the tunnels. The steam plant has two of everything which could either be used in parallel or as backup (the second machinery is normally used for backup purposes). When the water gets heated in the boiler system, the fuel used can be switched between Natural Gas and Oil, depending on the cheapest fuel source at the time. Needless to say, I didn't pay much attention on the manufacturing of steam since my main interest was one thing: the steam tunnels – the land of legends and mystery.

We hopped on the yellow electrical cart where he started to give me the tour of the tunnels. "The tunnels have a 6% grade," he said while

106 (Durham, Anderson & Freed 1968)

107 I couldn't catch his last name due to the loud noise throughout the steam plant, and I could remember only one thing on his maintenance uniform, a patch that said "Ed".

we slowly made our way through the enclosed space, "that means we are slowly going uphill." That explained the slow climb as we went through the main tunnel.[108] The tunnel connects to every single building throughout the campus (with the exception of the dorms). "As you can see," Ed explained, "it gets hotter and hotter as you move away from the plant. This makes sense since hot air rises."

The tunnel was large in both height and width, large enough to drive a semi truck through without the trailer[109]. Because of the large sum of racks carrying all the communication, electrical, steam, and water lines, the space is more confined where there is enough room for two to three people who are able to pass by each other with some extra room. Periodic escape hatches are placed every few yards along with fire extinguishers for emergency purposes. "Whoever designed this tunnel was really concerned about safety of the people stuck in the tunnels," Ed said while showing me one of the escape hatches, "I always feel really safe here even in an earthquake knowing that these things are here. If the water leaks, they have drains with sump pumps that will work so that way we don't drown down here."

It became apparent that the tour was over when the tunnel ended and split up into two directions. The left tunnel went to the LAB building and the right tunnel ended at Seminar I. Ed was right. The tunnel was really hot at the end of the steam tunnel. This was the end of the tour. So, I thank Ed and I was on my way. After the tour, I began to talk to other students and staff and began to find the stories of the steam tunnels.

The steam tunnels were open for contractors for anything from maintenance purposes to building concrete structures for the students. Unfortunately, those contractors were fairly careless from the 1970s well up to the mid-1980s by exiting through the escape hatches located throughout the campus[110]. Because of the carelessness of leaving the escape hatch unlocked or open, students soon discovered the steam tunnels running underneath their feet. Larry Savage, a long time worker of Police Services at The Evergreen State College said, "I once saw a

---

108 It turned out the electric cart had a low battery, which explains the slow climb. About half way through, we turned the electric cart around and then coasted our way back to the Central Utility Plant with a small push to the electrical outlet. I didn't mind walking……it was easier to take some picture!

109 The semi truck would get stuck if it had a trailer attached to it.

110 (Savage 2009)

teddy bear head on one of the racks of the tunnel back in the late eighties. I can't remember where and I am sure that is long gone by now."[111]

Another story I heard was about the mummified cat. The story goes something like this: *A small kitten accidently got into the steam tunnels one day in the 1990s and ended up stuck in between some floor boards. When it was soon discovered, the dead kitten was well preserved from the elements.*

The one story that seemed to be near true was the police that roamed within the steam tunnels. "One time, the police needed some training of their dogs to smell for bombs and drugs in extreme conditions. So, we planted a few of these bags throughout the steam tunnel for the dogs to sniff for them," said Savage.

"There were actually police officers running around with dogs without anybody knowing?" I asked.

"We let them. It was good training," he said.[112]

Nobody talks much about the steam tunnels now, but they do know they do exist. There were no aliens, unless the maintenance workers are actually disguised as humans (they seemed like real human beings!). There was no way for the National Guard to have access to the steam tunnels to take care of the protestors. It would not have been very simple nor be an easy access to the Red Square. Yes, the steam tunnels are big enough to drive large semis, but this would have been possible before the equipment was installed within those tunnels. I'd say these mythical stories are now de-bunked.

The 1000-Acre Woods

The 1000-acre woods are often a place where students go to escape and relax while performing their studies at the college. Surrounding the green brushy forest land is Geoduck Beach, Overhulse Road, F Parking lot, Driftwood Road, Sunset Beach Road, Lewis Road, and Marine Drive. The forestland isn't exactly a thousand acres, but it

---

[111] (Savage 2009)

[112] (Savage 2009)

gives more of a Winnie The Pooh type of feel. The woods are much more than just a place for students and the public to enjoy the natural beauty that surrounds them and the students like to camp out in the woods or even hang out for relaxation. This "hanging out" brings out things that pop out if you didn't know where to look for them.

Geoduck Beach

The Geoduck (pronounced as goo' ee duck) Beach was named after the Geoduck, a giant clam that lives on the naturally preserved beach.[113] Every spring, you can see them squirting the water as high as a fountain. Since the Geoduck is native in the Pacific Northwest, there seems to be an abundant of them in the southern part of the Puget Sound. Geoducks are fairly expensive with current rate in 2009 at $18 per pound,[114] but considered to be an Asian delicacy in sushi bars. The Nisqually Indian tribe first coined the animal as "dig deep" which is exactly what you have to do in order to catch them.

The beach has another reputation besides the natural surroundings of the Geoduck is more natural……exposure. For the longest time, Geoduck Beach had been known as a nudist beach. A once secluded place that only pertained to Evergreeners, Geoduck Beach eventually became popular from one independent out of print book written by an alumni, *100 Best Nude Beaches in North America.*[115] Since then, people from all around the world have been bearing all at the beach.

Nudity at The Evergreen State College is not a new thing. In fact, the college would hold a weekly nude swim meet every Friday for a full decade between the mid-70s and mid-1980s.[116] "They had to stop nude swimming much like they had to stop the nude beach," Larry Savage, a current dispatcher from The Evergreen State College's Police Department, said, "there were too many perverts hanging around."[117]

---

113 Digging a Geoduck is very highly illegal on this beach and if you are caught by an Evergreener, they would more than likely give you the death penalty – with torture.

114 (Taylor Shellfish Farms 2008)

115 (Savage 2009)

116 (Savage 2009)

117 (Savage 2009)

The beach is no longer nude due to the publicity and safety reasons.[118] One can not only get fined, but be labeled as a sex offender.

Gnome Swamp

The Gnome Swamp is a wetland within the woods guarded by Lawn Gnomes. In the middle of the swamp you will see a rustic tree house. Nobody lives in the tree house, but used by students. It is said that these lawn gnomes help fend off evil spirits that live within the swamp.

"Green Man" Tree

Approximately where "Gnome Swamp" is located is "Green Man" Tree and is often dubbed as "The King".[119] The tree would be decorated with metal trinkets. The "Green Man" is a large cedar stump with the roots of another cedar tree growing up through the side and then on top of the cedar stump. Because of the way the tree is growing off the trunk, one could see hair, two eyes, a nose, a mouth, and a beard from the root system.

The "Green Man" is best known from Celtic symbolism which derives from the Arthurian Legends of the "Green Knight."[120] It is believed that this face is on everything from trees to finely carved furniture in order to ward off evil spirits. The original story of the "Green Knight" came from the story, *Sir Gawain and The Green Knight*, a poem written by Geoffrey Chaucer.

Z-Dorm

The Evergreen woods are full of these extra shelters called "Z-Dorm". Z-Dorm was coined by Evergreen students because the dorm buildings on the campus only go to the letter "U". However, there some people who would prefer to go back to the "basics" and be on one with nature by camping. These students are often labeled as transients since it

---

[118] No safety problems or crime have been reported due to nudity at the beach.

[119] "The King" is short for "King of the Forest"

[120] (Malory 2009)

is illegal to camp out in the forest, but it happens more often than one might think.

With the results of these Z-Dormers, the Evergreen woods are filled with four tree houses bounded against the trees. These tree houses are hard to find unless you really look for them, but you will find them to be all sizes ready to sleep in for anyone who would prefer to risk the elements when it comes to their environmental studies.

There are several theories why these Z-Dormers actually exist. One theory is that they can't find a place to live (homeless) or couldn't get into the dorms or apartment at Cooper's Glen due to financial or time problems. The second theory is they are actually studying nature and want to see if they can actually survive by getting back to the natural basics. The final theory is that they are not students and is they are a part of the homeless problem. Sometimes it is hard to spot a Z-Dormer since they blend into the population at Evergreen well.

Memorial Tree

As you walk into the meadowlands of the Evergreen forest, and look hard enough in an out of the way spot, you will see a tree planted in memory of someone. There are trinkets, colored stones, and one picture. When I asked staff members who had been at the college since it began, none of them knew this woman nor do they know that the tree was planted. It looked liked it may have been planted sometime between the late 1980s to early 1990s since all I could see was the style of glasses that were popular at the time. Do you know who this woman was?

"The Red Baron Was Here"[121]

Baron Stean was concerned about the lack of credit of his fellow students when he attended The Evergreen State College in 1975 when it came to the building of The Evergreen State College's Organic Farm House.[122]

[121] Stean did not want to be recorded. He said that he would rather write it down because he didn't want someone to judge as a "crazy old man". This interview was based off solely of the memory of the author.

[122] This entire section is based from the January 21, 2009 interview of Baron Stean.

After serving his duty in the Vietnam War, Baron Stean became a contractor for construction. There was one thing that haunted him: finish up school with an undergraduate degree. He came onto Evergreen as a student for the nights and weekends program. When he said that he was a contractor, Evergreen was delighted and said that this was the place for him. He didn't know that Evergreen would have something for him because all he knew of Evergreen was the "basket weaving" classes.[123] Stean came onto the campus at the right time and became one of the students who designed and built the Organic Farm House.

The Organic Farm House was meant to be a "green" building, a building that was meant to be constructed with all natural materials and ecological friendly. Many attempts of building a "green" building were tested and often became a failure through the Environmental Design Group who proposed the Organic Farm back in 1971[124]. The Organic Farm was modeled after the Santa Cruz and J.I. Rodale organic farms[125]. In January 1972, Environmental Design created the Environmental Structure Project (ESP) with multiple temporary experimental structures.[126] Since the structures became condemned ESP was scrapped. With the original farm house about to be torn down for

With a contracting background, Stean figured there was a proper way of building: excavating the land with a backhoe lay a cement foundation, order the lumber, and etc. He soon found out that he had to learn an entirely a different way of building all together. Instead, the house was to disturb very little of the environment. If it was needed to be torn down, all of the building could be torn down, recycled, and the land would be returned to what it once was before building the structure. The house used cement blocks as the foundation with poles to hold the main part of the structure up. The wood was from the trees from The Evergreen State College forest land. The trees were taken to a local mill and then returned in order to build the house.

"Do you know how hard it is to work with green wood," Stean asked. Indeed, green wood is harder to work with when building a

---

123 Evergreen always had different titles for different classes. In this case, much of the community had always assumed The Evergreen State College was a joke for education. I had to basket weaving in quotes meaning it is a joke of a class even though it is probably a very interesting type of program worth learning.

124 The Paper, December 13, 1971, vol. 1 no. 2

125 Ibid

126 The Paper, January 10, 1972, vol. 1 no. 3

structure. The green wood is not only heavier, but the structure has tendency to move if it is not properly dried. "You should have seen the faces of my fellow contractors when they heard that I had to work with green wood," said Stean. When it came to the roofing, Stean asked if he should order the cedar shingles. The Environmental Design group said no. They wanted to get the cedar from the cedar trees from The Evergreen State College forest and split the shingles themselves. He was surprised that the students hand split the shingles by themselves. Unfortunately, they ran out of cedar shingles half way through the roofing, and Stean ordered more shingles from a lumber yard.

Stean had to teach the students the proper way of building and supplied the nails. "Most of the students didn't know absolutely anything about building or even how to use a nail and hammer," Stean said, "I held workshops to train them in the building technology and have pay stubs from the college to prove it." He left once he got his BA in 1975 with just the deck and the interiors uncompleted.

In an Evergreen Newsletter from February 8, 1980, Stean heard about the completion of the Organic Farm House and a dedication ceremony on February 14th and he went to the ceremony. Michael Barron was given credit for the Organic Farm, but other people who deserved credit (ie. the designing crew) was never mentioned. Stean stopped the former state governor and then college president, Daniel J. Evans. "Evans said that he was very busy and didn't want to look at the matter of who should take credit and who should not take credit for the work of the Organic Farm House," said Stean, "I don't know who this Michael Barron is, and perhaps he deserves credit for things that he did after I left, but I think the students who helped build the Organic Farm House should deserve the same credit as Michael Barron."

Here is a list of those students –

> Designers & Building: Ralph Allen, Kieth Brown, Nathan Chess, Mike Corke, Eva Foster, Tim Graham, Bruce Need, Vern Jensen, Merritt Mount, Barbara Pell, Neil Pritz, Baron Stean, Rhyno Stinchfield, and Lorie Schley.
>
> Staff Advisor and Contract Supervisor: William Knauss[127]

127 The Evergreen State College Organic Farm House booklet, back page

However, Baron Stean did leave his mark when he left The Evergreen State College's Organic Farm House. On one of the poles holding up the building is carved in the wood: "Red Baron Was Here".

The Mystery

On the morning of October 3, 1974, a female body was found in front of Dorm A of The Evergreen State College at 2:30 in the morning. She had appeared to be stabbed in the abdomen and thrown off of the tenth story of the building. The girl was identified as Vicki Faye Schneider[128].

The year 1974 was a troubling for The Evergreen State College. Aside from the national Watergate Scandal and the impeachment of Richard Nixon and the constant battle of the Washington State Legislature wanting to axe the college, crime was beginning to be more and more abundant. The campus was known for the high drug use, graffiti, and larceny, but not a homicide.

Unfortunately, 1974 did consist of a murder of a missing girl name Donna Gail Manson on March 21st while she was abducted while walking to a jazz concert at The Evergreen State College, later on murdered by Ted Bundy, but nobody knew about knew it was a homicide in 1974 since Bundy didn't confess and mentioned the location of her body until the day before his execution in 1989. Yet, Washington State was in full fear of the man they called "Ted".[129]

The year, 1974, also had a rape, but later on the male was captured and sentenced for incarceration. Also, during a celebration, one of the students got drunk, fell off the top library bridge. He was in a body cast and said that it was a very stupid idea. Along with the stupidity, there was another factor to blame that contributed such a high amount of crime throughout the campus: High Security. Many people thought their rights were often taken away before The Evergreen State College Police Services came into existence. Students were often padded down before entering the Library Building.[130] Many students were claiming that The Evergreen State College was becoming a police state and were really

128 (Kramer 1974)

129 (Rule 2000)

130 Temporary classrooms were set up in the library as well as other services such as SAGA (the food service), the bookstore, the administration, and the library.

concerned about the death of Vicki Faye Schneider (who lived in B-Dorm) who just started in Peter Elbow's program entitled, "Self-Exploration Through Autobiography". Very little was known of her at the time since she had just arrived at the campus on September 16th. She was a B-Plus student who graduated from Highland High School in San Antonio, Texas. There, she attended San Antonio College for more than a quarter. October 2, 1974 was her 18th birthday.[131]

Due to large news coverage from KIRO-TV, KING-TV, and KOMO-TV as well as The Centralia Chronicle, The Daily Olympian, Seattle Times, Tacoma News Tribune, and the Seattle Post-Intelligencer, rumors spread throughout the campus the death of Vicki Faye Scneider. Many people felt unsafe by linking the unsolved murders around Washington State. Others linked the rape that happened earlier that year and claimed that Schneider was sexually assaulted. One rumor claimed that drugs or drinking may have been involved, but these rumors were proven to be false.

The rumors were dispelled at a four o'clock all-campus meeting in the first floor library lobby. Some 150-200 people showed up to hear what Thurston County Sheriff Don Redmond (who was a part of the Manson case) had to say. He reiterated throughout the meeting "that there was no proof that Schneider's death had been suicide, but added that there was nothing to prove otherwise."[132] The sheriff did not want the rumors to flourish. However, there was a stranger who may have been linked to Schneider's death. He was described as a "man in his twenties, five feet 10 inches, 160 pounds, with short blond hair parted to one side. The man was wearing a white cowboy shirt with blue trim, tan dress cowboy pants, and shined cowboy boots...." He was seen sleeping on the floor of the 5th floor of A-Dorm and was seen playing pool with her few hours before her death.[133]

After interviewing three hundred people, Sheriff Don Redmond took it to court in order to close the case on October 29, 1974. It was an apparent suicide where Vicki Faye Schneider tried to commit suicide by stabbing herself in the abdomen an inch above the navel with a kitchen knife where the sheriff's detectives found the wood handle twenty feet from her body. Brett Adams, an Evergreen student, said that he was

131 (Daily Olympian 1974)

132 (Kramer 1974)

133 (Kramer 1974)

attempting to fall asleep when he heard a "loud thud". He looked out the window and saw a pair of legs. He put on his coat, ran down the stairs and asked for assistance while the McLane Fire Department attempted to resuscitate Schneider which eventually failed.[134]

Detective Paul Barclift speculated, "She came off the roof. There were only three ways to get there. One would have been out through a window that had a bookcase in front of it. Secondly, she could have climbed up a pole which security people at the college had greased to keep students off the roof. The third way to get there was to climb up louvers over an air conditioner. There were footprints on the louvers, but we couldn't positively match them with Vickie's shoes." Barclift figured that the she went through the louver route. "Although the knife wound wasn't deep, the pain would have been excruciating. She may have stabbed herself and then passed out, or she may have stabbed herself as she jumped."[135]

Thurston County Sheriff's department came to the conclusion of Vicki Faye Schneider's death due to boyfriend troubles where she became very depressed. After reading her diary, it was a basic suicide, not just her depression where she was planning her demise for a long time.

Even though Vicki Faye Schneider's case is tragic, suicides are somewhat typical but cannot be proven. You will find no higher education reporting such statistics. This story was chosen due to the myth that *The Evergreen State College has a higher suicide rate than any other college nationally*. There are too many variables that constitute a suicide when it comes to college campuses. The variables could be anywhere from a drug overdose, whether the person is considered to be a student when they are actually taking a quarterly break from their academics, or if they are considered to be a student off the campus. Due to the lack of statistics and too many variables involved, this could be a myth or a factual statement that The *Evergreen State College has a higher suicide rate than any other college nationally*. It could use further investigation by someone else.

134 (Daily Olympian 1974)

135 (Daily Olympian 1974)

Evergreen Ghosts

Many people have seen strange things throughout the campus other than the unusual behavior that happens occasionally or the occasional unusually dressed characters. Somehow, the supernatural had been hanging around the campus whether we want them or not. I'm talking mainly about ghosts. The Evergreen State College had ghosts well before the institution was dreamed up, not just former students, staff or faculty as once thought.

From an open letter written to the *Daily Olympian* from October 31, 1968, The Churchman Family said there is a ghost currently living in their home that they would be certainly glad to pass on to the college. Mrs. Churchman wrote[136]:

To The Future Students of Evergreen State College:

We, the Churchman Family of the Lewis Road, west of Olympia, wish to leave a legacy to The Evergreen State College, which will occupy the land we have called home for the last ten years.

We have left now, after a reluctant sale of our home to the State of Washington. We leave behind us one small member of our family whom we found it impossible to move. We leave you our household ghost.

He came to us about four years ago and his presence has been a part of our lives since the day he entered our home unannounced. He is often heard walking about the house and gravel paths and he is often seen and heard opening the doors of the home and other buildings. He seems to be quite at home and comes at all hours of the day and night. He has never attempted to harm any member of the family.

Not only are we used to his comings and goings, but the family dogs ignore him though he is heard walking within a few feet of them. Sometimes they will look when he opens a door but never make a fuss about it.

We wonder why he chose our home. Was there something here that we never understood?

We are going to miss him but we feel our friend will be a good member of the new college. We wonder which group of students he will choose for his new companions when the school is finished and occupied. We hope you will be kind to him, future students, and accept him as we have Treat him well. He is our legacy to you.

---

136 (Nelson 1968)

The Churchman Family

Who this man is, and we may never know, but he does more than leaving doors open and making footstep noises throughout the campus. He [the ghost] has the tendency to leave the water running and leaving the lights on. The former property had 22 wooded acres and the building is still standing. The rambler was still new in 1968 (it was built in 1960)[137]. That rambler home is currently contracted out to the Olympia Community School, a non-profit private school for K-5[138]. It also goes by another name as "The Geoduck House".

When Joyce Nelson, a *Daily Olympian ghost writer*, came to interview Mrs. Churchman, who at that time was living a retired life with her husband, George, in the Wynoochie Valley, she followed up with another experience of the ghost.

"One night, I looked out and the barn door open and the wind was blowing on those ponies and the lights were on. I said to George, you sure like to pay a big light bill. Well, it turned out that he hadn't been out to the barn. No, it couldn't have been a stranger sleeping in the barn, either. We checked.

Another thing, the lady who lives in the red ranch house over there swears she's heard music from over here. Not us. She says he likes rock 'n' roll."[139]

It isn't just the ghost from the Geoduck House. There are said to be ghost stories of former students that are haunting the land. When I asked around for some ghost stories throughout the campus two people finally said something. "I once gave a ghost a back rub," said a current male student. "It was in the B-Dorm of my room."

A female student piped up and said something that was more believable of her experience. "My mother was a friend of Donna Gail Manson," said the student.

> Donna Gail Manson became of victim of the Ted Bundy in 1974, where Ted Bundy finally admitted the killing and told the detectives the exact location of her body the night before his

[137] (Thurston County Assessor 2008)

[138] (Olympia Community School (OCS) n.d.)

[139] (Nelson 1968)

execution in Florida in 1989. The detectives believed they found the body, but couldn't identify it because her skull was never found.[140] So, when this female student said the name, Donna Gail Manson, then my ears promptly perked up in full attention of listening to her story.

"I was in the dormitory kitchen," the female student started, "when I felt a hand patting me on my right shoulder. That was when I turned around and saw Donna Gail Manson's ghost. The ghost said do you know my mother by name and I said 'Yeah," and began to point to a picture I had handy with me." She pointed to the notebook that she carries with her at all times, and opened it to the page with a picture of her mother and then closed the notebook. "Then, the Donna Manson's ghost disappeared."

I am sure there are plenty of ghosts throughout the campus being a close knit community. As a person who has walked the campus buildings in the middle of the night, you do find creepy places. Most people I've talked to had only felt something creepy within the campus buildings. The Library Building, one of the oldest buildings on the campus, is no exception. There was rumors of a ghost walking through the hallowed halls of the building, but may have changed due to the remodeling of the building. Still, people do claim that they still feel something unusual in the basement or the old cafeteria on the fourth floor. There was a ghost sighted in the periodicals section and the main stacks on the third floor of the Library. In the LAB buildings, some people claim that the whole building is creepy, but find the basement more creepier than the rest of the building.

I, personally, find the SEM II fourth floor of the building a little paranormalish in the middle of the night. This eventually came true on March 3, 2009 when I was doing my patrols for Crime Watch, a student night watchman position ran by The Evergreen State College's Police Services. At about one am I was doing my patrols of the fourth floor of LAB I. I was about to get myself a cup of coffee at one of the vending machines (hey, I was tired and I needed the caffeine!) when one of the machines

140 (Rule 2000)

started to act up across the room. After hearing about Scott Scurlock (aka "Hollywood" who robbed banks in Seattle), an Evergreen student who hid in the halls to make meth in the college lab, I said, "Scott, would you quit it?" Suddenly the machine stopped. I got my coffee and went to the elevator in order to go to the next floor. That was when I realized I saw a ghost/poltergeist. "Wow," I said aloud, "I just saw a ghost!"

Every student will find each building on the campus, in some way or form, very uncomfortable in certain areas. What frightens people the most is that each building is actually living with the noisy machinery going in order make the building a little more comfortable such as air conditioning, heating, and. Yes, buildings make noises. With the amount of ghosts throughout the campus, it explains the phenomenon of the paranormal world that The Evergreen State College students just have to live with. Perhaps, a little rock 'n' roll may settle your nerves.

The Evergreen State Prison (TESP)

Some of the stories I came across from students, staff, and faculty that had been repeated regularly is that The Evergreen State College was originally planned as a state prison; The State of Washington wanted to shut down the college and turn it into a prison; Or, the State of Washington hires out the same architects who design schools also design state prisons. Even though the concrete structures throughout the campus may seem like you are walking through a prison, these two myths are simply not true.

First, architects of Washington State actually specialize in one type of architecture when it comes to government buildings. In order to actually design a prison, one must go through vigorous federal and state background checks. The architect, Robert L. Durham of Durham, Anderson, and Freed, had historically never actually drawn up a prison in his lifetime. The Evergreen State College was the first four-year college that he had drawn up. His previous accomplishments were churches, elementary schools, and fire houses within the Seattle area.[141] Being his highest accomplishment, The Evergreen State College's architecture was named in the book, *The Campus As A Work of Art* by Thomas Gaines in

[141] (University of Washington Libraries 2009)

1991 as the sixth best laid out college campuses in the nation. Gaines explains, "The Evergreen State College's random but cohesive plan combined with exquisitely designed concrete volumes and voids set in the arboreal drama of Olympia, Washington, shows that administrations can aspire to perfection even with all the complex demands of campus making. The Evergreen does need more sculpture….and lacking to the existing master plan."[142] It wasn't just Robert Durham who was the architect of the layout of The Evergreen State College. Other architects also contributed to the making of the campus (See Appendix I for a full list).

The Evergreen State College had a battle with the Washington State Legislature for years. In 1964, a report was issued by the Council of Presidents, *A Plan for Public Higher Education in Washington*, where there was a recommendation to create a new four-year state college because of the projected high enrollment of students. In 1967, the dream came true with the purchase of 990 acres of land, including one of the oldest structures, a slaughterhouse for pigs (now the day care center and once the administration building). The battle with the legislature started after the buildings came up and the new type of education called "inter-disciplinary learning" based off Alexander Meiklejohn's book, *The Experimental College* and Joseph Tussman's *Experiment at Berkeley.*[143]

The battle became heated between the legislature and The Evergreen State College, mainly because of the lower than expected enrollment of students (the college was expecting 15,000 students enrolled by 1985[144]) and Washington State budgetary problems. The college, of course, was not the same college that was originally planned or what the legislatures thought it would turn out to be. However, the battle of proposals of shutting down The Evergreen State College was attempted several times because of these budget crunches.

The first battle started in 1971, when House of Representative James Kuehlne (R-Spokane) wanted to shut down the college and turn it into a police academy. "It is high time the Reed College of Washington State be closed," he said while proposing the amendment, "and that we build a police academy or good trade school or something of practical usage.[145]" Some legislative representatives weren't very impressed with

142 (Gaines 1991)

143 (Jones 1981)

144 (Durham, Anderson & Freed 1968)

145 (Kuehnle attacks TESC; seeks police academy 1973)

the students, either. For example, Representative Ken Eikenberry (R-Seattle) made a visit to the college. "We met one student in the library who had claimed he had been studying poetry for three years (the school had been open only one and a half years), which immediately raised a question of student accountability.[146]"

Representative Paul Barden (R-Seattle) commented more from the same trip, "[I] really saw no reason to keep it [Evergreen] in operation. We were on the campus for over two hours and never could find a class in session. It's a nice hotel, but I'd like to see some education going on there."[147]

This did not go well with Representative Barney Goltz (D-Bellingham) who defended the college with this limerick:

Mr. Kuehnle is back on the floor

Knocking down Evergreen's door

Though he will not owe it

To any one poet

I think he-uh-it should lay on the floor[148].

With the fear of under enrollment in for the 1976-77 school year, there was a final count of 2,636 students attending The Evergreen State College. Unfortunately, most of the students were from outside of Washington State[149]. Despite the enrollment, The Evergreen State College goes through another threat of closure due to budgetary problems. Senator A.L. "Slim" Rasmussen proposed Senate Bill No. 2866[150] that would have shut down Evergreen and the turn it into an annex of the University of Washington. Since the other universities in Washington State were at half capacity, Rasmussen reasoned that it would easier to take the students with near empty capacity (Evergreen)

---

146 (Katz 1974)

147 (Katz 1974)

148 (Kuehnle attacks TESC; seeks police academy 1973)

149 (Kruse 1976)

150 (Pokorny, Yet Another Evergreen Threat 1977)

and put them in a larger capacity (University of Washington)[151]. However, Rasmussen was proven wrong considering that The Evergreen State College was still cheaper to maintain than the rest of the state funded four-year universities[152]. The budget crunch was resolved with a tuition hike in higher education.

In 1981, a third and final call of a shutdown through House Bill No. 793 presented on November 11 by Representative Dick Bond (R-Spokane). Bond wanted to "moth-ball" The Evergreen State College due to budget cuts that would have saved the State of Washington $28 million. The Spokane legislature suggests that dorms may be appropriate for housing minimum security prisoners. He added that the college could be used to house state offices after the college was to be turned over to the state Department of General Administration. Over 80 percent of the students were from out of state and Washington State was paying for it. "It doesn't make any sense to fund that operation with all the troubles we got," said Bond, "All the four-year colleges have more students than we can pay for while Evergreen has to recruit to get enough students. It's ridiculous."[153]

Senator H.A. Goltz (D-Bellingham) fired back with the following limerick that saved The Evergreen State College from extinction:

A Kuehnle-like man from Spokane

Introduced a budget-cut plan.

Dan Evans, once-hero,

Got a Bond-rating zero,

Shed tears for the Evergreen clan.[154]

151 (Pokorny, The Man Who Wants to Close Evergreen 1977)

152 (Pokorny, Why Evergreen Costs Less, Costs More 1974)

153 (Olson, Barney's Barbs For Bond's Bill 1981)

154 (Olson, Goltz Aims Barb at Bond's Evergreen Bill 1981)

Happy Land

One of the most secret places is called Happy Land on campus. Unfortunately, I am about to break some rules of Happy Land that I will soon explain later in this written piece so it is more of breaking the power of ethics than it is of reporting about the secret place. There is a sad thing about Happy Land, which is an oxymoron since Happy Land should never be a sad thing and tears should never be shed in such a place. Happy Land will be no more when construction begins in 2009, thus giving people just memories of the old place and then leaving those memories behind them.

I was lucky enough to get the official tour in order to take pictures for the archives. The maintenance committee went on a long elevator ride into the basement of the CAB Building and ended up at door 14. Door 14 houses the storage for the student clubs. The key master opened the gate on top of a ladder and I climbed up it. I knew that I was headed to a magical place and not just a room full of junk. There were cans of food with vegetables that one would not eat set specifically: Del Monte® Cream of Corn, Campbell's® Cream of Mushroom Soup, and Libby's® Pumpkin sitting on the ventilation pipes. The graffiti began to increase as I got closer to the room. As I entered through the homemade door that was about four feet high, there was a paper sign taped on a ventilation pipe that read:

Welcome!

You've reached Happy Land: utility tunnel, cave, a section of the universe connected to other sections. There is much to do here. Before you leave take a moment to consider the value of this place. Consider the work that has been done here. Consider the placement of objects. Consider the amplification of the sound that shakes the floor, a din which has been here forever. Consider secrecy, don't speak of this place, instead make it part of yourself. Consider bringing someone here and letting the cave speak for itself.

The first rule of Happy Land is that it is not a place that one is suppose to talk about nor is it a place that exists but through the word of mouth (which is why I am breaking one of the rules by telling you about the place). The second rule of Happy Land is not only do you have to keep the place a secret, you must leave something behind and add your signature to the guestbook. If you hold any experiments, you must journalize that information as well (there was a book of experiments).[155]

As you enter the room, you see objects everywhere. The room is in rainbow colors of yellow, red, white, light blue, pink, and dark green. The color stripes do not repeat in the exact order. On the far wall, is a large sign painted on the cement: Happy Land.

The objects include a wheelchair, multiple pieces of electronics including television sets, a rolling light, figurines, and even some paintings to liven up the place. Many of the items date back to the 1970s, but nobody is too sure when Happy Land actually did start.[156] I've heard about the multiple decades of its beginning existence: 1980s and 1990s. Art projects such as sculptures, paintings, photographs, and memorials are rampant throughout the small room.

Some people who have been to Happy Land tell me their opinions of the place. Some say it is a room full of junk and needs to be cleaned up and cleared out immediately. Others say it is a valuable thing for the college to preserve for future students. Whether it is a room full of junk or not, Happy Land provides something that you had forgotten within your childhood. As someone once put it, "Happy Land is where my childhood left off in a psychotic kind of way." Perhaps Happy Land was a way for the college students to let go of their childhood and leave it behind as they become better adults in the future.

One thing is for sure: there is no other Happy Land outside The Evergreen State College. After much research by asking different college campuses around the world, Happy Land is still unique.[157] It is this uniqueness that should be preserved.

155 On the last day that Happy Land exists in the CAB, the books will be sent to archives for future filing. However, people are still showing up there unofficially on a daily basis.

156 There was so much eye candy, and since I was looking at the room, I didn't know where to start it when it came to picture taking. The guest books look fairly new, but they may not be too accurate.

157 Many students that I have talked to around the world actually do wish that they had a Happy Land to escape from the daily rut of daily academic studies.

Conclusion

What have I learned from studying these stories? Human beings have always been storytellers since the day they could communicate with others. We've seen it in cave drawings. Yet, they still survive and they do still tell the story of how they caught that animal. Throughout the study, I had to ask myself, "If objects could talk what would they say to me?" This is where I often looked for small things such as a marking on the wall or an associated object left behind.

There are several problems in hunting down the truth behind these stories. For one, the stories that do exist from word of mouth can normally be found not in history books, but old, musty newspapers, magazines, and the archives (which the college library has done a wonderful job of preserving these items). Objects and rooms are harder to track down as I soon found out. All I could do was to write my personal experience, describe, and take pictures. For example, I will try to find that picture of that woman and find out her name and perhaps give her an official plaque for her memory. It may not be today, this year, or even this decade, but I will keep on searching.

As I have examined the stories, I did find some sort of truth behind them.

- Students who saw contractors coming out of the steam tunnels between maintenance periods could lead to making up stories of UFOs living underneath them or National Guard having easy access to control any protestors or riots.
- We found that having recognition of something positive that you did for the community should always be recognized.
- Suicides do happen at any college, but not as many as we think. There are too many variables.
- There are ghosts throughout the campus if you believe in them. They are not there to hurt us, but to guide us spiritually. In other words, they love the college as much as Evergreeners do.
- We must fear any budget cuts that legislatures have it in for us. This could lead to the closing of the college.

Perhaps we should change our reputation to make the college more conservative, or better yet, find a representative who knows how to do limericks?

- The architects who designed the college did not design prisons, which defeats the ongoing theory of Washington state school buildings are ironically similar to Washington state jails and prisons.
- Until the CAB gets remodeled, there will always be a place to escape to known as Happy Land.

Finally, and I know this is a political statement, I found that libraries and the reference desks very handy when it came to finding these small things out. I have used four different library facilities when it came to investigating these stories: The Daniel J. Evans Library at The Evergreen State College including periodicals, government documents, and archives; The Capitol Law Library; Timberland Regional Library; and the University of Washington Library. Without these libraries, this report would be a bunch of stories I heard and it would be very boring. By all means, support your local library.

Bibliography

Cooper Point Journal. "New Building for Organic Farm." *Cooper Point Journal*, Juky 3, 1975: 4.

Cousins, Ken. *Ken Cousins' homepage*. March 2007. http://www.bsos.umd.edu/gvpt/kcousins/NW.htm (accessed March 7, 2009).

Daily Olympian. "College Coed Found Dead: Body Crumbled Below Wall-Knife Blade in Abdomen." *Daily Olympian*, October 3, 1974: 1.

—. "Coroner's Jury Finds A Death Verdict of Suicide." *Daily Olympian*, October 30, 1974: 1.

Durham, Anderson & Freed. *The Evergreen State College, Olympia, Washington: master plan phase 1 studies*. Seattle, 1968.

Gaines, Thomas A. *The Campus As A Work Of Art.* Westport, Connecticut: Praeger, 1991.

Jones, Richard M. *Experiment at Evergreen.* Rochester, Vermont: Shenkman Books, Inc., 1981.

Katz, Dean. "Evergreen and the Legislature." *Cooper Point Journal*, June 4, 1974: 16-18.

Kramer, Wendy. "Vicki Scheider's Death: News Coverage, Campus Reaction." *Cooper Point Journal*, October 10, 1974: 12-13.

Kruse, Steve. "Final count 2,636: Underenrollment Doomsayers Foiled." *Cooper Point Journal*, October 21, 1976: 1.

Malory, Sir Thomas. *Le Morte d'Arthur.* Sony CONNECT Inc., February 16, 2009.

Nelson, Joyce. "Evergreen's Set To Host A Ghost." *Daily Olympian*, October 31, 1968: 1 and 6.

Olson, Fred. "Goltz Aims Barb at Bond's Evergreen Bill." *Daily Olympian*, November 12, 1981: A1.

—. "Barney's Barbs For Bond's Bill." *The Daily Olympian*, November 12, 1981: A2 Col 1.

Olympia Community School (OCS). http://www.olympiacommunityschool.org/ (accessed February 10, 2009).

Paper, The. "Kuehnle attacks TESC; seeks police academy." September 24, 1973: 1.

Pokorny, Brad. "The Man Who Wants to Close Evergreen." *Cooper Point Journal*, February 24, 1977: 1.

—. "Why Evergreen Costs Less, Costs More." *Cooper Point Journal*, February 24, 1974: 3.

—. "Yet Another Evergreen Threat." *Cooper Point Journal*, February 24, 1977: 1.

Rule, Ann. *Stranger Beside Me, The.* W.W. Norton & Company, 2000.

Savage, Larry, interview by Ty Rosenow. *Oral History* (February 25, 2009).

Siatkowski, Andrea. "Campus Trail Maps (Map 2)." *The Evergreen State College.* http://www.evergreen.edu/tour/trailmaps.htm (accessed March 6, 2009).

Taylor Shellfish Farms. *Taylor Shellfish Farms.* 2008. http://www.taylorshellfishstore.com/geoduck-c-17.html (accessed March 4, 2009).

The Evergreen State College. "Evergreen Campus Tour." *The Evergreen State College.* http://www.evergreen.edu/tour/docs/evergreenmap.pdf (accessed March 7, 2009).

—. "Facilities Services at Evergreen." *The Evergreen State College.* http://www.evergreen.edu/facilities/buildings/101CAB/home.htm (accessed March 7, 2009).

Thurston County Assessor. *Thurston Geodata Center.* 2008. http://www.geodata.org (accessed February 10, 2009).

University of Washington Libraries. *Pacific Coast Architecture Database (PCAD).* February 12, 2009. https://digital.lib.washington.edu/architect/architects/1947/ (accessed February 23, 2009).

Woodbridge, Sally Byrne. *A Guide to Architecture in Washington State: An Environmental Perspective.* Seattle, Washington: University of Washington Press, 1980.

The Old Castle Tavern[158]

Drinks were finally served at the Old Castle Tavern, where travelers would often stop by and say whatever is on the mind, drink up and then walk out. But, more can be discovered throughout the ages of the Old Castle Tavern. The Old Castle Tavern was over 400 years old and yet, the stories still remain within its walls.

The tavern had seen lots of historical events within those 400 years. Buildings have gone up and buildings had gone down. People come and people go, each leaving a trail behind them that eventually gets passed on to others, thus creating a substantial amount of knowledge passed on from generation to generation like a father passes on to his son.

It hadn't always been called the Old Castle Tavern, even though there was a castle down the street. It had always been known simply as the Castle Tavern. One must remember that something becomes old only with age. The tavern didn't look old as past owners did their own interior decorating to fit the needs as the personal and cultural viewpoints changed over the centuries. But, the old tavern was still the same from the exterior with the exception of a little coat of paint on the sign and the word "Old" being painted before the "Castle Tavern".

What really makes the Old Castle Tavern, aside from the fact that it is a public house for both the travelers and the locals alike, is the stories over the centuries that made the old tavern as a gathering place of knowledge that gets passed on. And because of the logging of these conversations and stories, one could enter the special collections of the library, sit down, and then open the book with the white gloves on and

---

158 While I was in St. Andrews, I saw a small tavern up for sale on South Castle Road and North Street. Originally, I thought turning it into a business, but I know close to nothing about taverns and bartending, so I soon began to give the idea up. The building for sale and business was called "The Old Castle Tavern." Being a tavern that has been there right when the town began which may have been built sometime circa 1100 AD, my mind was exploding of ideas on what it must have been like from decade to decade and what stories the tavern could tell me if it were to talk. I could come up with very many stories since I was unable to write them in a short amount of time while I was in St. Andrews (I was only there for three months). However, I did add some other stories from "St. Andrews Ghost Stories" written by W.T. Linskill in 1921. It is public domain, but most of the stories were actually too good to pass up! I hope you will enjoy this piece reading it as much as I have written and read them! Hopefully, the next owner of The Old Castle Tavern in St. Andrews, Scotland will keep it the same business model. That tavern has a lot of history and a lot of stories to tell to the public.

start reading these entries bit by bit. That was what I did when I entered the special collections department of the library (by appointment, of course) and slowly copied down the some of the stories that I had come across of the Old Castle Tavern.

Not all stories of the Old Castle or super old. Volumes of these books were passed on from generation to generation while compiling these stories for future people and historians to enjoy. Hopefully, you may enjoy these stories as much as I have and be able to create some sort of a full understanding of what oral history of a strange town, a strange setting, and a strange set of people there really could be. However, considering this comes from the Scotland, the accent may be hard to understand rather than the story itself. This took me awhile to get an idea of what each person is saying because of the strong accents. Not all stories are heavy with accents alone. Without a further ado, here are some stories that I had come across from the book of stories that were told in the Old Castle Tavern.

Jonathan's Tale

London is full of people from different places. But not Jonathan, for he had lived in London for most of his life. He had often played in Hyde's Park near the Peter Pan statue and the Faerie Tree by the Princess Diana Memorial Playground as a child. He knew all of London and what he possibly could do there, including going up the London Eye to see the three hundred sixty degree view or to see the Big Ben. But, the watchful eyes of the cameras planted throughout town and the tourists cameras had caused him that odd feeling being watched in an Orwellian fashion.

Now, he had the freedom of escaping the big city and go out on holiday by going up north to calm his nerves from the years of broken down stress. The holiday, as prescribed by his psychologist, was to a quaint little town famous for its golfing along with the castle and cathedral ruins, homes and places of worship that had long been forgotten. The town still existed, despite its downturn of the economy and small selected interests. The beauty would relax Jonathan, for he would be going up to Scotland, since it is less stressful to not learn a new language. In Scotland, they speak English with a slight accent, but you can pretty much understand them despite their accents.

While coming from 26 Lambeth Walk, Jonathan headed towards the Lambeth North Tube Station, where he was to transfer from the Bakerloo line at Elephant and Castle to the North line and then go straight to the King's Cross Rail Station. After swiping his Oyster Card, he noticed the Tube was crowded with people – again. The people were mostly in the standing position only and crushed like sardines in a can. You must imagine how hard it is to keep your luggage with you at all times without it bothering other people surrounding you. It would be a form of disrespect, which the English often take it hard that being respectful of one another and their space. Jonathan knew of this and decided to mind is own business and move on.

As Jonathan got off the North underground train, he "Minded The Gap" and headed up a series of escalators and tunnels that criss-crossed each other. If one did not know where they were going or didn't read the signs, one could get lost in the Tube stations. Finally, Jonathan had made it through the last set of escalators and had made it inside the King's Cross Rail Station within the heart of downtown London.

All trains go in and out of London through the King's Cross Rail Station, making it one of the busiest rail stations within all of London. Crowds of people are waiting in front of the sign boards of arrivals and destinations hoping to make it to the train on time. Pigeons are hanging around the station looking for a scrap that a child or an adult may have accidently dropped. The scraps were public domain now and the pigeons would fly in to grab as much as they possibly can until the next set of footsteps of the floor sweepers clean up the floor and put it in the rubbish bin. Such great first impressions of riding a train for the first time, and to Jonathan, he was ready to jump on the old eighties train car for his destination.

He took his baggage and traveled down the causeway and stepped on to the train with his seat and coach in his mind: Coach D, seat 48. He had hoped that the seat would be a window seat where he could look out and take pictures on his way to the quaint little town. Unfortunately, that never happened. He had an aisle seat and some brat with a runny nose smearing snot on him throughout the journey. Oh well, so be it. It is not much different from a lousy airplane ride. After all, this was Jonathan's first train ride.

Smothered Piper of the West Cliffs[159]

It seems that in the old days no houses existed on the Cliffs from the old Castle of Hamilton to the modern monument near the Witch Hill. It was all meadow land, much used for the grazing of cattle and sheep, and also much frequented as a playground for bygone children. On and over the face of the cliffs, slightly to the westward of Butts Wynd, existed then the entrance to a fearsome cave, or old ecclesiastical passage, which was a terror to many, and most people shunned it. It had many names, among them the "Jingling Cove," "The Jingling Man's Hole," "John's Coal Hole," and later "The Piper's Cave, or Grave." A few of the oldest inhabitants still remember it. A few knew a portion of it; none dared venture beyond this well-known portion. Like the interior of an old ice-house, it was dark, chilly, and clammy ; its walls ran with cold sweat. It was partly natural, but mostly artificial—a most dark, creepy, and fearsome place.

In a description which I got of it many years ago, and which appeared in the *St Andrews Citizen*, I learn that "the opening of this cliff passage was small and triangular ; it was situated on a projecting ledge of rock, and it was high enough, after entering, to enable a full-sized man to stand upright. From the opening it was a steep incline down for a distance of 49 feet, thereafter it proceeded in a level direction for over 70 feet, when it descended into a chamber. At the further end of this chamber were two, if not more, passages branching off from it. Between the passages was cut out in the rock a Latin cross." This would seem to point to an ecclesiastical connection, and had nothing whatever to do with the more modern smugglers' cave near the ladies' bathing place.

But enough of description. In bygone days, in a small cottage, little better than a hovel, situated in Argyle, lived an old dame named Goodman. She occupied one room, and her son and his young wife tenanted the other little chamber. He was a merry, dare-devil, happy-go-lucky lad, and he was famed as one of the best players on the bagpipes in all Fife ; he would have pleased even Maggie Lauder. Of nights at all hours he would make the old grass-grown streets lively with his music.

---

159 These next four stories were written by W.T. Linskill's "St. Andrew's Ghosts" published in 1921. I had to cut parts of the stories to fit within the Old Castle Tavern.

" Jock the Piper," was a favorite among both young and old. He was much interested in the tale of the old West Cliff cave, and took a bet on with some cronies that on a New Year's night he would investigate the mysteries of the place, and play his pipes up it as far as he could go. His old mother, his wife, and many of his friends tried hard to dissuade him from doing so foolish and so foolhardy a thing; but he remained obdurate, and firmly stuck to his bet. On a dark Now Year's night he started up the mysterious cavern with his pipes playing merrily; and they were heard, it is said, passing beneath Market Street, then they died away. They suddenly ceased, and were never more heard. He and his well-known pipes were never seen again.

Somewhere beneath St Andrews lies the whitened bones of that bygone piper lad, with his famous pipes beside him. Attempts were made to find him, but without avail; no one, not even the bravest, dared to venture into that passage full of damp foul air. His mother and wife were distracted, and the young wife used to sit for hours at the mouth of that death-trap cave. Finally, her mind gave way, and she used to wander at all hours down to the mouth of the cave where her husband had vanished. The following Now Year's night she left the little cottage in Argyle, and putting a shawl over her wasted shoulders, turned to the old woman and said, “I'm going to my Jock." Morning came, but she never returned home. She had, indeed, gone to her lost “Jock." For years after, the small crouching figure of a woman could be seen on moon-light nights perched on the rock balcony of the fatal cave, dim, shadowy, and transparent. Wild shrieks and sounds of weird pipe music were constantly heard coming from out of that entrance.

In after years, when the houses were built, the mouth of this place was either built or covered up, and its memory only remains to us.

But what of "Piper Jock?" He, it is said, still walks the edge of the old cliffs; and his presence is heralded by an icy breath of cold air, and ill be it for anyone who meets or sees his phantom form or hears his pipe music. He seems to have the same effect as the ghost of "Nell Cook" in the dark entry at Canterbury, mentioned in the "Ingoldsby Legends," from which I must quote a few verses-

"And tho' two hundred years have flown,
Nell Cook doth still pursue
Her weary walk, and they who cross her path
The deed may rue.
Her fatal breath is fell as death I

The simoon's blast is not
More dire (a wind in Africa
That blows uncommon hot).
But all unlike the simoon's blast,
Her breath is deadly cold,
Delivering quivering, shivering shocks
Upon both young and old.
And whoso in the entry dark
Doth feel that fatal breath,
He ever dies within the year
Some dire untimely death."

So it is with him who meets "Piper Jock."

I only know of one man who told me that one awful night in a heavy thunderstorm he had heard wild pipe music, and seen the figure of a curiously dressed piper walking along the cliff edge, *where no mortal could walk*, at a furious speed. If I could only find now the mouth of that place, I bet another 'Jock' and I would get along it and find the whereabouts of 'Jock the Piper' and his poor little wife. Here is my hansom. Good night, don't forget the Piper.

Screaming Skull of Greyfriars

We were sitting over a cozy fire after dinner at the Old Castle Tavern. It was snowing hard outside, and very cold. Our pipes were alight and our grog on the table, when Allan Beauchamp suddenly remarked - "It's a deuced curious thing for a man to be always followed about the place by a confounded grinning skull."

"Eh, what," I said, "who the deuce is being followed about by a skull? It's rubbish, and quite impossible."

" Not a bit," said my friend, "I've had a skull after me more or less for several years."

"It sounds like a remark a lunatic would make," I rejoined rather crossly. "Do not talk bunkum. You'll go dotty if you believe such infernal rot."

"It is not bunkum or rot a bit," said Allan, "Its gospel truth. Ask Truffles, ask Jack Weston, or Jimmy Darkgood, or any of my south country pals."

“I don't know Jack Weston or Jimmy Darkgood," I said, "but tell me the whole story.”

“It was long, long ago, I think about the year 1513, that one of my ancestors, a man called Neville de Beauchamp, resided in Scotland. It seems he was an uncommonly wild dog, went in for racing and cards, and could take his ,vine and ale with any of them even in those hard drinking days. He was known as Flash Neville. Later on he married a pretty girl, the daughter of a silk mercer in Perth, who, it seems, died (they said of a broken heart) two years after. Neville de Beauchamp was seized with awful remorse, and became shortly after a monk in Greyfriars Monastery at St Andrews. After Neville's wife's death, her relations seem to have been on the hunt after him, burning for revenge, and the girl's brother, a rough, wild dog in those stormy days, at last managed to track his quarry down in the monastery at St. Andrews."

“Very interesting," I said, “that monastery stood very nearly on the site of the present infant school, and we found the well in 1880. Well, what did this brother do, eh?"

“It seems that one afternoon after vespers he forced his way into the Monastery Chapel, sought out Neville de Beauchamp, and slashed off his head with a sword in the aisle of the Kirk. Now a queer thing happened-his body fell on the floor, but the severed head, with a wild scream, flew up to the chapel ceiling and vanished through its roof."

"Mighty queer that," I said.

"The body was reverently buried," went on Allan, "but the head never was recovered, and, whirling through the air over the monastery, screaming and groaning most pitifully, it used to cause great terror to the monks and others o’ nights. It was a well-known story, and few cared to venture in that locality after nightfall. The head soon became a. skull, and since that time has always haunted some member of the house of Beauchamp. Now comes a strange thing. I went a few years ago and lived in rooms at St Andrews for a change, and while there I heard of my uncle's death somewhere abroad. I had never seen him, but I had frequently heard that he was very much perplexed and worried by the tender attentions paid him by the skull of Neville de Beauchamp, which was always turning up at odd times and in unexpected places."

"This is a grand tale," I said.

"Now I come on the job," said Allan, ruefully. "That uncle was the very last of our family, and I wondered if that skull would come my way. I felt very ill and nervous after I got the news of my uncle's death. A strange sense of depression and oppression overcame me, and I got very restless. One stormy evening I felt impelled by some strange influence to go out. I wandered about the place for several hours and got drenched. I felt as if I was walking in my sleep, or as if I had taken some drug or other. Then I had a sort of vision-I had just rounded the corner of North Bell Street."

"Now called Greyfriars Garden," I remarked.

"Yes! Well, when I got around that corner I saw a large, strange building before me. I opened a wicket gate and entered what I found to be the chapel; service was over, the lights were being extinguished, and the air was laden with incense. As I knelt in a corner of the chapel I saw the whole scene, the tragedy of which I had heard, enacted all over again. I saw that monk in the aisle, I saw a man rush in and cut off his head. I saw the body fall and the head fly up with a shriek to the roof. When I came to myself I found I was sitting on the low wall of the school. I was very cold and wet, and I got up to go home. As I rose I saw lying on the pavement at my feet what appeared to be a small football. I gave it a vicious kick, when to my horror it turned over and I saw it was a skull. It was gnashing its teeth and moaning. Then with a shriek it flew up in the air and vanished. A horrible thing. Then I knew the worst. The skull of the monk Neville de Beauchamp had attached itself to me for life, I being the last of the race. Since then it is almost always with me."

"Where is it now?" I said, shuddering.

"Not very far away, you bet," he said.

"It's a most unpleasant tale," I said. "Good night, I'm off to bed after that."

I was in my first sleep about an hour afterwards, when a knock came at my door, and the valet came in.

"Sorry to disturb you, sir," he said, "but the skull has *just come back*. It's in the next room. Would you like to see it?"

"Certainly not," I roared. "Get away and let me go to sleep."

Then and there I firmly resolved to leave next morning. I hated skulls, and I fancied that probably it might take a fancy to me, and I had no desire to be followed about the country by a skull as if it were a fox terrier.

Next morning I went in to breakfast. "Where is that beastly skull?" I said to Allan.

"Oh, it's off again somewhere. Heaven knows where; but I have had another vision, a waking vision."

"What was it?"

"Well,: said Allan, "I saw the skull and a white hand which seemed to beckon to me beside it. Then they slowly receded and in their place was what looked like a big sheet of paper. On it in large letters were the words -*Your friend,* Jack *Weston, is dead.* This morning I got this wire telling me of his sudden death. Read it."

That afternoon I left Allan Beauchamp. .

Since then I have constant letters from him from his home in England. He has tried every means possible to get rid of that monk's skull; but they are of no avail, it always returns. So he has made the best he can of it, and keeps it in a locked casket in an empty room at the end of a wing of the old house. He says it keeps fairly quiet, but on stormy nights wails and gruesome shrieks are heard from the casket in that closed apartment.

I heard from him last week. He said : - "DEAR W. T. L.,-I don't think I mentioned that twice a year the skull of Neville de Beauchamp vanishes from its casket for a period of about two days. It is never away longer.

I wonder if it still haunts its old monastery at St Andrews where its owner was slain. Do write and tell me if anyone now in that vicinity hears or sees the screaming skull of my ancestor, Neville de Beauchamp."

Beckoning Monk

Many years ago, about the time of the Tay Bridge gale, I was staying at Edinburgh with a friend of mine, an actor manager. I had just come down from the paint-room of the theatre, and was emerging from the stage-door, when I encountered Miss Elsie H--, a then well-known actress.

"You are just the very person I wanted to meet," she said "Allow me to introduce you to my friend, Mr. Spencer Ashton. He's not an actor, he's an artist, and he's got such a queer, queer story about ghosts and things near your beloved St Andrews."

I bowed to Mr. Ashton, who was a quiet looking man, pale and thin, rather like a benevolent animated hairpin. He reminded me somehow of Fred Vokes. We shook hands warmly.

"Yes," he said, "my story sounds like fiction, but it is a fact, as I can prove. It is rather long, but it may possibly interest you. Where could we foregather?"

"Come and dine with me at the Edinburgh Hotel tonight at eight. I'll get a private room," I said.

"Right oh!" said he, and we parted.

That evening at eight o'clock we met at the old Edinburgh Hotel (now no longer in existence), and after dinner he told me his very remarkable tale.

"Some years ago," he said, "I was staying in a small coast town in Fife, not very far from St Andrews. I was painting some quaint house and things of the sort that tickled my fancy at the time, and I was very much amused and excited by some of the bogie tales told me by the fisher folk. One story particularly interested me."

"And what was that?" I asked.

"Well, it was about a strange, dwarfish, old man, who, they swore, was constantly wandering about among the rocks at nightfall; a queer, uncanny creature, they said, who was 'aye beckoning to them,' and who was never seen or "known in the daylight. I heard so much at various times and from various people about this old man that I resolved to look for him and see what his game really was. I went down to the beach times without number, but saw nothing worse than myself, and I was almost giving up the job hopeless, when one night' I struck oil,' as the Yankees would say."

"Good," I said, "let me hear."

" It was after dusk," he proceeded, "very rough and windy, but with a feeble moon peeping out at times between the racing clouds. I was alone on the beach. Next moment I was *not* alone."

"Not alone," I remarked. "Who was there?"

"Certainly not alone," said Ashton. "About three yards from me stood a quaint, short, shriveled, old creature. At that time the comic opera of 'Pinafore' was new to the stage-loving world, and this strange being resembled the character of ' Dick Deadeye' in that piece. But this old man was much uglier and more repulsive. He wore a tattered monk's robe, had a fringe of black hair, heavy black eyebrows, very protruding teeth, and a pale, pointed, unshaven chin. Moreover, he possessed only one eye, which was large and telescopic looking,"

"What a horrid brute," I said.

"Oh! he wasn't half so bad after all," said Ashton, "though his appearance was certainly against him. He kept beckoning to me with a pale, withered hand, continually muttering, 'Come! I felt compelled to follow him, and follow him I did."

I lit up another pipe and listened intently.

"He took me," resumed Ashton, "into a natural cave, a cleft in the rocks, and we went stumbling over the rocks and stones, and splashing into pools. At least I did. He seemed to get along all right. At the far end of this clammy cave, a very narrow staircase, cut out of solid rock, ascended abruptly about twenty or thirty steps, then turned a corner and descended again into a large passage. Then a mighty queer thing happened."

" What might that be?" I enquired.

"Well, my guide somehow or other suddenly became possessed of a huge great candlestick with a lighted candle in it, about three feet high, which lit up the vaulted passage.

"'We now stand in the monk's sub-way,' he said.

"'Indeed, and who may you be? Are you a man or a ghost?'

"The queer figure turned. 'I am human,' he said, ' do not fear me. I *was* a monk years ago, now I am reincarnate-time and space are nothing whatever to me. I only arrived a short while ago from Naples to meet you here.'

"Good heavens, Ashton," I said, "is this all true?"

"Absolutely true, my dear fellow," said Ashton. .. I was in my sound senses, not hypnotized or anything of that sort, I assure you. On and on we went, the little man with his big candle leading the way, and I following. Two or three times the sub-way narrowed, and we had a tight squeeze to get through, I can tell you."

"What a rum place," I interjected.

"Yes, it was that," said Ashton, "but it got still rummer as we went up and down more stairs, and then popped through a hole into a lower gallery, and I noticed side passages branching off in several different directions.

"'Walk carefully and look where you tread,' said my monkish guide. 'There are pitfalls here; be very wary.'

"Then I noticed at my feet a deep, rock-hewn pit about two feet wide right across the passage. 'What is that for?' I asked. 'To trap intruders and enemies,' said the little monk. *'Look down.'* I did so, and I saw at the bottom, in a pool of water, a whitened skull and a number of bones. We passed four or five such shafts in our progress."

"Pon my word, this beats me altogether," I interpolated.

"It would have beaten me altogether if I had fallen into one of those traps," said Ashton. "Suddenly the close, damp, fungus sort of air changed and I smelt a sweet fragrant odor. 'I smell incense,' I said to the monk.

"'It is the wraith, or ghost, of a smell,' he said. 'There has been no incense here away since 1546. There are ghosts of sounds and smells, just as there are ghosts of people. We are here surrounded by spirits, but they are transparent, and you cannot see them unless they are materialized, but you can feel them.'

"'Hush, hark! ' said the monk, and then I heard a muffled sound of most beautiful chiming bells, the like I never heard before.

"'What is that?'

"'The old bells of St Andrews Cathedral. That is the ghost of sounds long ago ceased,' and the monk muttered some Latin. Then all of a sudden I heard very beautiful chanting for a moment or more, then it died away.

"'That is the long dead choir of monks chanting vespers,' remarked my guide, sadly.

"At this period the monk and I entered a large, rock hewn chamber, wide and lofty. In it there were numerous huge old iron clamped chests of different sizes and shapes.

"'These,' said the monk, 'are packed full of treasures, jewels, and vestments. They will be needed again someday. Above us *now* there are ploughed fields, but long ago right over our heads there existed a church and monastery to which these things belonged.' He pointed with a skinny claw of a hand to one corner of the chamber. 'There,' he said, 'is the staircase that once led to the church above.'"

Ashton stopped and lit a cigar, then resumed.

"'Well, on we went again, turning, twisting, going up steps, round corners, through more holes, and stepping over pitfall shafts. It was a loathsome and gruesome place.

"Out of a side passage I saw a female figure glide quickly along. She was dressed as a bride for a wedding; then she disappeared.

"'Fear not,' said the monk, 'that is Mirren of Hepburn's Tower, the White Lady, she can materialize herself and appear when she chooses, but she is not re-incarnate as I am.'

"Well, after we had gone on it seemed for hours, as I have described, the monk paused.

"'I fear I must leave you,' he said, suddenly. 'I am wanted. Before I go, take this,' and he placed in my hand a tiny gold cup delicately chased; 'it is a talisman and will bring you good luck always,' he said. 'Keep it safe, I may never see you again here, but do not forget.'

"Then I was alone in black darkness. He and his candle had vanished in a second. Quite alone in that awful prison, heaven only knows how far below the ground, I could never have gone back, and I feared to go forward. I was entombed in a worst place than the Roman Catacombs, with no hope of rescue, as it was unknown and forgotten by all."

“What a fearful position to be in,” I said.

“I should think it was," said Ashton. “The awful horror of it I can never forget as long as I live. I was absolutely powerless and helpless. I had lost my nerve, and I screamed aloud in an agony of mind. I had some matches, and these I used at rare intervals, crawling carefully and feeling my way along the slimy floor of the passage. I had a terrible feeling, too, that something intangible, but horrible, was crawling along after me and stopping when I stopped. I heard it breathing. I struck a match, and it was lucky, for I just missed another of those pitfalls. By the light of the match I saw a small shrine in an alcove which had once been handsomely ornamented. My progress forward was suddenly stopped by a gruesome procession of skeleton monks all in white. They crossed the main sub-way from one side passage and entered another. Their heads were all grinning skulls, and in their long bony fingers they bore enormous candles, which illuminated the passage with a feeble blue glare."

“It's awful," I remarked.

“On, and on, I slowly went. It seemed hours and hours. I was exhausted and hungry and thirsty. After a time I passed through open oak nail studded doors that were rotting on their hinges, and then-*then*, I saw a *sight so horrible* that I would never mention it to anyone. I dare not, I may know its meaning someday-I hope so-"

“What on earth was it?" I inquired eagerly.

“For heaven's sake let me go on and do not ask about it," said Ashton, turning ghastly pale. “The horror of the whole thing so upset me that my foot slipped, and I fell down what seemed to be a steep stairway. As I struck the bottom I felt my left wrist snap, and I fainted. When I regained my senses for a brief moment, I found that the White Lady, bearing a taper, was bending kindly over me. She had a lovely face, but as pale as white marble. She laid an icy cold hand on my hot brow, and then all was darkness again.

“Now listen! Next time I came to myself and opened my eyes I was out of the accursed passage. I saw the sky and the stars, and I felt a fresh breeze blowing. Oh! joy, I was back on the earth again, that I knew. I staggered feebly to my feet, and where on earth do you think I found I had been lying? "

“ I cannot guess," I said.

“Just inside the archway of the old Penda gateway at St. Andrews," said Ashton.

“How on earth did you get there?”

“Heaven knows," said Ashton, "I expect the White Lady helped me somehow. It all seemed like a fearful nightmare, but I had the gold cup in my pocket and my broken wrist to bear testimony to what I had gone through. To make a long story short, I went home to my people, where I lay for six long weeks suffering from brain fever and shock. I always carry the cup with me. I am not superstitious; but it brings me good luck *always."*

Ashton showed me the monk's gold cup. It was a beautiful little relic.

“Did you ever examine the place where you entered the passage?” I asked.

“Oh, yes,” he replied, “I went there some years afterward and found the cave, but it has all fallen in now.”

“By Jove! It's very late, thanks for the dinner, I must be off. Good night.”

I lit a pipe and pondered over that curious story. The entrance to the passage in the cave has fallen in; the exit from it in St Andrews is unknown to Ashton-only the White Lady knows.

On the whole, the story is wrapped in mystery, and does not help one much to unravel the wonders that lie in underground St Andrews. We may know some day or never.

Monk of St. Rule’s Tower

“By Jove, sir,” Captain Chester said, “that's the place for ghosts. Every blessed comer is full of them-bang full. Look at those fellows in the Castle dungeons, and Beaton and Sharpe and the men that got hanged and burned, and the old dev-- I mean witches. Years and years ago I took an old house in St Andrews, which was a small place then. Very little golf was played, and there was very little to do. But, gad, sir, the ghosts were thick, and the quaint old bodies in the town were full of them. They could spin yams for hours about phantom coaches, death knells, corpse candles, people going about in winding sheets, phantom hearses, and Lord knows what else. I loved it, it took me quite back to the middle ages.”

“Egad, sir," he said, “it was a curious time. Of all the tales I heard, the one that pleased and fascinated me most was the legend of the monk that looks over St Regulus's Tower on moonlight nights. I went thither every night, and constantly fancied I saw a figure peering over the edge, but was not certain. Then I got hold of a very old man, who related to me the old legend. It seems that years ago there was a good Prior of St Andrews named Robert de Montrose. He ruled well, gently, and wisely, but among the monks there was one who was always in hot water, and whom Prior Robert had often to haul over the coals. He played practical jokes, often absented himself from the daily and nightly offices of Holy Kirk, and otherwise upset the rules and discipline. Finally, when Earl Douglas and his retinue came to St Andrews to present to the Cathedral a costly statue, long known as the Douglas Lady, this monk made desperate love to one of the waiting women of Lady Douglas. For this he was imprisoned in the Priory Dungeon for some days. It was the custom of Robert De Montrose almost every fine night to ascend the tower of St. Rule and admire the view. The summit was reached in those days by means of ladders and wooden landing not, as it is now, by a stair. In those days, too, the apse and part of the nave were still standing, and the summit of the solemn old tower was crowned by a small spire. One evening just before Yuletide, when the Prior, as usual, was on the top of the tower, the contumacious monk slyly followed him up the ladders, stabbed him in the back with a small dagger, and flung him over the north side of the old tower."

"I thought, Captain Chester," I said, "that the murder took place on the Dormitory stairs."

"Gad, Zooks, and Odd bodkins, sir, I am telling you what I was told, and what I can prove, sir."

"All right," I replied, "please fire away."

"Well," continued Chester, "they told me the Prior had often been seen since peeping over the tower, and at times he was seen to fall, as he did years ago, from the summit. By the bye, his assassin was starved to death and buried in some old midden. One moonlight night as my brother and I were standing on the Kirkhill, to our horror and amazement we saw a figure appear suddenly on the top of the tower, loop on to the parapet, and deliberately jump over. Zounds, sir, my blood ran cold."

"We did not hesitate long, but jumped the low wall of the Cathedral. It was easily done in those days, and we were young and active, and hurried to the grim old tower. Just as we neared it, a monk passed us in the Augustinian habit, his cowl was thrown back, and for just one second we had a view of his pallid, handsome face and keen penetrating eyes. Then he disappeared as suddenly as he had appeared. We were alone in the moonlight, nothing stirring."

"That is very odd," I said.

"Zooks! sir, I have odder things still to tell you. We went home to the old house, had supper, and retired to bed thoughtfully. I woke about 2 a.m. The blinds were up and it was as clear as day with the moonlight. Imagine my blank astonishment when I clearly perceived, leaning up against the mantelpiece, the pallid monk I had seen a few hours before near the Square Tower. He leaned on his elbow and was gazing intently at me, while in his hand he held some object that had a blue glitter in the moonbeams.

"He smiled. 'Fear not, brother,' he said, 'I am Prior Robert of Montrose who quitted this earth many years syne, and of whom you have been talking and thinking so much of late days. I saw you to-night in our cruelly ruined Abbey Kirk. Alas! alas! but I come from ayont the distant hills and have far to go tonight.'

"'What do you want, Holy Father?' I said, 'and what of your murder?'

"'That is forgiven and forgotten long syne,' he said, 'and I love to revisit, *at times,* my old haunts, and so does he. You have in your regiment, me thinks, one named Montrose, a scion of our family.'

"'Yes,' I said, 'I know Bob Montrose well.'

"'See you this dagger I hold,' said Prior Robert, 'it was with this I lost my life on this earth many years syne on the tower of blessed St Rule. They buried it with me in my stone kist; I will leave it here with you to give to my kinsman, for it will prove of use to him e'er he pass hence-mark my words.'"

"He raised his hand as in act of blessing, and melted away. I fell back in a sleep or in a faint. When I woke the morning sun was streaming into my bedroom. At first I thought I had eaten too much supper and had a nightmare, but there on the table by my bed lay an old dagger of curious workmanship-the dagger that slew the Prior years and years ago. I faithfully fulfilled my vow, and my friend, Major Bob Montrose, has now got his monkish ancestor's dagger."

Love Letters In The Dark

"There was this loving couple who once roamed within the streets of St. Andrews." Captain Chester said as he motioned the bartender for another glass of beer. As you may tell, Captain Chester tells an ample of tall tales related to ghosts. But, there was some truth of the things that he had witnessed that relates towards to fact rather than fiction. Captain Chester had a quick sip of malt whiskey and then continued on with his story. "It seems more of a *Romeo and Juliet* type of story. The man loves a woman and a woman loves a man. They can't get together because of their families had been feuding for years and eventually committed suicide because their love is so deep. Only that was not what had happened."

"It didn't?" I asked. "How does the story really go, then?"

"Simple," said Captain Chester. He was getting somewhat annoyed with my interruptions, but he loved getting the attention. After all, Captain Chester was legally an attention whore and the story had to be blurb out the story. "It didn't end that way. They both didn't commit suicide upon themselves. Her boyfriend had written her many letters while they were alive. And, of course, she wrote back. Most of them were love letters."

"One day, her boyfriend was missing and she was no longer getting the love letters. It turns out that her boyfriend was killed by taking an overdose of sleeping pills given to him by his chemist. It was accidental, I'm sure of it. Anyway, she put the love letters into her hope chest and eventually forgotten about them." Captain Chester took another sip of his malt whiskey. His face became red from the high percentage of alcohol entering his body, a sign of an allergic reaction to the alcohol itself. He may have alcohol poisoning and not know it.

"Years passed and yet the hope chest was not opened. Because of it collecting dust and being unused, the hope chest was eventually transferred over to the attic to where it was to be forgotten. The lady had forgotten about the love letters and the hope chest. She decided to live on with her life and eventually looked for another man and had several children that she raised and loved and cherished everyday that they were growing up. Soon, decades passed and yet, the love letters inside the hope chest and the hope chest had still been forgotten." Captain Chester stopped his story while I, the owner o the Old Castle Tavern, put another pine wood log on the fire in the fireplace for us to keep warm.

"Pour me some more of that malt whiskey," Captain Chester said while motioning me that he wanted more. I couldn't decline, because I really wanted to hear more of this story. I gave him the finest top shelf Scottish malt whiskey, and said it was on me if he continued on with his story. He agreed, raised his shot glass, and then took a sip of his whiskey. He began to continue on with his story. "Where were we?"

"The love letters and the hope chest were forgotten for decades," I replied.

"The love letters inside the hope chest were long forgotten for decades. Even the hope chest was forgotten for decades. Eventually, the lady passed away of natural causes and one of her daughters was given her estate. So, her daughter figured it was time to, you know, re-decorate so that way she wouldn't be reminded of the loss of her mother."

"Funny how the loss of somebody causes one to try to forget them, and yet we have memorials located everywhere of the memory of that person," I said. Captain Chester took another sip of the malt whiskey out of his clear shot glass.

He continued, "So, her daughter decides to re-decorate, and, of course, in order for her to re-decorate the home, she had to go up into the attic to see what walls needed to be moved."

"Right, because if you destroy a load-bearing wall, then it may end up being the end of the roof or even the rest of the house," I said diligently.

"When the daughter ended up in the attic, she notices this hope chest, and just the hope chest in the attic. As she was curious to know what was actually inside this hope chest, she decided to open it and find the hope chest to be full of letters, all of which were bundled with red ribbon. She grabbed a bundle and slowly untied the ribbon, since the letters and the ribbon were in their fragile state. Once these letters were crumbled, there were to be no more. As she opened the letters, she noticed it was her mother's love letters, but from a different man."

"So, was she surprised that the love letters were not from who she expected, like her father?" I asked.

"Yes, she was quite a bit surprised, but she thought it was best to read more of these letters while she slowly pieced together her mother's childhood history that was never passed on to the daughter. When she was done with the love letters, she put them back into the hope chest. The daughter didn't know what to do with them, and thought perhaps that she could either preserve the love letters for prosperity or whether to destroy them. She did like the hope chest, for it was quite ornate." Captain Chester took another sip of his malt whiskey and I gladly poured another shot.

Captain Chester moved forward onto his story, "That night, she went to bed and began to think about the love letters. She wished that she had some attention, because she was a single woman who had never been married nor had any children. She wished that someone would write to her and send her some love letters as well."

"You might as well as say that she was jealous," I said.

"Not exactly," Captain Chester replied. "The daughter was more lonely than jealous. Loneliness can be hard to deal with and just everyone would rather be someone who cares about them."

"There has to be *some* exceptions," I said.

"There are always some exceptions to everything in the universe," said Captain Chester. "The daughter wanted a companion to look after her. Apparently, she had a heavy duty wish, that when she woke up the next morning, she found an aged letter underneath her pillow addressed to her. 'How strange,' she thought as she carefully opened the letter. It turned out to be a love letter from an anonymous gentleman. Imagine her surprise! What gentleman could be sneaking into her room, placing a letter underneath her pillow in the middle of the night while she was sleeping?" Captain Chester took another sip of his malt whiskey.

I asked, "How long did this last?"

"What lasted?" said Captain Chester. He was beginning to be little bit tipsy.

"Of the daughter receiving the love letters in the middle of the night," I said.

"Oh, this happened every night. She was receiving these letters on a nightly basis for several months. Somebody, apparently, was truly in love with her. She tried everything to catch her secret admirer, including staying up all night, but she still received a love letter underneath her pillow. I must say that she felt kind of freaked out because of the supernatural surroundings of her room. The daughter did not want to exorcise her home, because she did enjoy receiving and reading the love letters. It was something she looked forward to reading on a daily basis."

"One day, the love letter ended up becoming strange. I believe I have a copy of the letter here." Captain Chester pulled an old love letter that he happened to carry in his pocket. I could tell he was trying to tell this story sometime and couldn't wait when he first heard it. He unfolded the letter , sat the letter on the bar, and then pushed towards me direction with the lettering facing me for easy reading. "Read the letter out aloud," Captain Chester demanded. I poured him the last of the malt whiskey just in time to begin the closing of the Old Castle Tavern.

"My Dearest Lucinda," I read aloud from the letter. "I am sorry to say that this is the last of the letters and I must reveal who I really am. I am someone from your past, and yet, you may not know me. You must go to the St. Andrew's Cathedral on the edge of town and I shall meet you there at half past twelve tonight. Love, your secret admirer, Anonymous."

Captain Chester took the letter, folded it up, and then put it back into his pocket where he was saving it for a future re-telling of the story. "Well, the daughter was curious and wanted to see who her secret admirer and still wondered how got into her bedroom on a nightly basis and be able to put a love letter underneath her pillow. So, she decided to go."

"That night, she snuck into the churchyard (they normally lock up the churchyard at night because of the pranks of the University students) and was looking for the gentleman to carry her away into a romantic fairytale ending. She kept on hearing voices in her head and she followed them to where it lead to her to a grave site. The faint tombstone read, "Thomas Balfour" without a date of departure nor when he was born."

"'How odd,' she thought 'most tombstones have dates on them.' She looked around and saw spot in well manicured lawn where something was suppose to be there. Perhaps there was a missing tombstone? Frightened by the missing tombstone, she began to think that it was her grave and started to head out of the churchyard where she felt comfortable within the streets of St. Andrews along North Street and then quickly to Market Street, where others often move about from pub to pub. As she got to Dean's Court, she tripped over a piece of sandstone. It read, "'Thomas Balfour, jr.'"

"You see, tombstones and parts of building that no longer were functional were often taken and re-used as another building or a structure. Thomas Balfour, jr's tombstone was no exception, where memory becomes no longer neither was the need of the tombstones. It was quite common practice," said Captain Chester.

"So, her secret admirer was a ghost that wanted her to find his tombstone," I asked Captain Chester thinking that I was somewhat gypped from his story.

"Not exactly," said Captain Chester, "There really is a slight twist to this story where there is more than you think. She did find the missing tombstone, but as she was on the ground, a nice young man happened to be walking the street in the dark and ended up tripping over Lucinda. Lucinda saw the gentleman and there was love at first sight."

"She introduced herself, 'My name is Lucinda.'"

"The gentleman introduced himself, 'My name is Balfour. Thomas Balfour the third.'"

And they got married.

Afterword

There comes a time when you run out of stories to tell. I, personally, never thought this could happen so soon. Once the stories end, one must close the book and begin another book with more stories, but not necessarily from the same author.

I am sorry to say that this is my last book. The last time I punch down the keys on my laptop computer of the words from my imagination inside my brain and then transcribing it on paper. Now is the time to close the show and the end must happen sometime. There may be other books and there might not, I haven't decided yet. I would like to thank you, the reader, the listener, the observer, of this book something that you were willing to pick up and enjoy.

I am terrible at goodbyes. At times, it is hard for me to end something that is impossible to end. This could be a never ending story or a story with an impossible or implausible ending. So, here is my hug and a handshake of the wonderful times that I had taken you and may another author take you further into that journey.

I know that it is hard to find another author. My personal inspiration is Roald Dahl when he wrote adult fictional stories, but like Roald Dahl, I figured out other ways to move on. He chose writing children's stories. I chose history.

So, someday, you may find my future works of researching historical documents and reporting on them. Or, I may be enjoying myself in St. Andrews, Scotland. Wherever life takes me, I will be there.

Thank you for all of your support,

Ty Rosenow

February 12, 2009

Olympia, Washington USA

Extras[160]

Joke Translations:

Programmer "one liners"[161]

- 'Hello World!' 17 errors, 31 warnings
- It compiled? The first screen came up? Ship it! (Bill Gates)
- 1024x768x256 Sounds like one mean woman
- 2B OR NOT 2B = FF
- A bad day: 'Transfer completed (5720468 bytes, 1 CPS)'
- Apathy Error: Don't bother striking any key.
- Bad or Missing Sysop. Free files in all areas.
- Best 3D game? DOOK. I mean DUME.
- C:\PROGRAMS\FAULTY\TRASH \SICKJOKE\WINDOWS>
- Canadian DOS: 'Yer sure, eh? [Y,n]'
- CAUTION! Do not look into laser with remaining eye.
- Coming soon: Doom III - What The Hell?
- Daddy, what does FORMATTING DRIVE C: COMPLETE mean?
- DEVICE=LIFE LOCKED@AGE25 HEALTH=PERFECT
- Earth is shutting down in five minutes - please save all files and log out

---

160 These are extra stories that I came up with, but never really published them. After all, you could always waste your money on the previous books, or you could get a better deal on this one. Besides, extras can be more fun if you read inside a book!

161 This is the binary joke translation.

- Error 109: Error 108
- ERROR! Windows found! Formatting Drive C:!
- Ever noticed how fast Windows run? Me neither
- Evolution is God's way of issuing upgrades
- File not found. Nobody leave the room!
- Have a nice day - unless you've made other plans
- Honey, I Formatted The Kid!
- I t#ld yo#, 'Never#touch #he flop#y disk s#rface!'
- I wish life had a scroll-back buffer
- Insert disk 5 of 4 and press any key to continue
- Insert Mouse into drive A: and press any key
- JESUS SAVES; the rest of us better make backups.
- Life's too short to use a slow modem
- LSD: The ULTIMATE in Virtual Reality
- Error: Floppy not responding. Format drive C: instead [Y/N]?
- MafiaDOS: 'Thisa you lasta chance [Y/N]'?
- Moderator not found. Begin flame war [Y,n]?
- MOUSE.DRV not found, use RAT.DRV instead?
- On a hacker's tombstone: CONNECT 1964 - NO CARRIER 1994
- Only XT users know that January 1, 1980 was a Tuesday.
- Out of paper on drive D:
- Press ESC to enter or Enter to escape
- Real_men_don't_need_spacebars.

- REALITY.SYS corrupted. Reboot UNIVERSE [Y,n] ?
- Southern DOS: Y'all Reckon? (Yep/Nope)
- The Earth is 98% full. Please delete anyone you can.
- The Ultimate Virus: A self installing copy of 'Win95'.
- The world is coming to an end-please log off.
- There is a bomb on the premises. Please PANIC immediately.
- This copy of planet Earth has been unregistered for 4 billion years
- Track 0 bad?? Don't worry, there's lots of others
- Troubleshooting Shortcut #1: Shoot the trouble!
- Unknown Error on Unknown Device for Unexplainable Reason
- User Failure: Please Insert a Bootable Brain.
- Welcome to Hell! Here's your copy of WINDOWS
- Will Write Login Scripts For Food
- Windows 6345634.45a: please insert disk 95 of 5645
- Windows 8783837773.2c! We finally got it right. (Bill Gates)
- Windows: the $89 solution to your excess speed problem
- WindowsError:010 Reserved for future mistakes
- WindowsError:042 This virus requires Microsoft Windows.
- Your brain doesn't have enough memory, please make a boot disk
- Machines should work. People should think.

How God Created the Computer[162]

In the beginning, God created the bit. And the bit was a zero; nothing.

On the first day, He toggled the 0 to 1, and the Universe was. (In those days, bootstrap loaders were simple, and "active low" signals didn't yet exist.)

On the second day, God's boss wanted a demo, and tried to read the bit. This being volatile memory, the bit reverted to a 0. And the universe wasn't. God learned the importance of backups and memory refresh, and spent the rest of the day (and his first all-nighter) reconstructing the universe.

On the third day, the bit cried "Oh, Lord! If you exist, give me a sign!" And God created rev 2.0 of the bit, even better than the original prototype. Those in Universe Marketing immediately realized the the "new and improved" wouldn't do justice to such a grand and glorious creation. And so it was dubbed the Most Significant Bit, or the Sign bit. Many bits followed, but only one was so honored.

On the fourth day, God created a simple ALU with 'add' and 'logical shift' instructions. And the original bit discovered that by performing a single shift instruction, it could become the Most Significant Bit. And God realized the importance of computer security.

On the fifth day, God created the first mid-life kicker, rev 2.0 of the ALU, with wonderful features, and said "Screw that add and shift stuff. Go forth and multiply." And God saw that it was good.

On the sixth day, God got a bit overconfident, and invented pipelines, register hazards, optimizing compilers, crosstalk, restartable instructions, microinterrupts, race conditions, and propagation delays. Historians have used this to convincingly argue that the sixth day must have been a Monday.

On the seventh day, an engineering change introduced Microsoft into the Universe, and it hasn't worked right since.

162 This is the hexadecimal joke translation.

An Interview With A Leprechaun[163]

Ty: We have a special interview with Lucky McCurdy, the Lucky Charms Leprechaun in observance of St. Patrick's Day. Welcome to the studio, Lucky.

Lucky: Line!

Ty: Bob, could you please hold up Lucky McCurdy's cue cards a little bit higher?

Bob: Okay!

Lucky: (slowly reading) I…am…glad…to…be…here. (back to conversational mode) What the @#$% is this?! My agent told me this would be a respectable interview!

Ty: Lucky, there is a fable that all leprechauns have a pot of gold, is this true?

Lucky: No, we don't keep our gold in pots anymore.

Ty: You don't?

Lucky: No, that's ancient history! It seems that every time we said the word, "pot" the other person would try to smoke it. But, we started to invest in CDs.

Ty: You went to the bank?

Lucky: No, we went to the record store and invested in Compact Discs. We, leprechauns, see big money in CDs in the future.

Ty: What about our magical powers? I mean without your gold, aren't you powerless?

Lucky: It's a fib, I tell ya! We have a few drinks and get drunk and we're in high spirits and the rumors begin to fly about! That fib came about when I a guy got drunk and he had many hallucinations!

Ty: How do you create rainbows?

---

163 I actually wrote this piece while I was a student at Bates Technical College's radio station, KBTC 91.7 FM back in the mid-1990s. We produced and aired in time for the St. Patrick's Day. I was going to add other fictional characters such as the Easter Bunny and Uncle Sam, but I was slowly running out of some short scripts. Then, about a month later, I moved on with a job at KIRO 710 AM and started to learn the television broadcasting trade.

Lucky: It's easy! We use our CDs in bright sunlight!

Ty: Why do we not see any women leprechauns?

Lucky: Are you kidding?!

Ty: No, I'm not.

Lucky: There, there mate, just look for them.

Ty: But I can't see them!

Lucky: Then she is not for you, is she?

Ty: Lucky, I heard you came out with an idea for a cereal company you support, what was it?

Lucky: I tried red marshmallow skulls, but instead they wanted red balloons. Geez, they ask for my honest onion and they never take it.

Ty: Thank you, Lucky.

Lucky: (a good old fashion beating) Come here, ya stupid @#$%! I'll show you whose boss!

Ty: This concludes my special interview with Lucky McCurdy, the Lucky Charms Leprechaun.

The Best Invention Ever! Infomercial[164]

Narrator: You know, I have this wonderful project that I want to present to you. It has utterly changed my life! That's right, it is the hammer! The hammer would drive in those nails to keep those would products together! If you call now, we will add this beautiful wooden handle absolutely free of charge! Now, you can carry it with you! It's portable! While most tools, such as the crescent wrench, would only break nails and possibly the tool, the hammer would pound those nails quickly and easily. How much do you think I paid for this product? You, sir?

A: Eighty dollars!

Narrator: You madam?

B: Ten thousand dollars?

Narrator: I paid nine dollars and ninety-five cents for it. You can't get better than that! But, Ty, what if I make a mistake? I'll throw in something better. Something that most tools do not have: a nail remover! That's right! For nine ninety-five, you get a wooden handle, a hammer head, and a nail remover. Let's see a stapler do that!

---

164 I wrote this as a fun piece to show that you could sell just about anything. This piece was eventually put on the air on The Buzz 100.7 FM in Seattle, a talk radio format for guys.

About The Author

Everybody always wants to know more about me, the author. Like most cases, I have always had a hard time talking about myself since I feel my life is kind of boring. I was born in the mid-seventies as a fourth child. I found radio calling me when I was young, at the age of ten. Some friends and I on Vashon Island, Washington, USA ended up doing interviews of teachers and the school librarian and put it on a friend's small radio station with a one mile radius. I must say that those friends ended up very big in television, I stuck with radio broadcasting.

In 1990, I went to my high school radio station in Gig Harbor, Washington, USA called Peninsula High School. There, I learned the basics of radio broadcasting. I graduated in 1993, and then went to Bates Technical College in 1994 to learn about broadcasting and broadcast engineering. This includes both television and radio. The television in Tacoma, Washington was a PBS affiliate.

While I was at KBTC (Bates Technical College), I was laid off from the K-2 Corporation where I helped print the skis and saw a job opening at KJUN (The Country Gold Network). After a month of no pay, I went to KIRO-AM (news and talk) as a board operator and a producer for the weekend. This expanded from a simple fishing/hunting program to every other show. From there, I went to other radio stations that the company owned such as KNWX (news and business talk) and on to KQBZ (The Buzz, a talk station for guys). I worked on the morning shows and eventually moved on to Michigan.

I went to work WKLQ in Grand Rapids, Michigan. Since I hated working with certain set of people, I quit my job and moved to Ocean Shores with my parents. In Ocean Shores, Washington, USA, I co-founded a radio station called KOSW-LPFM. All radio stations I worked eventually were sold, changed formats, shut down, ratings dropped except KGHP-FM (my high school radio station) and KOSW-LPFM in which I only quit these organizations (never been fired from a radio station).

While I was in Ocean Shores and through Aberdeen, Washington, I attended Grays Harbor College, a community college with the full purpose of learning history. After three years of Grays Harbor College, I am currently at The Evergreen State College with same full purpose of learning about history and historical research. In fall quarter of 2008, I attended The University of St. Andrews in St. Andrews, Scotland, UK for approximately three months.

Currently, at the time of this book being written, I am searching a Graduate School with the ultimate career goal of archives or teaching. While I was in college, I wrote a total of three books, *Ty Roseynose: A Documentary, Ty's Book of Rubbish: Volume 20,* and *Ty's Book of Rubbish: Volume 19.* I guess I should also add this book: *Ty's BIG BOOK of Rubbish: An Omnibus,* the final of my books.

Cheers,

Ty Rosenow

April 14, 2009

www.ingramcontent.com/pod-product-compliance
Lightning Source LLC
Chambersburg PA
CBHW030822310726
48980CB00006B/593/J
9780578020778